Face Value

By
Ian Andrew

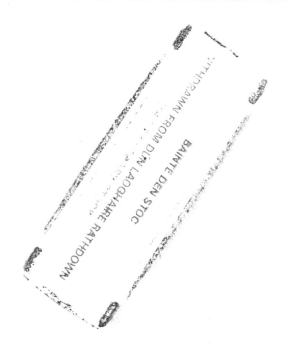

Cover Illustration: Web & Print Hub, Australia
Face Image, used under license from Shutterstock.com

Dedication

For
Johnnie and Bob
On your shared Birthday
Thanks for making us who we are

&

Taffy
The 1st of the 37th to depart

Also by Ian Andrew

The Wright & Tran Novels
Flight Path
Fall Guys

Other Titles
A Time To Every Purpose
The Little Book Of Silly Rhymes & Odd Verses

Be not deceived with the first appearance of things, for show is not substance.

Old English Proverb

1

Huntingdon, Cambridgeshire

It wasn't the prettiest place to die. But then again, where is? She was taking a shortcut through unfamiliar territory. He was running an illegal errand on ground he called his own. Neither would have wanted the street, with its vandalised lights and graffiti-covered hoardings, to be their final view of life. But we don't often get what we want.

She saw him first. The lone surviving streetlamp dropped a pool of weak yellow light that was just enough to reveal him rounding the corner, fifty yards away on the opposite side of the road. Despite the mild July night he was hunched over, his hands thrust deep into the pockets of his green nylon bomber jacket. Strands of straggly blond hair shielded a thin, cratered face. The Doc Marten boots, visible under too-short jeans, made no noise against the uneven, fractured footpath. Save for the lack of a skinhead haircut, he looked like he had stepped out of a documentary on right-wing hooliganism.

In the moment she thought to turn around and go a different way, he looked up, alerted by the click of her stiletto heels. As their eyes met he smiled and sneered simultaneously, his features distorting like a grotesque skull. She knew that turning away was no longer an option.

He took his hands out of his pockets. She could see the left was empty, but the right seemed to be concealing something. Steadying her pace, she shifted the chain-link strap of her clutch bag from across her body, so that it rested on her left shoulder.

He quickened his step and crossed the street. She moved into the middle of the footpath and kept walking, watching. He was a couple of inches taller than her and as he came closer, she could see he was thin and sinewy. Not a bodybuilder by any means, but he looked strong, agile, quick. Like an urban fox, thinner than it should be but capable, furtive, vicious.

When he was a few yards away, she grasped her clutch bag, letting the chain fall from her shoulder and moved to her right to avoid him. He blocked her. She stopped walking and stepped left, placing herself back in the middle of the path. He stepped to his right, directly in front of her again. She stood still and tried to be polite.

"I'm sorry. Please, after you," she said and extended her left arm to indicate where he should step.

He ignored her and stepped forward. "I don't fink so." His accent was rough-edged London. His lips were cracked and looked dry, yet as he spoke, spittle flew from his mouth. It hit her face. She didn't reach to wipe it away.

He smelt of cigarettes and body odour laced with an underlying stench of stale beer. Pale skin, almost vampiric was stretched over sunken cheeks that cowered under narrowed, dulled eyes. Pock marks had joined to form craters, valleys and crevices etched into his face.

He stepped closer. "I'm gonna enjoy this. Fancy a fuck?" His speed of movement surprised her. His right hand came up and elaborately flicked a butterfly knife open. Its four-inch blade shone briefly in the dim light. He held it just inches from her chest whilst his left hand thrust forward and caught her by the throat. She gagged at the force of his grip and began to feel him applying upward pressure. He was trying to lift her off the ground. She heard a voice from long ago.

'Kara Wright! How many times do I have to tell you? The first time you should see an attacker's knife is when it's exiting from your body. If you see it before then, you know it's all for show. They're full of piss and bravado.'

Kara gave a wry smile as the words of her first instructor rang out in her head. She swung her right arm up and over her attacker's left and plunged the side of her fist down into the bend of his elbow. The downward force ripped his hand away from her throat and she gasped at the release. Simultaneously, she flicked her left hand and arced the short chain of the bag around his right wrist. As she pulled down, his knife hand was drawn away and his whole body turned slightly, forcing his right leg forward. She planted her left foot solidly on the pavement and extended her right foot in a vicious front snap kick.

The four-inch stiletto heel she was wearing punctured the inner side of his right knee. Kara visualised the passage of it as it tore through the medial collateral ligament, sliced between the medial meniscus and passed behind the patella. She held the kick's form until the tip of her heel came to rest embedded in his anterior cruciate ligament. Her brain ticked off the damage in the time it took to happen.

Her attacker simply fell sideways to his right. The knowledge of the anatomical destruction done to him and the noise of the knife clattering onto the ground were lost in his screams.

'And remember Miss Wright, when we start, we finish.'

Kara snapped her right foot back, leaving her shoe impaled in the ruptured knee joint. She planted the ball of her bare right foot firmly, stepped slightly back on her left and executed a spinning hook kick. As her body pivoted around, she extended her left heel and met the head of her collapsing attacker in mid-air. The stiletto punctured the soft hollow that marked the pterion of his skull and the screaming stopped. His falling deadweight removed the shoe from her left foot.

Kara stood still, her balance regained. Her core muscles

tense but not strained. She could hear acutely the efforts of the night breeze as it caught on the tatters of billboard posters and gently swayed the precariously hanging corrugated sheets lining the backs of abandoned industrial units. She saw, in extreme clarity, the details of her would-be attacker's face, caught in shock and frozen in a death mask. His mouth shaping a now silent scream. She stayed still and concentrated on herself. Her breathing deepened and the quickening of her heart began to relax and slow. She looked down at her bare feet and mentally ran a checklist of her body. She had no injuries, no damage at all. As her heartrate slowed further her mind geared up and began to assess the options open to her. Giving weight to each in turn, she dismissed them almost as soon as she thought of them. As her heartbeat fully normalised she chose her actions.

Stepping back she reached down and retrieved her bag. Pulling her smartphone she opened an app called '1984'. The phone displayed a map of all CCTV coverage within a one mile radius of her current position. A large number of small red dots appeared on the display but only two were near where she was. That didn't surprise her. There was nothing of value in what was little more than a back alley running through an industrial area. She waited for the phone to synchronise with the cloud-based data. After a short time the two nearest dots adjusted their positions as the GPS fully resolved itself. They showed cameras at the front of a small car yard just behind her to the right. She walked back until she could see the rear of the yard and satisfied herself that there was no camera coverage in her direction. She zoomed in on a cluster of dots to her immediate north. The irony that she stood less than a quarter of a mile from the town's Police Station wasn't lost on her. However, she knew the line of sight to her position was blocked by a myriad of warehouses and industrial units. She zoomed the display out and checked to see where she would have last been observed on CCTV. The final coverage was when she had turned off Walden Road. Between there and here were at least ten cross streets and thoroughfares, with each one having multiple intersections and turn offs. There was no chance of anyone being able to conclude that the blonde haired girl in the red heels had come this way. Unless of course they found some evidence.

Kara walked back to the body that lay half on the pavement, half on the road like a discarded mannequin. There was little blood to be seen as the wounds were small, neat and conveniently plugged by her stilettos. She reached back into her clutch and removed a pair of latex gloves and a wad of tissues. Donning the gloves she crouched down and checked the pockets that she could reach without rolling the corpse. There was a ten-pound note in the front left jeans pocket and a half empty pouch of tobacco in the left jacket pocket. In the pouch, on top of the tobacco, was a packet of Rizla papers and two small Ziploc bags. One held a quantity of off-white crystals and the other a small amount of white powder. Sticking the money and the Ziplocs in her bag she set the tobacco pouch to one side.

Readying a few tissues, she very slowly pulled the shoe out of the knee joint. When almost clear she gently twisted it to make sure the complete heel, including the metal tip came out. Wrapping the tissues tightly to stop any blood drops escaping she set the shoe on the ground. Repeating the process she removed the other shoe from the skull wound.

Kara stood up and paused. She settled her breathing, turned a complete circle and listened for any approaching people or vehicles. When she was certain there was nothing and no one nearby she retrieved the butterfly knife from the road.

With a final look around, she crouched and inserted the blade into the knee wound and twisted a half turn. Given the relative dimensions she hoped it would mask the original stiletto puncture. Extracting the weapon from the knee she positioned the tip carefully against the hole in the skull. Pushing slowly forward with her full weight she implanted the knife into the wound and gave it a final sharp tap so the hilt contacted the side of the head. Then, with her arm at full stretch and her body leaning as far away as possible she withdrew the knife in a quick ripping motion. A small yet vibrant spray of blood and tiny fragments of bone rose and fell in the night. She stood up and reaching as high as she could dropped the knife, point first, onto the broken concrete footpath.

Picking up the tobacco pouch she threw it on top of the body and the light breeze teased at the open flap, helping to spread the fine brown threads like macabre confetti. Removing her gloves, she made a tight ball of them in the last of the tissues and popped it into her bag.

After a quick check of the '1984' app to plan a surveillance free route to her car, Kara gathered up her belongings. Pausing in the shadows she removed the blonde wig and wrapped the tissue-bound heels in it.

2

"So, how'd it go?" Tien asked as she swivelled her chair away from the banks of computer screens and hard drive racks that formed her workspace.

"Yep, all good. Easy in fact," Kara said as she offered Tien one of the two coffees from the cardboard takeaway tray she had brought with her.

"Oh thanks, is it the good stuff or…," Tien hesitated.

"Nah, it was the short Italian guy. I tried to wait for Ravi but there was a queue. Sorry." Kara flopped down in the spare chair.

"Ah don't worry. I still don't get how the Italian dude can barely make a drinkable coffee and the Sri Lankan is a master. Doesn't seem right." Despite her forebodings Tien took a long sip from the plastic-capped cup.

"Yeah, but be fair," Kara said, "Ravi's as much Sri Lankan as you are Vietnamese."

Tien giggled, "I know and look how far we've come. Both born in Hackney and both living the dream in Camden," she paused and Kara noticed the slight frown on her friend's brow. She knew Tien was going to switch back to business.

"So, last night, no problems?"

Kara answered smoothly and without hesitation, "No, in fact it's so much simpler than it used to be." She fished the smartphone from her pocket and handed it over. The younger woman took it and looked quizzical.

"Simpler?"

Kara nodded, "Yeah simpler. Much simpler. Imagine trying to follow someone into a nightclub armed with a clunky old camera. Wouldn't be exactly subtle. You'd have to get as close to them as possible without being seen and try to take shots without them noticing you pointing a ruddy great lens at them. Or the great big flash going off. Even if you managed it, you'd have to wait until the pictures were developed to discover if you had anything useable. It wouldn't even have been worth trying. All of that replaced by taking a false selfie."

"A what?" Tien asked.

"A pretend selfie. You just strike a bit of a pose so that it looks like you're taking your own photo, but you make sure the back camera of the phone is on and not the front. Looks completely normal nowadays and no one even gives you a second glance. It's easy and you can instantly check the result. How'd you think I did it?"

"I'm not sure I really thought about it. You know me, I just do what I do and let you do all the glamour stuff," Tien quipped.

"Yep, glamourous, that's what it is. I'm like a paparazzi ninja. Anyway, there's about ten shots on there, all in focus, well-lit and quite artistic if I say so myself," Kara smiled and poked her tongue out at her friend.

Tien laughed but looked back at the phone and sighed, "So it's true then? The client was right?"

"Afraid so."

"No doubt?"

"Nope. Not unless she was giving him mouth to mouth and I just misinterpreted. Anyway, she'd gone to a pub on her own. Picked this guy up, went clubbing and eventually left with him and didn't go back to her hotel. They just went straight to what

8

I presume was his house. I've copied the location onto the map." Kara nodded toward the phone, "You can get an identity for me?"

"Yeah, easy. Did you get more footage there?"

"Nah, not a thing. Mind you, I couldn't have picked a better spot. Could've stopped there all night. The house backed on to a cemetery but there wasn't much point. Upstairs light went on, blinds came down, curtains drawn across and that was that." Kara tried to give her best 'we all know what happened next' expression but Tien didn't laugh. Instead she just set the phone down and stared at it.

"I wonder what'll upset her most, knowing that her partner is screwing around or knowing that she's screwing around with a man?"

"Ah well, thankfully that isn't one for me to have to work out. It really shouldn't be a shock though. I mean as soon as we had same-sex marriage it was a cert we'd get same-sex divorce. Anyway, I'll write up the report and get it round to her by this afternoon. Can you get the images enhanced and printed by say," Kara checked her watch and saw that it was coming up to eleven o'clock. She hadn't got home until almost six and had only managed a couple of hours of fitful sleep before getting up and making her way into the early morning Camden Markets. She had made one purchase for cash and returned home. A half hour later she had walked the five minutes round to see Tien. "Two? Does that give you enough time?"

"Yep, no problem. You going home or working from here?" Tien nodded down toward the floor and meant the ground level office that sat under her apartment. Once a nail manicure shop owned by her parents it was now Kara's office.

"From here. Right, I'll go and get started." Kara pushed herself up from the chair and turned to the door, but Tien stretched out her left arm and stopped her. Kara felt the firmness of her friend's prosthetic hand against her leg.

"So, you had no dramas last night?" Tien asked with a slight tremor in her voice.

Kara breathed deeply but unobtrusively before turning to face her friend, "No, none. Why, what's up?"

Tien swung back round to the multiple consoles arrayed on her desk and opened up a browser window. She spoke whilst looking at the screen, "Have you seen any news this morning?"

"Only the BBC website, why, what's happened?" Kara asked as she leaned over to look.

"Did you just look at the headlines?"

"Yeah. Nothing much caught my interest other than the next round of defence cuts. I expect more of our old friends will be looking for work soon. What is it Tien? What'd I miss?"

Tien opened up the BBC's regional news page for Cambridgeshire. The short story was filed under a single stock image of an out-of-focus Police car and some Police Do Not Cross tape.

'Huntingdon, Cambridgeshire – (Reuters). A man was killed in a stabbing in Huntingdon overnight, authorities said.

The victim, thought to be in his late 30's and whose identity is not immediately available, was found dead in an alley in the Light Industrial Estate bounded by Brampton Road and Edison Bell Way about 6am when Police Officers attended a call from a member of the public, said a Cambridgeshire Police spokesman.

No one is in custody and detectives from the Bedfordshire/Cambridgeshire/Hertfordshire combined Major Crimes Unit are investigating. Police have asked anyone with information about the incident to contact the unit on 101.'

Kara straightened back up and spoke to the back of Tien's head, "That's terrible. Poor fella."

Tien spun round slowly and looked up at her, "So you never saw or heard anything?"

"No Tien, not a thing. Sorry. I'd let you know if I did and I'd let the cops know too. But no. Nothing. I just ended the surveillance and went back to my car. Drove home, slept and here I am now. Anyway, let me know when you get the photos and the ID done. I'll go and start on the report."

Kara turned away but Tien called her back, "Hey, you'll need this." Tien opened a drawer, took a new smartphone from it and threw it over to Kara.

"Thanks pet." Kara turned away from the monitors and Tien's watchful gaze. Breathing gently she walked unhurriedly from the room. She knew that whatever happened she would protect her best friend from her actions. If it ever came to it, she would not bring Tien down with her.

As the door closed behind Kara, Tien turned back to her consoles and pulled up a screen she had minimised just as Kara had first come in. It showed the master log from the '1984' app. Tien not only wrote each of the specialist apps that Kara needed for her field work but she maintained all the user data and app history. The screen showed the GPS read out for when and where the app was accessed and the CCTV locations it identified. Tien used it for correlation and enhancement purposes but because Kara would have called the development work, 'just all ones and noughts' Tien had never really told her about the level of monitoring that was possible. There was no need to. Kara did what she did and Tien did this.

The data revealed that the app had been accessed at 03:20 in the light industrial unit bounded by Brampton Road and Edison Bell Way in Huntingdon. The GPS track showed the movement of Kara's burner phone and Tien knew that Kara had been at the scene of the killing.

She shut the display down and unlocked the hard drive rack that was mounted on the wall to her right. Each separate drive stored the user data and history of each individual app she had ever developed. Each drive was, in turn, rotated for each operation she supported Kara on. That, coupled with the new burner smartphone she would furnish for each operation, made Tien's data records completely compartmentalised. The phones, preloaded with Kara's contacts and cloned down to the layout of the icons meant Kara always had her 'own' phone yet never carried a traceable mobile for more than a week at a time. Tien transferred the photos and the map location of the target address from the previous night's surveillance onto her PC. She would work on them later as Kara requested. Getting up from her desk she took the phone and the drive with the '1984' location trace into the small workshop set behind her kitchen. She placed both into the compact industrial kiln that sat against the rear wall and turned it on. Theoretically she knew there might be some algorithms that could erase data completely but she didn't trust that forensic computer squads couldn't get something back. She relied on more kinetically proven methods. A few hours inside the kiln and all that would be left would be a molten mound of plastic and metal. Once cooled it would make a great doorstop or large paperweight. It made equally good landfill.

Tien didn't reflect on what her best friend had done in the early hours of the morning. She knew Kara had lied to protect her. What she could do in return was remove any evidence of Kara at a crime scene. She knew that whatever happened she would protect her best friend from her actions. If it ever came to it, she would not bring Kara down with her.

3

Monday Morning.
Bedfordshire, Cambridgeshire & Hertfordshire
Major Crimes Unit, Huntingdon

He picked up the receiver of his Cisco desk phone on the third ring. "Tri-County Major Crimes Unit, DCI Tony Reynolds speaking."

"Tony, it's Jeremy."

Reynolds checked the clock display on the phone console, "Jesus Jem, you're up early. I thought you pathologist types didn't get up before midday."

"Yeah, very droll, but you're right, a quarter to seven isn't my usual start time. That's why this is me actually knocking off."

"You've been working all night? What on?"

"Your post-mortem."

"Mine?" Reynolds sounded confused. He couldn't think what would cause the doctor to work through the night on such an obvious case. "You mean the one from Huntingdon on Saturday?"

"Yes. How many dead bodies do you think you have?"

"Well, no," Reynolds hesitated. "That's my only recent

one. Just to be sure, we're talking about the druggie with the posh name and the great big knife wound to the head?"

"Yes. That's the chap. Manfield Bartholomew Hastings."

"But that shouldn't have taken you more than a couple of hours. Why did you pull an all-nighter on that?" Reynolds asked.

"Well, I got the call on Saturday morning but Shona was helping Professor Kennedy down in Uxbridge and I was over at a Norfolk road traffic incident. Given the on-scene assessment I thought it would be safe enough to put your chap on ice until I could get in on Sunday afternoon. Figured I'd get the PM done and have the report waiting for you when you came in this morning and all still within the time."

Reynolds knew the pathologist was referring to the normal 48-hour timeframe for a suspected murder post-mortem to be completed. "So what changed?" he asked. "I thought it was obvious."

"Yes, I'd normally agree and I did initially think that a large sharp force injury was quite persuasive as the cause of death. Especially given Mr Hasting's circle of influence."

Tony Reynolds couldn't help but smile. He had worked with Doctor Jeremy Rowlands as the main pathologist for the area for nearly ten years. Jeremy, or Jem to those he liked and Doctor Rowlands to those he didn't, had once been the pathologist for just Cambridgeshire. But now, with ever shrinking budgets, he was one of ten Home Office Pathologists assigned to cover the Greater London, South East and West Midlands area. He normally worked out of Cambridge and with Doctor Shona Johnston based in Chelmsford the two of them looked after the vast majority of the post-mortems needed within the counties of Essex, Norfolk, Suffolk, Hertfordshire, Bedfordshire and Cambridgeshire. It sounded like a lot but the violent death rate for those counties was one of the lowest in the UK. The other eight pathologists in the group spent most of their time working inside the M25 and were substantially busier than Jeremy and Shona. It was his relatively light post-mortem workload that allowed him to continue to hold a number of teaching and research posts. Given his expertise and ability his peculiarity of never referring to any deceased's criminal activities by name was fully acceptable.

But Reynolds couldn't resist teasing the pathologist a little, "His circle of influence, Jem? You make it sound like he was a member of the Huntingdon Drug Dealer's Rotarian and Lions Club."

"Now, now. What the poor fellow got up to in life is not for me to judge in death. You know I just try to find out what brought him into my care."

"A large knife to the head was my guess," Reynolds said.

"Yes, well that was my initial assessment too. The rest of the PM was quite as one would expect. You know, collapsed veins, multiple needle tracks, a liver that was displaying late stage Cirrhosis, lungs that had put in quite a shift and were now the worse for wear. All quite normal given the lifestyle. However, there's something not right Tony. The fatal wound is the head wound obviously, but I don't think it was caused by the knife you found. The bruising caused by the trauma to the temporal muscle is not consistent with a hand-delivered injury and the internal tissue shows a crater penetration. So I carried out a very thorough detailed sectioning and I've-"

"Back up a bit Jem, you've lost me."

"Sorry, right. Look, I'll get the report to you in full today but I think you should come over so I can show you. The gist of it is this Tony; the knife was used as a concealer. The fatal injury was not done by the butterfly blade but rather was a short stiletto shaped puncture surrounded by a much flatter and broader backing surface."

Reynolds considered what he'd been told, "So we're looking for a short stiletto bladed, broad hilted," he hesitated knowing how silly the idea sounded, "A sword? Are we looking for a short sword Jem?" he asked it with a trace of incredulity in his voice.

"Well, no not a sword. Like I said, I've looked a lot closer and I found some paint in the deeper sections of brain tissue."

Reynolds wondered what the pathologist was leading up to, but asked the obvious question, "What type of paint Jem?"

"That's what kept me up all night. It took quite a while to cross match the sample but I think we're looking for an actual stiletto."

"You mean a shoe, a stiletto shoe?" Reynolds asked it slowly.

"Yes Tony. I do believe Mr Hastings was killed by a very accurate and forceful kick to the head from someone wearing a red stiletto high heel."

4

Monday Morning. Camden, London

Kara met Tien on the pavement just outside Grafton Yard at 07:00.

"Which way?" Kara asked.

"Hampstead."

Both women turned north and set off on their morning run. They tried to stick to it as a weekday routine as much as life and other commitments allowed. Each picked the route on alternate days. Normally it was north to Parliament Hill Fields and the wide openness of the rest of Hampstead Heath where, by running a convoluted circuit around the various walking paths, they could knock out a reasonable five miles before arriving back at Kara's apartment. Depending on how either felt they could push the distance up in increments of two miles by adding in extra circuits and loops that took them up past the Highgate Ponds. To vary it they sometimes turned south instead and headed to Regents Park. Very occasionally, when Kara really wanted to blow out the cobwebs, she would take Tien all the way into the city for a circuit of Green Park and then back home.

Tien was a couple of inches shorter than Kara at five foot

five, a couple of stone lighter, much more slender and would easily match her mile for mile, but she would never have chosen the southern route. Kara knew it was nothing to do with the distance. They had been running partners off and on since back in 2009 when they first pounded round Kandahar Airfield together, but Kara knew Tien didn't get a buzz from the exercise like she did. There was no deep-seated, almost addictive need to exercise. Then again there also seemed to be no physical need either. Kara knew her friend could eat anything and everything, including a regular diet of Yorkie and Wispa bars and seemingly not put a pound on. Kara on the other hand needed the buzz that came from the exertion and she also needed it to keep her weight in check, especially since she had quit smoking.

"Was Saturday afternoon okay?" Tien asked as they turned into Grafton Road.

"Yep, she wasn't that shocked to be honest. Seems that the partner had been 'bi' before they'd got together. I think all we did was confirm what she knew."

"Any follow up needed?"

"No. She said she'd send through the final payments by direct deposit. I gave her the report, the receipts and the final invoice. We'll probably have the money by tomorrow and you can close down all the history." Kara glanced over and saw Tien nodding before she added, "She was hurt though. I know she was."

"Yeah, how come?" Tien asked as she checked over her shoulder before crossing Athlone Street.

"She asked me if I wanted to stay."

Tien pulled up quickly, "What?"

Kara turned and jogged backwards, "C'mon slacker keep up."

"Kara! What did you say to her?"

"I said I was very flattered but that I was straight. Now c'mon, keep up."

Tien ran to catch up and looked sideways at Kara, "Did she really ask you, just like that?"

Kara nodded, "Shocking isn't it. Tisk, Tisk, what is the world coming to?"

"Okay, you can stop teasing me now. It's not my fault. I just think people should be a little more..." Tien searched for the proper word.

"Prudish?" Kara offered.

"No! I am not prudish. Reserved. I just think we should be a little more reserved."

"So, you've no issue with her being a lesbian, or even asking me out. You just think she should have bided her time a bit more?" Kara asked, trying to keep her voice serious.

"Well, yes."

Kara couldn't stop from laughing, "You crack me up. And I'm only messing. Of course she didn't ask me out. I just wanted to see your face."

"Oh, you're incorrigible!" Tien said as she accelerated and Kara pushed to keep up.

They ran in silence until the three-way junction on the rail overpass at Barrington Close forced them to wait for the traffic to pass. Jogging in place Tien said, "Just to let you know there's been no word on that murder in Huntingdon yet."

"Oh, okay," Kara said it flatly and hardly had to mask her voice. She had spent Saturday night and all day Sunday visiting her parents down at their home in Somerset and hadn't given the events in the alleyway another thought. As far as she was concerned, it was over. She couldn't waste time thinking about it. Either she had cleaned up the evidence and disposed of the shoes and the drugs completely or she hadn't. If the Police were able to find any trace of them or her then she'd deal with it. If they didn't come looking for her, then as far as she was concerned a street predator had tried it on and come up short. He lost, she won. Move on. She waited for the gap in the traffic and pushed off again. Tien kept alongside and Kara got the weird feeling that she was going to say something else about the murder. Instead, at their next enforced traffic stop, Tien merely switched the conversation to ask Kara about her trip to Somerset. In turn Kara asked about Tien's traditional

Sunday ritual of chapel and lunch with her parents, her six older siblings, their wives and husbands and what seemed to be an exponentially increasing amount of nephews and nieces.

$$\phi$$

By ten Kara was back in her office and working on a surveillance plan for the horrendously named 'Lizard and Pickle' Pub a few doors up on the Kentish Town Road, the owner of which was convinced her bar manager was stealing from her. The normal cameras and till checks hadn't shown anything and so she came to see Kara and Tien. The work was easy, boring if anything and the fee was minimal but it would help pay the bills and that was always a consideration. Money was tight and every little helped. Kara pushed back from the desk and stretched her arms to work out the kinks in her shoulders. As she relaxed again into her seat the doorbell of the outer street door rang. Not expecting any callers she swivelled round and checked the intercom camera. A man and woman were framed in the fisheye lens that seemed to warp them and the interior of the small front porch like an old-fashioned carnival hall of mirrors.

Despite the comedic distortion they both looked to be in their late twenties and it was clear that although the man was much broader and taller there was a definite family resemblance between the two. Kara pushed the microphone button, "Hi, this is Wright and Tran Investigations, can I help you?"

The man bent forward so that his mouth filled the screen, "Hello, I'm Michael Sterling. This is my sister Zoe. Our parents have gone missing and we were told that you might be able to help."

5

Camden, London

Michael Sterling's muscular frame just managed to crunch into one of the occasional chairs set to the side of Kara's office. His sister in comparison seemed to glide to the chair next to him and settled into it like a soft sigh. Kara sat in a third chair that faced them both at a slight angle. She watched closely as the siblings composed themselves.

Zoe wore a knee length, multi-coloured, Bohemian Gypsy skirt, a casual black T-shirt and a light canvas jacket. Her bag looked to have been made from the same canvas material. She sat like a graduate of a charm school, knees together and feet placed side by side, with the toes turned slightly out. Her back was almost ramrod straight, her neck long and slender. Kara saw the woman's calves were exquisitely toned and her ankles looked almost muscular above her flat black pumps. Zoe's hands, clasped gently in her lap, wore no rings and her nails, although delicately manicured, had no visible polish applied. Her shoulder-length hair framed a natural complexion that also looked devoid of any makeup or adornment. Next to her grace and delicacy Michael Sterling looked like a battleship stuffed into a business suit.

His black brogues were polished but even they seemed to strain at the seams. The man wasn't really that tall but Kara thought he looked like a halfway point on the transition to the Hulk. All his clothes looked like they would burst if he so much as sneezed. His top button was undone, his tie loosened off and Kara wondered if this was simply due to the fact that he couldn't get a collar size large enough for his neck. As he shrugged back into the chair and looked over at her she noticed his right ear was slightly more cauliflower'd than his left and that his nose must have been broken a dozen times or more. Like Zoe, he wore no rings but she could see the distinctive tri-colour of a Help for Heroes wristband poking out from his right cuff. The watch on his left wrist was either a real Breitling Galactic, or an outstanding replica. Kara thought it was much more likely to be the former.

"So, Michael, Zoe. You said your parents are missing. May I ask, have you reported this to the Police?"

Michael turned to look at his sister. She nodded almost imperceptibly whilst keeping her eyes focussed on Kara.

He spoke with a slight London accent that had just enough of an edge to tie him to the City. Kara filed another observation away. "Yes, we went to our local station last week"

"And where was that?"

"In Fulham. We went to Fulham but they wouldn't do anything. They said there was no threat. It's a crock of-"

His sister cut him off, "They said there was no apparent threat of danger. Then they said they would keep it under review but wouldn't be actively pursuing it." Her accent was equal to her brother's, but a little more refined. Either she had concentrated on making it sound that way, or had mixed with a slightly different sphere of people. "Excuse me?" Zoe asked in a manner that was not haughty or arrogant, but held a firmness of conviction that halted any thought of progressing until she had been responded to. It was the 'Excuse Me' of a teacher to her student.

The question and its delivery caught Kara off guard. She looked directly at Zoe, "Yes?"

"Are you not going to take notes, write something down?"

"No. No, I'm not," Kara said it quietly, calmingly. She continued, "I'd rather just listen to you and Michael and get an understanding first. If I need specific details recorded later then my colleague will join us and we'll sort it out from there. But for now, all I want to do is hear what's happened. Can you tell me why you believe your parents are missing but the Police don't think there's a threat?"

Kara hadn't thought it possible, but Zoe managed to sit a little straighter in her chair before speaking again, "They said that because there was a message left and there's no sign of violence then there's nothing they can do."

"Sorry Zoe, can we start with the last time you and Michael saw your parents?"

"On Sunday last week. Eight days ago. We usually go to see them for Sunday lunch at least once a month. It depends on whether Michael's playing or not."

"And is their house in Fulham too?"

"No. Michael and I share a house down here. We both work in the city. Mum and Dad live up in Arlesey. It's a little village about halfway between Bedford and Cambridge."

Kara knew where Arlesey was but didn't interrupt Zoe.

"We went up there, had lunch and came back down. Then I phoned Mum on Tuesday but her mobile went straight to voicemail. Same with Dad's. So I phoned the house and got a recorded message. Michael and I went straight up there and the house was locked up. We tried to get the Police interested but they won't take us seriously. We've spent the week trying to figure out what to do but all we seem to have done is go round in circles. We contacted Mum's friends at the WI but they hadn't heard from her. Neither had Dad's friends in the Legion, but it isn't right. He would have told us if they'd been going away. They would have told us." Zoe's voice was becoming strained. Her clasped and manicured hands beginning to twist slightly in her lap. Her brother reached an arm over and gently patted her hands with surprising tenderness for such a big man.

Kara paused and waited but neither of the siblings offered

anything more. It seemed to her on first impressions that the Police might well have been right. Two grown-up children worried about their parents being away for a week seemed quite thin for a Missing Persons investigation. But the siblings didn't seem to be like the usual nutcases. They were obviously reasonably well-off, well-spoken, well-dressed, probably well-employed. 'Mind you,' Kara thought, 'Doesn't stop them from being well-crazy.'

She prompted them, "You said you listened to a recorded message and went straight up to their house. What did the message say?"

Michael reached into his pocket and drew out his mobile phone. He pressed a few buttons and handed it to Kara. The contact on the screen simply said 'Home'.

"Before you ring, there's something you should know," he said. "My Dad was an ex-Royal Navy photographer. He went all over the world for work and he and Mum have been on holidays all over the world as well. But not once has my Mum ever flown. She's got an acute fear of flying. I'm not talking just frightened, I mean it's debilitating. The medical term is severe aviophobia and it's not something she can master. She's been on courses of hypnotherapy and medication and none of it ever worked. In the early days of their marriage they even got as far as the airport, but had to cancel the flights when she couldn't get through the arrivals hall. So when we went on holidays we always went by car, boat or train. We travelled all over the UK and Europe, but not once to anywhere that needed a plane ride. Since the tunnel, Mum and Dad would take trains through to Europe and they've even taken a number of roundtrip cruises to further afield. But no flying. Ever."

"Okay Michael," Zoe said, having reclaimed her composure. "I think Kara understands. Let her listen."

Kara pressed the call button. The home phone in Arlesey rang five times before the message service kicked in.

'Hello. Brenda and I can't take your call at the moment.' The male voice had a distinct north-eastern accent. Smoothed out and made more generic over years spent far from home but definitely Newcastle. Kara registered it in the first few words and pegged it for Wallsend. She had a thing about accents and trying to get them to not just the area or the city but to the distinct vagaries of the individual town sites was something she did instinctively now.

She heard a hesitancy, slight but definite, before the male voice continued, 'We're going on a fly-drive holiday to America and will be away for a few weeks. Our mobiles won't work over there so if you need us just leave a message and we'll get back to you as soon as we get back into Heathrow.' There was a second of silence and then the beep. Kara ended the call and handed the phone back to Michael.

6

Camden, London

Kara concentrated on keeping the frisson of excitement that she felt out of her voice. Cases like this offered to raise her heart rate like a surveillance plan on a pub never could. "Before we go on," she said, alternatively looking at Zoe and Michael, "May I ask how you've ended up at my office?"

Zoe answered, "When no one would help us we contacted some of Dad's old Navy mates. They put us in touch with some other people. Eventually a woman called Victoria gave us your details."

Kara nodded and once more made sure to mask her rising interest in the Sterling family. She buried the flood of questions that had tumbled into her head upon hearing Victoria's name and instead conveyed a sense of surprise at the mention of an old friend.

But Kara needed to confirm a few things, "Victoria! Goodness me! Where did you meet up with her, what did she say?"

"We didn't meet her. It was all done over the phone. We were given a number to call her on yesterday. It seemed a bit strange to be honest. She told us to come see you and said you and Teen would be able to help us," Michael said.

Kara knew at the very least this part of their story was genuine. There was no chance they would ever have met Victoria in person and by Michael's mispronunciation of Tien's name she knew it really had been Victoria that sent them. It was just Victoria's way of leaving a calling card that was an easy and clean way of achieving corroboration.

"Yeah, that sounds about right for Victoria. Oh and I hope you don't mind, but my colleague's name is pronounced T-N, not teen. Just for when you eventually meet her. Anyway, let's get back to your parents. I can understand why the message would concern you. Surely you explained all this to the Police?"

"Yes, but they ran some checks and said that Mum and Dad had flown out of Heathrow on Tuesday morning. We told them it was impossible but they said their checks were conclusive." Michael sounded frustrated at the memory.

"Did they happen to mention what these checks were?"

"They said they'd cross-checked against the Border..." Michael hesitated, searching for the right word, "Patrol?"

Zoe spoke up, "Force. They said they'd checked against the Border Force and that Mum and Dad had left Heathrow heading to Miami on BA 207. Then they rang British Airways and the airline confirmed it."

"Okay," Kara paused, "Your parents said they were going to be away for a few weeks. Why not just wait for them to turn up?" Zoe's eyes flared angrily. Kara thought there was almost a viciousness in them, but then she thought again. It wasn't anger or viciousness, it was a deep hurt and a deeper fear.

Michael leant slightly forward, his gentle voice at odds with his bulk, "Are your parents alive Kara?"

"Yes."

"Would you wait?"

Zoe's eyes had taken on the shimmer of tears and Kara retrieved some tissues from a small kitchen area set off to the far side of the office. She knew that Zoe would have her own in her bag but Kara needed the half minute of time to consider her options. When she sat back down she had already made up her mind. "I'm just going to hold it there if we may, I think I've heard enough." Kara saw deep disappointment in Michael's eyes. "No, don't be sad. I'm going to help you. I'm taking the case. I'll get Tien to join us from upstairs and we can get everything started properly. We need to get some details recorded, establish a few facts and have you and I sign some documents. There's also the matter of agreeing a fee." The light returned to Michael's eyes and he smiled broadly, turning to his sister and laying his hand on hers again. Zoe didn't seem to share his conviction. Her fear and tears had once more been masked with the composure and carriage she had exuded when she had first walked in.

"Excuse me?" Zoe said it in the same manner as she had previously.

"Yes," Kara said and turned toward the sister.

"You've decided just like that? I mean it sounds terrific but we haven't necessarily decided on you. You didn't come recommended, you merely came referred from someone we've never met. There's a difference. I'd like to know if you have the pedigree or the capacity to do this type of work. I don't mean to be churlish and neither do I mean to belittle you or your business but a ground floor office on the Kentish Town Road, with your colleague upstairs, was not what I had in mind for a detective to investigate the disappearance of my parents."

Kara relaxed back into her chair. She was impressed. Zoe hadn't sounded churlish or belittling and had actually spoken in a pleasant and gentle tone. Nevertheless, the calm delivery had an inner strength, an edge that definitely communicated what Zoe had needed to say. She had basically told Kara she didn't trust her, didn't have much faith in the surroundings and wasn't that keen on engaging her. Yet she had done it in a way that made Kara want to genuinely thank her. That was a skill. In another setting, in days gone by, Kara would have seen a potential recruit in the woman that sat opposite.

"I appreciate your candour Zoe. I can only tell you that my colleague actually owns the apartment upstairs and where we are sitting was once her parent's business premises. They've retired and now live in a very fine Georgian Terrace villa, a few streets back from here. They also own the freehold on this building and I get a very reasonable rent for an office that is convenient for central London, has excellent road and rail access and is a five minute walk from my own apartment. As for me, I can't really provide details of other cases I've been involved in, as client confidentiality prevents that. What I can tell you is this. Your brother is an amateur rugby player. I'd hazard a guess at the Hammersmith and Fulham Senior 1st XV. They play in the London North West League-2 and mostly play their games on Saturdays. Occasionally they'll play Sunday Cup games. I reckon he's a loosehead prop and is an impressive size of a man, but just not quite tall or broad enough to carry into the semi-professional or professional ranks. Instead he concentrated on studies and now holds a lucrative job in the City, but the hours are irregular and so I would think he's an international trader or similar. The wristband he wears might be in recognition of your Father's service, but is likelier down to some of his City colleagues and friends having been ex-Service," Kara paused momentarily and looked to Michael. She saw the flicker of recognition in his eyes. "Given the circles he mixes in, I'd say some of them are ex-Guards, Household Cavalry, or perhaps even Honoura-ble Artillery Company." She had watched him carefully as she spoke and saw each assessment hit the mark. Kara looked back towards Zoe.

"You're a professional dancer. More specifically, a balleri-na. It could be the Royal Ballet, but if I had to make a call I'd be inclined to say probably not. More likely to be one of the other London Companies, maybe the English National. You've always been a dancer and probably graduated from one of the London schools. Obviously your hours are quite irregular, like your brother's, hence the shared house in town. As for your parents, I don't know what's happened to them but you've already told me your father was an ex-Royal Navy photogra-pher and I reckon he was at a Joint Service base near Arlesey for his last tour of duty. That means really only one place and that was confirmed by the fact that his ex-colleagues ended up putting you in touch with Victoria. Not many people have access to that lady. I really don't know if what's happening now has anything to do with his time in the Service, but it's a possibility. I think that outgoing message was left as a diversion, but whoever came up with the cover story didn't know about your Mother's fear of flying. That means something's not right." Kara paused and then couldn't resist adding a little icing on top, "Oh, and your Father was originally from Wallsend, just north of Newcastle and I'm not a detective. I'm a private investigator."

Zoe Sterling didn't quite smile but glanced across to Michael before looking back at Kara, "That's a very persuasive display. I would suggest it's okay for your colleague to join us now."

7

Camden, London

As the Sterlings were making their way back to Fulham, Tien had already broken into the various Global Distribution Systems that the major airlines used to validate bookings.

"So, what am I looking at?" Kara asked.

"On the left is Sabre, then Amadeus, Galileo, Apollo, Travelport and Worldspan. If the Sterling's parents made a reservation with BA it'll be in at least one of these."

"How the hell did you penetrate them so quickly?"

"Ah, these are easy and I've broken into them so many times I might as well have a login."

The computer screens beeped almost in a perfect sequence left to right and all of them flashed up the same record. British Airways Flight 207 departing Heathrow to Miami, Florida. Two seats. One for Christopher Harold Sterling and another for Brenda Joyce Sterling.

Tien interrogated the record details and compared it to the information Zoe and Michael had provided. "The names, address, dates of birth and all the other data we have matches. They got on a flight on Tuesday morning and went to America according to this."

"Well, someone did. Did they book business, first class?"

"Cattle class. No frills. Seats 45 B and C. Flight was booked and paid for," Tien paused a beat, "Oh that's interesting."

"What?" Kara said as she leaned over trying to interpret the screen of abbreviations and unfamiliar character sets that filled the central display.

"It was booked and paid for at 03:30, Tuesday morning from an Internet access. Paid for by a credit card registered to Christopher Sterling, so no details needed that wouldn't be on the card. Certainly no pin or signature required. It does show an IP address so if we can get the Sterling's home computer, then I should be able to verify if it came from there."

Kara laughed, "Interesting is an understatement isn't it? According to this Chris Sterling decided, on what appears to be a complete whim, to get up in the middle of the night and book himself and his airplane phobic wife on an impromptu flight across the Atlantic?"

"Yep, that would seem to be exactly what happened," Tien said as she swivelled her chair round. "So now what? There's no bookings in these systems for a hotel or a hire car. Their kids don't have a hotel name for them and according to the search I ran a couple of minutes ago, Trip Advisor says there are over 4000 hotels in Florida alone. The chances of us finding them are nil."

"So all we know is that someone booked a flight?"

"No," Tien said. "We also know that someone got on that flight and went to Miami." She swivelled back and pointed to the screen. "That 'pcf' next to each name means that the passengers completed the flight. It wasn't a no-show. Two people got on and sat in 45 B and C and then they got off at Miami without incident. They even had hold luggage of one bag each."

Kara sat down in the spare chair next to Tien. She steepled her fingers and leant her forehead against them. After a few moments she raised her head again, "How do we figure out who got on the plane?"

"Not easy," Tien said. "The chances of me getting to look at CCTV in the arrivals hall of Miami is nil. There's no way I'm getting into that and as for US customs, Homeland Security would be all over a breach attempt. So that's out. As for the UK, it might be possible but I really don't have the first clue who or what to target." Tien shook her head and then gave Kara her best smile, "You need to make a phone call."

Kara pulled a face that she hoped conveyed 'Oh Piss Off' but she knew Tien was right. "Fine, I'll go make a call. But you need to make one too. Call up Sandy Marrs at Chicksands and find out what Chris Sterling did in the Royal Navy. I want to know if he was mainstream or had gone over to the dark side. Once that's done can you get the car and we'll head up to the Sterling's house in Arlesey? I'd like you to get at their computer and I want to have a look at the place anyway. All good?" Kara asked as she pulled her mobile out.

"Yep," Tien said and began to shut down her computers.

φ

"Hi Sis, how's you?"

"I'm good. How's Alice and the kids?"

"Yeah great. Kyas fell out of a tree last week and nearly broke his leg but didn't. He was quite gutted that he couldn't have a cast. Apparently some other kid in his school has one and he thought it was 'coo-ool'."

Kara laughed, "And Marli?"

"Oh you know Marli. She started nursery school last week and loves it. Wants to go every day and was quite upset when we explained that even when she does go full-time she'll have to have Saturdays and Sundays off."

"Nursery? Already?"

"Yeah but it's just a pre-school playgroup for three year olds. We're only sending her there two days a week 'cos Alice started back part-time at the Yard."

"Is she enjoying being back?"

"Well, she says she is but she's knackered at the end of the week. Understandable though. It's been almost seven years since she left to have Kyas and she didn't go back at all in the middle. Saying that I'm sure she'll cope okay and be back full-time as soon as Marli goes to Primary. Anyway, how's you? How's the love life?"

"Ha! I'm good and the other is non-existent," Kara paused and waited for her brother to speak again but he didn't. "Umm, David?" she finally said.

"Yes Kara, what do you want?" His voice carried the slightly disapproving tone that he reserved for her when she phoned to ask him questions or elicit favours. She reflected that it was on these occasions that she felt like the younger sibling when in fact she was two years his senior.

"I just wondered if you could tell me something about surveillance at Heathrow departures?"

David laughed, "Well of course. Have you got all day?"

"Well not all of the systems, obviously," she stressed the last word and also reigned in her frustration. She loved her brother dearly but he could be an arse sometimes. "I only need to know what cameras would pick you up going through departures or where they store the scan of your passport when you go through passport control."

"Kara, seriously. I'm a Detective Sergeant in the Met. I don't have access to that information. It's all Border Force stuff. Anyway, what do you want to know for?"

"I have some people who allegedly went to the US but I'm not sure it was them travelling. I need to get eyes on them and the only place I can do that is when they went through departures here. Any ideas?"

"To be honest, no not really," this time David paused, "If they went through on false passports why aren't SO15 all over it?"

"Because the two people aren't a threat. They've no apparent links to anything dodgy and all the circumstances surrounding their trip check out. I have no evidence at all that it wasn't the real people." She didn't add that no one in the

Metropolitan Police's Counter Terrorist Command would want to take a second look at them now because that would mean having to admit to the US Department of Homeland Security that the Brits let two fakes get on a jet and head to the States. Kara had never worked for the Police but she knew enough about inter-nation military rivalries and doubted it would be any different for members of the 'thin blue line'. Cock-ups were not for sharing with your international friends.

"So why are you looking?" David asked bluntly.

"Because there's something not right about it."

"Your sneaky-beaky senses kicking in Sis?"

"Yep." Kara knew her brother well enough to wait out the silence on the phone line.

"Fine," he said eventually. "You know you could just save us a lot of time and tell me that the hairs on the back of your neck are up and you need some help."

"Yeah, but then I'd never hear all about Alice and the kids. You never call me!" she said the last with a comedic but melodramatic pout to her voice that made her kid-brother laugh again.

"I never call you. Huh! Hello pot, this is kettle. Hang on," he said and Kara could hear what sounded like the phone being placed on a surface. "I've put you on speaker. I just need to get a card for you. If I can find the damn thing."

She heard muffled scrapings and the background hum of traffic. She had visited his office often and despite being on the seventh floor of the New Scotland Yard building on Victoria Street, behind bullet and blast proof glazing, the hubbub of central London always seemed to permeate the space.

"Right, get in touch with a woman called Wendy Mead. I met her briefly at a conference in February. I think she's a consultant security advisor on the payroll of the Border Force. I know she works out of Gatwick. Thing is Kara, they're all as tight as a duck's arse when it comes to this sort of stuff. I mean, she might be able to clue you in on what happens but whether she will or not is a different matter."

Kara heard the background hum disappear as her brother

took the phone off speaker and raised it back to his ear.

"It's okay David. Trust me. You know I'll come up with a reason for her to tell me. I'll let you know what reason I've used, just in case she rings you. I wouldn't want us to get our lines crossed, now would I?" she said it with a hint of mischief in her voice.

"Kara, you will be the end of my career one day."

"Ah come on I wouldn't do that. Mine maybe, yours, never."

"Alright, I'll take a photo of her card and text it to you. Ok?"

"You're a lovely person David and God will reward you for this. You know that don't you?" Kara said in her best Sunday-school teacher's voice.

"Yeah, but not with a sister that I wouldn't swap for a decent Scalextric set."

8

Monday Afternoon. Arlesey, Bedfordshire

Breaking and entering was a lot easier when you had the house keys and alarm codes. Tien entered the 6-digit sequence that Zoe Sterling had given her and the chirping from the alarm control box ceased. The entrance hall and the rest of the large house fell quiet. Kara shut the front door and opened the first door on the right. Michael had provided them with a floor plan so she knew she was walking into the main lounge. What she hadn't expected was a Zulu war shield, cross-mounted with a short-staff assegai, mounted directly above the wide fireplace. Kara walked to it and examined it closely. She didn't know much about antiques but thought there was a chance this was an authentic version. Maybe even from the Zulu wars. Tien came in behind her and gave a low whistle. "I know," Kara said, "It's amazing." She turned to see Tien wasn't looking at the shield.

"That's a set of Bang and Olufsen Beolab 18's," Tien nodded towards the tall silver and oak structures standing in the midpoint of each wall either side of the fire.

"I thought they were sculptures," Kara said.

"Yeah, well, you could get cheaper statues. Those'll set

you back about four and a half grand."

"Really? Anything else worth that sort of money?"

Tien turned in a slow circle. "The TV is B&O too so I would imagine the rest of the audio system is as well. You've probably got upwards of thirty-K just in sound and vision equipment in this room alone."

Kara walked across to the French doors that led into a medium sized conservatory and looked beyond it into the garden. "His workshop's a lot bigger than I imagined," she called over her shoulder.

"Do you want to start in here or out there?" Tien asked.

"In here."

Tien started taking photos from each corner and midpoint of the lounge so she could recreate it later in a 3-D computer-rendered model if necessary. It was unlikely it'd be needed to investigate what happened to the Sterlings but Kara and Tien had routines. So now it didn't matter if it was going to be needed or not, Tien took the photos. The ability to revisit a place, examine the sight angles, the overall layout, the fixtures and the fittings had served them well in the past. When she'd taken all the photos she logged the dimensions of the room using a laser distance measure.

Kara waited in the conservatory. Her brother had joked about hairs on the back of her neck standing up when she felt things weren't right and that was exactly how she felt standing in the Sterling's house. Zoe and Michael had said they hadn't disturbed anything when they first came up almost a week earlier and Kara believed them. However, they had said that whilst their parents were clean and tidy they thought the house looked 'too neat'. She had to agree. Just from looking at the lounge and conservatory she could feel something was wrong. There was a slight dust on surfaces, exactly what you would expect from a week of inactivity, but there was also a clinical feel to the place. "I'm going to go look through the rest of it, you follow as you're ready," Kara said and Tien nodded from behind the camera.

Off the main hallway was a door to what had once been a

formal dining room but was now a study, another to a kitchen-cum-breakfast room and a last one that opened on to a downstairs toilet. All the rooms were similarly neat, clean and overly tidy.

Kara went upstairs, passing family portraits of the Sterlings that tracked their progress from the wedding of Chris and Brenda through to the graduations of Zoe and Michael. Upstairs she found four bedrooms, an en-suite, a main bathroom and a large linen cupboard that was big enough to contain a drop-ladder to the roof space. The rooms were tastefully furnished in what looked a casual manner but had obviously had a lot of time and care devoted to the effect. Each room had quality artwork on the walls and dotted here and there were fine art sculptures, including a set of exquisitely cast bronze ballerinas in what Kara assumed had been Zoe's room. But as for obvious clues to where Brenda Sterling and her husband Chris had gone, there was nothing.

She waited for Tien to join her in the master bedroom and take the final set of photos, before both of them donned gloves and began to conduct a thorough but cautious search of the rooms. When Kara opened a drawer or a cupboard Tien photographed the exact state of the contents before either of them began to move anything. It was slow and painstaking but necessary. Depending on what had happened to the Sterlings the house might yet become a crime scene and neither Tien nor Kara had any desire to destroy or disturb evidence that could be of use later. Before closing the cupboard or drawer they replaced the contents and compared the results to the original photo. They did the same with objects on shelves or on top of cupboards and made sure everything went back exactly. They took pictures off walls and checked behind them, lifted rugs and mats and searched under mattresses and in pillow cases.

It took them two and a half hours just to finish upstairs and at the end of it they had found nothing of use. The only saving grace had been that the roof space was empty other than the insulation batts and whilst Kara and Tien didn't pull them up it was obvious from inspection that no one else had either.

Returning downstairs they carried out the same search procedure in the lounge, conservatory and kitchen with the same results. That left the formal dining room come study. It offered their last and possibly best hope of eliciting any clues as to what was going on.

Kara looked around it. Besides the computer desk and a small offside working area, it was lined with half-height bookcases. The library held, along with the occasional pulp fiction, mostly books of military genres, both fiction and historical reference. The walls were bare of artwork except for a stunning print of The Defence of Rorke's Drift, by Alphonse de Neuville that dominated the main space of the main wall. The search of the desk drawers, bookcases and behind the print revealed nothing. Only the computer remained. Tien turned it on and waited until the 'enter password' screen appeared.

"Do you think you'll get anything off the Mac?" Kara asked with an air of optimism that she didn't really believe.

"It's password protected but that shouldn't be a problem," Tien said as she took a small USB drive from her jeans pocket and waved it in the air. "I'll be able to get the IP and compare it to the ticket booking but that's all I'd hold out hope for."

"I'm going to take a wander outside whilst you finish. I want to look at the workshop. Catch me up," Kara said and went to leave but turned back. "Tien?"

"Yes?"

"What does this house look like to you?"

Tien looked up from the computer and gazed around the study. She pursed her lips and then shrugged, "Honestly? It looks like the way we would've left a safe house if we'd had time before bugging out."

"My thoughts exactly," Kara said.

"But when I spoke to Sandy Marrs he said that Chris Sterling didn't go across to special ops. He was a photographer who became an Imagery Analyst and eventually an instructor back at Chicksands. We know heaps of folk that have done that and none of them got trained in the sanitisation of safe houses."

"Maybe Sandy didn't have the whole story?" Kara said, but without conviction. Sandy Marrs was the Executive Officer at the Defence Intelligence College at Chicksands. It was the nearest Joint Service establishment to Arlesey and had been the favourite bet of where Chris Sterling had spent his last tour of duty. But if Sandy said Chris hadn't done special ops training then he more than likely hadn't.

"You think they've been involved in something and now they've done a runner before being caught?" Tien asked.

"It's one possibility but it doesn't explain why they'd leave a message like they did. It's an obvious false flag to the kids."

"What's the other possibilities?"

"They might have been relocated by someone to protect them." Kara looked around the room again. "But that's doubtful for the same reasons. Agencies would have looked after the loose ends better. They wouldn't have tipped the kids with the message."

"That leaves taken against their will. But by someone who was constructing a diversionary story and didn't know anything about the fear of flying thing. Is that what you're thinking?" Tien asked.

"Probably. What do you think?"

"I guess so, but for now it doesn't really matter. Either way, free-running or dragged; what you need to do is figure out why and where. Then we'll go find them, reunite the Sterling Family and live happily ever after." Tien gave a little smile and turned back towards the computer.

Kara made her way through the back door of the kitchen and out into a large garden that she reckoned was almost half an acre of land. The house, sitting as it did at the end of a single-track lane about five miles from the small town, had no neighbours within a good stone's throw so the garden was a place of seclusion and tranquillity. Three offset screens of trees were cleverly placed to divide it into distinct planting areas. The first, nearest the house, was a simple run of well-tended lawn. The second had the workshop located off to one side with low shrubs and medium height plants opposite. Kara thought they looked nice but couldn't identify any of them. The last garden area had seemingly been left to nature and had the look and feel of a summer meadow. In the warm sun of a July afternoon it radiated in colour and fragrance.

She breathed in the mix of freshness, light overtures of fine perfume and the slightly heavier notes of the surrounding country. Walking forward to the sound of water she found a small pond with a number of water pipes feeding into it. Not big enough to be a feature fountain, but enough to keep the water moving and oxygenated, it was home to half a dozen goldfish that swam around in the gaps between submerged plants. As she looked at this last third of the garden Kara realised the meadow effect had been achieved with a lot of hard work and thorough planning. The natural look and feel of it was carefully cultivated. She relaxed in the still lingering heat of the sun for a short while and then headed back to the second garden area and Chris Sterling's workshop.

According to Zoe and Michael their father had left the military in 1992 after serving twenty-two years, then had established a small photography business in Bedford. He shut up the shop and took early retirement in 2005 aged fifty-five. Not content to do nothing he apparently kept a small photo practice running out of home. He did the occasional wedding, took and sold some art shots and framed pictures. It was more a hobby than a continuing business according to Michael. The workshop was where he ran it from.

Closer up it was even more substantial than it had looked from the conservatory. Stretching about forty feet in length, Kara also noticed it had a very large padlock on the door. She reached into her pocket and took out a small fabric fold that contained a set of picks. After a few moments the lock gave a soft click and the hasp popped up.

"Nicely done," said Tien who had come up behind her.

"You all finished inside? Anything on the computer?"

"No, nothing. Well, not relating to why they're missing. It seems Mrs Sterling uses it for recipes, sewing patterns, what looked like scrapbooking, a lot of gardening sites and researching her family history. All of which is quite interesting on its own. It would appear she or her husband, to be honest I couldn't figure out which, is related to one of the defenders at Rorke's Drift. Hence the shield, spear and painting I presume. However, one thing I can tell you for certain is that it was the computer the airline tickets were booked on. So, what's inside here?"

Kara pushed the workshop door open and allowed her eyes to adjust to the dimmer interior. There were windows along either wall but the ones at the far end of the space had blackout curtains drawn across them. She found the light switch and three long fluorescent tubes lit up, revealing that the space was functionally split into two. Nearest to the door was a compact woodworking area with benches, a vice and an array of saws and planes. At the far end, with the blackout curtains, was what seemed to be a photo studio including backdrops and screens.

Tien stepped inside and made her way to the far end. "Nice studio setup. Bigger than you'd imagine. I guess half of it was a darkroom at some point." She raised her camera and began to take photos as she had in the house.

The two women spent the next half hour methodically searching each space, cupboard and drawer, making their way back up the length of the workshop. Eventually Kara raised a drop-leaf side bench next to the main woodworking area and she and Tien stopped.

Set into a steel frame and masked from sight by the drop-leaf that had been specifically shaped to conceal it was a three foot tall by two foot wide combination dial safe. As the drop-leaf came horizontal the safe door swung slowly open.

"That's a disappointment," Kara said as the inside was revealed to be completely empty.

"Still," Tien said. "That's a big safe."

"Maybe he kept his cameras in here? We haven't found any trace of them."

"True, but a combination safe this size? Bit of over-protection, don't you think?"

"I do," Kara agreed. "Let's finish the rest."

The next double cupboard was also empty.

"Well I don't know what it was, but there was definitely something in here," Tien said. "Look at the discolouration around the edges but not in the middle of the shelves. I reckon at least one of these outlines was a printer."

"Right. We've got no cameras and no printer. Was there any photo software on the Mac in the study?" asked Kara.

"Nope."

"So we're probably also missing a laptop or desktop computer?"

"Yep," agreed Tien. "But there are no fine tools either. No small screw drivers, no model knives, no small tacks or small hammers. There's no mounting glue or tape. All the stuff you'd use when framing pictures. Maybe all the little stuff was in whatever was on these other shelves."

Kara shrugged and closed the cupboard.

A half hour later, as the sun was beginning to set into the Bedfordshire countryside, they closed the padlock on the door to the workshop. The last out-building to check was the garage. As Zoe and Michael had told them, Brenda Sterling's Peugeot 508 Station Wagon was there and Chris Sterling's Jaguar XFR wasn't.

"They must have been doing okay. That Peugeot's not the cheapest car," Kara said.

"Not half as expensive as the missing Jag," Tien said as she photographed the otherwise empty garage. "Even more so for having personalised plates," she said referring to the fact that Zoe had been able to recite the YI700N of her father's registration. With an appropriately placed fastening bolt the plate would read 'Why-Aye Toon'.

Kara laughed, "Yeah, but it is only a Newcastle United supporter's plate. Probably cheap as. Be different if he'd got LFC1."

"Oh yeah, sure," Tien said sarcastically. A life-long Arsenal fan, Tien never missed the chance to tease her friend about supporting Liverpool Football Club. She received a raised finger in response.

When they were done, Tien locked the house and reset the alarm whilst Kara made a quick call. They met back at their car.

"According to Zoe the safe was for his cameras but as to what else might have been in it she doesn't know. He did do all of his photo processing work on his laptop and yes, there was a hi-grade photo-quality printer in the workshop. Michael and she hadn't realised anything was missing because they never went in to the workshop last week."

"Why not?"

"They don't have keys for the lock. Apparently their dad keeps them on his keyring."

"Kinda strange?" Tien mused.

"Not really. Apparently he only had the workshop built after he retired from the photography shop, by which time Zoe and Michael weren't living at home. I suppose there was no reason for them to have keys for it. If there's a spare set they don't know where."

"Did she ask how we got in?"

"Yeah but I told her that's what she was paying us for. Anyway, it confirms we're missing some things."

"But we can't go to the Police and tell them that it all went missing last Tuesday, can we?" Tien said as she slid into the driver's seat of the automatic. It was fitted with a steering wheel knob that allowed her single-handed operation of the vehicle.

Kara glanced over her shoulder and watched the Sterling's house receding. "Nope, because the cops will say that the cupboards and safe could have been empty for ages. They'll also tell us that it's more than likely Mr and Mrs Sterling left for a fly-drive photo tour of the States, taking their camera, laptop and printer with them. Is that what we're meant to be thinking?"

Tien nodded, "Yeah, sounds about right. Problem is, I don't know where we go from here. You'll need to get me an in to the Heathrow system if we're going to prove it wasn't them that flew out. Failing that all we have is nothing. An empty safe and some missing gear."

"Let's hope this woman Wendy Mead comes up with something tomorrow. We'll need to do some prep in the morning."

9

DCI Reynolds looked over at his Detective Chief Superintendent and shook his head.

"No Ma'am. Not a thing. My team interviewed the man who found the body but he'd merely stumbled upon it and we learnt nothing of note. We've talked to almost all of Hastings' normal acquaintances and although that sounds good, it was actually easy to achieve. He had a sheet as long as your arm and was known to us for assaults, domestic violence when he still had a wife, possession, minor supply and major supply. He'd been working his way up the distribution hierarchy of the South Cambs suppliers but then got back into using and quickly worked his way down again."

Reynolds paused to allow the DCS to make comment but she just waved for him to go on. She had an unnerving way of staring whilst receiving briefings but Tony had worked for her for long enough to not be fazed by the quirk.

He continued, "If this had been a simple knife to the head, drug deal gone wrong we'd have a likely list of players to work through. As it is, with Doctor Rowland's discovery of the real cause of death, we need to start again. None of the usual druggies in the town tend to wear stilettos or be capable of standing upright let alone kicking someone in the head with that amount of force. I'd have said, based on nothing more than instinct, that this could have been a self-defence killing. But in that case I'd have expected to have found lots of DNA left at the scene. Instead, we've got nothing. In fact, it was so devoid of traces it almost looked like a professional clean up. There's nothing that gives any indication of who we're looking for except for the red paint found in the wounds."

Detective Chief Superintendent Laura Mitchell held her hand up and stopped him, "Tony, what if it was a pro-hit? Is there a chance the red shoe is the false lead? Was he clubbed to the head afterwards with a stiletto heel to make it look like a shoe?"

"According to the secondary tests Doctor Rowlands ran, the wound was delivered with a force equivalent to almost a thousand pounds. It was definitely a kick," Reynolds hesitated waiting for Mitchell to ask something more but she didn't. She just looked neutrally at him and waited, so he continued, "The results we got back last night on the paint reveals it's used on quite literally millions of shoes imported from the Far East. I've had a five strong team trying to discover who the assailant is and we've had no return. It's been more than three days now, so I'd like your authority to take a fresh approach. I want to review all the CCTV from Friday night and Saturday morning."

"From where?"

"The whole town."

"That's an immense amount of data surely?" Mitchell said.

"Yes Ma'am, but the person who did this had to come from somewhere and go to somewhere afterwards. We currently have a body in the light industrial area, where there's no CCTV coverage and an unknown assailant who seems to have appeared out of nowhere and disappeared back into the same. If we're going to find them then I need to-"

Mitchell cut him off with a gentle wave of her hand. "Okay Tony, but the budget is going to be tight on this and whilst I will never acknowledge publically that we shouldn't be spending time on the death of a known drug user and dealer..." She stopped and merely tilted her head and looked over her glasses at him.

"Yes Ma'am, understood."

"So wrap this up quickly. If it runs over or we get a higher priority then it goes on the back burner and," she paused before stressing her next word, "*if* it turns out that it is an upstanding, law-abiding citizen acting in self-defence, then we and the CPS will need to sit down and have a good long talk. Clear?"

Reynolds was a realist but his detective instinct baulked at the prospect of the case being dropped by the Crown Prosecution Service because it wouldn't play well in the media. He would need to get the case completely watertight so that they had no option but to proceed. For now, he merely said, "Yes Ma'am."

He left Mitchell's office and returned to the Major Crimes Unit on the fourth floor. Detective Sergeants Gary Mason and Moya Little were waiting for him in the operations room.

"Did she agree?" Mason asked.

"Yep, so let's go get a copy of it all."

Mason and Little both pointed towards a cardboard box sitting on the desk behind them.

"We figured you'd talk her round, so we sent Pop over to Eastfields already." Little said, referring to the Huntingdon-shire District Council's CCTV control room. "They gave him 51 DVDs. One for each individual camera in the town and they confirmed all of their feeds are in colour nowadays. However, it's still going to be difficult to accurately see red shoes in the glow cast by the street lights," she added.

"So, how do you want to do this Gov?" Mason asked.

"I think we'll miss less if we double up," Reynolds said. "Gary you sit in with Pop, Moya you take John and I'll go with Anna. According to Doctor Rowlands it was no earlier than eleven on Friday night and no later than five on Saturday morning that Hastings was killed. So we'll bracket from nine through to seven. Ten hours and seventeen cameras each. I want a quick scan of all the tapes. Mark up any of them that show red high heels or if you can't determine the colour just a set of heels will do for now. We'll concentrate on single females only, not groups and not with males and they'll need to be in the west of the town or heading to it. Once we've got a shortlist we'll reconvene."

"Why only singles?" Mason asked.

"Because I don't think our Mr Hastings would have approached a couple or a group. I don't think he was a sociable type."

"It still might not be that short a list. We're going to be covering the chucking out time from every pub and club in Huntingdon. How many of the locals do you think will be wearing heels?" Mason asked.

"God alone knows but there can't be many that are capable of inflicting a kick to the head with the force and accuracy that killed Hastings, so that might help us a bit. Anyway, we start by whittling it down and then we go from there. Agreed?" Reynolds looked at both his Sergeants. They smiled and nodded.

"What are you both smiling at?"

"You," Moya said. "You've been moping about for the last two days as we got nowhere and now look at you. All happy and enthused about sitting in a video suite to watch hours of CCTV just because you think it might be a lead."

Reynolds smiled back at them. "Yeah, well it's only dampened by knowing I still have you two working for me. Are you actually going to do any work or just take the mickey out of your boss?"

"Perhaps. C'mon Gary. I suppose the sooner we get started the sooner we make him look good again. Let's go get him a shortlist," Moya said and winked over at Mason as she stood.

Six hours later they were back and pleasantly surprised that their list was very short indeed.

10

Tuesday Morning. Camden, London

"**H**i Wendy, you don't know me but I'm David Wright's sister. I believe you met him at a-"

"Oh! David," the woman answered in a voice Kara thought was normally reserved for cute puppies and kittens. Mead continued a little hurriedly, "How is he? I do hope he's well. Such a nice guy."

Kara stopped herself from saying anything smug or cynical. She knew growing up that her brother had obviously been okay looking as he'd had girlfriends, but to be honest she had always thought he had punched way above his weight when Alice agreed to marry him. She definitely knew he was a flirt. She had seen him hold the attention of many a member of female company by talking and laughing with them. But she hadn't expected him to have had a lasting effect on a fifty-something woman he met at a conference five months ago. Saying that, Kara knew Mead had been getting over a break-up at the time, so perhaps David had made an impression simply by being kind and taking an interest in her. He was nice like that.

Kara bit her lip slightly at the thought that she and Tien's last ninety minutes of effort might have been superfluous, but on reflection, she figured probably not. Research was never wasted and anyway, she and Tien had routines before a first contact.

They had arrived into the office early after a shortened morning run and started doing preliminary background research using Wendy Mead's prolific social media presence. Starting with her Facebook account, Kara and Tien knew that Wendy was single, fifty-one years old, the eldest of three girls and her two younger sisters were both married and had kids. Wendy had been married and divorced in her thirties with no children from it. She'd had another long-term partner but split up from him sometime between summer and Christmas of last year and since then had been single. They knew her full résumé from LinkedIn and it was quite impressive. Leaving school at eighteen but not going to university, which Tien thought likely meant she had failed her A-levels, she started work as an administrator for an armoured-van security company. The job was easy and Wendy Mead was obviously a great deal smarter than her probable A-level results gave her credit for. Within five years she was an accounts manager, within ten a senior security manager. The company diversified into fixed point security and Wendy's career had continued to impress. After twenty-five years she left and formed her own solo security consultancy. She had won a few small jobs over the last eight years including a couple of one-year Government contracts before being the sole consultant commissioned to provide a report into airport procedures.

That was as far as they had got on LinkedIn but a cross reference to a Government tenders website revealed a little more. Given the relative dates, it was probable that Wendy had won a contract to write a study paper on the 'Provision of Electronic Scanning Within UK Arrivals'.

Pinterest had provided a few more clues to the woman's likes and dislikes, as had Twitter; Mead owned a cat, enjoyed baking, mostly cupcakes, and read historic fiction. Her favourite novelist was Jane Austen, or so she said and she supported the Coventry Blaze Ice Hockey team. She might also have had a real passion for Rugby Union or as Tien had reckoned, she just collected photos of the New Zealand All-Blacks for aesthetic reasons.

Kara had formulated an approach that she figured would give her the best chance to get the information she needed. Now, Wendy Mead, with her reaction to the mention of David had, in one sentence, given Kara a completely different angle to work from.

"Oh he's very well Wendy, very well. Made me promise to make sure I said hello for him and to tell you he'd been asking after you."

"Really, oh how lovely," Mead giggled in a strangely adolescent way and Kara suppressed more cynical comebacks. "Well," continued Mead, "that's just so nice."

Kara thought she'd rarely heard someone more genuinely pleased. She decided to lay on a little more flattery. "I really hope you don't mind but David said that you'd be able to help me. In fact he insisted I ring you when he found out what I was working on. He said that he'd met you at the conference and was blown away by your in-depth knowledge of the whole security field. I do hope you don't mind him imposing me on you?" Kara said with a hopeful tone.

"Of course not, no, of course not. Aw, that's lovely that he thought of me like that," Mead enthused.

"I hope I'm not taking too much advantage of your good nature, Wendy?"

"No, certainly not. So what is it you're working on and what can I do to help?"

Kara improvised and adapted her original strategy, "I'm doing some research for a course I'm taking. Apparently I need to get a security qualification because my experience doesn't count and I keep losing jobs to people with Bachelors and Masters."

"That's just pathetic," Mead said. "It's pompous ass graduates who don't know their way to the toilet by themselves that are the problem."

"I know Wendy, I know," Kara agreed, "but, I've caved in to the pressure," she laughed a little nervously. "So David said you could you help me out?"

Mead didn't hesitate, "Of course Kara. You fire away."

Kara started with banal questions about airport transit procedures and Mead answered them succinctly. After about five minutes of to and fro with Kara taking hurried and completely fictional notes, she simply changed gears and figured that if she had reeled Mead in well enough the answers would just keep coming.

"Wendy, this is great. David was right about you. You certainly know your stuff."

"Oh, I, well, I suppose," Wendy almost simpered.

"So, when people are leaving the UK do the Border Force have to check all their passports too?" Kara asked. "That would be slightly depressing seeing all the happy faces leaving on holiday."

"Ah well, no. The Government really wants to reintroduce passport controls for all departing passengers from all points, to all points, but that programme is behind schedule."

"Phew, that's alright then. I couldn't think of anything more happiness-sapping," Kara said, managing to mask her actual disappointment at the news.

"Ah, but Kara, they do have to do it for all international air passengers. Everyone has to present their passports at UK air departure points." Mead had said it in the tone of a teacher instructing a diligent pupil.

"Really?" Kara said it as flatly as possible, once more hiding her real emotions that this time had been elated at the news. "But that must be thousands of people? Where on earth do they store all that data? And who would ever have time to look at it?"

"Oh it's not stored. The passport chips are read or the machine code scanned for the old passports with no chips. Although they're out of date completely in a couple of years. Everyone will have to have a chipped passport by 2016. But there's no data capture. That would be impossible. The system just runs a check against some databases, no-fly lists, Interpol lists, that type of thing. If it doesn't sound alarm bells then that's it. Have a nice trip!" Mead said with a light tone.

Kara played along, "Gosh! And there's me thinking there was a whole collection of photos taken of everyone leaving the country."

"Ha!" Mead laughed, "No, nothing like that I'm afraid."

"So no Big Brother stuff? How sad. I imagined you could have tracked people through the airport? You know, follow them on CCTV and do all that spy stuff."

Wendy laughed, "It would be almost impossible to do that unless you knew what they looked like already and were using it to follow them in real time. The Police and anti-terrorist guys do use it for that sometimes, but I really can't talk about those operations. The CCTV is controlled by the Transport Police, except ironically in the car parks. But we've got five separate parking options and over 3000 spaces, not including the off-site parking that runs into thousands more. The chances of tracing a specific car would be dependent on knowing which car park was used and a rough time window of when it came through. And we are small when compared to Heathrow," Mead paused, "But listen to me rabbiting on. You know I love this stuff and I could talk about it for days but you want to know about the passengers and the impact on them."

"No, no this has been great. Really Wendy, fantastic. David was right, you really are an expert in this. I can't thank you enough, but I do realise you must be busy and I think I have enough to be going on with for now."

"Oh, well, you know, that's so nice of him to say so. You ring me anytime you like and good luck." Mead was back to being a slightly infatuated schoolgirl.

"It really has been terrific. Thanks so much Wendy."

Kara hung up the call and sighed. Her worst imaginings were confirmed. The Sterlings, or whoever had sat in for them, were gone and there was no way of knowing if it was the actual Mr and Mrs Sterling or not. She hadn't really known what she would have done with the information had it been available, but she didn't have anything to work on now. Even if Tien was able to perform a brute force attack on the UK Border Force main database they wouldn't find anything useful. All it would show was that the Sterling's passports and someone who looked enough like them to get through the system had got on that flight. Tien had ruled out the hack anyway. She said that breaking in was difficult enough but insisted it would certainly be traced regardless of what deception plan she ran around it. They might get in but they would get caught. It would take the Government agencies a while but they would catch up with them. It didn't matter now. There was no point breaking in to the equivalent of an empty safe. Kara got up from her desk and went back to her apartment.

φ

Grafton Yard was a converted Georgian Terrace that had once been a series of very fine London townhouses and was now a series of very fine, but much smaller, London apartments. The bonus for Kara was that the rent was therefore affordable in an otherwise unaffordable area. She also liked the fact that there was one conventional way in, but potentially five non-conventional ways out. She knew she didn't have to think like this anymore but she doubted she would ever stop. The habits of self-preservation had been hard won. So she was happy to know that the car park was small, gated and protected by pin-coded entry and the apartment's main entrance was accessed from it. Her apartment had a small balcony to the rear that overlooked the car park and three main lounge room windows to the front that overlooked the Kentish Town Road. If she squeezed up close to the left hand side of the left hand window she could just see her office and Tien's apartment, one hundred and fifty yards down the road.

She kicked off her shoes and stripped off the rest of her clothes as she walked through to the bathroom. A half hour later she was relaxed, soaking in a hot bath and sipping a straight Maker's Mark bourbon. The hoarse, gruff, velvet voice of Ted Hawkins was playing on her Sonos system and the music drifted into her mind, soaking her soul with its sadness. She loved his melancholy, the power of his voice and the truthfulness of his delivery. The drifter Mississippian, whose life was beset by prison and addiction knew how to live the songs he sung. Kara could still remember the first time she heard him sing his cover of the old Country song 'There Stands the Glass'. He infused the song with a depth and a need that addicts and those who knew them could recognise instantly. She had once watched a documentary that featured the original performed by a Honky Tonk Country singer called Webb Pierce. The song had been a huge No.1 hit for him back in the 'Grand Ole Opry' days of the Fifties but as far as Kara was concerned, Pierce's original was a thin and wispy twang in comparison to Hawkin's deep and soulful plea of desperation. The sadness she felt as she listened to Hawkins always reflected her sense of missed opportunity for him. How he had come so close to achieving an easier life, and had it snatched away by death. As the playlist progressed from the 'Best of the Venice Beach Tapes' to the 'Kershaw Sessions Live at the BBC' she sunk her head under the water and tried to think about a new way to track down the Sterlings. The water was almost cold and the playlist had ended by the time she got out of the bath with not so much as an inkling of an idea.

Sitting on her sofa, wrapped in her dressing gown, towel still on her head and contemplating what music to play next, Kara's thoughts were interrupted by the opening riff from 'Baby Please Don't Go' by 'Them'. It was her personalised ringtone for Tien. She answered the call before the guitar chord played out.

"Hi, we need to go back to Arlesey," Tien said with no preamble.

"Okay. What for?"

"Their roof space is too small for the rest of the house."

11

Tuesday Afternoon. Arlesey

Kara drove them the forty miles up the A1 in a little over fifty minutes. There was light traffic heading north in the middle of the afternoon and her only restraint was the average speed cameras that lined the route. On arriving they turned off the alarm, donned gloves and went straight to the upstairs linen cupboard. The drop-ladder came down smoothly and they both went up into the roof space. Tien flicked on the switch to an unshaded single bulb and the space showed what it had on their last visit. Insulation batts and no sign of disturbance.

"So where's the discrepancy?" asked Kara.

"I'm going to guess the far end from here. It's darker and would be easier to hide a false wall."

They turned on the torches they had brought and gingerly made their way across the space, stepping from one rafter to the next. As they covered the twenty or so feet toward the eastern end of the house Kara could still see nothing that looked odd. The wall she was approaching seemed exactly like the end wall near the access hatch. But as she stepped right up next to it she suddenly realised the 'bricks' were flat.

"It's a photograph! It's a photograph on high quality paper

pasted in sections," Tien said, as she flashed her torchlight the length of the false wall. "Oh Kara, this is good work. There's no chance you would see this normally. No reasonable search team would have found this. The paper is thick enough to not crease or flex. Mind you, it's also thick enough to reflect the laser measure I used, so in effect it let itself down."

"And you found this from just messing around with your 3-D model. How much space is it concealing?" asked Kara.

"About three and a half feet in depth. I couldn't tell how wide it was from the measurements I had but looking at it now, it would seem to run the whole thirty feet width of the house." Tien moved down the length of the paper screen feeling for an opening. "And I wasn't messing about."

"What were you doing?"

"I was bored," Tien said.

"Other people watch TV. You make 3-D models of houses that we don't need?"

"It would seem we did need it, now doesn't it? Ah ha!" Tien reached through a black cut-out concealed right at the bottom corner where the photo screen met the floor space and the roof hip. She felt for and found a catch. Shining her torch she called Kara over, "It's got a lock, did you bring your picks?"

"Of course."

Crouching in the narrow gap Kara took slightly longer than usual but after a few minutes the lock gave a soft click. Kara backed off and stood up to stretch whilst Tien reached through and pulled the catch. A two-foot wide reinforced door on a plywood frame swung in. Tien stepped through and swung her torch up the length of the space.

"What's in there?" Kara called. There was no answer. "Tien, what's in there?" Kara stepped across the gap of the rafters and ducked in through the door. Tien was stood just to her front. "What is it Tien?" Again there was no answer, but Tien stepped off to her left and allowed Kara's torch to light the space. On four wooden boards spaced along the width of the roof space were small, neat stacks of twenty-pound notes.

"Holy fuck!"

"Language Kara. But yes, that about sums it up," Tien chided her with good humour.

"How much is there?" Kara asked.

Tien crouched and swapped her torch for a single stack of the notes. As Kara shone her light on it Tien balanced the stack in her prosthetic palm and counted it quickly before shuffling forward from rafter to rafter to look at each of the four boards in turn.

"There's ten grand in each stack and each board, except for this one, has ten by ten stacks. This board has thirteen stacks missing. So all in all, assuming all the stacks are the same there's three million eight hundred and seventy thousand pounds."

"Holy-" Kara stopped herself from swearing again. She didn't need to ask if Tien was sure. Her friend had many talents and mental arithmetic at speed was one of them.

"This rather changes the game, doesn't it?" Tien said as she looked back along the length of the space to Kara, "What do we do now? Get the Police involved? Surely they'll be interested with this lot?"

"We leave it where it is," Kara said as she gazed at the stacks of notes. "For now."

"Really?"

"Really, Tien. But we're going to have to move it and sharpish."

"Why?" Tien asked and then added, "And where? Where are we going to move this to?"

"Not sure where, but I'll figure that out. The why is easy. Let's say that the Sterlings are being held against their will. Let's assume it's because of this lot. If they break and the people who have them come back here and get the money then there's no reason to keep the Sterlings alive. So we need to shift it. If it turns out that Chris and Brenda come back on their own, well I'm sure we can come to some arrangement."

"You sure we shouldn't be going to the Police?" Tien asked with a fair amount of scepticism in her tone.

"Look, if we take this to the Police then it'll disappear out of our hands. The whole case will be in their lap. Look at how much money is here." Kara shone her torch over the notes.

"Yes, I get that it's a lot but what happens if the Sterlings come back on their own and this is just their savings? What-"

Kara interrupted her, "C'mon Tien. That's not likely. This isn't from a sailor's pension. If they come back on their own I'm sure we can return it and suggest at the same time that Mr and Mrs Sterling make it worth our while to keep their extra roof insulation quiet?"

"You think they will?"

"I don't know. But we could really do with a proper payday. This could actually make us solvent. I could stop having to turn tricks at King's Cross," Kara said and winked at her friend in the low grey light of the torches.

"Kara!" Tien said and scowled at her.

"What we have to do is get it out of here in the next couple of days and in the meantime you'll need to set up some form of tripwire so we know if anyone comes in here."

"That's easy. The Sterling's Wi-Fi modem is still running and I've got a couple of Nanny-cams in the boot of the car. I'll rig one of them up and piggy-back onto the signal. It's motion sensitive and it'll stream the footage straight to my phone if it activates. Good quality image too if I put it up near the hatch door where there's good light."

"Thanks MacGyver," Kara said.

"Oh ha ha. You'd be lost without me," Tien said and held the torch up to her chin and poked her tongue out.

Kara laughed.

As they turned to leave Tien's torch played over a shape nestled in the far corner of the space.

"Hang on Kara, there's something here." Tien crouched and shone her torch to reveal an old-fashioned children's duffle bag with cord string-pulls that when taut closed off the neck of the bag.

"What's in it?" Kara asked as she held her torch steady for Tien to navigate by.

Tien struggled for a few moments and then turned back to Kara, "I can't get the string," her voice was heavy with a barely concealed frustration. It wasn't often Kara saw it in her but sometimes, and normally with the most mundane tasks, Tien's annoyance with her left hand would come to the surface.

"It's okay, I'll get it." Kara shuffled across the rafters and took the bag. Easing the stiff cord away from the neck she angled it down so Tien's light could shine into it. There were four UK passports nestling at the bottom of the otherwise empty bag.

"Who are they for?" asked Tien.

Kara reached in and retrieved them. "This one's for Mr Adam Johnson who looks remarkably similar to the photos of Chris Sterling that we got from Michael. This one's for John Adamson and look at that," she held the passport round into the light so Tien could see it.

"It's the same photo!"

"Yep." Kara juggled the documents and opened the other two. "This is for Mrs Anna Johnson and this one, Mrs Joanna Adamson. But both of the photos are of Brenda Sterling."

They searched the rest of the concealed space thoroughly but there was nothing else hiding in the shadows. Taking the passports, they locked everything else back up the way they'd found it.

The drive back into London took longer in the late afternoon traffic but it allowed them time to talk. As they were pulling back onto the Kentish Town Road they had a semblance of a way forward.

"I still don't trust him," Tien said.

"Well neither does anyone else in their right mind. He's a thief and a cheat and a conman. But he's also the only person we know that might have an idea who can produce forged passports. So I don't see we have a choice. Do you want to ring him and set it up?"

"Not really, but I guess I'll have to. Do we try and get him to your place?"

"Well that would be nice but he won't go for it. He always wants to choose the ground. That's fine. We'll let him think he's running it."

"I'll ring the boys then?" Tien asked.

Kara nodded by way of reply, "And I'll get a message through for Victoria to get in touch. Agreed?"

There was a pause as Tien considered Kara's question. Finally she said, "Agreed."

12

Tuesday Night. Central London

Tien sat at the alfresco table warmed in the glow of a sunset and caressed by the slightest of breezes. With her smartphone on the table, headphones in and the gentle rocking of her head she looked like she was enjoying her own musical accompaniment whilst drinking wine and eating a beautiful Italian meal. Her sunglasses, not strictly needed for the late evening sun that cast narrow and lengthening shadows to her front, nonetheless added a touch of urban chic. She occasionally adjusted them. Being first-generation British Vietnamese didn't diminish from the natural beauty of her Vietnamese genes. She looked like a thousand other Asian tourists in London on a beautiful July evening. Her small mouth, with its perfect Cupid's bow and soft lips required the occasional dab of her napkin. The reality of her situation went unnoticed by the multitude of passers-by.

Tien sat at the outside corner table of the alfresco seating area with clear sight lines to Leicester Square and Irving Street. There was no music playing in her headphones, just the faintest static hiss of an open radio channel. The wine glass to her front held cranberry juice with a dash of blackcurrant and although she spun meagre amounts of spaghetti on to her fork at slow intervals, she ate very infrequently. The adjustment of her sunglasses and the dab of her napkin covered the raising of her right cuff-mic to her mouth.

Kara was sitting diagonally opposite, at a German themed restaurant, some three hundred feet away at the far end of Irving Street with her back to Charing Cross Road and the Garrick Theatre. She wore no sunglasses and had no meal on the table. A glass of mineral water sat in front of her and a spare chair waited opposite. The almost invisible earpiece, nestled deep in her left ear, made a small 'tic' sound just before she received a transmission. 'Tic.'

The faint, yet perfectly audible, sound of Tien's voice filled Kara's ear, "He's stopped at the entrance to the Odeon." Kara glanced up and saw Tien bending her head down, as if to blow her nose. Her soft voice sounded in Kara's ear again, "I told you he'd bring company Kara. He's got two with him. Both mid-twenties, maybe younger, black, six feet plus, short cropped hair, both wearing jeans. One has a dark blue T-shirt the other a light maroon colour. That's what we'll call them. They look exactly like the sort of muscle you'd expect Ty to bring with him. He's sending them both this way. Wait."

Kara reached up and covered her mouth as if to yawn. "Now, now Tien. Don't be petulant that he brought some cover. We brought ours."

Dan and Eugene O'Neill, or 'the Boys' as Tien normally referred to them, were sitting quite close to Kara. Eugene was directly opposite her at an alfresco table outside another Italian restaurant. His brother Dan sat on the same side as Kara but a few yards behind her on a small wall surrounding an oak tree set in a concrete triangle. Sheltering under the oak was a tour company kiosk and the whole space acted as a divider for traffic on the Charing Cross Road. 'Tic'.

"Yeah but we don't look like your sort of friends, now do we?" Dan said softly.

Kara suppressed the urge to laugh. She had to admit that not only didn't they look like her sort of friends they also didn't suit their names. Adopted by an Irish couple in Mill Hill, London in the 1980's Dan and Eugene's birth parents were both of Nigerian descent. Each boy was the same rich ruby-black colour of their adopted Catholic-Irish father's preferred drink. Graduates of the exclusive Mill Hill School, both boys excelled at rugby and boxing with Eugene winning the under-16 British schoolboys heavyweight title and Dan the English ABA Middleweight Championship. Dan especially shocked his coaches by deciding to quit the gloves and follow his kid brother into the army.

After nine years in the Parachute Regiment, including two tours of Afghanistan for each and one of Iraq for Eugene they left and established a private security firm. Kara had first met Eugene in the backstreets of Basra and now, when she and Tien needed some support, they were her first call. Or in this case, Tien's first call. 'Tic.'

"Maroon in lead, on way to you. Seen?" Tien asked.

Kara saw the first of Ty's entourage turn into Irving Street. She tapped her right index finger on the table by way of acknowledgement. Both Eugene and Dan clicked their mics once. 'Tic.'

"Dark blue is holding at the entrance to Subway Restaurant. Ty's getting them to bracket you. He's moving now. Fifty yards from me." There was a pause and then Tien spoke again, "Twenty-five."

As Ty Hendry turned into Irving Street and walked past where Tien sat, she merely tapped her finger twice on the table and got three soft clicks in return. Tien held a major advantage over Ty. Although she had spoken to him on numerous occasions, they had never met face to face. She knew there were a few old photos of her out on the Internet but she could be fairly sure that to anyone who had never met her, she would look much like any other Asian girl in London. Tien was quite happy to rely on the stereotypical inability of other races to separate her from the masses. But she knew Ty. Every time Kara had met him, Tien had been there, in the background, providing security.

She and Kara knew this meeting was likely to be completely risk free. They had contacted Ty late in the afternoon and he had had no pre-warning. The risk to them was minimal. There was no reason for the O'Neill boys to be called in to provide additional security. There was no reason for Kara and Tien to have scouted around the meeting point an hour in advance. There was no reason to have set up Tien as surveillance on the western approaches and Dan on the eastern. No need to have Tien check for others accompanying Ty, no need for Eugene to be carrying a concealed 9mm Glock-17 pistol in a shoulder holster under his jacket. But Kara and Tien had routines. Routines they never forgot to implement regardless of the permissiveness of their environment. 'Tic.'

"He's all yours Kara."

Kara didn't acknowledge Tien's message. She just relaxed knowing that her friends had her back. It allowed her to concentrate on the task at hand.

"Hi. You're looking good as usual," Ty Hendry said in his rich, almost sultry voice tinged with the hint of a Jamaican accent. He pulled out the spare chair and sat down.

"Thank you. You're looking okay too. Life treating you well?" Kara asked.

"Well enough." He glanced up as a young waitress appeared at his side, "Just a glass of house red please. Nice uniform. You look lovely," Ty said, referring to the faux-Bierkeller costume the girl wore. She smiled broadly at him and unconsciously flicked her hair away from her face before returning to the restaurant door.

"That was quick. I normally have to sit here for half an hour before anyone comes near me," Kara said.

"Perhaps you're not the fräulein's type?"

"I think it's more that you are."

Ty smiled a broad smile. His perfect teeth and the slight glint to his eye all added to the impression of the man. A completely false one, but an impression that he cultivated to assist him in his chosen career.

"How's business?" Kara asked. "Lots more schmucks in

London this year? Managed to con anyone to buy Westminster Palace?"

"Kara, I'm insulted. I don't con. I'm the equivalent of the lottery."

"Really?" she said it with a large inflection of cynicism.

"Yes. Really. People spend money on a ticket with the hope of winning big. They don't and they lose their money. No harm, no foul. I just give them the same opportunity. They can spend their money with me on the chance of winning big."

"Mmm, I think the difference is that they spend big with you and there is no actual prize."

"Well, if you're going to get technical," and again he gave Kara his best smile. She easily understood how people could believe anything of the man if he put his mind to it.

The waitress had reappeared and set the wine in front of Ty, "Would you like something to eat?" she asked. Ty in turn looked at Kara and raised his eyebrows in query.

"No we're fine for now thanks. My colleague and I might have something later," Kara said cutting across the young girl's focus on Ty. The waitress turned with a rather bemused look and Kara actually thought she was going to say, 'I wasn't asking you' but instead she simply gave Kara a rather stern stare and moved away.

"A colleague, is that what I am now?" Ty gave a deep, resonant chuckle. 'Tic.'

"Kara. His maroon T-shirt guy has gone just south of the corner of Irving Street. Holding station with eyes on you. Phone to his ear, probably talking to his partner. Tien confirm," Dan's voice was relaxed, unconcerned.

Tien responded in a similar tone, "Confirmed. Dark blue has a phone up."

Kara gave no indication of hearing the voices in her ear. She merely continued her conversation, "Well Ty I can hardly say, me and my con-artist, thief and ne'er-do-well cohort here, now can I?"

"You know how to flatter me, don't you Kara? So, what can I do for you?" he asked and took a drink of his wine. Kara saw him glance to his right over his glass and knew he was making eye-contact with his maroon T-shirted buddy.

"I'd like you to take a look at these." She reached into her jacket, took two passports out and set them on the table.

Ty picked the top one up and opened it. "UK, European Union passport in the name of," he paused and flicked to the last page, "Mrs Joanna Adamson. Who, even allowing for a passport photo, is quite an attractive older woman." Ty looked up and Kara rolled her eyes.

"What else Ty?"

He glanced back down at the passport, "Issued on the 15th February 2006 by the UK Passport Agency. Has a set of entry and exit stamps for Australia, New Zealand, Singapore, a temporary visitor visa issued on entry to Indonesia. A couple of stamps for Malta and Algeria. Oh and a set for the US tucked in here at the back." He closed the passport and held it up, "What am I meant to be looking at Kara?"

"It's a fake," she said and watched his eyebrows raise in appreciation. He looked back down at the document and flicked through it again but this time much more slowly. He finally arrived at the last page again with the holder's details on it. Holding it close he tilted the laminated page back and forward to catch the fading light and reveal the holographic image overprinted on the photo of Joanna Adamson. Finally he set it back down and reached for his glass. Kara waited for him.

"I hope you paid top money for this Kara." He looked up and she held his gaze.

"Go on," she prompted.

"It's quality work. In fact I don't think I've ever seen as good. A dodgy copy to get you through cursory checks in Europe or Africa will cost you a grand. This sort of product will set you back ten or twenty times that. Maybe more. I don't know if the travel stamps are real or not but there's every chance they're valid. This is good enough to get you through the UK, Aussie and US checks." He moved the passport to one side to reveal the second one on the table. "I'd have said that it could be done by some people I know but only if it was a one-off masterpiece example of their work. But I'm guessing this is the same?" He indicated the second document, "May I?"

Kara nodded in reply.

This time Ty examined the outer cover carefully and as the lights covering the alfresco area came on with the sun slipping lower in the sky, he opened the passport and began a careful examination from the inside cover forward. After a good few minutes of appreciative nods and the occasional soft blowing of air from the lips of an admiring connoisseur of fakery, Ty opened onto the last page. As he rotated it to look at the holder's details in the correct orientation, Kara saw his expression freeze.

She watched him very carefully. He had stopped nodding, stopped any form of appreciative gesture, his eyes hadn't widened like a cartoon expression of surprise but rather had focussed intensely. His grip on the passport had tightened to the point that the pages had bent slightly. His breathing had deepened and a small bead of sweat had formed near his temple before running freely down the right hand side of his face. He stared at the page for a moment or two longer and then, instead of turning to examine the inside cover in the same manner as had been doing up until then, he simply closed the passport and placed it back on the table. His gaze remained down and his fingertips rested lightly on the bottom of the passport's front cover. Kara watched as he breathed again, settled back in his chair and then looked up with his customary broad smile and gentle eyes.

"Definitely great work. Both of them. Do you want me to take them off your hands, is that it?" He managed to keep his voice neutral but Kara could see the tension in his neck, the spreading outbreak of sweat on his forehead and top lip.

"No. I just want to know who could do this level of work and how I get in touch with them."

"I don't know Kara. I'm sorry."

"Really? You've no idea where these could have come from. With all of your contacts?"

"Yeah, really. I'm sorry." As he said sorry again Ty moved his right hand down by his side, out of sight of Kara, masked by the table. 'Tic.'

"He just waved off Maroon," Dan's voice sounded in her ear.

"Listen Kara, I can't see that I can offer you much help. But, thanks for the drink. Pleasure seeing you, as always." Ty drained his glass and began to stand.

In the years that she had known Ty he had presented many personas and most of them false, but in all that time she had never seen him scared. She didn't have a clue what had rattled him but whatever it was she decided she needed to find out. Kara drummed the fingers of her left hand lightly on the table. "Sit down Ty."

He continued to rise and laughed a little as he looked down, "Or what Kara?"

"Or the man who is coming across here will make you."

Ty laughed but the nervousness of his uncertainty sounded through it, "Is this where you want me to look behind me?"

Kara said nothing but merely held Ty's gaze as she stood up. She reached forward and placed her hand on his arm.

"Move your fucking hand off me Kara or I swear to Christ I'll drop you in the middle of this fucking street," he made the threat quietly enough not to attract the attention of other diners but there was a quiver to his voice.

She didn't move and if anything tightened her grip a little. Ty's bluff had been called and he knew it. He shrugged her hand off and made to leave but turned straight into a broad, tall, well-dressed man in a tailored business suit. The man towered over Ty and was almost twice the width of the slim Jamaican. He reached over and put his large left hand on Ty's left shoulder. With what appeared to be an almost nonchalant gesture, Eugene pressed Ty back down into the chair. He leant forward and put his mouth next to the conman's ear, "Sit the fuck down Tyrone or I will hit you so hard you won't be able to get up for a month."

Kara heard Eugene deliver the threat but watched Ty's

eyes darting to where he hoped his Maroon muscle was going to appear like the 7th Cavalry. The confusion of what he was looking at caused Kara to turn a little and gaze behind her.

Maroon had stepped away from the wall he had been leaning against as soon as he saw Ty make his under-table gesture but his path was immediately blocked by what appeared to be a homeless guy. As he put his left hand out to move the shuffling derelict from his path, the shorter, hunched homeless man delivered a withering set of three rapid punches into the left hand side of the maroon T-shirt. The damage was already done but for good measure as the maroon T-shirt bent forward Dan O'Neill delivered a left upper cut. It snapped the head of his opponent back and forward so fast that the tourists milling around Charing Cross never registered a massive assault had occurred next to them. Dan cradled the slumping body and moved back to the small wall surrounding the oak tree. When Ty looked over all he could see was one of his protection team resting in the arms of some homeless guy. 'Tic.'

"Eugene. Dark blue moving, fifty yards," Tien's soft voice carried no panic.

Eugene turned on his heel and keeping his left hand on Ty's shoulder watched the second of the muscle back-up make his way down towards him. Like his maroon companion, this member of Ty's entourage was full-set and would have looked completely comfortable doing the door security at any of the big London clubs.

Kara, still standing, watched as the man wearing the dark blue T-shirt began to slow his pace. She watched him looking at the scene in front of him, she watched as he glanced beyond her to the scene on the concrete wall. She watched as his gaze returned to Eugene. She saw Eugene move the flap of his suit jacket momentarily to reveal the concealed weapon he carried. As the approaching man slowed more she saw Eugene shake his head to convey the simple message of, 'No, you do not want a part of this, go away.' The message was well understood. Kara saw the change in the man's eyes. Between leaving the entrance to the Subway Restaurant until getting to within ten yards of where she stood, Ty's muscle had realised that the people he was walking towards were in a different league of violent intent to him. He turned on his heel and walked back along the length of Irving Street. 'Tic.'

"He's kept on walking. You're clear. No one else noticed a thing," Tien reported.

As Ty's last hope of relief walked out of Tien's view, Kara retook her seat. Eugene stayed behind Ty and Dan laid his sleeping companion in the flower bed of the oak tree.

"Ty, we really should get better acquainted," Kara said and looked across the table to a very frightened and thoroughly confused petty thief.

"Wha' d'ya mean?" he asked and even his refined accent had slipped. The heavy brogue of Jamaica had reasserted itself.

"You and me have had dealings in the past but I don't think you ever appreciated me for who I am or what I've been. In the last," she glanced at her watch, "two minutes, you should've figured out that I'm with people you do not want to fuck with. Clear?" Kara looked directly into his eyes. He held her gaze for less than a second before he looked down and nodded.

"What scared you about the second passport? Did you recognise the photo?"

Ty nodded again.

"Who is it?"

"No chance mon. You migh' be scary but dey are fuckin' animals."

"Who are?"

Ty's fear caused a fire to return to his eyes, "Listen girl, 'cos you obviously not hearin' me. Deese people will cut my fuckin' heart out an' eat it."

"Only if they catch you. The difference is I already have you. You need to fucking focus Ty. You're here, right now. These people you seem to be scared of are fucking nowhere and they will never know what you tell me. They will never know any of this happened. But if you decide to be the hero for some weird bunch of fuckers, I'm going to let my very big friend behind you twist your head until all the bones snap one by one. He won't do it quick. He won't kill you. He'll leave you in a wheelchair for the rest of your life. So you get to choose. Tell me what I want to know or don't tell me and have your life fucked up. Permanently. Which do you fancy?"

Kara reached forward and poured a little more of her mineral water into her glass with an unflinchingly steady hand. The young waitress turned up again and gave another winning smile to Ty. He didn't even register her presence. Kara sent her away to get Ty a straight Scotch.

"Ty, you can think about this all you like, but I'm not leaving until you tell me what frightened you so much. Who is in that photo?"

The silence drew on, the waitress brought the Scotch and Ty downed it in one. Kara let the alcohol hit the Jamaican's system before she spoke again.

"Ty, do not think I won't do this. Do not think I will not have my colleagues take you to a remote location and make you hurt so much that you beg to tell me what you know, just to make them stop. Now make your choice."

"I don't know what his name is." Ty's accent had returned to what Kara was used to.

"Okay, but what do you know?"

"He works for Chekov."

Kara had no idea who that was other than a dead Russian author or the Star Trek helmsman but she didn't let it show, "What does he do for him?"

"I don't know. I just know he works for him."

"How do you know?"

"Cos' he was there. With all the rest of Chekov's crew."

"Look Ty, you need to concentrate and start telling me a coherent story. I don't have time for this. Who is he, what does he do, where did you meet him? Start to finish."

"Well how the fuck do you get your hands on these passports if you don't fucking know him? You're taking the fuckin pi-" Ty stopped short as Eugene leant his considerable weight down on his shoulder and said quietly, "You need to answer her questions or I'm going to start breaking things like she promised."

Ty calmed himself and nodded up towards the bulk that was behind him. "Okay. Okay."

Kara repeated herself, "Start to finish."

"I saw the man in the passport photo once. With Chekov. I was doing a job in the run up to the Olympics that needed some extra women hanging around. The mark had a liking for foreign girls. Chekov has the biggest stable in town so we came up with a deal through an intermediary. When it was over I was a day late in getting the money to the right place. It was a genuine mistake but Chekov thought I was being disrespectful. I was brought to him. Don't know where, some big shed. He had a line-up of people watching on."

"And this man in the passport was there? You're sure?"

"Yeah he was there. He was one of the spectators."

"Go on Ty, tell me about it. All of it." Kara said and nodded up to Eugene who leant his weight off Ty's shoulder.

"Chekov had them all lined up to watch. Like it was a warning to them that no one fucks with him. Not even a little bit. Not even if it wasn't intentional. I mean I had all his money. I had all his fucking money and he still wouldn't listen to me. He said I had treated him like a peasant. I told him I didn't mean no disrespect but..." Ty's voice was shaky, hesitant and he looked like he was going to be sick.

"Go on," Kara insisted.

"He... it was... he just... turned some of his guys loose on me," Ty's voice cracked and Kara could see him struggling to swallow.

Kara softened her approach. She reached forward and set her hand on his, "Tell me the rest Ty."

"He fucked me up," Ty paused again and Kara recognised the struggle he was having. The memories of trauma and the shame of being unable to stop it when it happened. The inability to control your emotions when you remembered it. She knew he would tell her but she also knew it would cost him. She considered leaving it, telling him he could stop, but he was her first decent chance of finding a link to where Chris and Brenda Sterling were. She had no option.

"Finish the story Ty." She nodded up to Eugene who put a small amount of pressure back on to Ty's shoulder.

"Okay, okay, please don't hurt me," Ty gulped air and Kara watched a tear roll down his face. His voice was reedy, thin, almost childlike. "He beat me, but he made sure I stayed conscious. Two others held me up. He didn't touch my head so I could see and hear and feel every fucking thing." Ty sniffed and rubbed the back of his hand across his nose, the marks of his tears wetting both cheeks now. "Then Chekov was right there, with a knife to my nuts and another to my throat. Leaning right into me, both blades pressed against me. Shouting that no one betrays him. Then he asked," Ty looked down and Kara saw his tears fall freely onto the gaudily coloured paper table cloth. She waited.

Ty's head remained bowed, "Then he asked if I wanted my nuts or would I take a whipping."

Kara knew her face was registering the shock that she could see reflected in Eugene's. She was going to stop Ty, but before she could say anything he continued, "They tied my arms up and he whipped me. He whipped me like I was some fucking slave and he made all of them watch. That's why I remember this fucker in the photo. I remember all of them, every face from the six that Chekov made watch. They all stood and stared at me."

"Okay Ty. It's Okay," Kara nodded at Eugene to stand back. "We're going to take you home Ty. I'm going to have some of my friends watch over you and your house. Chekov and his people won't find out that you spoke to me. I can promise you that, but I'll provide protection for you anyway. Just to make you feel safe. Until you can get your own people back." She pushed a slim envelope across the table. "Your fee is in there. We'll take you home now."

φ

The phone screen showed 04:00 and 'No Caller ID'. She struggled to sit up and took a couple of extra rings to prepare to speak, "Kara Wright."

"Good morning sleepy. I believe you wanted to talk?"

Kara's mind cleared as she swung her legs out of the bed and sat upright, "Yes I did. How long have you got?"

"Not long. What do you need?"

"A full background on the man whose kids you put in touch with me."

"I can, but if you contact Sandy Marrs he'll be able to do it a lot easier than me."

"We already did, but all he gave us was the standard file."

"That's the full scoop. There's no special file. The guy in question was just an Imagery Analyst. Nothing of significance. Other than being a bit strange in that he was ex-Navy yet specialised in Russian Tactical Air Forces."

"So why did you get contacted if he was just a run-of-the-mill?"

"Because he and I go back years and some people knew that. It was more helping a mate than anything involved with our world. I mean he was within our circles but at a completely different level. He wasn't an operator. I met him on board a Royal Naval Frigate that I was hitching a ride on. We bumped into one another off and on over the next lot of years. You know how it is. Some people you see regularly and others you don't run into again."

"Hitching a ride on a Frigate?"

"Long story. Don't ask. What's next?"

Kara hesitated before asking her next question.

"C'mon kiddo, I'm on the clock here. What's next?"

"Do you still have contacts within organisations like your ex-hubby used to work for?"

"Yes. Why?"

"I need to open an account."

"Do you mean in that particular jurisdiction?"

"Not fussed but it needs to be completely opaque."

This time the pause came from the other end of the line.

"Completely, as in not traceable?"

"Yep."

"Okay, that's not a problem. I'll have someone contact you. They'll use the initials of the band to verify. You can take it from there. Next?"

"That's it. Other than, how's things, are your boots tight, is the mail getting through, do you need me to send socks?" Kara teased.

Victoria laughed, "I think I'm fine thanks and the socks might be a bit much."

"Can you say where?"

"Sunnier, sandier climes that continue to display an unending ability to set their days and nights to a background symphony of RPGs and AK-47's. You need anything else you know how to get me."

"No worries. You keep your head down and thanks."

"Too easy, anytime. Say hi to Teen-girl."

"I will. Be safe."

Kara disconnected the call and decided to get up. Her mind was too busy to be able to get back to sleep.

13

Wednesday Morning. Central London

Dan and Eugene were handing over the physical protection of Ty to a couple of their associates. The brothers had maintained a vigil all night and were now heading off for some well-earned sleep. Tien was installing the suite of hidden cameras into the Lizard and Pickle Pub and briefing the owner on how it all worked. Kara was in Victoria Tower Gardens, on the western bank of the Thames with a skinny latte and a Marks and Spencer's jambon-et-fromage croissant. Although she did wonder what had happened to the days of a cheese and ham sandwich and a white coffee she couldn't help but feel that out of the rest of them, she had the best of the morning so far. She sat on the low steps of the Buxton Memorial Fountain as the coolness of the morning sun hadn't burnt off the dew on the grass.

Gazing up she could see half of Big Ben's face and only the very tip end of the minute hand as it tried to hide completely behind the tower and spires of the Palace of Westminster. Off to her left and not to be outdone by its more famous counterpart, the clock on the eastern end of the former Church of St John's was hiding behind the full foliage of the trees that lined the gardens. Kara watched as the breeze stirred the leaves and the hands of the Baroque edifice's clock peeked into view. It was 07:25. She watched the minute hand slew to twenty-six and saw David turning into the far end of Dean Stanley Street. He walked with confident, long casual strides and Kara couldn't help but reflect that the once Police Constable might have left behind his uniform days, but still meandered like he was on 'the beat'.

He smiled and waved to her as he came through the gates to the gardens. "Don't get up," he said sarcastically as he plonked himself down beside her.

"Charming. I could just keep these for myself," she said gesturing towards a takeaway cappuccino and the second Marks and Spencer's croissant.

He leant over and gave her a peck on the cheek. "What would I do without you, oh favourite sister of mine?"

"That's not much of a compliment, oh only sibling of mine," she teased him back.

"So, what do you need?" he said as he twisted the plastic lid off his coffee.

"David, why do you think that every time I drop in to see you, or call you, or arrange to have an alfresco breakfast snack with you that I naturally want something?"

He didn't answer but she saw his eyebrows raise over the rim of his cup.

"Well, I might need a little thing," she admitted.

"Of course you might," he checked his watch. "But we'll have to get a move on Sis, I have a briefing on the move to go to."

"What move?"

"The building move. Remember? The whole of New Scotland Yard is being shifted."

"Oh yeah," Kara said a little vaguely. She remembered reading some stuff in the press but had slightly tuned out to David's explanation of what was happening when she had gone round for dinner a few months ago. She didn't feel too bad. Alice had tuned out just as much if not more. "So you're all moving to," she hesitated and her brows furrowed.

He shook his head and said a little exasperatedly, "Embankment. We're all, well not all, but about half of us, are going to Embankment. Anyway, never mind concerning yourself about that. Obviously. But, I have to be in the office fairly sharpish. So what do you need?"

"No problem. It's just a bit of background. Should be simple for you. I came across the name of a fairly nasty thug yesterday but I've no ideas on him other than he's brutal and runs prostitutes. Wondered what you guys had on him? The name's Chekov, I assume it's an alia-" Kara was silenced by the look that passed over her brother's face. He had been about to take a bite from his croissant but had stopped short. He set it and the coffee back down.

"Kara, did you meet this man?"

"No David. I just heard about him. What the fuck's the matter? You've gone grey."

"You listen to me Kara. I am not messing about here. Did you see him or were you seen by him?"

"No, I wasn't David. I told you."

"Yeah I know you told me and I also know that sometimes you don't tell me the truth 'cos you think you're protecting me from all the weird and daft shit you get up to. But this is different."

"David," she said it forcefully. "I promise I've had no contact with this man. Now who the fuck is he? You're worrying me."

"Well you should be worried. The guy is an animal."

"Yeah, I know that already from the story I was told. What I don't know is who he is. You obviously do. What's his real name?"

"We have no idea. We know of him, but we've never got close to getting him. He's an ex-pat Russian who's been over here for fifteen, maybe twenty, years. In all that time I think we have one photo of him and we're not even sure it's him. We do know what he does and some of the specifics he's got up to, but we've never had one shred against him. On the one occasion we thought we were getting close the confidential informant we had just disappeared. No trace, ever."

"So what sort of stuff are we talking about? I heard he ran girls?" Kara asked.

"He does. High and low-end prostitutes and when I say high I mean really top end, thousands of pounds for a couple of hours. He controls a chunk of the amphetamines coming in to the East End and possibly controls the traffic lanes from Amsterdam. We certainly know he provides protection around the east and north of the city. We've lifted low-level people who work at the street end of his operations but they've never even seen him let alone interacted with him. He always keeps them at a distance. And frightened. He keeps them very frightened. From what we do know, we figure he has about seven or eight key people who run the operations side for him. They control the street ops and keep the fear pressing down on the lower end."

"I'd guess he has six key people working for him David. And yes, they are well motivated to keep their people in line."

David looked genuinely startled, "How can you possibly know that?"

"Because I met someone last night who was flogged in front of them to keep them focussed."

"Jesus Kara. Who was it? We need to talk to him."

"That's not going to happen David. Even if I gave him up, he wouldn't talk to you and he certainly wouldn't be standing up in a court. You can't scare him as much as Chekov does."

"So why did he talk to-," David stopped himself asking the question. "Don't bother. I don't want to know."

"Okay, so you're not telling me much new here. Chekov's a thug and a nasty one, does drugs and prostitution and protection. Anything else?"

"As well as our CI that went missing, he's suspected of being involved in a stack of murders or disappearances in the UK and a whole litany of others back in his home."

"Which is?"

"Somewhere in that bit of Russia that's squeezed in

between Poland and Latvia."

Kara shook her head.

"What?" David asked.

"I think you mean the Kaliningrad Oblast and I think you'll find it's between Poland and Lithuania. Did you actually take Geography at school?"

Her kid brother raised his middle finger.

"Mature, nice. Suits you. Now, can you get me a look at his file?" she asked with no embarrassment.

"Nooo! Of course I can't Kara."

She lifted her coffee and drank it without taking her eyes off him.

"Stop it," he said and looked away. She continued to stare and waited for him to look back. "Kara, pack it in. I can't get you in to look at his file." She held her stare.

David tried to eat the rest of his croissant and drink his coffee without making eye contact with her but in the end he gave up, like he always had when they were little and still did even now. "Fine! I'll read the damn thing myself and talk to you later. Okay, satisfied?"

Kara smiled, shimmied over to him and kissed him on the cheek. "You are the best brother a girl could want," she laughed as he stood up. "Oh and the photo of him would be handy?"

"You're the worst sister a bloke could want and fine, I'll get you a copy of his photo. But you have got to be careful Sis. This is-"

She cut him off by holding her hand up like a traffic policeman on point duty, "David, it's me and Tien you're talking about. We'll be careful. We're always careful."

"Okay," he said and smiled a half smile, half grimace down at her. "I've got to get into this meeting Kara. I'll come see you tonight. Try and be good."

"Oh, I will, but tell me, did you get up to something naughty with Wendy Mead at that conference this year?"

David paused and Kara watched as he had to place who Wendy Mead was. That told her most of what she had thought but David confirmed it anyway.

"No I didn't! She was a nice person. We spoke at the majority of the interval breaks. I think she was just a bit lonely that's all. Why? What on earth did she say?"

"She didn't say anything bad, relax. In fact she just enthused over how simply spiffing and wonderful you are. And I can see her point." Kara reached her hand out and David helped her up.

"I am spiffing and wonderful," he paused, "And so are you."

They hugged and as David left the gardens to the west Kara left them to the south. Her mobile began to ring as she turned onto the footpath that ran along the side of the river. She pulled the phone from her pocket but didn't recognise the number.

"Kara Wright."

"Hi Kara. My name is Timothy Yorath. I believe you wanted to talk to me about an account?"

"Yes I think I did," Kara said as she perched herself on the low concrete wall above the flowing river. "Before we go on, my friend gave you some information so I could verify you?"

"Yes. I must admit I thought it was a little cloak and dagger but I suppose no more unusual than some of the things my industry does."

"So?" prompted Kara.

"Ah yes, she said to say S, L, F and to let you know that I used to work with her husband in the Union Bank of Switzerland before we both moved on to new ventures."

"Excellent. Where can we meet?"

14

Wednesday Morning. Huntingdon

Detective Constable Annabelle Walsh and Detective Sergeant Moya Little were coming out of their third bar of the day and it wasn't even lunchtime.

"Where next Sarge?" Anna asked.

"The King's Arms I guess," Moya answered.

"That's way out of the centre."

"Yeah but these women drink somewhere before they head into town and go to the clubs."

"Oh joy," Anna sighed as she got into the car.

"Ah it's not too bad at this time of day."

"Why, do they change all the staff into nice people?"

Moya laughed and pulled away from the kerb. "No, but at least the clientele should be a bit thinner on the ground and a bit less plastered."

The journey took less than five minutes but it transported them from the heart of the pleasant market town to the middle of a 1960's social experiment that had gone wrong. The low-rise and high-rise concrete houses for the masses had, like in every other similar estate, turned into a low-rise and high-rise concrete ghetto for the poorest of the society they were meant to inspire. The King's Arms pub was designed to be the hub of the community. A place for families to relax and enjoy their neighbour's company whilst watching the children playing in the beer garden. Instead it turned into a hub of heavy drinking and drug supply where neighbours watched each other's children push prams at too early an age. The large concrete car park adjacent to the pub was known locally as 'the Madison' after Madison Square Garden due to the amount of fights that occurred at closing time on Fridays and Saturdays.

Little pulled the car into it and reached for the car's radio. "Papa Mike Dispatch, be advised DS Little and DC Walsh on-scene at the King's Arms in the Cowfield Estate."

"That's nice for you," the voice of Sara Reed, the local radio dispatcher, answered. "Be sure to give them our love."

"Thank you Sara," Moya laughed as she hung the hand-mic back in its bracket.

Anna led them through the door marked 'Lounge' and into a bar devoid of people. She took up a place against the wall whilst her DS walked up to the counter. By peering through to her left Moya could see into the public bar on the other side. A television was showing a rerun of the British Formula One Grand Prix and she could see four men sat at the bar and three more in seats set back against the walls. There was one barman on duty. Little knew all the staff at the King's Arms by name.

"Hey Harry," she called and as he turned, so did all the other heads she could see.

Without moving Harry said, loud enough for the whole bar to hear, "Detective Sergeant Little, what can I do for you?"

Three of the men at the bar got up and turned away from her before heading straight to the main door. They were joined by two more from the seats at the wall and no doubt a few more she couldn't see from her vantage point. Harry took a glance around before making his way over to Little.

"Nice touch Harry. Well done."

"Don't know what you mean Detective," he said as he leant on the counter and looked beyond Moya to Anna Walsh.

"Nice. Is she 'wif you then?"

Moya leant into him and spoke softly, "Yes Harry she is. She also has a name, a rank and a fuck off big can of pepper spray that she would gladly empty down your miserable fucking throat at one word from me. You keep up your Essex-wide boy chav act and I shall call her over and tell her that you just assaulted me. Are we clear?" She clamped her hand on his wrist and held it down against the bar.

Harry's ruddy complexion went a clammy white. "I didn't mean no offence, honest. Detective, you know me. I was just-"

"Well don't. Anna!"

Anna walked forward reaching into the inside pocket of her jacket. Harry squirmed under the pressure of Moya's hand on his wrist. He was trying to pull himself free with no success. "Aww, c'mon Detective I wasn't sayin' anyfink. I wasn't. I'm sorry."

Moya straightened up as Anna got to the bar and laid seven pieces of paper down on it. Each one showed a still frame taken from CCTV footage.

"Good Harry. Apology accepted," Moya said as she released his hand and Harry almost stumbled into the racks of optics behind him. "Now, look at these photos and tell me who these women are."

Harry glanced nervously at the public bar to his right.

"It's okay Harry, you did a great job of moving them on. No one left is going to care. Now get back over here and take a look at these photos."

He slowly came back to the bar and looked down at the set of A4 sized close-ups that Anna had laid out.

Walsh and Little both watched him closely. Before he had even opened his mouth they knew he recognised at least some of them.

"Nah, I don't know any of 'ese."

Moya looked up at Anna, "DC Walsh. Would you care to explain to Mr Cook how much shit he is in?"

"Certainly," Anna looked down at Harry. Although he was standing on a slightly raised bar floor behind the counter it made no difference as she had a good five inch height advantage on his five foot six. She stared hard at him and he seemed to physically wilt.

"Mr Cook, if you tell us who these women are we shall go away and leave you to your happy bar serving. We know you know some of them. Your afternoon will have a small interruption and we will move on. If you don't tell us we will take you down to the station right now. You will be arrested and charged with conspiracy and we shall spend a few days talking to you. That will be more than a minor interruption."

Harry went even whiter. "Conspiracy? Conspiracy to what? I haven't done nothing."

"Anything," Moya said.

"What?"

"You haven't done anything Harry," she said.

"Yeah, that's right. I haven't."

"Yes, that is right," Moya added. "And if you don't identify these women we will take you in for not helping us. You will be charged with conspiracy to murder-"

"Murder!" he yelped the word and the remaining customer at the public bar leant forward.

Harry stepped right into the counter and out of sight of the interested onlooker. "Murder," he said more softly. "I'm not involved in-"

"We know," interrupted Anna. "Just tell us who you recognise here."

When Moya and Anna left the bar they had the names of four women who lived on the Cowfield Estate. It was blatantly obvious Harry didn't know the other three on the shortlist.

φ

DS Gary Mason and DC John McKay were leaving the much calmer and postcard photogenic surroundings of the Pheasant and Heron. The landlord, Stanley Reese, had been more than cooperative and kindly generous with the offer of a small half on the house for both of them. He definitely knew one of the women in the photos. She was his niece, Tanya. It had been her one Friday night off each month.

"Night off?" asked Mason. "From where?"

"From here. She's working in our restaurant out the back. Do you want to talk to her?"

φ

It was almost 2pm when Tony Reynolds and DC Colin Oldman finished.

They had been given freely volunteered copies of the security videos from Huntingdon's three nightclubs and had reviewed each of them to match with any of the seven women previously identified from the town's CCTV.

"What a great cross-section of humanity we shortlisted," said Oldman.

"Now, now Pop. You're just jealous you weren't out there with them. Especially with that nice young lady caught throwing up in the corner," Reynolds laughed and turned the screen off. "So what do we have?"

"Three definite, one probable and three no, Gov."

"Let's go see what the rest have turned up."

φ

The main operations room had a full-length magnetic board against the far wall. Moya stood next to a display of the seven enlarged CCTV snapshots.

"Okay, what do we know?" Reynolds asked her as the rest of the team drew their chairs closer.

"We have IDs for five of them. Sisters Shirley and Cheyenne Thompson, Brittany Lancashire and Courtney Stiles. All four of them are off the Cowfield Estate. We also have Tanya Reese from Ellington but Gary will take us through her later. As for the four Cowfield women, Cheyenne Thompson is nineteen and went home early to meet her boyfriend, Drew Iveson, at his house. That corresponds with what we saw on the original CCTV. We also have a statement from his mum that Cheyenne arrived in just after eleven, Drew came home

89

off nightshift about half an hour later and that the pair of them were there through to the morning. It gives a small window of opportunity for her but I don't reckon on it. We caught up with her at work in Iceland. She was on the tills but took time to talk to us. There was no panic, no aggression. If anything, for a Cowfield resident, she was pleasant and kind. Anyway, we took her to her house and recovered two pairs of red heels from her room. I don't think either pair is what we're looking for but they've gone to the lab. Anna also walked over to the Iveson's place, got the statement from the mother and checked their house."

"Any red heels under the boyfriend's bed?" Reynolds asked as he looked down the line of his team.

"No Gov," Anna answered. "No heels at all matching anything we were looking for. Also, the mother was more than helpful. Young Drew is a student nurse down at Hinchingbrooke so I reckon he and Cheyenne are planning to move up and out of their surroundings."

"Assessment?" Reynolds directed the question to Moya.

"Highly unlikely," she answered. "There's no history of any fight training. She's young and fit and I would assess agile but showed no signs of anxiety or trying to cover anything."

"And her sister?" asked Reynolds moving the conversation on. As far as he was concerned if Little didn't put Cheyenne in the frame then that was good enough for him.

"Mmm, yeah. Shirley Thompson. She was at home when we went back with Cheyenne. She's twenty-eight and has twin boys, aged twelve. They all live together with Cheyenne and Shirley's dad, Billy Thompson, and his partner Maggie Blake. Shirley wasn't as forthcoming as her sister. A real attitude and extremely resentful that her little sister was so helpful. Eventually we got to the point where she finally admitted going to Rocky's Nightclub. Got off with someone, no idea of his name, came back in to the club after a short trip up the side alley with her new beau and then she stayed in the club until chucking out time. She's the one you found on the video being sick in the corner. Says she can't remember what happened next but she knows she got a cab home. That tied in with us seeing her staggering about on her own on the CCTV cameras H82 and H89. Also explains why we didn't see her on H83 because she cut through to the High Street and ducked into Franci's Taxis. We checked with Franci and he confirmed she was in his office waiting for a cab. Remembers her because she offered him a blowjob for the fare."

There was a combined groan from all the detectives.

"It's okay. He says he didn't accept as she was barely capable of sitting up straight. I didn't ask if he would have accepted had she been sober. Anyway, he got one of his female drivers to take her home. Dropped her off about half two. Short of the most miraculous recovery from being drunk and deciding to head back out to the industrial estate, she didn't do this."

"What did you find in her room?" Reynolds prompted.

"Nothing. She refused us entry. We'll need a warrant if we want to go back to her but I don't think it's worthwhile. She did do boxing in high school and definitely looks like she could hold her own on a normal Friday night in the Madison but from what we saw on the CCTV and from what Franci said there was no way she could have kicked anyone in the head last Friday."

"Okay, Next."

"Brittany Lancashire. The one you found on the video from Joanna's Nightclub, Gov. She's twenty-five, works in Mission Hire out on the industrial estate. That's only three streets away from where the body was found. Lives on the Cowfield in a top level flat on her own. She wasn't delighted to talk to us until we told her what it was about and then she became an open book. She met up with three friends in the club, which corroborates what you and Pop saw. She said she was heading back to one of their houses in St Ives but needed to go and get some money first. We checked with the HSBC and they confirm a transaction from her account at ten to one. We can get their ATM camera footage if you want but I held off with the warrant for now," Moya paused.

"Fair enough," said Reynolds. "Did we get confirmation she went to St Ives?"

"Anna caught up with all three of the friends by phone whilst I sat with Brittany and they all confirmed the timeline," Moya answered.

"Rehearsed?" Reynolds turned to look at Anna again.

"No Gov. All individual, no collusion or covering."

"Okay. The fourth Cowfield girl?" Reynolds asked and noticed out of the corner of his eye Anna Walsh smiling slightly. He knew that she was pleased that he had taken her assessment without question. 'Good' he thought. His young Detective Constables were developing nicely.

"The fourth is Courtney Stiles. She's the one we saw on the CCTV hanging around the front of Rocky's and then eventually going in. She exited later and wandered off on her own up Prince's Street."

"Yeah," said 'Pop' Oldman. "She was weird in the club. I tracked her for about half an hour on the CCTV and she looked really twitchy."

"She should have," Moya agreed. "She was meant to be meeting her boyfriend. His name's Andy Louth. He stood her up, or so she thought. She eventually left and wandered up Prince's Street to get a cab to take her back home. Then she got into her car and drove to his house in Peterborough. Except she didn't get there. Instead, she got a call telling her that Andy had been admitted to the Emergency Centre at Peterborough City Hospital after being involved in a road accident as he'd been driving south to meet her. Andy's parents had forgotten to call her to let her know until then. We checked the call log on her phone and there were multiple calls out to his number in the evening, all unanswered obviously and then the one from his Parent's number. It all checks. Andy's comfortable but still in hospital. So, she's not in the frame either." Moya sat down.

"Gary?" Reynolds looked at Mason.

"Tanya Reese, from Ellington. Works at her Uncle's pub. Has one Friday night off a month but has to be home relatively early to get up for work on Saturday. Her brother picked her up at 11pm and drove home. We checked the registration with the number plate recognition cameras on the A14 and the car definitely made the journey. Her brother and parents confirmed the arrival time. As for Tanya, she was completely open. Came back to her house with us and voluntarily allowed us to search her room. We have one set of heels in the lab but much like the others, unless this kid is a future Oscar winner, then I don't peg her for this." Mason sat down and Reynolds stood up. He took a red marker and put diagonal lines through the five pictures they had ruled out for now.

"That leaves us the brunette, seen on street CCTV but not on the nightclub tapes. She's heading out of town in the wrong direction but might have doubled back." He reached up and put a small tick mark next to her picture.

"And finally the blonde. She shows up in Rocky's Nightclub taking multiple selfies, doesn't drink too much, doesn't dance, doesn't hook-up with anyone and leaves on her own. Then she shows up near the cemetery on CCTV and after a considerable time turns up again over on Walden Road. She's the only one in the right area of the town at about the right time. Interestingly we never get a clear look at her face in any of the camera footage. Not once, not on any camera." He reached up and put a large red tick on her picture.

"We need to find these two women. Especially this blonde."

15

Wednesday Afternoon. Camden, London

Kara and Tien were in Tien's apartment looking at the photo of Chekov. David was leaning with his back to the window and dunking a bourbon biscuit into his tea.

"I know this is going to sound weird David, but he looks familiar to me," Kara said.

Tien nodded, "Yeah, he does. But I can't place him."

"Really? How familiar?" David pushed himself up and moved to sit on the sofa. "Where did you see him?"

"I don't know," said Kara. "He just seems familiar."

"But you both think so. Was it somewhere overseas when you were serving? When you were on ops? In Iraq, Afghanistan?"

Tien took the photo in her hands. "No, I don't think so. Much more recent. Kara?"

"I agree. It wasn't from any of our ops. It's recently, but I can't think where. Don't worry David. It'll come to me. Us," Kara said.

"Well make sure you tell me," he said looking directly at his sister. Kara nodded like a chastised child.

"I must admit I was expecting a sort of Rasputin type of

look. You know, big and hairy and menacing. He's actually quite handsome," Tien said as she looked at the semi-profile picture of a man, probably in his fifties, wearing a suit and smiling at someone or something that was out of frame. The shot had been taken at distance so fine details were impossible to see but his neatly groomed hair still had a lustrous dark brown sheen, he was clean-shaven and most prominent of all the features was a distinctive, almost classically proportioned, Roman-nose. "He has quite a cute smile to be honest."

"Well I'll take your word for it. But just remember, we aren't even sure this is him. The photo was found on a small digital camera about three years ago, in the digs of our missing CI. The CI was gone so we just had to assume."

"Can't you run it against all the hi-tech face recognition we hear about?" Kara asked.

"Nope, not a chance. The quality isn't that great for a start but it's a profile. We don't have anything that'll do a side-on match."

"Okay," Kara said. "So what else *do* we know?"

Her brother set his cup down, interlocked his fingers and stretched both his arms out. Kara hid her smirk at her brother's habit that always reminded her of a pianist about to start a virtuoso performance. When he had finished his stretch, David said, "We haven't got a name other than Chekov. We know he's very, very security conscious. We do know from Interpol sources that he likely came from Gusev in the sticky out bit."

Tien looked confused, "The what?"

"The Kaliningrad Oblast," Kara answered and rolled her eyes. "My brother is a dolt but at least that explains the Chekov bit."

"Does it?" David asked.

Kara sighed in an overly dramatic fashion, "Ho hum. Seriously? Was there not an explanatory note on file?"

"Um, seriously Kara, I have no idea what you're getting at," David said.

"Gusev might be a town in the Oblast but it's also the title of one of Chekov's short stories."

David looked at her in disbelief, "Really? How the hell do you know that?"

"Aw c'mon. You know I learnt Russian when I first joined up."

"Yeah but I figured they'd teach you how to say 'tank' and 'gun' and 'for me the war is over'. I thought you joined up as a linguist, not a literary critic."

"Very funny. I had a hard time with the language at the start so I used to read novels by Russian authors. Chekov was good because his stories were short and vibrant."

"Well there you go. You really never do cease to amaze me Sis."

"Thanks, I think. Right so he comes from Gusev and?"

"And he maintains some links back there. We also think he has some links in the Russian Far East. Thing is we have no idea how he smuggles his girls in. Any that we've picked up have been schooled to say they came in through Stanstead or Heathrow or wherever. They're terrified of what will be done to them or their families if they tell us how they actually get in to the country so they stick to their stories."

"What happens to them after you've arrested them?" asked Tien.

"Unfortunately, when we get to them they have no ID and very little money. The ones we've found have traced back to rental apartments leased through false names and the trail stops dead. Like I said he has a very tight organisation."

"Yeah, but the girls. What happens to them?" Tien pressed him.

"We get their real names and where they came from and," David paused and knew that what he was going to say would hurt Tien. He knew the struggles her family had gone through to get out of a desperate situation.

"And?" she said, her voice neutral.

"And they get deported back to wherever they originated from," David said.

"You know that they'll simply be scooped up again and forced back into the life, don't you?" she asked, again keeping her voice neutral.

"I know Tien. We all know. But..." David couldn't finish the sentence. He merely looked at Tien and shrugged.

Tien stood, wandered over to the kitchen and put her cup into the sink. She turned and looked back into the open plan living area. Gazing over the top of David's head to Kara she gave a small nod to continue.

"What else David?" Kara asked.

"That's it. We haven't got close. We don't know his name. We don't know where he lives. We know he's the background 'Godfather' of an organisation that runs drugs, prostitution and protection. He has obvious international connections and has been mentioned in a number of probable murders and disappearances. He runs a compartmentalised organisation that maintains tight security and never, never connects back to him in a way we can trace."

"I assume you've followed the money?" Tien asked from behind him.

"Yes, but not too well. We tried a tracker in notes given to one of his girls and followed it to a house," David paused and pulled out his mobile phone. He accessed the photo he had taken of Chekov's thin file, "in Essex. A small village called Earl's Colne. It sat there for six weeks before returning to London. Then it was spent in a restaurant by one of the girls. The only conviction was for the couple who owned the house in Essex and they provided no leads further up the chain. They just stayed quiet. In fact they insisted they were running the girl. Eventually they got three and a half years suspended for living off immoral earnings. We're fairly sure the restaurant is a clearing house for a number of organisations but again, not enough proof. We get clever, they get cleverer and they have more money than us."

The room fell quiet and the atmosphere seemed to reflect the frustration that was being felt by all three. Kara felt a rising anger at a criminal justice system that apparently favoured the criminal and was light on the justice. However, she also knew that she and Tien, the O'Neill brothers and the other associates that they could call on for assistance weren't shackled like her poor brother and his colleagues.

"More tea?" Tien asked.

Kara laughed, "My how British you are Tien Tran. Yes, I'd love another cup."

φ

Tien was making another three mugs of tea and one coffee. David had gone home and her living room was now playing host to Kara, Eugene and Dan. The photo of Chekov lay on the table between them.

"So that's everything we know," Kara said.

"Which isn't a lot," Eugene said.

"And we're taking the leap that the Sterling's disappearance is down to this guy?" asked Dan.

The full weight of Dan's question wasn't lost on Kara. She really had nothing to go on that linked Chekov to the disappearance other than some very tenuous coincidences.

"It's not certain but Chris Sterling is tied in with a major old-school gangster. His house looks like it was sanitised and he and his wife sure as heck didn't get on a plane to Miami. It's what we have," she said as Tien handed out the drinks and retook her seat.

"That's a thin assumption to be chasing," Dan said.

"I know but either Chekov's directly responsible or a rival gang is moving against him by targeting his associates. Either way Chekov is the only thing we have so we go after him until we get something better. Tien and I thought we could start by trying to find out who the girls report to. They must have some form of low-level pimp who reports up and up. If we can track and follow, then maybe we get to one of those that Ty saw at his flogging."

"We could waste a lot of time doing that and it'll also be expensive," Dan said. "Those type of girls won't come cheap and their minders normally take the fee up front."

"I know," Kara agreed. "But if it is Chekov that took the

Sterlings then we don't know how long they've got left. It might all be too late already. But we have to do something and we can only go with what we have. As for the money, the clients have provided an advance of sorts." Kara saw Tien shake her head and smile, unseen by the brothers.

"Okay, I can see the logic. What do you want us to do?" Dan asked.

"Keep your babysitters on Ty and find out from him how he got in touch with the girls he hired in the first place. I want to know how we get one of the top-end escorts. Once we have that and confirmed that Ty's muscle is back in place, we can pull out of there."

"Aren't we worried he might go to Chekov and tip him that we're looking for him?" Eugene asked.

"I can't see it. I don't think you go to someone like Chekov and admit you told us all about him but now you're here to 'fess up and get brownie points for giving him a 'heads-up'. I think all Chekov does is kill you for talking in the first place. So no, I think Ty will be safe enough. You can leave someone on him if you want but I think he'll be okay," Kara said.

"Okay, anything else you need?" Dan asked.

It was Tien who responded, "Yeah. Assuming we end up finding where the Sterlings are we'll need a few more helpers. We were wondering if Sammi and her crew were in the country or are they back overseas?"

The brothers shared a look between them that was obviously a precursor to some bad news.

"I'm going to guess you didn't hear?" Dan asked and looked across to Kara and Tien who both shook their heads in unison.

"Taff never made it back from their last run into Kabul. He was hit in the mortar attack that took out the US Senator and his entourage. Do you remember that, about six months ago?"

"Vaguely," said Kara. "But I didn't know Taff was involved."

"Normal reporting," said Eugene. "A civilian contractor. You know how it works."

"Bollocks. I liked Taff. I mean he was a bit of a nutter, but when it came down to it you could trust him with your back," Kara said.

"That's really sad," Tien said. "He always made me laugh when we were out in Helmand." The friends sat for a moment in collegiate sadness at one of their own having passed.

Kara reached for her mug, "Here's to Taff." The soft clink of china was as much as they could do for him now. As was their way, the moment was marked and Kara nodded for Dan to continue.

"Funeral was a quiet family thing. We didn't find out until about two months after it happened when we met up with Sammi. She was okay. Chaz had some shrapnel to his thigh and Dinger had part of his own Osprey body armour blown into the top of his arm but they're all recovered now. I know they decided they weren't going back anymore so we can give them a call and round them up if you want."

"Yes please, that would be great. Now you both need to get going as Tien and I have an errand to run.

φ

The white Ford Transit van was about as non-descript a vehicle as you could possibly get. It was the reason Kara and Tien had invested in one for their business a couple of years earlier. As a surveillance platform it was almost unnoticeable. On the A1 from London to Arlesey it blended in to the hundreds of similar vehicles like a white wildebeest on some strange migration.

With the Sterling's house being relatively isolated and with no overlooking neighbours, Kara reckoned they would be able to complete their task surreptitiously enough. She had been assured by Timothy Yorath that the offloading of their cargo in the basement of his central London bank would be equally unobserved. The difference was his staff would do that aspect of it so Tien and Kara wouldn't have to break sweat. But the loading in Arlesey was down to just the two of them. With no interruptions they reckoned it wouldn't take too long to fill the thirty small backpacks that Tien had bought earlier in the day.

Each backpack could easily fit more than the allotted thirteen stacks of notes, leaving a few less for the last bag; it wasn't the volume that was the issue. Tien had worked out that the problem was much more likely to be the weight of almost four million in cash. So she had gone for a limit of about seven kilos in each bag. More trips up and down the stairs, but easier to manage.

They re-entered the house, turning the alarm off and the lights on before making their way up to the loft. Once inside the space masked by the false wall, Tien held the torch and Kara packed the bags. Working in the hot and restricted confines of the loft it took them just over forty-five minutes to pack the notes and move the bags to the top of the loft ladder. It was another fifteen minutes to get the bags down to the landing, secure the false wall access door and leave the loft as it had been before. Minus the money.

They each hoisted a pair of the compact backpacks and began down the stairs.

It was on the way back up from her fourth trip that Tien stopped still on the sixth stair from the top. Kara was already on the landing swinging another back pack up on her shoulder.

"Kara," Tien said.

"Yeah?" she answered without looking at Tien.

"Put the bag down and come here."

It wasn't what was said but the way Tien had said it that caused Kara to immediately do as her friend asked. As she stood on the stair above Tien she followed her friend's pointing finger and looked at Zoe Sterling's Graduation photo.

"Fuck me!"

"Not quite my thoughts exactly, but close enough," Tien said.

16

Thursday Midday. Central London

Zoe sat at a window table in the curved gallery of the Royal Albert Hall's Italian Kitchen Restaurant. As Kara entered and saw the graceful figure waiting she couldn't help but think that the setting and the sitter complemented one another perfectly.

She had rung Zoe at 06:00, quickly assured her she had no news as yet but needed to meet with her or her brother. Apparently Michael was sleeping after a late night of international trading and Zoe had to go to the London Coliseum for early rehearsals, but after those she was due at Markova House, the home of the English National Ballet, for a production meeting. Zoe offered to meet Kara for lunch at the splendid Italian Kitchen just across the road.

"This is very nice Zoe. Thanks for taking the time to meet," Kara said as she leant her bag and the wrapped parcel she had brought with her on the window ledge next to the table.

"No problem," Zoe passed a menu over, "Are you going to eat?"

"Do you recommend anything?"

"Do you want light or heavy?"

"Light I think," said Kara.

"The Arancini Siciliani is a starter but it's good for a light lunch," Zoe said, pronouncing the Italian flawlessly.

"Sounds great."

Zoe caught the attention of a waitress and ordered two of the starters. The waitress returned momentarily with a carafe of mineral water.

Once the young woman was out of earshot Zoe asked, "So you said you needed to talk. How can I help?"

"You know Tien and I have been up and down to your parent's house checking for anything that we might have missed?"

Zoe nodded. Kara reached for the parcel and eased the tissue wrapping from it. She took out Zoe's graduation photo, still in its frame. "I was wondering if you could tell me who the people are in this photo?"

"Where did you get that?" the question was asked with a surprised tone rather than any shock or anger.

"From the wall next to the stairs in your parent's house."

"Oh yes, quite. I'd forgotten they had it there. How sweet," and Zoe laughed before the sound caught in her throat, smothered by the remembered fear that her parents were still missing.

"Can you tell me when this was and who these people are?"

"That's my graduation from Central in 2003-"

"Sorry Zoe, Central?"

"The Central School of Ballet. You were correct when we first met. I did attend a London School. As for who, well that's me obviously, Michael and Mum and Dad," she answered and pointed to each in turn. "That's my Nana, Mum's mum. I'm afraid all the rest of the Grandparents had passed by then."

"And these two people?" Kara asked, indicating the male and female who stood at the far left of the group photo.

"Oh that's my best friend Nat and her dad, Uncle Illy," Zoe said as she pointed to the other girl dressed in gown and cap and the man next to her. The one who looked like Chekov.

Kara's kept her voice as even as she could manage, "Uncle Illy?" she asked.

"Oh not a real Uncle. You know how it is when you're little. Family friends get Uncle and Auntie when they're not really."

Kara nodded and feigned her best smile to show she knew what Zoe meant, "Can you tell me about Nat?"

"Well yes, but I thought you wanted to know more about my parents."

"I do Zoe, but for now it's important to know about Nat and her father. It's very important. I wouldn't ask if it wasn't." Kara considered the fine features and high cheekbones of Zoe Sterling and saw a confusion in the other woman's eyes.

After a brief pause, Zoe shrugged, "Nothing really to tell you about Nat. Her proper name is Natalya. She was born in Russia but came over here when she was little. She's the same age as me and we went the whole way through Central's prep and senior school together. After graduation we both got contracts with the English National."

"Do you still see her, are you still in touch?"

"Oh yes, of course. She's the assistant choreographer on our current production. I saw her this morning in rehearsals. Why? What's the matter with Nat?"

"Nothing Zoe, nothing. Well not as far as I know. I'm sure she's fine. You said she's a choreographer?"

"Yes. She got a career-ending injury in," Zoe frowned as she tried to remember exactly when, "Gosh it's nearly ten years ago now. It does happen to a lot of us. I'm a rare beast that is still dancing in the Corps de ballet at my age."

"Do you mind me asking?" Kara said and smiled to hopefully lessen the intrusive nature of the question.

"Oh no, not at all. I'm rather proud of the fact. I'm thirty-three and still dancing. Although I'm probably in my last year or two and even now I can't do mid-week or Saturday Matinees. I'm down to one show a day at best."

Kara could hardly believe it. "Wow! You're only a year

younger than me. I wish I knew your secret because you don't even look like you're out of your twenties. You look amazing." Kara meant every word. Zoe blushed.

"Ha! I wish I *felt* in my twenties. But thank you. That's very kind. And you don't look old Kara."

"Maybe not, but I do look my age."

"Perhaps, but I think I've had the easier ride being a dancer than what you chose to do."

"How do you mean?" Kara asked, a little hesitantly.

"Well it's obvious you must have been in the Army. Dad's mates put us in touch with other Service people initially. Michael and I assumed that you and the lady who eventually phoned us were all in the military together at some time. I know Tien definitely was."

"Not Army for me; Air Force. But yes I was in and the lady you spoke to still is. How do you know Tien was definitely in?"

"I Googled you after our meeting. You don't show up much other than your website for Wright and Tran Investigations. But Tien showed up in quite a few news stories."

Kara nodded and took a small drink of the mineral water. "Yeah, I suppose Tien and I tend to forget about that. It's not like news used to be. One day's paper is tomorrow's fish and chip wrapper. Now it's out there for ever."

"She's a genuine hero," Zoe said with a tone that mixed a strange blend of awe and gratitude. "They don't give out Military Crosses for fun. The news reports said she saved a number of fellow soldiers and was badly injured. Is that how she lost her hand?"

Kara, halfway through taking another sip of water didn't answer immediately and Zoe misinterpreted her delay.

"Oh God! I'm sorry Kara. I didn't mean to pry. I meant no offence, I'm- "

"It's okay Zoe," Kara said with a calming motion of her hand. "No offence taken. You're right, that was how Tien got injured. From memory I'm fairly sure the news reports were mostly spot on because it came from the official citation. She put herself in the path of bad people whilst she dragged three colleagues to safety. I think the only annoying thing was that she didn't get the Victoria Cross. But yes, I'll totally agree with you, my little friend is a true hero. Although she would say that Ziagul was more heroic."

"Ziagul?" Zoe asked, cocking her head in a way that reminded Kara of a puzzled puppy.

"A little Afghani girl, no more than seven. She braved Taliban crossfire and probable retribution just to bring Tien water that day."

Zoe said nothing straight away but Kara could see a dawning realisation in the woman's eyes. "Like I said, I've had the easier ride being a dancer."

Kara smiled in reply.

The aroma of spicy tomato and saffron signalled the approach of their food and the conversation stopped as the two women sampled the Sicilian rice balls.

Kara bided her time until Zoe was half way through the small dish, "Zoe, I don't suppose you know where Nat came from in Russia?"

"Oh yes. Hard to forget."

"Sorry?"

"She came from Gusev," Zoe said with her fork poised in mid-air.

Kara was slightly taken aback at the way she had just been handed the likely confirmation that Uncle Illy was Chekov. "I'm sorry to ask, but how can you be so sure? Most people think everyone in Russia comes from Moscow."

"Have you heard of 'Le Corsaire'?" Zoe asked.

"No, I don't think so."

"It's a ballet, but rarely performed in full. We put on the first ever production in the UK in 2013. One of the most famous versions of it is by Pyotr Gusev," Zoe must have recognised the lack of recognition in Kara, "He was a very famous Russian dancer and choreographer. Anyway, when we were in pre-production Nat mentioned that Gusev was the name of the town she'd been born in. I hadn't known that before. I knew she'd lived in Kaliningrad, that's where she first went to Ballet School but I don't think she'd ever mentioned Gusev before or I'd have remembered. We all know who Pyotr Gusev is."

Kara realised she must have still had a slightly blank look on her face as Zoe added, "Well, no I didn't mean that to sound so patronising. I meant we all do as dancers. I mean, you do if you're involved in ballet." She smiled awkwardly trying to deflect any perceived slight.

Kara laughed, "It's okay Zoe. I must admit I'd heard of neither Pyotr nor 'Le Corsaire'. But that's interesting about Gusev." She decided now was as opportune a moment as any of the lunch, "Can you tell me about Nat's father. Uncle Illy? It would help me if I knew as much about him as you know."

Zoe, now much more relaxed in Kara's company, opened up without hesitation, "He and Dad go way back. They met at our recitals and became friends. He came over here years ago. Ninety-one or two I think. We started Central in ninety-four. Me and Nat, not me and Uncle Illy." She laughed and took another forkful of the rice, dipping it into the tomato and saffron.

"What about his wife?" Kara asked.

"No, Nat's mum died when she was three or four I think. Her Aunt Yanina, her real Aunt, looked after her."

"Her aunt's here too?"

"Yes, but I know she came later. I think we were in the second or third year of the school, something like that."

"So is Yanina Illy's sister?"

"Umm, no," Zoe said a little awkwardly.

Kara raised an eyebrow.

"Aunt Yanina was Nat's mum's sister. It could get a bit confusing for everyone because Nat and I both called her aunt. When we were growing up I never thought too much about it but now we all know that Uncle Illy and Aunt Yanina are a thing. I guess they were both lonely in a new country and it was natural."

"What's Illy's name?" Kara asked between mouthfuls.

"Oh, it's really grand. We always joked that he should have been a prince with a name like Illarion Yurevich Sultanov." She laughed again and dabbed her mouth with the heavy linen napkin.

Kara laughed too, "That's a great name. So is he a prince or does he have to work?"

"He runs a modelling agency. The Krasota Agency."

Kara registered the Russian word for beauty and knew that Zoe had probably given her enough to be able to find the man. She still had no idea if he was responsible for taking Chris and Brenda but if he wasn't he was probably out there looking for them as well. If he was responsible, then Kara had to hope he hadn't been callous enough to kill his old friends.

"Thanks for this Zoe. It's all been really useful and it'll certainly help Tien and me to move things forward." As she said it she saw the sadness return to Zoe's eyes. Kara reached over and took her hand. "It's okay. We'll find them." Zoe sniffed and nodded.

The conversation lulled again as both women finished their food. Kara poured them more water and waited a moment longer. Then, as casually as she could she asked Zoe, "So did you contact Illy about your parents going missing?"

"Oh yes, he was one of the first calls Michael and I made. He tried to tell us they'd probably just gone away on holiday but when we told him about Dad's message he was really surprised and shocked. He told us to go straight to the police."

Kara pondered the information, "Did Illy know about your Mother's fear of flying?"

Zoe looked a little puzzled, "How do you mean?" she asked.

"I was just wondering. You said he was shocked. I'd have thought, being such a close family friend, Illy would have known about her fear of flying?"

"No. I wouldn't have thought so. Mum was really embarrassed about it. She'd get really upset when it was mentioned. When we were little I remember I whinged about not being able to go to Disneyworld and she started crying. It was awful.

I felt terrible. So we never really talked about it. It was just there but not discussed. Even by us, so I wouldn't have thought Uncle Illy would have known. He was certainly surprised when I told him about it."

Kara thought, 'I'll bet he was.'

If Illy was responsible for taking Zoe's parents then all that hard work to get a good cover story, even to explain away the inoperable mobiles phones by being in America, was all undone by a simple unknown fear. Still, she couldn't help but be impressed that if he was behind the disappearance then he must have had supreme confidence he had covered his tracks to recommend Zoe go straight to the Police.

'Cocky son-of-a-bitch,' she thought. She kept her voice light, "That was good advice. Did he offer anything else?"

"He and Nat came round to see us that night. He was really upset that the Police weren't listening to us. I thought he was going to go through the roof. I honestly thought he was going to go to the Police Station and demand to be seen."

"He didn't?"

"No," Zoe drew the vowel out like it was something she would never have expected Uncle Illy to do. "I know he's been here a long time but I think he still mistrusts authority. I think it's a hangover from his days under communism. I don't know what happened to him back there but I'm pretty sure it was bad. So no, he didn't go round. But he has told me to keep him informed every day and to let him know if we need money to pay for your work."

"Right. So he knows you've hired me and Tien?" Kara kept the tension she felt out of her voice and reached down to scratch an itch on her knee.

"Oh yes. He was really impressed that I had found you through Dad's old mates. Like I said, he asked for me to keep him up to date with what you're finding out so he can help if he can," Zoe said.

'Tic.'

Eugene's voice sounded in Kara's ear. He was sitting at a table on the far apex of the curved gallery with clear lines of sight of the whole restaurant floor. Tien and Kara had thought it a reasonable precaution just in case the man in Zoe's graduation photo had indeed been Chekov. Once again Kara thanked her reliance on good practice and excess caution, regardless of situation. "Kara, I'm on it."

He didn't need to say anymore. She saw him lifting a mobile phone to his ear and knew he would make sure that Dan moved to immediately secure Tien. She also knew that Tien would start revisiting their last few days to see if they'd been compromised at any turn. For now, all Kara could do was turn her thoughts back to Zoe and improvise as best she could. She had to assume the worst case. If Chekov was involved in the abduction then she needed to stop him getting any more information about what she and her team were up to. Even if he wasn't involved she didn't fancy a Russian gangster having an inside track on her activities. She reached for a drink of water and used the time to invent a reason for Zoe to keep her mouth firmly shut and away from Illy's ear.

"That's marvellous Zoe. I'm really pleased you have someone there for you. The thing is though, I have a favour to ask and it might seem a bit strange but I hope you'll bear with me."

Zoe's brow had creased and she was concentrating fully on Kara's face. "Yes?" she asked with a seriousness to her voice.

"The thing is, I haven't been completely truthful when I said we had no news this morning. We actually think we might have a slight lead," Kara said and watched Zoe's expression change to one of hope. Kara once more made a calming motion with her hand. "It's not much and I can't tell you if it will even come to anything but, Tien thinks she's discovered some monitoring equipment in your parent's house."

Zoe now looked simply confused, "I'm sorry. I don't know what that means."

"We found what seems to be a microphone and listening devices."

Zoe's eyes widened, "You mean like a bug?"

Kara spoke softly, "Yes. But we don't know what it's there

for. We can't take it to the Police without knowing where it transmits to or why. They'll just tell us to go away like they did to you. I think this all might be to do with what your dad did back in the Navy all those years ago. I take it you didn't know what he did?"

"Well not at the time. I was only ten when he left. But since then, obviously, we know he was a photographer."

"Yes, but do you know what else he did?"

"Well," Zoe hesitated and looked down to the table.

"It's okay Zoe, I know what he did. I just need to know how much you and Michael know."

"Well I suppose it'll be okay to tell you given you were in the Army." Kara almost corrected her again but didn't. She let Zoe continue, "We know he eventually worked for Navy Intelligence," Zoe said it very softly and quickly followed it with, "But we were never allowed to speak about it. Dad and his old mates would come round but it was never discussed openly. Certainly not the details of what he did. We knew he worked as a teacher in the Intelligence School, but that was it."

"Good," said Kara. "That's good that you knew what he did. Yes, he was in Intelligence and we just don't know for certain if this is related. We could start looking at everyone who knows about this to see if they are being monitored too, but that will take a lot of time. I don't think we should waste resources on it when we can be cleverer and that needs your help." She paused and leant forward a little. Zoe reciprocated her movement and the women's heads almost met in the middle of the table space.

"We don't have the technical ability to check your house and your phone, or Michael's phone," Kara lied. Had there really been bugs Tien would have negated the threat with minimal effort. Kara paused again for what she hoped would be effect, "This is the favour, Zoe. I need you to not tell anyone about what we're doing. Nothing at all. As far as anyone else is concerned we've got no further news. None. So you can't even tell Illy or Yanina or Nat about what we've discussed here. That way they'll be kept safe and in the clear.

If they ask, or if you need to keep Illy up to date, just tell them we met and I've got no further news. It's really vital that whoever is listening in gets nothing from you. Do you understand?" Kara sat back a little and said a silent, quick prayer that the rubbish she had said had been delivered in a credible enough way to scare the sense out of Zoe.

Zoe nodded, "Yes, certainly. I totally understand."

"Great, that's fantastic. I've reached out to some friends who might be able to do a bug-sweep and if they do then we'll be able to check your place and maybe even your Uncle Illy's and Nat's. I'm guessing Nat isn't still at home? "

"Oh gosh no. She's married and lives out in Loughton."

Kara shook her head, "Loughton?"

"It's up near Epping Forest."

"And Illy?"

"Somewhere on the other side of the forest from Nat. He moved a couple of years ago and I haven't actually been to the new house yet. Gosh! That's shameful," she said, shaking her head slowly, "We all used to be in and out of each other's houses all the time. I suppose life just gets in the way?"

Kara nodded her agreement.

"Mum and Dad have been there. Apparently it's beautiful. Uncle Illy certainly has come a long way from a little terrace in Highbury."

Kara nodded her agreement again but for different reasons than Zoe thought.

"I can text him and get the address if you need it?" Zoe said reaching for her bag.

"No, that's fine," Kara said as casually as she could but her stomach had lurched at the prospect of Zoe tipping Illy that someone wanted to know where he lived. "If I need it I can get it later. I'll let you know, but for now the less details being passed on phones or in conversations the better."

Zoe looked as if she had realised the laxness of her offer, "Oh, of course. How silly of me. Someone might be listening and then they would know too."

"Yes, that's it exactly," Kara said and wondered why

civilians believed it was so easy to bug phones and listen in. 'Hooray for Hollywood,' she thought.

It was a shame Zoe didn't know the address, but Kara couldn't risk Illy being tipped off. She was going to have to hope Tien could dig out an address later. But she needed to know one piece of information Tien wouldn't likely be able to turn up.

"You said Sultanov. I remember meeting a Russian man once by that name. He bred the most beautiful pedigree dogs. Is that Illy?"

"No. Aunt Yanina doesn't like dogs so they've never even had one let alone bred them."

"Ah well, I just wondered. Sometimes the world is so small." Satisfied, Kara switched tack, "Will Michael be at home tonight?"

"Yes, but I have a performance so I probably won't see him until late."

"Okay, so if you're on the phone to him, no news. Then take him outside the house to tell him what we know. Tell him to be careful on the phone and in the house with what he says. Okay?"

"Yes, absolutely," Zoe paused and her eyes became teary, "Do you think Mum and Dad are still safe?"

"I have to believe that they're still safe Zoe. We will find them. I can promise you that. We will find them."

The graceful ballerina had started to weep, very softly and very discreetly. Kara caught the eye of a waiter to bring the bill and by the time she had settled their account Zoe had regained her composure. The women stood and Kara offered to accompany Zoe across to Markova House. As they left the restaurant Kara passed Eugene and received the subtlest of nods.

As the women waited to cross the narrow Kensington Gore, made more constricted by a huge tourist coach disgorging its camera wielding horde, Kara felt that she should say something to try and lighten Zoe's mood with a good memory.

"It must have been great that your dad used to come to your recitals?"

Zoe gave a small, limp smile, "Yes, he never missed. Such a sweetie really. And always gave Mum a full report."

Kara half turned, "A report?"

"Yes, Mum hardly ever got to come in person. I think that's why Illy and Dad became such good friends."

Kara guided Zoe around the last of the tourists and saw Eugene waiting at the end of the street. He reached up and dusted his left shoulder. All clear. She responded with a similar gesture telling him he could safely leave her from here on.

"Why was that?" Kara asked.

"Oh you know, most of the people there were mums and they were the only two men who turned up regularly."

"Right. I just assumed that your mum would have gone too. Did she not like ballet?"

"No, nothing like that but Dad was self-employed in the camera shop and could take the time off."

"Of course. I see. I'm really ashamed to say I had assumed your mum hadn't worked."

"Oh no, she always worked. That's one reason we moved to Arlesey. It was close to Dad's last tour of duty but it was also on the main rail line to Peterborough and Mum had worked up there for years. It was an easy commute."

Kara nodded.

Zoe turned at the stub of Jay Mews that sheltered the entrance to the English National Ballet, "Well this is me. Thanks for lunch Kara and I shan't say anything until I hear from you. I promise. I'll also talk to Michael as soon as he gets in."

"That's great Zoe. And chin up and stay positive?"

Zoe nodded and reached forward to give Kara a kiss on either cheek.

17

Thursday Midday. Huntingdon

Detective Constable 'Pop' Oldman came through the operations room door brandishing a piece of paper. Tony Reynolds looked up and was beaten to the punch by Moya Little, "What's that Pop, peace in our time?"

"Huh?"

The rest of the room laughed.

"Never mind Pop, what is it?" asked Reynolds.

"It's the ID for the brunette. A Mrs," he referred down to the piece of paper, "Agnes Shawcross called in to say that she saw the flyer in the Post Office and she knows who the girl is."

"And?" prompted Reynolds.

"And I thought we could go and check it out," said Pop smiling over at him in a beguiling, if slightly blank, way.

Reynolds merely looked over to Gary Mason who was the Sergeant that had mentorship over Pop.

"I think the Gov wants to know the name of the ID Pop," Mason said and wondered yet again if the young man was really cut out to be a Detective. Unlike his surname, Pop was actually the youngest of the squad. At just twenty-five he was keen but sometimes a bit short on common sense.

"Oh right-o. Mmm, she's called Martina and lives opposite Mrs Shawcross in Lark Crescent. She doesn't know what the girl's surname is but she reckons she's a foreign student staying with a family in the street."

"So we don't actually have an ID for the brunette then?" Mason said.

"Well, no Sarge but, I thought, you know, we could..." Pop didn't finish the sentence and stood with his mouth slightly agape.

"Mmm, maybe a bit more thinking needed. C'mon," Mason stood and grabbed his jacket from the back of the chair, "Let's go see Mrs Shawcross and see where she points us."

Pop cheered up again and turned on his heel. Mason looked round at Little and Reynolds and raised his hands in mock prayer.

As Mason and Pop left, Reynolds' phone rang.

"Gov, it's Anna. Can you come into the video suite?"

"Sure, what's up?"

"I've been taking another look at some of the CCTV. I think I've found something."

Reynolds and Little both went into the suite. One screen was paused on a scene from the dim interior of Rocky's Nightclub, the other on the well-lit main foyer.

"What've you found?" asked Reynolds.

"It's the blonde. The one taking the selfies."

"Go on."

"I don't think she's taking selfies. Can you see just here," Walsh pointed to the dimmer, interior screen where a couple were sitting in the corner. "I think she's taking photos of that couple. She's followed them around the room. I've checked all the interior cameras and she is definitely tracking them, albeit very, very subtly. Eventually she leaves a couple of minutes before they do."

Reynolds pulled out a seat, "If she left before them how's she tracking them?"

Anna pressed play on the remote and the image from the dim interior played forward. "Because Gov, they do all the normal stuff when you're ready to leave. Finish drinks, get coats, the woman gets her bag." She paused the screen again. "But the blonde; that's her just there on the edge of the screen. I think she sees all that and just goes straight to the entrance. Much easier to start a surveillance trail if you're out before your target. Gives you time to get set up and looks less obvious." She pressed play on the foyer screen and the blonde walked straight through the image.

"I still find it interesting how she angles her head," Reynolds commented.

"You mean the way we never see her face?" Anna asked.

"Yeah. I mean if this is the woman who ends up killing Hastings then did she know she was going to do it, even at this stage of the evening? I find that hard to believe. I think she's trained to avoid surveillance. It's like she's almost unconsciously doing it."

"At least we can say she's medium height, medium to slim build with blonde hair," Anna offered.

"Well, blonde hair that night," Moya countered. "It could be dyed, could even be a wig if she was really concerned about masking her appearance. She becomes more interesting all the time."

As they talked the video played on and the couple came into view on the screen. Walsh paused it at the moment when they were in the middle of the brightly lit nightclub entrance and left the image frozen on screen. She ejected the DVD of the dim interior and replaced it with another disc. "This is from the camera next to the petrol station. The one up near the cemetery where we saw the blonde. I went back and looked at it again." She pressed play and fast forwarded until she got to the view she wanted.

"We didn't notice this earlier. Watch." The image was a wide-angle view of the entrance roads into a petrol station and the corner of the main shopping centre complex in the town. A small segment of it also covered the footpath and pedestrian crossing on the corner of Priory Road.

As Reynolds and Little watched, the couple from the

nightclub walked up to and crossed at the pedestrian crossing. As they disappeared out of shot to the top of the screen the blonde entered in the bottom right. She followed the same path and eventually exited screen-top. Again, not once did she lift her head to give a clear shot of her face on camera.

"Okay, I'll go for it. So what is she?" Reynolds asked.

"I don't know Gov. PI maybe?" Anna said and looked to her Sergeant for support.

Moya considered what she had seen and eventually said, "It's possible. Definitely possible."

"The timelines work. If she was conducting a surveillance that would explain why there's such a gap between this view and her turning up down on Walden Road a couple of hours later," Anna said and looked expectantly at Reynolds, awaiting his verdict.

"That's really good work Anna, well done," he said. "Moya, take Anna and see if you can turn up anything on this mystery couple. Talk to the nightclub staff again. See if anyone can identify them. If they're subject to a surveillance we want to play this really carefully. We have no idea if we've just stumbled into something that's official and way outside our paygrade, so if you find out who they are you *do not* go after them. Are we clear?"

Both women nodded.

"Okay. Whilst you do that John and I will make the rounds and see if someone's been operating on our patch without letting us know. I can't see it but you never can tell. The anti-terrorist chaps have a tendency to do first and apologise later."

φ

Mason and Pop were back by early afternoon. Martina Costa was an Italian exchange student staying with the Lilly family in Huntingdon whilst she attended the College of Animal Welfare. The twenty-two year old was in the second year of her Diploma in Animal Management and was currently on a mid-term break. She hadn't gone back to Italy this time as she was, in her words, 'saving for a car'. Mason had called ahead and Tony Reynolds was waiting for him in the annex to the interview suites.

"Hi Gov. I'm not sure if she's hesitant because of her language skills or if it's something else. What I do know is that she wasn't able to tell me what she'd been up to on Friday night. The lady she lives with, Lorraine Lilly, said Martina has her own key so she has no idea what time she got in."

"Okay,' said Reynolds, "I called for an Italian interpreter when you first rang, but apparently the nearest one is Cambridge so we'll have to wait. I'll have Pop standby to bring them in when they get here. Did you find any heels?"

"No. But I didn't search the house. I asked her if she had a pair of red high heels and the best that I could make out was that she'd thrown them away because the heel was broken. But to be honest her English went rapidly downhill the minute we announced we were Police."

"Convenient that they broke?" Reynolds said sarcastically.

"Yeah, but that and her hesitancy weren't the only reasons I brought her in Gov."

"Okay, so what else?"

Mason took his phone out and turned it to show Reynolds the picture he had taken in Martina Costa's room. The photo showed a double floating shelf on a wall above a single bed. On it were six gilt trophies with black and gold ribbons hanging from each.

"What am I looking at?" Reynolds asked.

"These are hers. She's a First Dan Black Belt in Qi Kwan Do. I'd never heard of it before but according to Pop it's a specialist self-defence form. It's the other reason Miss Costa is studying in Huntingdon."

18

By the time Kara made it back to her office she knew the wagons had been circled. Eugene and Dan were sitting in the occasional chairs that Zoe and Michael had sat in not seventy-two hours earlier. Tien leant against the window that looked out over the back of the small courtyard to the rear of the office. It was a reminder that the whole building had once been a house dating to the late Victorian period. Back when the likes of Karl Marx claimed the neighbourhood as home. Kara stopped in the doorway and leant against the frame, "Status?"

Tien gave a slight shrug, "It's no worse and no better than you might think. We know it's highly unlikely that Chekov penetrated any of our meetings up until now. Even more remote is that he had eyes on the meeting with Ty and hugely doubtful that any of us have been followed since we took on the case," she paused.

"But?" asked Kara as she walked over and took her seat behind the desk.

"But the remotest of possibilities exist that since he learnt of us from Zoe and Michael he could have decided to come have a look. For all we know he has expert, ex-Russian

Service operators and we might have been slack. They might not have moved against Ty because we've had babysitters on him."

"Do we still have?" Kara asked.

Dan nodded, "Yep. I kept one of my guys in loose hold around the perimeter after we'd spoken last night but since Eugene called in I've upped it back to four. We can keep a pair on him day and night. I don't think you've met them but they're all solid people."

Kara acknowledged the news with a nod, "What about here?"

"All the covert surveillance cameras are up and running. Tripwires are in place," Tien answered and pointed to the open laptop on the small coffee table between Dan and Eugene.

"Physical assets?" Kara asked.

"I've called in Jacob and Toby. They're front and back on an outer perimeter but at that point we've run out of people," Eugene said.

Kara was pleased that they'd called in Toby Harrop and his younger brother Jacob for extra protection. They were both ex-RAF Regiment and although Kara had never worked with them whilst in the military, she and Tien had used them on a couple of investigations in the previous year when Dan and Eugene hadn't been available.

"So we're going to have to get inventive," Eugene continued. "Either Dan and I provide the second pairing for here and you and Tien stay connected at the hip or, we drop to one-on-one and relocate inside. Either way we'll run it in twelve hour shifts. It's the best we can do."

Kara considered the logistics, "I think the two pair on Ty is a good call. We promised we'd keep him safe and until we know we haven't been compromised we should make sure he is." Kara looked to each in turn and got nods of agreement. "But Tien and I can cope with one of you in close for each of us. However, I do think we all need to start carrying. From what we've heard of Chekov he's not the 'call round for a chat' sort of bloke." Kara looked to Tien.

Tien answered by raising the left hem of her jumper to reveal a snug waist holster with just the grip of her Glock26 Gen4 sub-compact pistol showing above the waist band of her jeans. "Yours is in your desk," she said.

Kara opened the top drawer and saw her Sig Sauer P239 nestled in a concealed-carry leg holster. The eight-round magazine sat next to it. She removed the pistol from the holster, checked it was clear and slid the magazine into it. Pulling up the left leg of her jeans she secured the holster to the inside of her left shin before pulling her loose jeans back down over it.

"Thanks Tien. So what else have we got?"

"I just need to remind everyone that whilst we have to take precautions to be safe, we really have to remember that we still don't know if Chekov, or Illy, or whatever we're going to call him, is involved in the abduction," Tien cautioned.

"I totally agree," Kara nodded to reinforce her point, "but I also think he's our only avenue of investigation, so we have to proceed. Even if we know it's based on an assumption."

"What about the idea of going after his girls and their pimps for information?" Dan asked.

"Like you said yesterday, that could take weeks to reveal anything. We know who Chekov is now and worse, he knows who we are. I think the only thing we can do is go direct to the source," Kara answered.

"And do what?" Eugene asked.

"Isolate him. Talk to him. Find out where the Sterlings are if he has them or find out who might have taken them if he didn't." Kara once more looked at each of them in turn. She didn't get nods of agreement this time but she got shrugs that meant they couldn't think of anything better.

"Okay. Then I guess that's a plan," she said. "Tien, have you managed to turn anything up on him with the information Zoe gave us?"

Tien moved to the other soft chair and picked up the laptop from the table. She opened up a couple of browser windows and angled round so Kara could see.

"Nothing on Illarion Yurevich Sultanov. And I mean nothing. No papers in his name, no registrations, no house address, phone records, driving licence, nothing. I tried all the variations of the name I could think of but all blank. He obviously has run all or any official paperwork in another ID."

"That's not too big a surprise is it?" Kara asked.

"Not really," Tien agreed. "But we do have good news. The Krasota Modelling Agency is a real agency based out in Waltham Cross."

Kara nodded, "That makes sense. If the house is on the western side of Epping Forest."

"Yep. They even have real models doing real shoots from what I can find on the web, which to be honest surprised me. I reckoned it was just a front for the escorts."

"I'm sure it's a front for something," Kara assured her.

"Probably. Anyway, Aunt Yanina is Yanina Bobrik. She holds all the papers on the business. It's registered in her name and her very attractive face is on the website, along with a 'Get to Know the CEO' profile. She's a member of the local trader's association, the local, and very exclusive, golf club and seems to be mentioned in connection with a fair few charity events in the Hertfordshire and North London social calendar. No home address though. Everything's addressed to either the business or Company House. There's also no mention whatsoever of Uncle Illy. He's the ultimate silent partner and if he attends these events with her he's been very careful to make sure there are no photos out there. But as for her, there's quite a lot to choose from so I've printed out a couple so we can get familiar."

"What does the profile say about her background?" Kara asked.

"Allegedly she was born in a place called Kaunas in Lithuania, grew up in Kaliningrad and moved to the UK in ninety-nine after a successful international modelling career. No way of verifying any of that but the dates tie in roughly with what Zoe gave you and her photos do show a beautiful woman," Tien said.

Kara clasped her hands, looked down and took a deep breath. The other three waited. After a moment she raised her head, "Right, obviously the news that our most likely candidate is now bosom friends-" She was interrupted by Dan's phone ringing.

He checked the screen, "It's Jacob." The tension in the room was immediate. He pressed the answer button, "Go ahead."

Kara felt the strange mix of fear and excitement that she had known so many times on operations in the UK and overseas. She knew it was the thrill of the uncertainty and the potential danger. But deep down in places she didn't think about or examine too closely, she knew it was also the possibility of violence and mayhem. It quickened her.

Dan raised his free hand and made the 'ok' for them all to see. The tension in the room dissipated and the tiniest of regrets ebbed into Kara's mind.

"Roger that," said Dan and ended the call. "Tien, your cameras are about to pick up three people coming into the entry porch. It's all good."

Tien's phone sounded a series of soft chirps. Kara watched as Tien looked at the screen and saw recognition in her friend's eyes. "Sammi's here," Tien announced and went to open the door.

The UK armed forces had many skillsets but inventive nicknames had never featured highly. Samantha Davis, James Bell and Charles Randal had, since their first days in uniform, been known as Sammi, Dinger and Chaz. Their former Welsh colleague Taff, now laid to rest in his native soil, had been further proof of the lack of effort that went into the process. But, as obvious as they were, the names had followed them into civilian life and their pseudo-military activities.

Kara and Dinger had brought some more chairs into the office, Tien and Sammi had gone upstairs to get four more laptops and Eugene and Chaz had made mugs of tea for all. Dan had stayed as the watchful point of contact for Jacob and

Toby.

"If you've got 'em, smoke 'em," Kara called and all seven of them glanced around.

"Really, not one of us smokes anymore?" Dan asked and was answered by six shaking heads.

"Well fuck me, aren't we all fuckin' saints now," Dinger said, exaggerating his Scottish accent.

"Yep, all fit and healthy, going bald and getting fat," Eugene laughed.

"Speak for yourself," Sammi said.

"I was actually talking to you," he answered.

Sammi raised her middle finger, "Happy to check your prostate any time."

"Mmm, I'll pass," Eugene chuckled, "You've got hands like a welder."

"I really don't. It's just the last time I held your cock it was so small it made my hands look enormous," Sammi said with a superior flick of her head and Tien, Dan and Chaz nearly choked on their tea. When the laughter had subsided and Sammi had blown a mock kiss to Eugene, Kara knew it was time.

"Okay, we need to start."

An hour later, and despite Tien's best efforts, they hadn't managed to narrow down which house near Epping Forest belonged to Illy and Yanina. But they had managed to construct a rough working plan that depended for its further refinement on the whereabouts of Yanina Bobrik.

"Why can't we just go back and talk to the kids again?" asked Chaz.

"Because whilst they might be able to get his address they might spook him. If Zoe and Michael haven't visited for years then a sudden desire to come see Uncle Illy might be strange," Dan offered.

"But given the circumstances, you know, the missing parents, Zoe might want to go round for a visit," Chaz pressed.

"I did think long and hard about it Chaz, but I'm not prepared to risk he gets even an inkling," Kara answered. "I also don't want to advise Zoe and Michael that a lifelong family friend might actually be holding their parents against their will until I have definite proof. If we need to involve them later, we will."

"Fair enough," Chaz conceded.

"Okay. Let's make the call," Tien said and handed Sammi a pre-paid phone. The room quieted, Sammi dialled the number and put the phone onto speaker.

"Thank you for calling the Krasota Modelling Agency. My name is Francesca, how may I direct your call?" The efficient voice of the receptionist was tinged with the trace of practised elocution lessons or a happy circumstance of being raised in the mid-Atlantic.

Samantha Davis was a native of Knightwick, a small village in Worcestershire. Her natural voice still carried the slight burr of the West Country despite having left to join the military years before. But the young Samantha had discovered by the age of ten that she could mimic almost every dialect of English she encountered. It was her party trick until she ended up as a Human Intelligence Operator at which point it became elevated to a very handy skill and on one occasion, a life saver.

The voice she chose now to reply to Francesca was Kensington and Chelsea upper-class, old-moneyed English with drawled Rs and instant familiarity, "Oh hello Francesca. I'm calling to speak to Yanina. Oh I do hope I haven't missed her. It's such a bind if I have. Could you possibly be a dear and put me straight through, could you?"

"May I say who is calling?"

Francesca's accent had kicked up a notch or two. She had gone from well-spoken middle-class to an attempt at matching Sammi.

"Oh why yes my dear Francesca. It's Tamsin. I work with Kate at Tatler. We simply must talk to Yanina. I'm looking for a fresh face and all the one's I'm being shown are so tired. I must have a new look for our cover. Have I missed her?"

"Oh no, certainly not, I can put you-"

Sammi nodded. Tien and Kara yelled out loudly, "Tamsin,

126

Tamsin, come at once, you must come at once."

"Oh Francesca, are you still there darling?" Sammi asked.

"Yes," the eager receptionist had almost yelped her reply.

"Oh dear sweetie. I've been summoned. I have to run. Please be a love, when does Yanina leave for the day?"

"She normally stays until at least five. Shall I get-"

Sammi nodded. Tien and Kara yelled out again.

"Oh darling! I must go. Now tell Yanina not to fret I shall call her today before she heads off. Oh, I must run. You've been a treasure. Ta ta." Sammi ended the call and the six others gave a round of applause. Sammi gave a mock curtsey in response.

"Okay, so we've got her fixed. Now all we need to do is figure the rest out," Kara said. It took a further hour for them to improvise a workable action plan.

"This is pretty thin," Sammi said.

"It is," Kara agreed. "But is it enough to be feasible?" She looked around the room. All of the team were frowning slightly, but they all gave a nod to confirm their agreement. "Then we do it and figure the rest out when we get more to work on. Sammi, book us a base of operations somewhere near to the forest. Tien, get as much kit as we have here. We don't have time to make this pretty."

Tien raided her supply locker and issued all of them with pre-paid smartphones cross programmed with speed dials for each other. She also issued ear pieces and cuff-mics for the digital radio system that they would carry, but cautioned them that it was only good for short range work. She knew they knew but it was always worth the reminder.

After giving Sammi, Chaz and Dinger a laptop each and tethering them for Internet access she cleared the rest of the miscellaneous electronic equipment from the locker. Unlatching the four metal shelves she handed them rearward to the waiting team and pressed a small latch on the now bare back panel. The whole of what had been the rear of the locker hinged right to reveal a hidden series of shelves holding an array of specialist equipment gathered by Kara and Tien over the years. Some of it was legal to own and some of it less so. Some had been gifted to them and some they had 'liberated'.

"Nice," said Chaz peering over Tien's shoulder, "Are they Fourteens?" he asked referring to the night vision devices on one of the shelves.

"Yep," she said and stood back. "Help yourselves, but I want it all returned when we're finished."

Once they had taken all they needed Kara led them back downstairs, "Any questions?"

She was answered with silence.

"Right, see you all later," she said and went out the door with Dan. Tien and Eugene went next, Sammi and her team left last. Toby and Jacob stayed in place.

19

Thursday Afternoon. Huntingdon

Martina Costa's hands were trembling, her dark hair, damp from sweat, clung to her coffee-coloured Mediterranean skin and her expression was like the proverbial rabbit in headlights. Police Constable Pia Giovanni sat next to her talking in a low but distinct tone. The rising and falling cadence of the Italian language struck Tony Reynolds as a beautiful incongruence to the otherwise austere drabness of the interview suite.

He was watching, along with Mason, Pop and John McKay, on a live feed piped into the monitoring room that sat next door to the interview suite. He didn't have a one-way mirror like all the American TV shows but instead had a twenty-six inch TV screen and a handheld camera controller. With no indication in the interview room itself, other than a small green light to show the interview was being monitored, he could zoom in on suspects as they answered the questions posed to them. More often or not it wasn't the Interviewing Officer or their colleague sat next to them who saw the inconsistencies, the changes in body language or the deliberate concealments of a suspect but rather the monitoring officer via the screen in this room.

Giovanni had been briefed to inform Costa why she had been asked to come to the station and what was going to happen from here forward. Reynolds had left them alone in the hope that a familiar accent and the friendly disposition of Giovanni might calm down the increasingly distressed Costa. The Police Constable indicated to the camera she had done as requested. From what Reynolds could see it hadn't seemed to change Costa's demeanour much at all.

"Right, on you go," said Reynolds and Mason led Pop into the suite.

Reynolds moved the camera angle to take in the whole scene as Mason and Pop took seats opposite Costa and Giovanni.

Despite having video monitoring the interview suite also continued to use audio recordings. Mason turned to the control panel on the wall and pressed record.

"I am Detective Sergeant Gary Mason, also present is Detective Constable Colin Oldman, Police Constable Pia Giovanni and Miss Martina Costa. If you could please identify yourself for the purpose of the tape."

"Detective Constable Colin Oldman," Pop said.

"Police Constable Pia Giovanni, Police interpreter," Pia said before turning to Costa and explaining what she needed to do.

"Martina Angela Maria Costa."

"Miss Costa, you have not been charged with any crime at this time. You voluntarily came to the station so I could continue to question you with the aid of a Police interpreter. Is that correct?" Mason waited for Giovanni to translate. Costa nodded rapidly.

"Can you please answer for the purposes of the recording Miss Costa?" he said.

Reynolds noticed that Mason's voice was smooth, controlled, efficient; yet that didn't lessen the impression of how brutal it sounded when compared to Giovanni's version of the same sentence repeated back.

"Sì," Costa said, the nervousness of the young woman perfectly framed in the tremor surrounding the single word.

"Yes," Giovanni said.

Reynolds figured that the afternoon was going to be a long drawn out affair.

φ

Moya Little and Anna Walsh were waiting in the same casual seating area of Rocky's Nightclub that the unidentified couple had sat in on the CCTV. Although open on a Thursday, Friday and Saturday night the Club's main doors were still firmly shut in the early afternoon. Other than a few bar staff doing stock checks and a few cleaners making their last rounds, the place was empty. A non-descript door tucked into the far corner of the bar area opened and a tall man of about thirty, wearing a very smart business suit, came through and headed in their direction. He walked with a slight swagger. Nothing too extravagant, nor in any way arrogant. Just a confidence that seemed to exude from him and was somehow reflected in the tailoring of his jacket, the crispness of his shirt and the neat knot of his tie.

"Hi, I'm Steve Lyttle, the Duty Manager. How can I help?"

Both women stood and showed their warrant cards.

"Umm, that's a coincidence. I'm Detective Sergeant Moya Little," she said aware of the slightest of smiles the man had given her.

He bent forward and looked at her warrant card. "Ah but mine's spelt with a 'Y' which is good. It would have been terrible to find out we're related," he said and gave the cheekiest of looks to Moya. She stifled a laugh but before she could respond in any meaningful way Anna took up her defence.

"I'm sorry Mr Lyttle but what did you say?"

Steve turned and looked at the woman who matched him for height. He raised his hands in mock surrender.

"It's okay," he peered forward to look at her warrant card,

131

"Detective Constable Walsh. I merely meant that had we been related I couldn't ask the Detective Sergeant out on a date. Wouldn't be fitting for cousins, now would it?"

Moya again stifled a sudden urge to laugh and watched as Anna seemed to flounder, completely lost for words. Deciding that her near-namesake could probably charm the birds from trees, Moya took a breath and, as Anna still hadn't responded, moved the conversation on, "Well, I shall take your flattery as a compliment Mr Lyttle and I shall also ask my young colleague not to lift you up and bodily throw you across the room for being cheeky. Would you care to sit down and have a look at some photos for us? We're trying to establish the identity of some people that we found on the CCTV recordings your owner gave us earlier in the week."

"Certainly, I'd be delighted," Lyttle said and sat opposite Moya.

Anna stayed standing and placed two gloss prints on the table.

Steve picked up the top one that showed the blonde walking through the foyer. "No idea, can't see her face. She could be one of hundreds." He set it aside and picked up the picture of the couple that had also been taken in the foyer. "Haven't a clue who the woman is but the bloke is Paul Harris"

Moya sat forward, "You're sure?"

"Yeah. Huntingdon's a small place in the scheme of things. Me and Paul went to school together. Out at Hinchingbrooke."

"Do you know where he lives?" she asked.

"Afraid not. Like I said, we went to school together and still acknowledge each other on passing but I don't think I've properly spoken to him for years. He's okay like, no dramas with him. Just not in each other's circle of friends really."

"What about where he works?" Moya asked hopefully.

"I'm pretty sure he used to be out at Lola Cars, you know the Formula One setup that went bust?" Moya didn't but nodded like she did to keep the momentum going. She could find out later and looked up to make sure Anna was taking notes. "But I'm not too sure where he is now. Sorry," Lyttle said and Moya got the impression he was being genuine. She looked at him and saw, like her, he wasn't wearing any wedding band on his finger. He was about the same age as she was, well presented, handsome'ish and confident. Above all, confident. But not overly so.

"Do you know if he's married?" she asked.

"Mmm… I don't think so, although… I wouldn't swear to that. We're not even Facebook buddies so I don't really know," Lyttle said and gave a tight, half-smile.

It took another few minutes to tidy up the details and then Moya and Anna made to leave.

"Oh, I almost forgot," Moya said turning back, "If you think of anything else that might be of assistance you can ring the number on that card."

"Is this your number?"

"No Mr Lyttle it's not. It's the operations room for the Tri-County Major Crimes Unit," Moya said with mock severity.

Lyttle reached into his suit pocket and handed over a card of his own. "Well perhaps, if I forget to call, or I don't have anything to call about, you could check up on me? On Sunday perhaps?"

She glanced over her shoulder to make sure Anna had walked on through to the foyer. "I might just have to do that. Duty of care and all that sort of thing."

"Exactly," Steve Lyttle said and smiled in a boyish way that Moya reckoned was well practised but she still found incredibly attractive. She turned and caught up with Anna.

"Everything okay Sarge?"

"Yep. I think that was a result. Let's go see what the Gov wants us to do."

ϕ

Once they'd sorted themselves out with coffees and teas, Reynold's team and PC Giovanni settled in the operations room.

"We've officially detained Costa," he explained to Moya

and Anna. "The charge clock's ticking so Gary, John and Pop will have to find something of use otherwise we'll have to let her go. We've nothing at the minute other than something's not right and I want her where I can see her for now. The warrants for the search of her house are being signed off hopefully as we speak."

"What's her story?" Moya asked.

"She said she went into town on Friday night, met some friends, had a drink and went home early because she was feeling tired. That ties in with what we saw of her on the CCTV. Problem is that after that we have nothing. No one was at home, or rather her landlady didn't see her come home. We don't have the shoes she was wearing because she says the heel broke off one of them and she threw them out. She's a black belt in a specialist self-defence form of martial arts and most of all she is really agitated. Way too keen to answer yes to everything she can yet not able to answer anything we need. Avoids eye-contact and is generally showing all the traits of someone trying to hide something and doing it badly. So, we'll wait for the duty solicitor to turn up and then we'll have another go. Any other questions?"

"Only if you managed to find out if someone was operating on our patch?" Moya asked.

"Not a thing. I asked the Super to check it out at her level too and it all came back clean. So the blonde, if she's doing surveillance, is doing it privately. Why's that? Did you find something?"

Moya let Anna take the rest of them through the identification of Paul Harris. "We ran his name and he shows up as living in Priory Grove, backs onto the cemetery and ties in with where we saw him heading on the video. Don't have a work address for him, but if we aren't going to be stepping on anyone's toes we thought we could go to his house and see if anyone's in. If not we wait for him."

"Yes, definitely," Reynolds agreed. "But be discreet. If we assume that the blonde was hired to follow them then we might be wading into a civil divorce case or some other such nonsense that we don't need to involve ourselves with. My guess would be that it's probably his partner who's hired someone to follow him so if she's there you're going to have to talk to her separately. Don't lose focus that it's the identity of the blonde we need." Reynolds said it not for Moya's benefit but for Anna's. She, John and Pop were all in their first couple of years out of uniform and whilst they were shaping up nicely for the most part, he always liked to take the occasion to reinforce their skills.

Anna and Moya finished their coffees and headed out. As the door was swinging shut a uniformed constable came in with the warrants Reynolds needed.

"Right," Reynolds said taking the papers and handing them over to Mason, "Go see if you three can find me some evidence."

20

The Krasota Modelling Agency may have been a beauty by name but the address that claimed to be its International Headquarters was less than aesthetically pleasing. The office sat on the top floor of a small complex of shops that seemed to sag under the weight. The little row of outlets looked as if they had been stuck on as an afterthought to the front of the Pavilions Shopping Centre in the middle of Waltham Cross. On closer inspection it was obvious the modern centre had been built afterwards, right up to their back doors, like some large bully trying to edge them off their tenuous hold on the pavement. The gaudy façade of the Pavilions loomed over them from behind like a leering giant.

The modelling agency's front door and narrow stairwell were squeezed between a charity shop and a building society. The first floor windows, dressed by vertical blinds that hid all indication of activity within, bore a striking logo of a curved 'starstreak' with Krasota written across its centre in a westernised, Cyrillic-style font. Tien thought the 'starstreak' effect looked a little like the old Soviet sickle.

She and Eugene were watching from the corner seat of a

fast food restaurant obliquely across the pedestrianized precinct. Just visible to the right of the Eleanor Cross that gave the town its suffix was the agency's doorway. In the previous hour they had seen one young woman exit with a large format portfolio under her arm, but since then the door had remained closed.

"Another coffee?" Eugene asked.

"Oh no, if I have to try drinking anymore coffee I'll burst."

"Soft drink?"

Tien made a fake retching sound, "Definitely not."

"Well we need to pick something or find a new place to lay our heads. That big officious pain in the arse who came over earlier is hovering again."

Tien looked past Eugene's shoulder to the long mirror that reflected the whole of the small restaurant. A teenage girl with five stars on a badge that wobbled and jostled as if trying to hang on to a uniform shirt that gaped at every seam stood, with hands on hips, openly glaring at them.

"What on earth is her problem do you think?" Tien asked.

"I would assume that for each gold star they've given her the more of a pain she's become," said Eugene. "Or, she is awestruck by my handsome good looks and is insanely jealous of you."

"Yep, I agree," Tien paused, "She's got worse with every new star they gave her."

Eugene started to laugh but was stopped short by his phone ringing. He scooped it up, "Go… Yep… On our way." He pocketed the mobile and began to slide out from the seat, "Turns out we shall avoid the wrath of Miss Five-star. That was Kara. Dan has eyes on Yanina and another woman who is presumably Francesca. They've gone out the back."

The problem with the pedestrianised precincts so common to English towns was they left multiple options for where a town-centre worker could park their car. Waltham Cross was no exception. During their initial planning Kara's team had determined the extent of their 3-D puzzle and knew it would be touch and go. There were seven car parks within walking distance of Yanina's office. They didn't know what car she drove so they couldn't hope to find it and wait for her and they couldn't rule out she'd be picked up by a driver. None of that took into account the chance she used public transport, but that was the least likely proposition. The obvious disadvantage was not knowing where Yanina's home destination was going to be but at least they would know where she was going to start from.

Tien and Kara, accompanied in turn by Eugene and Dan monitored the front and back of the agency. Sammi, Dinger and Chaz, prepositioned in their separate cars along the most likely routes out of town, waited for cueing onto the target.

Knowing that Illy and Yanina's house was likely on the western side of Epping Forest was an advantage of sorts. The remnants of the ancient woodland stretched for miles but the main expanse, bounded to the north by the M25 and to the south by Chingford was only about six miles in length. However, if the house was in the scattered patches of forest that stretched southwards past Chingford then life would get considerably more difficult.

Kara and the rest had designed the best solution they could manage. Tien and Eugene had taken up their place in the restaurant; Kara settled on a bench seat that covered anyone coming from the rear door of the agency and turning to exit through the Pavilions Shopping Centre whilst Dan got the least comfortable post. He had oversight of an alley that could be accessed from the rear door of the agency, led to the centre's waste bins and eventually came out next to the offloading dock of a supermarket.

Once they were all in place the first thing was to confirm Yanina was still in the office and presumably waiting for 'Tamsin' to call back. Unfortunately Sammi didn't have an appreciative audience this time and made the call from her car. After chatting for a few minutes and insisting Yanina sent her headshots of her most auspicious nominations for Tatler to peruse, Sammi wound it up. She gave the almost salivating Yanina a false 'Tatler' email address that Tien had rigged and promised to be, 'In touch as soon as I find that face I'm looking for. Love to you sweetie. Ta ta.'

She ended the call and texted to the whole team, 'She's still in there.'

That had been half an hour earlier. Now Yanina had finally decided to leave for the day. Dan had spotted her and alerted Kara who in turn alerted the rest of them.

Tien and Eugene were moving in opposite directions. Eugene to recover their car from the Eleanor Cross Road car park to the rear of the town's bus station and Tien to intercept Dan and take over the surveillance of Yanina if needed. Kara was moving to recover the car she and Dan had parked in the main High Street car park and Dinger, Chaz and Sammi held position until they knew which one of them would be in the best place to take the lead.

Tien heard a small whistle in her ear followed by a broken series of words, 'Rad- ch-k, o-' She pulled her mobile and phoned Dan.

"Radio's not working mate, too many buildings in the way. If you need to talk you'll need to call. What's up?"

"Two women exited from the rear. One confirmed as Yanina, assume the other is Francesca," Dan said in an efficient but unrushed manner. "They dumped rubbish bags into the skip bins and then headed for the multistorey on top of the shopping centre. They've taken the stairs and I've had to break off. Can you cover the exit lane?"

Tien turned on her heel and walked back past the restaurant she had come out of. Ten yards further on and directly opposite the only exit lane of the multistorey car park, a throng of people were formed in distinct and orderly queues lining the front apron of the town's main bus station. Tien joined the end of the queue that gave her the best view of cars coming down the steeply sloped exit ramp.

She still had the phone to her ear, "In place. Describe the other woman."

"Early twenties, five nine, brunette, shoulder length, free flowing, straight fringe, hazel eyes, high cheekbones, thin nose, wearing a black mid-length jacket with a fur-trim on the collar, white blouse under," Dan said keeping the description to the attributes Tien would likely see of a driver in a car. "Copy?"

"Copy. And Yanina?" Tien asked.

"ID as per photography. Good likeness. Wearing pink blouse under dark blue business jacket. Gold loop drop earrings."

"Okay. I'll initiate a multi-way once I get Sammi up. You talk to Eugene, tell him to hold at the car park, I'll come to him. Sammi is placed to take the lead. Copy?" Tien said quietly into the phone that she held to her right ear whilst masking her mouth behind her raised prosthetic hand. The man immediately to her front in the bus queue turned to look down at the small Asian woman but, on seeing the false hand, he smiled embarrassedly and looked away. Tien considered that on occasion her hand could be a good deterrent to too much attention.

"Roger that. Out," Dan said.

Tien disconnected the call. She knew Sammi was less than one hundred yards to her right in the car park of a KFC that was shielded from view by a modernised block of apartments. The fast food outlet also sat perfectly positioned to intercept cars coming from either the multistorey or the car park behind the bus station. She tried the digital radio but with no luck. Tien figured with Sammi in a car and her standing under an aluminium bus shelter it was all a bit too much for the close range system. She hit the speed dial on her mobile.

"Sammi, Yanina's in the multistorey. Has to turn left on exit. Once I get the car ID I'll give it, then you'll have the lead."

"Too easy," Sammi said and Tien heard through the phone the sound of her car's engine starting up. "I'm swapping you over to hands free. Wait," Sammi said.

During the pause Tien watched a small and slightly battered red Ford Fiesta edge down the exit ramp of the car park. The young girl driving was very attractive, had dark, lustrous brown hair, cut with a straight fringe. Her hair nestled on top of a fur-trimmed collar. Tien heard the click in her phone.

"How Copy?" Sammi asked.

"Fives. Standby, standby. The girl we reckon is the receptionist, Francesca, left with Yanina at the same time. Her car now exiting from the car park. Red Ford Fiesta, plate is Echo Zulu Zero Seven Romeo India Romeo. Assume Yanina not far behind. Copy?" Tien reported in her calm, unhurried and precise manner.

"Roger that," Sammi acknowledged.

As the Ford stopped at the foot of the ramp and Francesca checked it was clear to pull out, a sleek black Lexus saloon with heavily tinted side windows came into view at the top. When it turned onto the down ramp Tien thanked whatever laws stopped tint being applied to windscreens. Yanina Bobrik was clearly visible behind the wheel. Tien actually thought her photo didn't do the woman justice. She was Tien's mental idea of the archetypal Russian beauty. A perfectly oval face was framed by blonde hair that curled and fell across her shoulders in a way that made Tien think someone had styled the woman just before she stepped into the car. The intensity of her blue eyes was clearly visible across the gap that separated her from Tien. She was either a lot younger than they had assumed or had aged remarkably well. Tien went for the former. She must obviously have been Natalya's mum's younger sister by quite a margin.

"Sammi. Black Lexus saloon. No idea of the model type. Plate is Lima Mike Won Fife Sierra Quebec Delta," Tien said using the standard radio pronunciation to make sure there was no misinterpretation of the numbers. "Copy?"

"Tien. Black Lexus, Lima, Mike, Won, Fife, Sierra Quebec, Delta. Confirmed?"

"Roger. Fifty yards from passing your front. You have the lead. Now hang up until I can get the multi-way established. Out." Tien ended the call, waited for Yanina to drive past, then sprinted to the rear of the bus station and the car park where Eugene was waiting for her.

Sammi eased her car forward and watched as first the red Ford passed by and then moments later the black Lexus. There was no opportunity to leave standard gaps as the Lexus was about to enter the biggest traffic roundabout in Waltham Cross and she had to know where it exited. She eased into the main road right behind the target vehicle. The tinted rear screen of the Lexus meant she had no idea if Yanina was checking her rear-view mirror but Sammi knew it was highly unlikely that a target car would notice anything as long as she didn't follow for too long.

Tien slid into the passenger seat next to Eugene and as he accelerated to catch up with Sammi, she started to call the numbers of the other cars. Kara first, then Chaz, Dinger and finally Sammi. As each answered she pressed 'add call' on her iPhone screen and eventually pressed the merge calls button. They now had five-way communications that would be reliable over distance.

"Sammi, it's all yours," Tien said.

Sammi had managed to get a car between her and the Lexus as they entered on to the roundabout and stayed in a one-car separation as it exited straight across, staying on the A121 heading directly eastbound. In her mind she could see the geography of the playing field that she had taken charge of.

Epping Forest provided the right hand, eastern wall to a large rectangle, the top edge of which Sammi was currently travelling along. Chaz had been stationed up to the top left corner in case Yanina had either headed west or been parked in the western car parks. Dinger was sitting near the top right of the box in case Yanina had headed east. Sammi had been the close-in pivot capable of moving to whichever central car park Yanina might have left from. Sammi also knew Eugene and Tien would be about half a mile behind her providing secondary backup and that Kara and Dan would hold until things became a little clearer but could move to the bottom of the rectangle to provide potential intercepts later in the game.

"Dinger, I'm straight on the A121 eastbound. If she stays on here past the turning to the old Gunpowder Mills I'm going to bug out and let Eugene take it. If she heads south I want you to take her from there. Copy?"

"Copy," Dinger said from his position in a McDonalds car park on a main corner junction. Its location allowed him to exit back onto the top of the rectangle or head south and east on a road that aimed for the midpoint of the forest.

The traffic was quite light and it took less than a minute for Sammi to cross the bridge that traversed the twin waterways of the River Lea. The main junction was just ahead.

"Dinger, she's indicating right, right, right. Standby."

"Roger." Dinger eased his car towards the exit that would lead him onto the southbound section of the A121 known as Meridian Way.

Sammi stayed in the left lane. Green lights meant she could do nothing else but head straight across the junction.

"Dinger, she's in the right hand lane waiting to make the turn. I'm clear through and about to lose eyes on. Confirm black Lexus, plate Lima Mike Won Fife Sierra Quebec Delta. She's all yours. Copy?"

"Copy. Lima Mike Won Fife Sierra Quebec Delta," Dinger repeated.

The tension within and between the five cars was palpable. Eugene and Tien were fast approaching the junction and could probably deal with any route changes the Lexus might throw if Yanina was running counter-surveillance techniques, but it was never good to have a blind moment.

"Dinger we're coming over the bridge now. The right hand signal has gone green," Tien said.

"Roger that."

"She's turned. But we'll be caught on the change of lights," Tien added looking the hundred or so yards ahead to the busy junction.

There was a pause of almost half a minute which in the

scheme of the operation seemed to stretch for an hour. Yet no one chipped in, no one prompted for responses. A good few years had gone by since all seven of them had worked together but the trust and confidence in each other hadn't diminished. Back then in the dust and sand and heat, when they had formed a specialist team with particular expertise in close quarter observation, the bad guys had been worse than ruthless. It had honed Kara and her friends. They had no need to hassle Dinger. He would answer when he was ready.

"Tien, I'm visual south on Meridian Way. Kara can you follow behind Eugene and Tien? I think we're going to need to hand off quicker," Dinger said.

"Roger," Kara responded.

"Chaz, same with you. Make as good time as you can mate," Dinger said and figured Chaz and Kara might not get to him quickly enough. The risk was that he and then Tien would be forced to follow for too many miles. He was pleasantly surprised by Chaz's answer.

"Dinger, I'm eyes on Tien. I started heading east when Sammi first called it, so I'm probably way in front of Kara."

"Okay. Good news. Kara let me know when you get to the McDonald's turn. Tien tell me when you see me." Dinger knew all of his colleagues had the picture of the local area committed to memory so he knew they could follow along in their mind. All he needed to do was provide the commentary, "Going round a long left-hander. Now east on Meridian Way."

A native of Skye, in the Scottish Inner Hebrides, the tall, broad and fair haired Scot spoke with a clarity, cadence and softness that Kara had once teased would have made for a great voice-over artist.

"Straight across the first roundabout."

"Continuing east, approaching second roundabout."

The next roundabout was also the next major decision point for what parts of the rectangle stayed in play. If Yanina went straight across she would be heading for the northern stretch of the forest. If she turned right and went south that would open up the whole southern half of the space. Dinger had three cars between him and the Lexus.

"She's not indicating but she's moved into the right hand lane at the Dowding Way roundabout. She's going right, right, right. Southbound onto A112. Tien are you close enough?"

"Yep, we can take it," Tien answered.

"Roger that. She's gone right, I'm out. You have her." Dinger continued eastbound on Dowding Way.

"Eyes on, southbound A112, we have four vehicles between her and us. Chaz how far back are you?" Tien asked.

"I'm just approaching the roundabout. Have about six cars and a couple of trucks in between us."

Tien was pleased that the homeward bound rush hour was making the tail relatively easy but it could also be a pain if it got too busy. Suddenly too much traffic was the least of her problems.

"Oh damn. She's indicating left, left, left. Heading for," Tien paused and checked the map on her smartphone, "Avey Lane. She's turning into Avey Lane. Oh this isn't good. It's nearly single track. Multiple turn offs. We'll have to go with her but the traffic's going to be thin."

The Lexus turned onto the small road that angled across and intercepted the main expanse of forest at almost its midpoint. No other cars turned after it which meant Tien and Eugene would be highly exposed.

"Duck down," said Eugene as he prepared to make the turn. "She can see me but it's not a good idea she sees both of us. Get me a pull-in down here that we can hand off to Chaz."

Tien, doubled forward almost into the foot well and tried to check her map but Kara responded first.

"Tien. Halfway down the lane, on the right there's a nursery. Turn in there. Chaz can take it. I'm just turning at McDonalds. About five minutes behind Chaz. Copy?"

"Copy. Chaz are you good?" Tien asked.

"Yep all good. I'm just coming up to the lane turning."

The Lexus was about a hundred yards ahead of Tien and

Eugene with no traffic between them.

Tien had finally got the map in focus, "Eugene, once you clear the first buildings on the left, there's a stretch of empty fields, then the next buildings on the left are opposite the turning for the nursery."

"Okay. Roughly how far?" he asked, concentrating on keeping his distance from the Lexus, near but not too near.

"Less than a mile."

A little under two minutes later Tien, still huddled in the foot well, heard Eugene put the indicator on.

"This is us," Eugene said.

"Chaz. You're in," Tien said.

"Copy that."

Chaz watched as Eugene turned off down the even narrower lane to the nursery and just glimpsed the brake lights of the Lexus as it negotiated a gentle left hand bend ahead. Avey Lane was lined with high hedgerows and had the occasional passing place cut into the verge. He hoped nothing was coming the other way that would cause the Lexus to stop and mean he would close right up on the target. He calculated that if he could keep at least a bend between them he would be safe from detection and still be able to follow. But he didn't get the chance. Less than half a mile further on he rounded the next bend and almost drove into the back of the target car. It was making an acute left turn into the driveway of a house set back some distance from the road. Chaz didn't flinch but merely slowed enough to allow the Lexus time to make the manoeuvre. Then he drove straight past, checking all he could in his mirrors.

"Target has turned into a house on Avey Lane. No opportunity for observation. Now what?" he asked.

"We meet at RV1. Copy?" Kara said.

21

Thursday Evening. Huntingdon

Paul Harris parked on his small concrete drive and stepped from his car. Like the rest of the 1950's semi-detached houses in the narrow cul-de-sac, the parking space had come at the cost of most of the former front garden. But at least his house had retained some greenery. His neighbours had either concreted the whole space to cater for two cars or attempted to plant rose bushes in the remnants of exposed soil. Paul had stuck with simple lawn. Well-tended and neat but with a size less than the smallest of putting greens, it didn't require much maintenance to keep it that way.

Moya and Anna had arrived earlier and with no answer from the house had parked up, half on, half off the pavement, a few yards further along on the opposite side of the road. They'd spent the last twenty minutes listening to the coverage of the Wimbledon tennis on the radio. Now they waited a little longer until Harris was putting the key into the front door. He turned at the sound of their footsteps.

"Mr Paul Harris?" Anna called.

"Yes," he said, a little startled by the approach of the tall young woman and her shorter, older companion.

"We're from the Tri-County Major Crimes Unit. Can we have a word with you?"

Moya kept her expression neutral but was pleased inwardly at Anna's use of the Major Crimes title. It was always a good thing to throw at someone when you wanted them knocked off balance. She watched the colour drain slightly from the man's face. She knew he was the same age as the nightclub charmer Steve Lyttle; they had been at school together. But where Lyttle was tall, trim and confident, Paul Harris was shorter, slightly heavier than he should have been for his height, appeared a good few years older and looked distinctly unsure of himself. Moya considered the pictures she had seen of him and the girl leaving the nightclub together. She thought, and considered it unkind even as she was thinking it, 'You must have money or a great personality, or just had one helluva lucky night, Mr Harris.'

Stepping back against his front door, he stammered through the usual responses trying to find out what they wanted, what this was all about, why did they want to speak to him, but Anna deflected all of his questions very ably. Moya was impressed. It only took a few minutes until they'd identified themselves formally and Harris had invited them to sit down in his living room.

"Are you married Mr Harris?" Anna asked.

"No, no I'm not," his voice was hoarse, strained and he sat forward on the edge of his chair.

"Have you ever been married?"

"No. Never. Look what is this about a major crime?" he directed the question at Anna but Moya interjected.

"We'll get to that Sir. But first, we really need to know, do you have a long-term partner?"

Moya thought he looked like a spectator at Wimbledon as he turned first to look at her, then Anna, then back to her again. His movement was smooth but his expression was getting increasingly perplexed.

"No. No I don't. I don't have a partner. And it would be a woman, so you can save the political correctness," he said, a little more strain noticeable in his voice.

"Are you currently seeing anyone, even casually?" Anna asked.

His tennis spectator action began to slow a little but he continued to alternately stare at both of the detectives. His breathing was steadying from the initial surprise and Moya could see his eyes searching their faces for clues as to what was going on.

"Sir?" Anna prompted.

"No. Not seriously," he said with a hesitancy.

Moya nodded and Anna took out the photo of Harris and his female companion exiting the nightclub.

"Who's this Sir?" Anna asked.

Moya watched as Harris' face reddened even more rapidly than it had drained to white at their arrival. The intensity and speed of the blush was startling. He went to speak but then closed his mouth. He did that a few times. Moya thought he had gone from Wimbledon spectator to fish out of water.

She decided it was time to ease his worries, "Mr Harris. You are not in any trouble. We're merely trying to ascertain a few things in the progress of an inquiry. We believe you and this woman were the subject of a surveillance operation last Friday night. We suspect a private investigator photographed and followed you and your companion. All I need to know is why. So, if you are not married and you don't have a long-term partner. Sorry," Moya corrected herself, "Girlfriend. Then can you think of any reason that someone would have you followed?"

Harris' mouth had come fully open now. He stared back at Moya with a deeply furrowed brow and an almost comedic expression of confusion. She waited.

"Sir?" Anna prompted a little more severely. It had the desired effect.

"No. I've not got a wife or a girlfriend. I have some women I see off and on but that's it. There's no reason for anyone to follow me."

"What about work? Is there anyone from there that might

want to know what you're up to?" Anna asked.

"No. I'm self-employed. I don't have any staff."

"What do you do Paul?" Moya asked.

"I'm a mechanic."

"Did you set that up after Lola closed?" Moya asked and knew she was taking a slight risk. If her previous information was wrong then it could make Harris less amenable but if it was right then it would cause him to think she knew more about him than she actually did.

His confused expression became shaded with even more concern. "Uh, yeah. How did-"

"Any customers that you've maybe had a run in with?" Anna interrupted him.

"No, no. I get on well with them. They're all mostly regulars. Seriously I don't have any reason to be followed."

"Any debts Paul?" Moya asked.

"No. I got paid out for Lola. I got enough to clear the house and set up my business. Seriously, you have the wrong man."

"Has anyone been in touch about last Friday?" Anna asked.

Harris answered quickly and a little aggressively, "Only you."

Anna raised her eyebrows and looked like she was about to retaliate but Moya spoke first, "Okay Paul. Let's just take this one step at a time. If no one is following you then they must be following your date. Who is she?"

His redness, that had begun to recede, flared anew.

They waited for a moment and with nothing forthcoming Moya sensed Anna was about to go on the attack again. She thought that might do more harm than good so she played a hunch and spoke first, "It's okay Paul. We've all been there. Do you know her first name at least?"

He looked down and nodded his head.

"And you either didn't get a last name or you don't remember it?" Moya asked with a gentler tone.

His voice was resigned, "I don't remember it. I'm not even

sure she told me it."

Moya looked sideways at Anna and saw what she thought was quite a disapproving look on her young face. She'd have to have a word later. Personal feelings and displays of emotion were not helpful in stimulating empathy in an interview.

"Okay, look it happens," Moya said. "You haven't heard from her since?"

"No," he said it with a trace of real sadness.

"So this was a one night stand. You've never seen her before?

"No. She was only up here for a conference."

"But you really liked her?"

"Yeah. Look at her," he pointed to the photo, "She was really pretty, funny, clever and-" he stopped short.

"And?" Moya asked.

Harris raised his head and looked at her, "And, you know," he gave a strange tilt of the head which Moya could only guess meant one thing.

"Good in bed?"

Harris blossomed red again and went back to gazing at his knees. He nodded.

"In the morning, did you swap phone numbers?"

"I gave her mine," he said, continuing to stare down.

"So you gave her your number. Didn't you ask for hers?"

"Yes," he said the single word like a truculent child being forced to admit a misdemeanour.

Moya waited but Harris said nothing else.

"And?" she prompted.

"And she wrote a number down. I rang her on Sunday but it was...," his voice tailed off completely and he stopped again.

"It was?" Moya asked a little more sternly.

"It was a mobile dog washing service."

Moya was relieved that Harris still had his eyes cast down at his knees so he didn't see her nearly bite through her lip to stop from laughing. She thought that when she spoke to Anna about masking her emotions she would have to have a word with herself.

She swallowed hard and went on in a steady and sympathetic voice, "Okay Paul. That's fine. Let's tell me what you do know about her. First name, this conference she was attending, where she lives, anything you have."

He looked up, the redness beginning to dissipate and his voice a little steadier, "Her name's Diane. She said she was from Hayes in London and she's a civil engineer but that might all be rubbish."

"What conference was she attending?"

"She said it was a conference on engineering. She was up for Thursday, Friday and Saturday but was going back to London on Saturday night. After I tried to ring her on Sunday and got nothing I Googled it. There was a conference in the Marriott about engineering."

"The Marriott in Huntingdon?" Moya said referring to the large hotel to the west of the town.

"Yeah."

"That's great Paul. We'll go and have a chat to the hotel and see if-" Moya was cut off by Harris.

"But that's not where she was staying. I dropped her off early on Saturday morning at the George."

"In town?"

Paul nodded and Moya decided the chances of finding Diane had just improved dramatically. The Marriott was a large modern hotel. She had no idea how many rooms it had but it must have been in the hundreds. Whereas the George was a sixteenth century coaching inn and Moya reckoned they couldn't have more than a dozen rooms. Of course there was no guarantee Diane had actually stayed there.

"That's great." Moya said and turned to Anna.

Anna picked up the questioning, "How did you two meet Mr Harris?"

"I went out for a drink with some mates. We were in the Three Tuns and she wandered in on her own. I was at the bar and she just started talking to me. My mates left me to it. When it was closing time I asked if she fancied going to a club."

"Did you notice this woman at all?" Anna showed him the picture of the blonde leaving the nightclub.

He stared at it for some time and then shook his head, "No. But you can't see her face. Do you have one that shows it?"

Anna shook her head.

"Then no, I don't recognise her at all. Is this who you think was following us?"

"Yes," Anna said. "This was taken on Friday night so this is what she was wearing. You don't remember seeing a woman like this, dressed like this?"

Harris thought about it for another few moments and again shook his head, "No. I'm sorry. I was preoccupied with Diane."

Anna finally softened her tone, "Don't worry Mr Harris. From what you've told us I would imagine she was following Diane and not you."

"Yeah but what if Diane was married and I'm in the middle of some weird thing with her husband. I mean he could be a psycho. What happens if he comes after me?" Harris had begun to look strained and anxious again.

"I'm sure nothing like that is going to happen," Moya said. "It's incredibly unlikely and even if Diane was in a divorce you'd have nothing to answer for Paul. And anyway, we know about it now so if anyone contacts you then you contact us and we'll come running. Okay?"

"I guess so," he said a little unconvinced.

Moya stood, "That's all for now Paul. We'll keep you informed if we find out what this is about and why you were being followed. But in the meantime, if there's anything else you can think of, anything at all, no matter how trivial, I want you to get in touch with us directly. My colleague will give you her card and if you think of anything, or you get contacted by Diane, or anyone else claiming to be associated with her, you ring us straight away. Understand?"

Harris nodded and taking Anna's card he led the two police officers to the door.

The George Hotel was less than a half-mile walk from Paul Harris' house but to get there by car meant a near two mile journey around the ring road and various one-way streets. As they pulled in to the small car park a team of workmen were on high ladders taking down large canvas banners that had been strung across the rear entrance of the hotel's four hundred year old courtyard.

"Ah, that's that for another year," Moya said as Anna swung the car into a parking bay.

"How'd you mean?"

"The banners. They were advertising the Shakespeare they always put on here in the summer. It finished last week."

The pair walked across the car park and around the ladders.

"Did you go?" Anna asked.

"Yep. I always try to go. This was my fifth year."

Anna made a sort of non-committal grunt.

"Don't knock it till you've tried it Anna. Anyway, if you stay in the town for a while you'll end up going. Shakespeare at the George is a local institution. You'll have to embrace your cultural side," Moya teased.

The reception counter displayed a small desk stand announcing that not only was the George delighted in welcoming them but that the bright and effervescent head receptionist who smiled warmly at them was called Rhiannon.

Once she was satisfied with Anna and Moya's credentials it took less than five minutes for her to help identify Paul Harris' date. It transpired the hotel had more than twice the number of rooms Moya had first thought but the twenty-six potentials soon became seven that matched with a check-in on the Thursday and a check-out on the Saturday. The seven reduced with the dismissal of the two family rooms that had been occupied by parents and accompanying children.

"That just leaves these five guests," said Rhiannon.

"Would you mind showing us the short registration cards?" Moya asked.

"Certainly, but there's only one female," Rhiannon said as she handed over a single card.

Moya was immediately grateful for the security requirements of hotels in the post 9-11 world. The short registration card showed the name, address, phone number and car registration of the individual checking-in. Anna copied down all the data, they both thanked the helpful Rhiannon and made their way back out through the old courtyard.

The one-way system worked in their favour this time as they drove the less than half-mile back to the Police Station.

"Her name is Diane Worrell. She's listed as living in Daleham Drive, Hayes, in the west of London. It seems to be a pleasant area and the house is a nice looking semi-detached according to Google. She drives one of the new Vauxhall Insignias and was up here for a Civil Engineering conference. No record of marriage and the only other person listed at the address is the owner of the property, a Miss Catherine Boon. So either she's house sharing and a fiancé or boyfriend is having a private-eye check up on her, or she's in a relationship with Miss Boon and it's Boon that's doing the checking, or we have missed the reason completely and it's so far out of left-field that Anna and I haven't thought about it." Moya ended her report to Reynolds.

"Good. Nice work, the pair of you," he said. "I assume you want to go to London tomorrow?"

"Yes please Gov."

"Alright. Just give the Met a ring and let them know what we're up to. Okay?"

"Yep."

Reynolds sighed, "At least it's a way forward. Unlike Costa."

"Have the lads not turned anything up?"

"On the contrary. We thought we'd hit the jackpot. The general waste bins up in Lark Crescent are only collected every other week and they're not due to be picked up until next Thursday. Costa's red shoes were in it. One heel broken off just like she said. Gary got John to rush them straight to the lab but the Med Tech' on duty reckons the actual shape and size of the stiletto doesn't match the profile identified by Doctor Rowlands. He still has to do a full blood check to see if there's any forensic match with the victim but he's not hopeful." Reynolds sighed again and rubbed his hand over his face.

"But, never say never. Anyway, you two get off home and give me a call tomorrow from the big smoke."

22

Thursday Night. Epping Forest

RV1 was the Lord Cardigan Rise. A combination pub, restaurant and motel annex perched on top of a small hill in the gently undulating countryside to the west of Epping Forest. It had been Sammi's best guess for a base of operations. Midway along the main expanse of woodland, it was in a small hamlet of houses and had a fairly good road running past it east to west. That road connected at both ends to relatively good north and south routes. Overall she had picked it because it offered rapid access to all of the surrounding area. When she had called and enquired about four rooms she was told that the separate motel annex only had six rooms in total and three of those had already been let. Sammi took the last three and agreed with the owner to have a small cot bed put into the third. Not that they would need it but it was what would have been expected of more normal guests. What she nor the rest of the team had known was just how remarkable her choice of a base had been.

The seven of them crowded into one of the bedrooms and variously smiled, laughed or shook their heads at the fact that from where they were sitting to the back of what they presumed was Illy and Yanina's garden was less than five hundred yards in a direct line. The pub did sit to the wrong side of the east-west road and they would have to negotiate it before they could get to the rear of the house, but other than that it was a superb location.

"I'd say well done to me, but it was pure fluke," Sammi said.

"Don't knock it. I'd say it was about time we had some luck on this," Kara responded. "All we have to do now is make sure that the house is actually hers and not a friend she was visiting."

It had just gone 19:30 and despite their best attempts at drive-by observations there had been no way to see if Yanina's car was still parked at the house she had pulled into. Given the narrowness of Avey Lane there was also no way to leave a couple of cars in situ without them being easily spotted should Yanina drive back out.

What they needed was for it to get dark but they had at least an hour and a half to wait for the sun to go down. Double that for the night to get dark enough for them to venture forward and reconnoitre the house and its grounds.

"You never know Kara," Dinger said from his cross-legged perch on the floor next to the room's bed, "Our luck might well be changing. It's the new moon tonight so all things being equal it'll be as dark as we could want. But, right now, I'm fucking starving so what are we going to eat?"

They decided they had too much to do to allow for a visit into the Pub's restaurant so elected instead to have a mixture of Chinese and Indian take-away delivered.

While they waited, Dan, Eugene and Dinger started to check all the equipment they had brought. Tien moved to the room's small table and set up three laptops. Chaz, Sammi and Kara stood behind her.

"Bloody hell," Sammi said, "That's amazing quality. How the hell did you get that?"

Tien looked up, "Which one?" she asked looking back to the three screens, each one displaying a different resolution image of the target house.

"Any of them to be honest, but that one on the right. It's phenomenal."

"It's all commercial grade imagery and available to anyone nowadays," said Tien.

Chaz shook his head, "Jesus, this is better quality than we had off the military systems when I started out."

"Yeah, but you did start out a long time ago. Weren't they still using balloon observation in your day?" Kara teased and stepped quickly to the other side of Sammi, using the broad shoulders of the keen swimmer as a mock shield from the lithe Mancunian's reach.

"Not quite and don't think she's going to protect you," he laughed. Chaz was the oldest amongst them but not by much. What he was by a long stretch was the best exponent of self-defence and martial arts out of the seven in the room. Even Eugene and Dan knew that if it came down to an all-out, no holds barred fight Chaz had the taking of them. Kara winked at him from behind Sammi.

"They appear to have a lot of house for what's probably only the two of them," said Tien refocussing them back on the screens.

Sammi was peering forward over Tien's shoulder, "Seriously though, how do you get this quality? It's way more detailed than Google Earth?"

"Yeah, but it's still commercial. You can buy this off the Net. We've got access to three of the big satellite imagery companies. They've got birds flying now like WorldView-3. It's got thirty-centimetre resolution. But this on the right," Tien said pointing to the screen that showed the house in fine detail. "That's low-level aerial imagery taken by a small UK outfit. Local councils use it for planning and homeowners can buy prints of their house. That sort of thing. It's really excellent and very similar to what we would have taken on an op. Between all the sources we can normally get imagery taken within the last few months. It's not perfect, it's not real-time and we certainly can't task it to go look where we want at the time we want but for what we do, it's the best available."

"This must cost a fortune," Chaz said.

"No idea really," said Kara. Sammi and Chaz turned to look at her with small frowns of confusion. "Tien broke her way in ages ago. We have actual accounts, it's just that when we need the imagery we don't get billed for it. She managed to shut that bit of the process down for our particular account. It's sort of like having an all-inclusive, access-all-area pass. And no one comes looking for us 'cos they don't know we're stealing it." She gently patted Tien's shoulder.

"I shouldn't have been surprised," Sammi said. Tien looked up and smiled at her in acknowledgment of the compliment.

"So you have access to all of this great imagery but how do the two of you non-trained, poor excuses for ex-intelligence analysts manage to cope?" Chaz said, trying not to smile but his eyes betrayed him.

Sammi started to laugh at his stirring of an old pot between those who had been trained in Imagery Analysis and those who had been trained in Signals Intelligence. Sammi, with a foot in either camp, loved the banter that invariably occurred at the first inkling that Kara or Tien could look at photos or Chaz could understand signals. All four of them had been trained in human intelligence techniques so they couldn't wind each other up over that.

"Well I just don't know Chaz. I guess it can't be that hard. We managed to figure it out without having to go to a school for four months," Tien said quietly.

"See! Now you've kicked it all off," Kara said with an air of fake reproach. "If Tien's coming out swinging then you've overstepped the mark."

Chaz put his hand on Tien's shoulder and with mock graveness said, "I am so sorry Tien. I know a fantastically trained person who specialised in electronic gathering such as yourself, could do anything. I was meaning your linguist friend over there who, let's face it, struggles to speak English let alone any other language. How did she manage to hold an image up the right way, let alone analyse it?"

"Eh bien, je ne sais pas comment vous parvenez à vous habiller," Kara said. Tien and Sammi laughed. Chaz, not understanding the phrase but fairly sure it contained an insult, flicked the V-sign at her.

"Well, if you have all finished talking gibberish at me," he said in as posh an accent as his Manchester dialect could manage, "I suppose one of us better do some work."

Tien stood up and gave Chaz a hug, "Love ya really," she said. "It's all yours and there's a printout coming soon." The portable colour printer she had set up wirelessly on the other side of the room started to whirr and feed paper in confirmation.

Chaz took the seat and he and Sammi began to examine and analyse the grounds and surrounds of the target house on the high resolution image.

Kara and Tien slipped outside and in turn went into the other rooms they had booked. They dressed them so that to a housekeeper coming in the next morning it would look like someone had stayed and slept in the beds. Then they stepped back into the courtyard and waited for the food deliveries.

They also noted the faux coach-lights hanging to the front of each room in the motel annex and the additional lighting that illuminated the rear of the Pub and the beer garden.

φ

At 22:30 Chaz came out of the en-suite bathroom and looked at the rest of them, "I'd love to see that Chinese delivery guy's face if he knocked on the door now."

Each of them might have had their own preferred makes or designs of equipment and clothing but it didn't detract from their uniformity. They all wore black high-leg boots, black combat trousers, black T-shirts, black combat smocks and black gloves. Each was bedecked in two-tone camouflage cream on face and neck and the only slight difference was in the choice of either dark green or black rolled woollen caps perched on their heads. Each had a small day pack, similar in size to the ones Tien and Kara had used to transport the money, slung over their shoulders.

Sammi grinned, her white teeth showing menacingly from darkened face and lips, "I reckon we'd probably have got away without paying."

Laughing, they began a series of buddy checks to make sure there were no rattles of tell-tale objects or glints from exposed metal. Tien had them check their digital radio systems that, given the openness of the countryside and proximity of their observation points, she had assured them would work much better than in the town earlier. But she had them take their phones as backup, just in case.

"You all sure they're switched to vibrate?" Kara asked.

A series of nods confirmed.

"Okay, let's go," she said.

They switched the room light off and Tien slipped out the door into the dark courtyard. Between the food being delivered and getting changed, she and Kara had removed all the bulbs from the coach-light lanterns.

She stood still in the small porch and waited until she was sure the occupants of the other three rooms weren't out and about. Then she moved along the edge of the wall that separated the motel annex from the neighbouring golf course entrance. Once satisfied that their path was clear she went back and gently tapped on the door. The rest filed out quickly and Dan slipped in front of Tien to lead them.

Although in a direct line they were only five hundred yards northeast of their target, on that line was the main east-west road, a collection of houses that constituted a small hamlet, an open stretch of ground and two small tributaries that fed into the Lea River. To get to the target house unseen and dry they would need to go in a much more circuitous route. So they started by following the trees at the edge of the golf course and headed northwest for four hundred yards. Then they swapped that cover for a high roadside hedge that swung southwest for three hundred yards before it merged into a small thicket. A hundred yards further and they had reached a point where they could double back to the south east and reconnect with their original line. With no houses in sight and no vehicles within earshot they quickly crossed the road with little chance of being observed. Another three hundred yards further and they regrouped at the edge of a line of trees. This was the final cover they would use to make their approach to the target house.

Dan and Dinger used the two most modern sets of night sights that had been in Tien's cupboard to scan the whole of the approach to their next point of reference; two hundred yards to their southwest a T-junction of large trees marking the corner of Illy and Yanina's garden. Or so they hoped. With no observation on the house since Chaz had seen Yanina drive in five hours earlier there was a chance that they were on a wild goose chase. Kara knew it but there was nothing to be done but press on. She moved beside Dan and put her hand on his arm.

"All clear for me," Dan whispered.

"Same," Dinger concurred in a similar tone.

"Okay. Dan you have point," Kara said softly. She and the rest of the team had much older-generation monocular night sights that were good for use in static observations but difficult to use on the move, so they set off again into what, for five of them, was almost absolute darkness. She smiled to herself, remembering the first time she had ever gone out of town and into properly rugged country.

Fifteen years old, with eleven other Air Cadets and a couple of instructors she had been on a Duke of Edinburgh Awards expedition over the August Bank Holiday weekend. They'd headed for Exmoor and the minibus had dropped them off early on the Saturday morning at a little village she had never forgotten the name of- Simonsbath. It sat on the edge of the Exmoor National Park and from there they had walked to the head of the River Exe before heading in to the rolling downs of the Long Chains Combe.

That first night under canvas and under stars had been a revelation to her. She had never truly appreciated what dark meant before. Her small hometown of Crewkerne wasn't exactly a metropolis but every street had streetlights. Exmoor didn't. There was no artificial light other than the torches she and her friends had carried. The silence of the night and the majesty of the stars that she glimpsed through scudding clouds took her breath away. The following day they had set off to walk almost clear across the moor to find the point where the East Lyn River formed. That second night, colder with no cloud cover, had made Kara cry. Not from cold or tiredness but from the sheer spectacle.

She had never before seen stars like that. Innumerable dots in a vast sky. Unable to tear herself away, she had stayed up almost the whole night staring into the universe, helpless to not think how small she was in it. Yet she was also inspired. That night forged an ambition in her to live a life of boldness. She didn't know then just what or how but she knew she must. It had been the thought of how desperately sad she would have been had she never experienced those stars until her old age. She figured many people had never seen things the way they should be. In their raw state. She swore to herself that evening on Exmoor to travel, to experience new things, to take on challenges and overcome them.

Staying up into the small hours had been somewhat regrettable given that the next day they had trekked the length of the river to where it met the West Lyn. But, even for her tiredness, as she followed the water and watched it flow into the sea at Lynmouth she felt refreshed, relieved. She went back home enthused and desperate not to live what she imagined had been the stationary lives of her parents and grandparents. She had joined the military three years later. Shortly after that she had discovered the truth about what her grandparents had done on both sides of the family and realised she was following in footsteps rather than breaking new ground.

The darkness surrounding Kara as she trailed Dan was also country dark. There were no street lights, no spill from houses that were shielded by high hedges and tall trees. But it wasn't Exmoor. Less than fifteen miles southwest of where she stood was the centre of London. The immense sprawl of artificial light from the city contaminated the night sky with a glow that obliterated most of the spectacle that she knew was up there, waiting.

Dan stopped at the junction and waited for the rest to catch up. "We sure there are no dogs?" he asked.

"As sure as we can be," said Kara. "If this is the right house then the information I got said Yanina doesn't like them. Chaz and Sammi saw no dog runs or feed bowls, fencing or anything else that looks dog-related on the imagery."

"Okay then. Let's hope we're right." He and Dinger slid forward and breached the point that marked the rear of the garden. From now on they were all communicating via radio.

"Right folks," Dinger's soft accent came through to all of them. "We have a medium height, densely thick hedge running from where we are now across the rear of the whole garden before it finally turns left and forms the right hand side of the boundary. It goes as far as the tight knot of trees to the front right of the house. That was where Chaz said the first OP should be?" he asked referring to the observation posts that they were going to try to establish around the house.

Chaz and Sammi had spent their time well in analysing the imagery. Not only had they seen no evidence of dogs, they'd identified a range of close in security features like under-eave lights and motion sensors. Given the limited angles available on the photography they had selected, as best they could, five points that they assessed would make ideal places for long-term surveillance. The garden, or more properly the extensive grounds of the house, were dotted with the occasional single specimen, but more usually knots, of small copses. The Oak, Hornbeam and Birch trees were testament to the fact the house sat on partially cleared ground that had once been within Epping Forest itself. However, the selection of points from a photo still needed to be confirmed with conditions on the ground and Dan and Dinger were their eyes to establish the truth.

"Roger that. That copse is OP1," Chaz confirmed.

Dinger continued, "To our front left is a tennis court and to the right side of it a weatherboard shed, probably for keeping the tennis equipment and lawn tools in. It provides a line-of-sight block between us and the house. If we need to penetrate further we can use it as a blind spot."

Dan, lying to the left of Dinger took over, "To the left of the tennis court is that long stretch of trees extending all the way back to Avey Lane. I'm moving now to check. Wait."

As Dan moved in a crouch to the left, Dinger moved further to the right and eased through the hedgerow's dense roots to get a clear view of the house itself, sitting some one hundred yards from where he lay. The night sights showed a large, solid building that according to Sammi must have been built in the late 1800's but had been substantially remodelled and enlarged in more recent times. A raised area extended from the back of the house and was surrounded by an elaborate balustrade. Midway along its length it broke to allow three steps to lead down into the garden and grounds proper. Dinger knew that the large area within the balustrade was an open-air pool and swim-up bar. The expansive pool-surround abutted the rear wall of the house and was accessed by a wide stretch of window-doors which were closed and curtained. The curtained darkness was repeated on all the windows that he could observe on the T-shaped house, but he could only see a limited amount from his position opposite the bottom right of the long leg of the T. If they were going to observe the property in full they needed to get more OPs in place. He looked left and saw the faint shape of Dan reappear at the bottom edge of the trees that marked the left side boundary.

"Okay Kara," Dan said into his radio. "These trees are thick all the way back to the road. We can easily put OP5 in here and it'll have eyes on the garage as well. There's also a large car parking area in front of the house. Currently got one Mercedes E-Class, a top end Range Rover, a Toyota something, it's a family looking saloon car, not sure what model, a Mazda MX-5, a Nissan something or other, not sure of the model either but small and sporty, a Ford Mondeo and a

VW Scirocco. No sign of Yanina's Lexus but the garage is big enough to hold two cars so I'll assume hers is in there."

"Roger that. Are we clear to move?" Kara asked.

"Clear," Dan said.

"Clear," Dinger confirmed.

"Let's go then," Kara said. Neither she nor the four with her moved at all. Their monocular night sights would have been more hindrance than help in navigating the darkness, so they waited. Dinger came back through the hedge and led Eugene and Tien off to the right and into position at OP1. Once settled in their location, nestled opposite the top right corner of the T-shaped building, the monocular sights would allow them to observe the front right and right side of the house.

Dan led Sammi and Chaz up to OP5 from where they would monitor the front left and left of the house.

Eventually Dinger came back and led Kara to OP3, the original point where he and Dan had breached the garden. It sat dead centre rear and allowed her to observe the back of the house and right to where Dinger would be in OP2 and left to Dan in OP4. They in turn had eyes on not only the rear and sides of the house but also the other OPs to their respective fronts. Between the five points they had almost full 360-degree coverage.

Each OP was set no more than a hundred yards from the target property but each would be completely invisible to the occupants of the house. The team knew they might well have to stay in position for a couple of days and so they used the cover of darkness to prepare their locations thoroughly. The long hours of surveillance were the least glamourous and least advertised of the skills they had all once been trained in, but potentially the most valuable. Certainly in years gone by and now possibly again.

It didn't take them too long to get settled and less than any had expected for them to confirm the house was home to Illy and Yanina.

"From OP5, we have eyes on Tango," Sammi's voice came

through to them all and even though their military years were behind them, old habits died hard. She had referred to Illy as a Target. "Tango's in a bathrobe, first floor front, first window on right. Likeness to the photo isn't bad."

"From OP1, we have a female silhouetted in the bathroom window, first floor, right hand side of house, middle window of five. No ID due to glass but fits Yanina's hair styling, hair colour, height and build," Eugene said.

Another ten minutes passed before he spoke again, "From OP1, bathroom light is out."

Another five minutes went by.

"From OP5, we have both Tangos confirmed. First floor, front right window. Designate master bedroom. Copy?"

All the rest responded that they had copied.

Another solid half hour passed with no activity and then the whole rear of the garden lit up like a floodlit stadium.

Dan and Dinger were temporarily blinded in both eyes by the flare of the light in the sights they had been using to observe. Kara suffered the same but only in the one eye that was looking through her mono lens. All three of them shut their eyes quickly and lowered their heads slowly to the ground. There was no calling out and no major movements.

"Who has eyes?" Kara whispered.

Chaz's voice sounded in her ear, "The whole of the rear of the house just lit up with the under-eave lights, but I've got no personnel in sight," he said. Although he and Sammi had identified the lights on the photos of the house they hadn't been able to assess how effective they were. That had been well and truly answered now.

"I have movement," Tien said. "I can see a shadow at rear right of property but no ID on person. Looks like we have at least one heading in your direction."

"Dinger, can you see?" Kara asked in hushed tones.

"Negative. I got complete flare-out when the lights went on. I'm a minute or two from even having blur."

"Dan?" Kara asked, still hushed.

"Negative. Same as Dinger."

Kara eased her eyes open and the right one was a myriad of bright flashes of light and dark dots floating through her field of vision. It was watering profusely and her left eye was reacting in sympathy for its mate. She concentrated on the garden area and could see a very blurry figure walking down the steps from the pool into the garden. He seemed very big but other than tall and wide she couldn't make out any other detail.

"Do you want me to break cover?" Chaz asked with a hint of urgency to his voice.

"Negative. Negative. We wait for a minute."

"Kara, if you're compromised a minute is too long," Tien said without a trace of anxiety. Her calmness was infectious.

Kara's mind relaxed. She knew her friends would cope, "If I'm compromised I expect you to tear the perpetrator and this house to pieces. But for now, just wait. Wait and consider how fucking stupid we are for not making sure one of Dan, Dinger or me weren't using sights simultaneously. Lessons people."

She slowly blinked her eyes and after a few more seconds the figure, now seventy yards from her began to resolve itself.

After a few more seconds she could see he wore trousers, a business shirt with a tie and he was raising his hand to his mouth. As she figured out what she was looking at, Tien sounded in her ear again.

"I can smell cigarette smoke."

"Roger, I can see enough of him now. You're right, he's smoking," Kara confirmed. She blinked more and the fine details began to resolve. The man's shoes were dark and the high shine glinted in the harshness of the halogen lights. As she continued to blink and he continued to pace back and forward in the garden her right eye began to relax from the shock of the flare and her left stopped watering. The man, now walking around in circles, was big. Kara reckoned he must have been about six feet six inches tall and somewhere near the eighteen or even twenty stone mark. But he wasn't fat. He was solid. As he turned back on himself again and took the last draw from the cigarette, Kara's eyes properly refocused. His path turned him sideways onto her and she realised that over his business shirt he wore a shoulder holster.

She spoke as gently as she could, "All. One male, armed with pistol, left shoulder holster. Pacing back and forward in rear garden. Smoking. Nil threat. Dan, Dinger, relax he hasn't seen us. Are you functional again?"

"Just, but don't ask me to shoot anything for a few more minutes. He's still a bit of a blur but I can see him," Dan whispered.

"Me too. He's a big son of a bitch, isn't he?" Dinger said.

"Yep. What shall we call him?" Kara asked.

Each time the team encountered a new person on a surveillance operation they would assign them a name. It made it easier than trying to refer to them as numbers or by their description. It was also a necessity that long ago they had turned into a competition.

"Nicolai," said Dan.

"Okay," Kara said hesitantly, "why's that?"

Eugene's gentle chuckle sounded over the radio, "Big Russian heavyweight boxer, seven foot tall. They called him the Beast from the East. His name was Nicolai."

"Don't think our boy's that big, but Nicolai it is," Kara said.

Dan, Kara and Dinger, their eyes fully adjusted, watched and waited. Dinger took a couple of photos of the big security guard before Nicolai plodded his way back up the pool steps and in through the window-doors. He put latches in top and bottom and then drew the curtains. The floodlights extinguished and the garden was plunged into blackness.

"Do we have anything?" Kara asked.

All of the team reported in turn. There were no lights and no movement visible in the house.

"Okay, sort your shifts out people and get some sleep. Dinger, Dan I'll take the first two hours. Who's up next?"

"I'll take it," said Dinger.

"Okay. Dawn's at five. I want a full visual half an hour before to make sure we aren't poking anything out in the breeze. Copy?"

All the OPs copied and the team settled into their surveillance.

φ

At 04:30, as the first glimmer of light began to illuminate
their surroundings the team made buddy-buddy checks on their
respective OPs. Situating them in the dark was the most
practical but darkness could also hide the obvious that showed
up plainly in the day.

Other than a minor repositioning of the cover to the front
of Sammi and Chaz the five locations were all but invisible to
the naked eye.

"So all we have to hope for is that no one in the house
possesses an IR camera," said Tien.

"Let's be fair Tien, not everyone's as technically adept as
you and most aren't as security-paranoid," Dinger answered
her.

"Well, see Dinger. Look what happens if you're not. Seven
strangers come and lie down in your garden," Tien said with
mock indignation.

"I feel like Snow White," Dan said.

"Lol," Chaz said.

"Seriously, did you just say Lol?" Dinger asked.

"Yes mate. I'm cool and hip," Chaz responded in a broad
version of his Manchester accent.

"Fucking replacement hip more like," Dan chimed in.

"Oh boy, I forgot what you lot were like. This is going to
be a long day," Eugene said and laughed softly.

23

Friday Morning. Cambridgeshire

Tony Reynolds tried to keep to his morning routine as much as he could manage. Up at 05:00 he would splash enough water to clear the sleep away and try to stop his unruly brown hair from frightening any other early risers. He'd don cross-trainers, shorts and singlet, then head down the flight of stairs from his first floor apartment and out onto the narrow Church Lane that ran past his front door.

Turning left, away from the centre of the village, he would set off south on a gentle jog. A mile later he turned left into the car park of the Old Ferry Boat Inn and having long before gained permission from the landlord, cut through it to a gap in the trees. The gap led to a small field that was no more than fifty yards across. Through another gap in the tress on the far side, he joined a private track that again, long ago, he had got permission to use. A mile more, heading almost due east he came out at the bottom of the quaintly named Overcote Lane. Another mile angling back north west and he came into the Village's rather grandly, if a bit over-ambitiously, named High Street. Two quick left turns and he was back at his front door. It was just over three miles in an almost exact triangle and he loved it.

He tried to do it every morning regardless of weather for in some strange way it summed up the purpose of his work for him. The three miles led him past the site of an ancient well, three small nursery gardens, a boat marina on the Great Ouse, a scattering of private houses, three pubs, two churches and a war memorial that despite the number of times he passed it staggered him for the amount of names it included. The village was small now and Tony always wondered how it had given up so many when it must have been so much smaller in 1914. The sense of community encapsulated by the variety of the buildings and structures he ran past seemed to him to be a microcosm of the Cambridgeshire he loved and which he served to protect.

Never the fastest runner the jog normally took him just on twenty-five minutes. He knew he could probably go faster but it was enough for him to get up and go. He also knew that doing it at all was driven by a casual vanity. He was happy that nature and genetics had allowed him to keep enough hair for it still to be unruly in the morning. There was little he could do to claim credit for that, but he could work to stave off a belly that would betray the fact he was well into his forties.

After showering, shaving and dressing in his standard suit and tie, with a fresh shirt that he always ironed the previous evening, he'd make a quick breakfast of toast and coffee and be out the door again by 06:20. He was on schedule if he caught the 'Review of the Papers' segment on BBC Radio Cambridgeshire's Breakfast Show.

The eight-mile drive to the Police Station took no more than twenty minutes, even on a bad day when he got caught by every set of lights. He quite liked those type of mornings. Over the years he had come to value the time he shared with the various presenters of the Breakfast Radio Show. The present incumbent was a bubbly and charismatic woman called Dotty. He liked her style and invariably she made him smile on his way to work. He had a much more hit-and-miss connection to the evening presenters because he never really knew when he'd end up driving home, but the Breakfast Show was a touchstone for him. Just after 06:30 he would get the travel and main news headlines from a variety of correspondents that again he felt he knew. Sandwiched between these would be the weather forecast more often than not delivered by a lady called Elena who made even the worst weather conditions sound pleasant and manageable.

So it was this morning when she warned Tony that a band of heavy rain was heading south across the whole country. A bright and reasonable start would turn overcast with drizzle, followed by light rain building to heavy downpours later. Eventually easing it would clear completely to reveal a pleasant and warm evening. As he pulled into the road approaching the Police Station car park his windscreen testified to the accuracy of the prediction. He flicked his wipers on and smeared the drizzle.

As he came into the station a uniformed Sergeant was waiting for him.

"Morning Sir."

"Morning Colin, you're looking serious, what's up?"

"There's a Mister Carpenter waiting for you in Interview Suite-1. He arrived about ten minutes ago. I didn't call because I knew you'd be on your way in."

"What's he want?"

"Says he's here to alibi the Costa girl."

24

Friday Morning. Hayes, London

Other than the addition of a very small garage to the left of the house and a relatively small porch projecting to the front, the semi-detached property listed as Diane Worrell's home address looked so much like Paul Harris' house in Huntingdon as to be quite disconcerting.

"Not much imagination going on in house design back when these were built, was there?" Anna said as she got out of the car and stretched her back muscles.

Moya, doing the same, looked around at the neat street lined with neat semi-detached houses and probably once neat gardens mostly surrendered now to paving for car parking. "I suppose they were all too busy simply building replacements to worry about the design."

Anna looked a little surprised, "How do you mean?"

"The war. London lost over a million houses alone," Moya said it somewhat perplexed that Anna hadn't automatically known.

"Oh yeah. The war. I suppose."

Moya bit her lip. A quarter to seven in the morning was not the time to lose her temper with the young constable. But she felt genuinely disappointed at the lack of awareness.

"Yeah, the war, I suppose," Moya said quite sarcastically. "Probably want to bear that in mind sometimes Anna. Lots of people still alive that remember it."

Anna might have been a little unaware about history but she was fully aware when her Sergeant was miffed. Moya saw her nod meekly in response.

"Okay, let's go do this. After you," Moya said and waved Anna up to the door.

They had left Huntingdon at five in the morning in an effort to catch Diane Worrell before she left for work. Moya was keen to talk to her in isolation and not get into the middle of whatever potential domestic circumstance was going on. The goal was to identify the PI. Nothing else.

The early start meant the traffic had been light for most of the distance. It had only taken an hour and three quarters against the two and a half hours Moya had allowed for in her head. She had even managed to phone the Duty Sergeant on the Metropolitan Police liaison desk and inform him what they were up to.

Anna pressed the bell fitted to the left of the door and was greeted by the Westminster Chimes playing loudly in the porch-cum-hallway. They waited patiently given the early hour and after a few minutes a woman's head appeared in the small glass panel of the door. Her hair was wrapped in a towel and she was looking at them with a rather concerned expression.

Anna raised her warrant card and held it open to the glass, "Police, Ma'am. May we have a word please?"

The locks were thrown and the woman opened the door. She was dwarfed by Anna but was about the same height as Moya. Wrapped in a towelling robe and in her bare feet she stepped back and ushered them into the house.

"Go straight through and on your right," she said in a definite London accent but one that was without any estuary edge to it.

Moya and Anna walked into a tastefully furnished lounge-diner whose dining room wall had been half knocked out to open up the kitchen area and form a breakfast bar. Overall the open plan was surprising in a house of this age yet Moya thought it really worked. As per their strategy, agreed on the way down, Anna took a seat and Moya stayed standing.

"I'm Detective Sergeant Moya Little and this is my colleague Detective Constable Anna Walsh. Cambridgeshire Police. Can you tell me who you are please?"

The woman, her arms wrapped tightly around herself, stood just inside the lounge door. "I'm Cathy Boon but I'll assume I'm not a random house call for the Cambridgeshire Police, so you already knew that."

She spoke in a plain, calm manner and Moya was quite impressed. To have two police turn up at your door in the morning hours would normally be quite disconcerting. Cathy Boon on the other hand seemed to be fully in charge of her faculties.

Boon continued, "Given the distance you've come this isn't a next of kin notification. You would have had your colleagues in the Met do that for you. So you've come specifically to see me for some other reason. So if it's okay with you DS Little, whilst you decide on what to ask me, I'm going to make a cup of coffee. Would you like one?"

Moya and Anna both nodded and watched as Boon walked into the kitchen, filled the kettle and turned it on.

"Is there anyone else in the house at the moment?" Moya asked to the woman's back.

"No. Just me."

Moya took the time to process her options. She decided, given Cathy Boon's demeanour, to be open and straightforward. She walked over to be near the breakfast bar.

"Miss Boon-"

She was interrupted, "Cathy, please."

"Cathy. Is Diane Worrell here?"

Cathy didn't turn from reaching for cups, but spoke brusquely, "Nope. She's not here and she won't be back."

"Would you mind telling us why?"

Cathy set the cups on the worktop and turned to face

Moya, "DS Little, she won't be back because I threw her out on Sunday. It would have been Saturday but by the time she got home it was a bit late for her to get alternative accommodation. So I waited until Sunday to give her the news. This is my house and she was no longer welcome. Now why do the Cambridgeshire Police want Diane?" She turned back to a larder cupboard and retrieved a sugar bowl and an instant coffee jar.

Moya watched as she stepped over to the fridge and took out a milk carton. "Cathy, what prompted you to ask her to leave?"

Boon turned again and looked back over the breakfast bar at Moya. "I would say that the reason I asked her to leave is none of your business. Now, why don't you tell me what you want with Diane?"

Moya was on thin ground but given the previous answer she was fairly certain that it was Cathy who had hired the PI. She decided to just push ahead, "Am I correct that she wasn't just your roommate? Were you in a relationship with her?"

Cathy stepped back and wrapped her arms around her body again. Her voice was a little edgier, "That's not a crime."

"No. I know it isn't Cathy and thank goodness for progress," Moya smiled at Boon and saw that the woman's outer demeanour was an act. Her eyes were beginning to well with as yet unspilled tears. Moya spoke in a softer tone, "Cathy, I don't need Diane. I don't want to pry into your personal life and I certainly have no desire to be rude or callous but I do need to know if you threw her out because you hired a PI to follow her. I need to know if that PI provided evidence to you of some unusual activity Diane had been involved with in Huntingdon."

The kettle clicked off and Cathy turned on her heel and started making the drinks. In the reflection from the glass splashback Moya saw her reach up and wipe her eyes.

"Cathy?"

Boon's voice was strained, breaking, "Unusual activity. Is that what we're calling shagging some fucking stranger? Well

178

okay then. Yes. I threw her out because of some 'unusual activity'. The fucking whore." Cathy stayed facing away from Moya but she was no longer making the coffee and her shoulders were silently heaving up and down.

Moya walked into the kitchen and guided the sobbing Cathy Boon back to the lounge.

φ

Anna had finished making the coffee and the three women sat in the lounge. Cathy had stopped crying and Moya sat next to her on the sofa passing across more tissues. She was desperate to ask the question and get the identity she needed but she knew that to bide her time was the right thing to do. The humane approach. The friendlier tactic. She also knew that Anna would be even more frustrated at the delay than she was and it would be a good lesson for the younger officer. Eventually Cathy had wiped all the tears and blown her nose enough. She had taken the towel from her head and her long hair hung down past her shoulders. Damp and dark it offset the woman's pale complexion. Her green eyes were rimmed red and her face looked rather crumpled from the crying.

Moya knew it was time, "It's okay Cathy. We don't need the details. All I need to know is who you hired. I just need to track her down because as well as following Diane that night she might have inadvertently witnessed a crime in progress. I need to find her."

Cathy nodded and stood up. Crossing to a side buffet she retrieved an inch-thick manila file from the top drawer and placed it on the coffee table in front of Moya. It was over stamped with an offset W&T logo and displayed the name, Wright & Tran Investigations, London.

Cathy retook her seat and said, "The full report and pictures are in there. The woman's name is Kara Wright."

25

Friday Morning. Huntingdon

Tony Reynolds was observing Interview Suite-1 on the monitors. The early morning visitor, Mr Carpenter, appeared to be in his late twenties, average height, average build, average looks, yet he also gave an impression of solidity. Normally people fidgeted or stared about, conveying a sense of unease with being in an interview room. Mr Carpenter seemed to exhibit none of these. He sat still, almost becalmed. Gary Mason came into the room behind Reynolds with a sheaf of notes.

"Thomas Peter Carpenter. Age twenty-nine. Lives in Alconbury. Married to Audrey. Two kids, a girl aged four and a boy aged one. He works at the local library as an archivist. Drives a Mazda-3 saloon and has no priors. That's all we have on him officially, but a quick Internet search shows that he's a fourth-Dan Black Belt in the same style that Costa does. He's one of the senior instructors in Cambridgeshire. In fact he's one of the highest qualified in Europe."

"So now we know how he knows her. He seems to be practising his meditation techniques or whatever it's called. He's all calm and trance-like." Reynolds checked his watch.

"Where are Pop and John?"

"I told them to start at eight. We didn't finish out at Costa's house until gone two this morning."

"Fair enough. And we got nothing other than the shoes?"

Mason just shook his head.

"Okay, well I'm going to go in and see our Mr Carpenter here. Find out if his calmness is more than surface deep. You go see the Lab and find out what they've turned up on the shoes. Come and get me when you know."

"Gov," Mason said in acknowledgement and left.

Reynolds pressed record and went through to the interview suite. Carpenter stood up as he entered. He was actually a bit taller and a lot more solid than he had appeared on the monitors.

"Good Morning Sir, I'm Detective Chief Inspector Tony Reynolds. I'm sorry to have kept you waiting."

"No need to apologise, I haven't been here too long."

Reynolds held his hand out to indicate Carpenter should sit. "My desk sergeant said that you wanted to speak to us about Miss Martina Costa, is that right?"

"Yes. She didn't do whatever it is you think she did."

"Okay. And what is it that I think she did?" Reynolds asked and watched the first flicker of doubt appear in Carpenter's eyes.

"Well, I don't know. He didn't tell me that."

"He?"

"The solicitor that called me last night."

Reynolds guessed he was referring to the Duty Solicitor that had been provided to Costa as soon as she'd been held officially, but he still needed to check.

"The solicitor? Can you recall his name and what he *did* say?"

"He was from Peacock and Laing, the local firm. His name was Gotts. I didn't get his first name. He told me that Marti was being held in here and that she had asked him to call me," Carpenter spoke not exactly slowly but in a very considered way. "He told me she was being held on suspicion of being involved in a very serious crime on Friday night."

"Marti?" Reynolds queried.

"Martina. It's what she's called normally, Marti."

"Okay. So how do you know she didn't do this serious crime that you don't actually know about?"

"Because I was with her from nine on Friday night through to seven on Saturday morning," Carpenter said and blushed. It was the second chink in the calm exterior Reynolds had seen.

"Doing what?"

"We're both in the same martial arts class and we were train-"

Reynolds cut him off, "Before you go on Mr Carpenter I want you to consider something. You coming in here to provide an alibi is one thing but as soon as you lie to me you'll be an accessory. Miss Costa is being held for a very serious crime as you were told but maybe I can clarify it for you. She's being held for suspected murder. So you think long and hard before you tell me the two of you were doing some Bruce Lee shit for nearly twelve hours. And while you think about it you answer me one question. Where does your wife think you were on Friday night?"

Carpenter looked surprised and shocked. His composure had obviously been a thin veneer and it had fractured completely under the first proper impact of reality. Reynolds always found it interesting how the mention of murder still rocked people. He would have thought they would have been immune from it given all the TV shows that revelled in it, but it was different in a real interview room, faced with a real detective.

"Mr Carpenter? Where does your wife think you were?"

"She thinks, I'm, well she, I…"

"Right, stop. Just stop. Here's the facts Mr Carpenter. You tell me the truth and if I can prove it without dragging Mrs Carpenter and your kids into it, I will. If you tell me the truth and I need to go talk to Mrs Carpenter, I will. But, you tell me crap and I will make it my personal duty to go talk to your wife, your friends and her friends. I'll talk to your four year old and I'll probably wait for your one year old to get old enough but be assured I'll talk to him at some point in the future. I'll also talk to all your colleagues at the Library and all your training buddies at the Dojo. Or," Reynolds paused for effect, "You tell me what you know and it might all be kept in this room between you and me. So?"

Reynolds was prepared to wait until Carpenter had thought through his options but the man obviously had considerable speed of thought when faced with stark choices. It didn't take him more than a breath to come to the realisation he was beat.

"Okay. I was with her at the house in Lark Crescent. I met her there at nine."

"No one saw you arriving?"

"Marti let me in by the back door so the old battleaxe of a landlady didn't see us." Carpenter stopped. Reynolds thought he was going to start speaking again but nothing more was forthcoming.

"I'll need more than that Mr Carpenter and to be honest I'm getting fed up trying to draw teeth. So, take a deep breath and tell me what was going on. Let's start with how you manage to be at Marti's on a Friday night. Where was your wife?"

Carpenter actually did take a deep breath. "My wife was off with the kids at her Mum's in Ipswich. I was meant to be at home. I waited for her to call, to say she'd arrived safe and then I went out. Marti's landlady goes to bed early and gets up late so we knew we were okay for the night. My wife wouldn't be phoning me again until before she was leaving to come home on Sunday. I got up at seven and went home because I had a class to teach on Saturday morning, but Marti and I spent Saturday night together as well." He drew another breath.

Reynolds had the sinking feeling that Carpenter was telling the truth, but he still needed more. "Do you have any way of proving this to me Mr Carpenter? I mean it's a great story. I have no doubt that when Miss Costa walks out of here as a free woman she'll be more than grateful to you, but I need more than your word on it. So, any corroboration?"

Carpenter dropped his gaze to the desk. Reynolds could see his jaw tensing, like he was almost grinding his teeth trying to think. He raised his head again.

"Would me being able to describe her tattoos be of use?"

"Do you mean Miss Costa's?"

"Yes of course."

"Shall I assume they're normally covered with clothing?"

"Yes. They're on her th-"

"No, Mr Carpenter," Reynolds held up his hand to stop the confession. "Other than telling me you've seen her naked or partially naked, it won't work for proving where she was on Friday night."

Carpenter dropped his gaze again and once more went through the process of seemingly thinking very hard. Eventually he raised his head.

"You can do stuff with GPS and phones?"

"Stuff?"

"You know, tell where a phone was, when photos were taken?"

"Yes, we can do that. But that'll tell me where your phone was; not where you were."

"It's not my phone. It's Marti's. Have you checked Marti's phone?"

"For what?"

"For the photos on it."

"No, I don't believe so. What photos?"

"We, um, I mean, we..."

"The time for embarrassment is over Mr Carpenter, spit it out." Reynolds waited for Carpenter to square away whatever remaining hesitation he had. Eventually he saw Carpenter's requirement for self-preservation win out.

"We took photos during the night. I couldn't have them on my phone so Marti took them. Could you use them to check the times?"

"Yes Mr Carpenter, we could."

There was a knock on the door and Reynolds turned to see Gary Mason beckoning him.

"Stay here Mr Carpenter. If this checks out I'm going to have some of my detectives come in and record your statement, okay?"

Carpenter nodded as Reynolds left the room.

"What's up Gary? Give me some good news."

"Well, if making sure an innocent walks is good news, then it's good news," Mason said.

"The Lab I presume?"

"Yep. No forensics on the heel at all."

"Ah well. It ties in with what I've just got. When Pop gets in you can both go back in there and get dickhead's statement."

"That good eh?"

"Oh yeah, mastermind in there probably has a full alibi for Costa but took a month of Sundays to give it up. It'll still need a quick check of Costa's phone by the techies but I imagine it'll be solid," Reynolds almost sighed.

"Her phone?"

"Yeah. I'll take you and Pop through it when he gets in. Save me repeating myself. Once you get Carpenter on record you'll have to take a new statement from Costa. Pia Giovanni will be in soon so you can do it after you talk to Carpenter. Once all the paperwork is squared and the techies have proved the phone give me a shout. I'll be there when we release her."

"No problem. Maybe Moya and Anna will have better luck Gov."

"I hope so Gary. They're the only game in town now." Reynolds led Mason over to the coffee machine and noticed the rain against the kitchen window had increased in intensity as per the Breakfast Show's forecast.

26

Friday Morning. Epping Forest

Kara was using standard binoculars to watch through the now open curtains of the wide window-doors. Illy and Yanina were sitting at a grand table and their breakfast was being served to them by a young woman who the team had decided to call Cinders. Kara wondered what it would be like to have so much money that you could afford staff. Cooks and servers, cleaners and gardeners. Bodyguards. She mainly wondered what it would be like to have them running around all the time. Even if you had money how did you settle yourself being waited on hand and foot? But then she wondered what your conscience had to be like to afford it all on the back of crime. The young Cinders could even have been one of the girls Illy used for other purposes. She was cut off in her thoughts by Sammi's hushed voice in her ear.

"Head's up folks. We have a car pulling into the driveway. Ford Focus ST, Red. One male occupant. Wait."

The team all checked their watches; 07:16.

Sammi continued, "One male occupant. Mid-twenties, about six foot. Slim, athletic. Short dark hair, grade one or two all over. Handsome. High cheekbones and straight nose. Wide eyes and relatively square jaw. Black suit, white shirt and maroon tie, black shoes. Shined. Tattoo to back of right hand. Not identifiable. Currently standing beside his car. Just lit up a cigarette. Wait."

After a short delay Sammi spoke again, "Second car pulling in. VW Golf, GTI, Red, one male occupant. Pulled up alongside the Focus. Wait."

Again the team checked the time; 07:19.

"Well that saves me a lot of effort. Take the description for the Focus driver and it's the same for the Golf GTI driver. Bar the tattoo on the hand. He doesn't have any ink visible. But they seriously might as well be twins. In fact let's designate them Reggie and Ronnie. Reggie's got the tatt. Both just waiting out front of the house."

Another few minutes passed.

"Third car coming in," Sammi said. "Beginning to look like this is the day shift arriving. Time now, 07:23. Oh, that's nice. Silver Porsche 911. Old style. Very nice. I always wanted one of those. Wait." Sammi watched as the car pulled in beside the Golf and Ronnie stepped over and opened the driver's door.

"Okay, older male, probably late thirties. He's a little shorter than them, five ten, a little stockier but not by much, still looks capable. Brown hair, with a left hand side parting, neat cut, off the collar and ears. His ears stick out a little more than the norm, round face, bit flushed and a nose that might reflect a love of the vodka. Black suit, shirt, tie and shoes same as the others. Reggie doused his cigarette pretty quick when he was pulling in and Ronnie opened the door like a footman. From their positioning and greeting I would say he's the boss of the twins. Designate him Smirnoff. All three of them heading to the front door," Sammi paused, "Interesting, Smirnoff has a key," she paused again, "And they've gone in. Door shut. Chaz has photos of the cars and all our new arrivals. Being uploaded into Dropbox now."

Kara remembered the conversation she had had with Tien about taking surveillance photos in a nightclub. Back in the day it was so ridiculous it wouldn't have been attempted. But even in a concealed surveillance like this one, any photos would have been useless until you had extracted out of the position and got them developed. It was only then you would have known if you had enough for the operation, or enough for the courts, if it was that type of surveillance. Now, Chaz had taken the photos and all the team would have access to them on their phones inside five minutes. In fact five minutes was slow but you couldn't always rely on the telephone network. She laughed to herself at the thought that waiting five minutes was an inconvenience.

"How are we all doing? Let's go round," she said.

"We're good. No observations other than Cinders and Mrs Beeton in the kitchen," Eugene reported using the designator they had given to the cook who Tien had first seen shortly after 06:00.

"I'm good. Nothing for me since Nicolai came out for another smoke at six," said Dinger.

"I'm good and have our targets in sight still eating their breakfast," Kara reported to the rest of her team.

"I'm all good with nothing to report," said Dan.

"We're good. Sammi's been farting but other than that we're okay," Chaz said. He waited a second then added a quiet but dramatic, "Owww!"

Kara settled back down into her comfortable observation of Illy and Yanina.

φ

"Front door just opened up," Chaz reported. "Time now 07:56. Seems that last half hour was shift handover. I've got Nicolai heading down into the parking area. Jesus, he is a big boy isn't he? Another male behind him. Both dressed in black suits, white shirts, maroon ties and black shoes. Looks like our target's security have a corporate uniform. Second male is about five ten, stocky, solid. Short dark hair, not shaved but neat. Probable mid-twenties. If you ever wanted a picture of a thug this guy would do it for you. Big forehead, sunken eyes, nose that's been well broken a few times, long face, cleft on chin. Tattoos on both hands, including all fingers. Rising sun on back of left hand. Designate Sunrise," he paused and watched the men walk towards the car parking area.

"Nicolai is getting into the light blue Ford Mondeo. Far out. You can visibly see that car's suspension dip when he gets in. We have a third person exiting the house," he paused again until the front door opened fully.

"Okay third security is a woman. About five eight. Slim to medium build, yellow-blonde hair cut to shoulder length, no fringe. Same black suit but white blouse, no tie. Black shoes, no heel. Quite a square face, wide eyes, proportioned features. No visible tattoos. Reminds me a bit of that American actress."

"Wanna narrow that down a bit?" Dinger said.

"I'm getting there Mr Impatient, Sissy Spacek," Chaz said.

"Designate her Carrie," Dan cut in.

"Nice," said Chaz.

"Sunrise is in the VW Scirocco," Sammi added.

There was a pause and the rest of the team could hear the cars starting up in the front driveway.

"Carrie's in the Nissan," Sammi said. "She's leaving first because like the sensible woman she is, she reversed in. Okay, it's a Nissan 350Z. Nice car, very sporty. She's at the gate and she's gone right, right, right. Nicolai's next. He's going right as well. Confirm Nicolai is right, right, right. Sunrise is last out and he's gone left, left, left. Time is 07:59 and no harm to any of you but I'm starting to get soggy. Who ordered the weather?"

27

Friday Mid-Morning. Central London

The problem with London parking wasn't a problem if you had a space in the underground car park that sat beneath the most famous revolving Police sign in the world.

Anna drove whilst Moya rang Tony Reynolds to give him an update and followed that by calling the Met's Duty Sergeant she had spoken to earlier. Eventually, even with the heavy morning traffic and the drizzle that had begun to fall, they arrived into New Scotland Yard.

"Ugh!"

Moya looked over the roof of the car and laughed.

"Oh thanks Sarge. Thanks a lot," Anna said, shutting the door and wiping her face from the water that had dripped onto her.

"I'd forgotten that the Met's car park leaks like a sieve," Moya said. "Even when it's not raining. Maybe their new building will have a dry one. Have you been here before?"

"Only on a visit during my original training. But we didn't come through this way," Anna said whilst towelling her hair with a tissue. "I think we got the VIP tour to impress us and try to tempt us to transfer."

"Yep, that'd figure. They're quite happy to poach us once we've been trained at someone else's expense," Moya said as she led them into the lift and selected 'Visitor Reception'.

Even with their warrant cards and the fact they were expected, it took them a good ten minutes to get through the security of the building. Eventually, at 08:30, they were ensconced in a 'hotdesk' working space equipped with a secure phone, a computer connection into all the Police databases and a separate computer with Internet access. Half of the third floor of the building was given over for the use of visiting Officers and almost all of the desks were occupied.

"Where are all these people from?" Anna asked.

"There are eight million stories in the naked city," Moya said in a slightly frail American accent.

Anna looked back at her blankly, "What Sarge?"

Moya shook her head, "Never mind. The people in here are just like us. Trying to track someone or something down in the city. Anyway, let's get to work. You try the official databases and I'll go surfing."

φ

"Heads-up folks," Sammi said. "Yanina's just left the house. Time now 08:43. She's heading to the garage. You'd have thought with all their money they'd have an interconnecting corridor. She's going to be all wet and bedraggled by the time she gets in," she said watching Yanina hunkering under an umbrella whilst waiting for the automatic garage door to roll up.

"Maybe the garage used to be a stable block," Tien commented from the other side of the building, blind to the garage and Yanina. "You wouldn't have wanted that connected to your house."

"S'pose not and it does look a little stable'ish," Sammi said before giving a low whistle as the garage door opened fully. "Oh that's nice. I'd take a free one of those."

"What is it Sammi?" Kara asked, knowing that her friend

liked cars and no doubt whatever the garage had revealed was on some wish list of hers.

"Well the Lexus from last night is there and Yanina's getting back into it but there's a beauty of a Jag XFR beside it. Gorgeous, black metallic, looks like the full body kit and the twenty inch Draco alloy wheels. I'm drooling."

"You're a lovely, but very strange, woman," Dinger said and was about to continue with the banter but he was cut off by Kara and Tien talking over each other.

"One at a time ladies," Sammi admonished politely.

"Can you see the registration plate of that Jaguar?" Tien asked before Kara could speak again.

"Yep, hang on. Yanina's at the exit to the lane, she's gone right, right, right. I'd have to assume she's heading back to work," Sammi added as the car went out of sight.

"I'd agree. But answer Tien's question Sammi. What's the plate on the Jag?"

She managed to read it off just as the automatic garage door came back down to obscure it, "Yankee India Seven Zero Zero November."

"Or 'Why-Aye-Toon' if you'd like," Kara said and smiled a broad smile that none of her team could see but that she knew Tien would be sharing. "We have some news folks," she said and began to explain the significance of the number plate as the sheets of fine drizzle thickened into showers.

φ

"Miss Costa, you're free to go and we'd like to thank you for assisting us with our enquiries." Reynolds indicated for Pia Giovanni to translate. Once done he turned a piece of paper around on the desk and pushed it across. Pia explained to the young Italian that it was the transcript of the interview and that it had to be signed and dated.

Reynolds turned to Mason. "Interview terminated at 09:25," Gary said and clicked off the recorder.

φ

"Gov?"

"Yes Moya. How's the research going?"

"Okay. We have solid information on Wright and Tran Investigations."

"Great. I could do with some good news."

"What's up?"

"Costa's walked."

"Oh," Moya said realising that she had almost forgotten about the young Italian girl. "No luck with forensics then?"

"No. We released her about two hours ago. There was no evidence on her shoes but it was trumped by her instructor from the local Qi Kwan Do Training Academy turning up. Seems him and her were with each other on Friday night."

"Training?"

"In a way. Horizontally."

"Ah, I see. Why on earth didn't she tell us?"

"Because Mrs Instructor wouldn't have been too happy, I'm guessing."

"Bloody hell Gov, can no one in Huntingdon keep it dry on a Friday? Between Costa and Harris all we seem to have is people tapping off with people they shouldn't."

Reynolds laughed, "Yeah, it would seem they're all at it like rabbits. Anyway, his story checked so he's alibied her and that was that. We even think we know why she was terrified of us. Pia Giovanni found out that when Costa was a little girl she'd been in Genoa during a massive riot surrounding a G8 summit. Lots of carnage and most of it done by the local Police. According to Pia, if you weren't scared of authority before then you were after. It explained Costa's attitude. Anyway, she's gone and you and Anna are our last hope now," he paused a beat, "no pressure."

"Gee thanks Gov," Moya laughed but didn't say more.

The line stayed quiet and Reynolds knew there was a problem. He almost dreaded asking, "So, Moya. You and Anna are off to pick up our PI?"

"No Gov. Hence the call."

Reynolds turned to stare out the rain lashed window and almost sighed. The neat result he had hoped for was obviously going to be more complicated, "What's up?" he asked.

"Two things. Her profile shows she was ex-military. I talked to the Ministry of Defence and got access to their online records but Wright's are heavily redacted."

"Yeah, and?" Reynolds wondered what his Detective Sergeant meant.

"Well, I thought they might have covered something up. Military offences or Courts Martial. You know the military can be even more sensitive about PR than us. I thought it might give us an angle if it turns out all the blacked-out pieces of the files are hiding something relevant. Maybe her being chucked out for violent conduct or similar."

"Mmm, fair enough. So what do you need?"

"I want to go over there Gov. Do you know anyone we can talk to?"

"Yeah, I can call up a few folk. When do you want to go?"

"As soon as possible. Then I want to take a drive-by the office of Wright and Tran and have a look at it on our way home. I figured a review with you and the team before we go any further would be smart?"

"That sounds good. You said there were two things about Wright?"

"Her brother's a DS in SCD1," Moya said referring to the fact that David Wright worked in the Met's Homicide and Serious Crime Command.

"Ah," was all Reynolds said despite his desperate desire to fling expletives. "I assume we haven't tipped him off?"

"No Gov. Turns out he's only four floors above us at the minute, but no, I didn't think it would be advisable to go and have a chat."

Reynolds could hear the slightly sarcastic edge to Moya's voice. He knew it was justified, his question had been demeaning. "Fair enough Moya. I didn't mean to be an arse. I'm just frustrated." He paused and turned away from the window and focussed back in the operations room. "There's nothing we can do about her having one of us as a brother. We go where it takes us. Get over to the MOD and see what you can find out. I'll call you with a name to talk to."

"No problem Gov. We'll see you this afternoon."

"Yep, but take your time and drive carefully, this weather's bloody awful."

φ

Despite the fact that she now knew Illy had been involved in the Sterling's disappearance, Kara was beginning to worry. Chaz and Sammi had seen the security guards swap over and Yanina go to work. Tien and Eugene had the occasional sighting of Cinders tidying up in various rooms and Mrs Beeton at the kitchen window. They'd also seen Smirnoff watching TV in what they had decided was a sitting room, Dinger, Dan and Kara herself had seen the Twins come out to the rear garden to have a smoke, but none of them had seen Illy since he had left the breakfast table at 07:36. Kara didn't know where he was, didn't have a full handle on the layout of the house and had no idea how they were going to get at him.

"Front door is opening," Chaz said slightly louder than had been the norm, just to carry over the sound of the hammering rain. "We've got a new one. Time is 12:40. Male, about six feet, maybe a little shorter, athletic build, blond hair with a pony tail. Goatee beard and moustache, very light colouring. Same outfit as the others but he's minus his jacket. No holster visible. He's got quite sharp features. Looks like a cross between a Viking and a hippy. In fact, cut his ponytail off and give him a shave he'd look a bit like Dinger. He's sorting himself out with an umbrella. Wait."

Kara felt a mixture of emotions. She was hopeful that Illy would be coming out behind the new guard but she was also fretful at the revelation that there was a new guard at all. How had they missed him previously?

"He's moving towards the Merc parked on the drive," Chaz continued. "Just opened the rear door and retrieved a

195

plastic folder. Heading back inside. What do we want to call him?"

"No sign of our main man?" Kara asked.

"None."

"Fine, call the new one Thor. Listen folks, we're not getting far here. What do you think?"

"Are you saying you want to hit the house now?" Dan asked with a trace of trepidation in his voice.

"God no!" said Kara. "If we try to hit the place now it'd be like the Charge of the Light Brigade. We wouldn't have a clue how many Russian guns we'd be heading into."

"So what are you thinking?" Tien asked over the increasing sound of the downpour.

"I really don't know. I'd hoped there'd be minimal security at the house. Hoped it'd be empty during the day, hoped we'd be able to penetrate it and work out a way of getting to Illy. Hoped he'd tell us if he was involved in the abduction or not. But now we know he's definitely involved and we definitely need to talk to him I still can't see a way of doing it. He has a three-strong team during the day and a different one at night. He's got at least one other guy that we didn't even know about. Maybe he's a live-in so who the fuck knows how many more are in there. It's not like we can storm the place and rip it to bits. This is Hertfordshire, not Helmand. So, truth be told Tien, I'm open to offers."

The rain seemed to increase when she finished talking. Kara looked out from the dense hedgerow and struggled to see the house, just a hundred yards away. The curtain of water was almost opaque and the area of the garden immediately ahead of her was already flooding. She was soaked from the wool hat on her head to the insides of her high-leg combat boots. Every layer through to her underwear was sodden. The only bit that had been dry, her front, was now squishing into a wet layer of mud that had finally succumbed to the torrent.

She knew the rest of her friends were suffering in the same way and there was nothing to be done. They would be just as uncomfortable, tired, wet and miserable. But they had all been equally uncomfortable in many other places on many other occasions so she knew they'd be fine.

"Kara," it was Sammi. "We might need another two days scoping this house and even then we might get nothing. How long do you think we have before the whole thing's a busted flush?"

"No idea. It could be too late even now. I'm hopeful that the few weeks Chris Sterling mentioned on his phone message means something but that's pure speculation. I do know I'd rather not spend another few days here and get nothing."

"We have new movement," Eugene said neutrally.

The hopefulness Kara felt every time one of the team reported a new sighting reasserted itself.

But Eugene's voice reflected the dullness of the actual observation, "It's just the Twins and Smirnoff entering the kitchen with Cinders and Beeton."

"Roger," Kara acknowledged with a hint of dejection at the necessity of the report and the fact it did nothing to improve their prospects.

"Hey Kara?"

"Yes Eugene, what's up?"

"What about forgetting about our friend Illy and going after a weak spot?"

"Meaning?"

"You remember the cleric in Basra, Kazim Al-Zubayr?"

The rain began to ease a little from the zenith of its efforts. Kara thought about a faraway place where the oppression of the weather had been in the form of dust and heat. Minutes ticked by and none of the team spoke. Kara contemplated the suggestion. Finally she asked, "Who would we take Eugene?"

"Not saying it isn't a gamble Kara, but do you think the Sterlings were lifted in the day or night?"

"Probably night, no proof but it's what we would do. Easier, cleaner."

"Well then, we take the risk and hope he used his night crew to do it and not some others he has kicking around that we don't know about."

Kara thought through the implications of the move Eugene was suggesting. It was a risk like he said but perhaps time was running out. Perhaps it was the best plan. She thought about the assets she would have to bring to bear. "The timing would need to be exceptionally tight," she said.

"Agreed," Eugene said. "But nothing we can't cope with."

"And it'll put us on a definite deadline."

"Agreed," he said again. "But you said it; we might be too late anyway. A bit of pressure isn't a bad thing."

The rain eased further. The noise from the downpour lessened and was replaced by the incessant trickling of small rivulets and streams trying to escape the confines of the garden. Kara found herself torn between her desire to go through Illy to find the answers she needed and the practicalities of her situation.

Her best friend gave her the push she needed, "Kara, you taught us over and over that if something isn't working out then we improvise, adapt and overcome."

"I know Tien, you're right. What do the rest of you think?"

"Gets our vote," Sammi answered for herself and Chaz. Dinger agreed and Dan reminded them he hadn't been in Iraq so he'd go along with whatever the rest thought.

A few more minutes passed and a small break in the cloud allowed the first rays of sun to shine down onto the garden. Not one for signs Kara nevertheless smiled at the coincidental timing. "Okay, we stay here until dark. If nothing changes in the interim we're outta here. Dinger, you'll move up to OP5 and stay behind to be our ears and eyes. Agreed?"

"Roger that."

φ

The afternoon sun was shining through the tail end of a light shower and casting odd-shaped shadows on the operations room floor. Reynold's team had been joined by Detective Chief Superintendent Laura Mitchell and it was she who signalled for them to begin. Anna Walsh placed a slightly pixelated, A4 photo enlargement of an auburn-haired woman up on the magnetic whiteboard. Next to it she put an older, black and white image of the same woman.

"Ma'am," Moya began by indicating the colour image. "This is Kara Wright from her driving licence photo taken about three years ago. She turns thirty-five at the end of this month and lives in Camden, London. She's also the only person wearing heels in the near vicinity of south west Huntingdon during the time window of Manfield Hastings' death. We have her on CCTV for a twenty-second segment walking across Walden Road at 03:02. We also have her car going through the A1 number plate recognition cameras near Caldecote at 04:17. Between those times we have nothing. No sight, no forensics, not one shred of evidence. However, Wright definitely has the skill set to pull this off." Moya stopped and nodded at Anna.

"Kara Wright, no middle name, born July 1981 in Crewkerne, Somerset. We checked her out on all the databases but she's got no record. The DVLA have a speeding fine from two years ago for doing seventy-two in a sixty zone but other than that, nothing. She has a brother David, who's a Detective Sergeant in SCD1 with the Met and-"

Laura Mitchell held her hand up to cut Anna off. She turned in her chair to Reynolds, "Tony have we informed SCD1 that we have an interest in this woman?"

"No, not yet Ma'am. That's one of the reasons we're here. To figure that out and defer to what you think will be best."

Mitchell turned back to the front and waved for Anna to continue.

"Wright has a note for Military Service so we contacted the Ministry of Defence and got access to their online records. That's also where we got this photo from," Anna said pointing rather awkwardly to the black and white image on the board before continuing. "It's about fifteen years old and one of the few things we were able to get unedited. Almost all of Wright's records had been amended to obscure the details. Thinking the missing information might be relevant to our enquiries we went to the MOD and spoke to a Colonel Howard Denny. He couldn't let us see the original documents but he did confirm that Kara Wright had an exemplary Service record. In fact, she's been mentioned in dispatches on three occasions fo-"

"That still exists?" Mitchell interrupted.

"Ma'am?" Anna looked a little blank.

"Mentioned in dispatches. I thought that was something from the Boer War days?"

Anna, having practised her brief on the way up in the car, was a little thrown by the DCS' question. She looked over, somewhat plaintively, at Moya.

"Yes Ma'am. It still exists. Wright's had three of them. One for Afghanistan and two for actions that are still classified," Moya said.

"So what do we know that *isn't* classified?" Reynolds asked.

Moya looked back at Anna who stepped forward again. "She joined the Air Force as an Intelligence Linguist in August 1999 and after basic training was posted to RAF Digby until May 2004. From May to November of that year she was in Iraq and when she came back from there her record becomes rather sparse. According to Colonel Denny she was identified as a potential talent. He wouldn't elaborate on what that actually meant but said she was approached to join a very small sub-unit of the Special Reconnaissance Regiment that was due to be established in 2005. What we do know is she was definitely back in Iraq during late '05 through early '06. Then she was posted to Hereford."

"As in SAS Hereford?" Mitchell asked.

"Yes Ma'am. According to Colonel Denny that's where the specialist unit is based."

"Do we have a name for this unit?"

Anna glanced down at her notes, "The Field Intelligence Tactical Team. They're known as the FITT," Anna paused and looked at Mitchell.

"Carry on."

"Yes Ma'am. It appears that over the next four years she

was either at Hereford or on operations. Probably in Iraq and Afghanistan but most of that period is blacked-out on her file and Colonel Denny wasn't forthcoming. What we do know is she was an instructor at the Human Intelligence School at Chicksands in 2008 through to 2009 and after that went back into Afghanistan. In April 2010 she was injured at a place called," Anna paused again and checked her notebook. "Marjah. It's in Helmand Province. That was where she got the Mention in Dispatches that we do know about."

"For what?" Mitchell asked.

The junior Detective Constable had sweat patches appearing on her blouse under the arms. Moya knew Anna hadn't briefed a Detective Chief Superintendent before and thought the young woman had made a good impression so far, but she could probably do with a break.

Moya stepped forward and took over. "We couldn't find an actual citation for Wright and initially the Colonel was very reticent but eventually he told us that Sergeant Wright, as she was then, was wounded in the head by a sniper bullet as she attempted to drag an injured soldier back into cover."

"Shot in the head and she's still alive?" Mitchell asked.

"Apparently it was only a minor graze to the top of her skull, but the sheer velocity of the bullet knocked her unconscious in the middle of a major ambush. The good news is that despite the Colonel's reluctance to tell us anything more, it seems Wright's actions happened at the same time that her business partner, Tien Tran, was also decorated. We've pieced together most of it from the publicity that surrounded that."

"Publicity?" Mitchell asked.

"Yes Ma'am," Moya confirmed. "Tran is first-generation British Vietnamese. She was only twenty-three at the time and was only the fifth woman ever to have received a Military Cross. Extremely photogenic she would have made a great recruiting poster for the Army. But it was rather unfortunate that she was up to her eyes in a secret unit doing unacknowledged operations. Colonel Denny did admit that Tran would probably have received a VC but for the nature of the team they were part of. Although the Army couldn't avoid a certain amount of publicity, the difference in scale had it been a VC would have brought all the surrounding circumstances into the full glare of the media."

"I see. Do you have the details?" Mitchell asked.

"Yes Ma'am."

"Okay, carry on. I'd like to know what sort of adverse backlash we're likely to run into from the tabloids if Wright is our murderer. I can see the headlines now, *Veteran Hero Slays Drug Monster*. Just how much of a hero was she?" Mitchell asked.

Moya looked at her notes, "Both Wright and Tran were part of a reconnaissance team supposedly supporting a major offensive push into a village known to be a stronghold for the Taliban. I think they were probably doing something much more clandestine but it's neither here nor there now. As they were moving forward the lead vehicle of a three-vehicle convoy initiated a roadside improvised explosive device. Two of the occupants of that vehicle were killed and two injured. The second and third vehicles then came under small arms fire. Tran and Wright were in the second vehicle."

Moya lifted a copy of Tran's citation that had been printed in the Army News. "Ma'am I asked Colonel Denny about the report and official citation and he explained that where no unit name was given or where the names of the other personnel were left out it usually meant an operation whose details would never be fully explained."

Mitchell nodded her understanding.

Moya read the article verbatim, "Lance Corporal Tran having recovered from the initial concussion of the blast and having witnessed her Sergeant suffer what she thought was a fatal wound whilst trying to extract two injured soldiers, left her position of cover. Unaided and exposed to constant enemy fire she ran into the open and dragged one of the wounded infantry men some fifty yards into safety. Ignoring the continued efforts of the enemy she immediately exposed herself again to hostile fire to extract the second injured soldier. At this time, Tran sustained a severe wound to her left hand all but rendering her arm useless. It was following this extraction that she also realised her Sergeant was not fatally wounded as previously thought," Moya paused and looked up.

"We're assuming that this Sergeant is Wright," she said and saw the audience of detectives all nod slowly. Laura Mitchell was leaning forward in her chair.

Moya continued, "Tran rallied the rest of her unit to provide suppressing fire into the enemy positions. Ignoring her own wound and refusing to be treated for it, she made a third journey into open ground and dragged her Sergeant out of the firing line and into cover. With absolute disregard for her own safety, she repeatedly risked her life in order to rescue wounded comrades and extract them from danger. For her outstanding gallantry, selflessness and personal example in the face of a particularly ferocious attack from a determined enemy, Lance Corporal Tran is awarded the Military Cross." Moya set the citation down. The operations room was silent.

It was Mitchell that spoke first, "That's quite humbling."

Moya merely nodded her agreement.

After a few moments Mitchell spoke again, "Bring me up to date with them then."

Anna opened her notebook, "Tran lost her left hand and was medically discharged in early 2011. Wright left in August 2011 at her twelve year option point. They set up Wright and Tran Investigations based out of business premises on the Kentish Town Road that are still registered to Tran's parents. Tran lives above the office and Wright lives just around the corner. They mostly do security surveillance, divorce cases, missing persons, all the normal Private Investigator bread and butter. Good reputation in the industry even though they're relatively new. Popular with female clients and they're known to collaborate with a firm called O'Neill Brothers' Security, the proprietors of which are former paratroopers."

"Why did you say she has the skill set for the Hastings' killing?" Reynolds asked.

"Because of what the 'FITT' are," said Moya. "They're not acknowledged on any Army website or official records. It was only you calling ahead to Colonel Denny that even gave us the briefest of insights Gov."

"He owes me a favour or two. We were neighbours about ten years ago and when his eldest applied to be a constable with Thames Valley I did a reference for him. So what did he say?"

"The 'FITT' are a reconnaissance outfit designed to get into enemy territory and attempt to recruit enemy personnel for intelligence gathering missions. They're trained in stuff that sounds like it comes straight out of a boys-own book of adventure. He told me the actual syllabus was-,"

"Classified?" Reynolds said with a sarcastic tone.

The whole team smiled, even the Chief Superintendent.

"Yes Gov. But he gave me a list of the basic topics. Physical fitness, covert photography, infiltration, camouflage, advanced driving, small arms, explosives, sabotage, communications, close-quarter battle skills, close observation reconnaissance, mobile reconnaissance, agent recruitment and agent handling," Moya paused and took a breath.

"It also includes a plethora of psychological and influencing techniques and strategies. Finally, or as much as Denny would share, they're all trained in advanced self-defence. According to Wright's record she was an exceptional exponent of unarmed combat. When I pressed Denny as to what that meant he read an extract from a performance review that was written in 2008." Moya stopped and once more looked to Anna.

The Detective Constable read from her notebook, "Wright sets a terrific example to her team with her knowledge of unarmed combat. Always willing to train and mentor others she is restrained, controlled and yet empowered with an explosive ferocity of aggression when required. Her skills are honed and if necessary would be lethal. She-"

Laura Mitchell held her hand up again and once more Anna stopped.

Tony Reynolds turned to his boss. "Ma'am?"

"I'm afraid we'll need more," she answered. "Having the skills and being in roughly the right place at roughly the right time are not enough."

"Ma'am?" Moya spoke as she walked over to a small desk offset to the side of the main briefing board.

"Yes DS Little, what is it?"

Moya lifted the Wright and Tran Investigations report that she had been given by Catherine Boon. "This report that was produced on the surveillance of Diane Worrell is as comprehensive a piece of work as we would compile."

"Okay, and?"

"It contains times, locations, photography and a written narrative that uses GPS time stamps taken from a mobile device. We know the forensic technicians can retrieve almost anything even if someone has tried to erase it. I thought maybe if we could place Wright at the exact location at a fixed time, then given the rest of what we have, it might be enough."

Mitchell held her hand out for the file. She slowly flicked through it and the rest of the room waited. Eventually she handed the file back to Moya and stood. The rest of the team stood too.

"Okay Tony, let's get search warrants drawn up. If she's that tech savvy I don't want her having the chance to ditch or destroy anything. I'll sort out the liaison with the Met but it'll take time. Plan to do the knock early tomorrow morning. As for her brother, there's not a lot we can do. If she did this and it brings negative publicity to the Force then we'll just have to cope. First things first, let's see if there's any evidence. We'll go from there."

Mitchell left and the rest of the team began to get busy. Reynolds turned to Moya who had crossed back over to the whiteboard.

"It's funny," she said, looking at the picture of Kara next to the crime scene pictures of Hastings. "But at first sight, on face value, you'd think that Manfield Hastings, drug dealer, drug user, thuggish looking, would be the one to avoid bumping into on a darkened street. How wrong you'd be."

ɸ

DCS Laura Mitchell was back in her office, with the door shut. She used her mobile and dialled a number from memory.

"Hi, it's me."

"Hello," the man's deep voice sounded soothing.

"I think I might have found a potential."

"Continue."

28

Friday Evening. Epping Forest

The rain had finally fizzled out and the evening was turning into quite a pleasant one. Some of Kara's clothing had dried out due to body heat but her feet were still sodden and the mud directly under her was still soft and oozing.

"Look alive folks and say thank you to whoever you've been praying to," Chaz said in her ear. "Nicolai's back. Looks like this must be the shift handover. Time now 19:20. If this goes like we think, then the whole handover should be complete in half an hour."

In the time since she had made her decision about what to do Kara had waited to see if events would confirm the likely plan. It all hinged on whether the security guards worked a twelve hour shift or a twenty-four hour shift. If the latter then Kara would have no choice but to wait at least another couple of days. But, if it was a simple day and night shift arrangement, then she and her team would be able to move into action the next morning. Whilst waiting, Yanina had come home at five and for the first time since the morning they had seen Illy, when he joined her in the dining room. Now it seemed a twelve hour shift handover was being confirmed.

"Carrie and her sexy sports car are here as is Sunrise in his VW Scirocco. Time is 19:22," Sammi said.

Kara rolled a little to her right and retrieved a muesli bar from her jacket pocket. She ate it in small, delicate bites and waited patiently. Half an hour ticked by.

"Looks like we're on," Chaz said. "The Twins are out. Followed by Smirnoff. They're all getting back into their cars. Wait."

Sammi took over, "Reggie has gone right, right, right. As has Ronnie. And Smirnoff. That's right for all of them."

As the Porsche's engine roared away up Avey Lane the quiet descended back down onto the large house and gardens.

φ

The sun was thinking about setting. The rainy day had transformed into a gentle evening and the low rainclouds had retreated in the face of their high cirrus cousins who stretched lazily across the deepening blue. They provided a wispy, textured canvas that the sun was dappling in reddening tones.

Kara had most of the plan straight in her head. It was merely a matter of waiting until the night got dark enough for them to extract out and regroup back at RV1. She was thinking through the list of equipment they would need when Sammi's voice sounded in her ear.

"I have eyes on Nicolai and Carrie exiting the house. Wait."

Kara felt her heart quicken. The adrenaline kick was immediate.

"Nicolai is checking out the Range Rover on the driveway and Carrie is checking the Merc. They're doing a bomb sweep of the cars. Geez, they must be paranoid. The whole house has been protected all day and they're checking the cars for booby traps."

"It pays to be paranoid," Tien said quietly. A ripple of gentle laughter played across the radio net.

"Okay, they just signalled all clear. Thor and Illy are

exiting the front door followed by Sunrise. Seems we have an outing planned," Sammi paused again.

"Illy is dressed in a dark leather jacket, over a black T-shirt, jeans and black boots. He's got into the back of the Merc. Nicolai's in the front passenger seat and Thor's driving. Carrie is driving the Range Rover with Sunrise in the passenger seat. Range Rover's going first, Merc behind. Heading to gate and going left, left left."

It made sense to Kara that the cars would go left. It was the quickest route into North London. From what she had learnt from her brother about Chekov's business interests it was more likely for him to go into the city than into rural Hertfordshire.

Her attention was drawn back to movement to her front. "Head's up, movement in the dining room. I have Yanina and," she paused and lifted her binoculars up for a closer look. "I have another bloody security guard. Female. About five seven. Dark skin, looks slightly Mediterranean. Slim, but busty, dark hair, long, tied back in a ponytail. White blouse with visible shoulder holster under right arm. No tie. Dark trousers, no visual on shoes. Quite a long face, long nose, small mouth, high cheekbones. She has gold stud earrings."

"How many more are in there?" Tien asked.

"I don't know. Maybe it's just a male and female live-in team for personal protection and maybe Yanina doesn't like to take hers to work. We weren't here early enough last night to see through the dining room windows. Anyway, what are we calling her?"

"Well, I have eyes on her too and she reminds me of Penelope Cruz so I vote for Penny," Dinger suggested.

"Penny it is," Kara said.

Kara put the field glasses down and went back to her mental planning.

It was almost 02:00 when the Range Rover and Mercedes pulled back into the driveway. Illy and the rest went back into the house. A few minutes later Nicolai came out for a smoke in the back garden. When he went back in and switched off the halogen floodlights Kara decided they had seen enough.

"Right folks, let's move out."

It took another fifteen minutes for Dan and Dinger to bring Chaz, Sammi, Tien and Eugene back to the extraction point. Then Dinger got himself settled in the OP where Sammi and Chaz had been. Dan led the rest of them back to RV1.

Once back at the motel they made use of all three rooms to have long hot showers. Dan called Jacob and Toby back at Camden and gave them Kara's equipment list. It was almost 04:00 when the tall and stocky Jacob and the slightly shorter, but equally stocky, Toby arrived at the motel. All eight of them squeezed into Kara and Tien's room and got ready for what the next shift handover of Illy's bodyguards would bring.

29

Saturday Morning. Camden, London

At precisely 06:15 Tony Reynolds, having forgone his morning run for a very early drive into the city, buzzed the intercom button for Kara's Grafton Yard apartment. Pop Oldman stood next to him with a set of search warrants.

At the same time Moya Little and John McKay were knocking on the door of Wright and Tran Investigations and Gary Mason and Anna Walsh were doing the same at the entrance to Tien's upstairs apartment. Each detective pairing had a five-strong, armed back-up team assigned to them from the Metropolitan Police. Arranged by Laura Mitchell, through one of her counterparts at Scotland Yard, she had also ensured all mention of the operation had been kept far away from David Wright's ears.

With no response at any of the premises Tony Reynolds authorised the use of the Enforcer door rams. Within seconds all three locations were breached.

"They're going to have to pay for the repairs," said Tien.

Kara murmured her agreement. She and the rest of the team were looking over Tien's shoulder at the video being streamed from the security cameras back in Camden, via Tien's mobile, on to the screen of the centre laptop on the motel room's small table.

"Anything you want to tell us Kara?" Sammi asked with a playful tone.

"Nope. Don't think I've got any overdue library books," Kara said and managed to keep her voice light but her mind was spinning. She was rapidly cross-checking all that she had done since her trip to Huntingdon.

"Any chance that we were compromised and Illy has called in some bent cops to try to lift you?" It was Dan asking and the question was logical. Kara doubted it but couldn't explain to her team why she actually thought twenty-one police were searching her life.

Tien flicked the second and third laptops on. She had video feeds from Kara's apartment, her own and the office streaming live now. Kara watched her plug in a set of headphones to her phone.

She was worried what her friend would hear. Reaching down she put her hand on Tien's left arm. Her friend reached across and laid her hand on top. "It's alright Kara, I'll keep an eye on this. You need to get everyone moving."

Kara felt Tien's finger tapping lightly. She held her hand still for a few seconds, then squeezed her friend's arm and turned away from the screens.

"Right, you heard Tien. God alone knows what's going on back at our place but whatever it is doesn't change what we're about to do. So, I want you all to forget that shit and get focussed."

The rest of the team turned away from the screens and followed Kara over to the bed where a large flipchart lay open. It showed a sketch of Avey Lane marked up with the passing places that Chaz had noted between the nursery turnoff, that Eugene and Tien had used, and Illy's house.

In the other direction, what would be left from the house's driveway, it showed that Avey Lane ran in a shallow right hand bend for almost a mile before passing two driveways, one off to the left and one off to the right. Both led to large properties set well back from the road. Avey Lane then straightened out for a further half mile and passed through the middle of an offset crossroads.

"Okay, let's go through it once more," Kara said.

φ

Gary Mason pulled out his mobile and called Reynolds, "Gov, I think we've hit paydirt."

"What've you got Gary?"

"A drawer full of mobile phones, racks of hard drives and enough computer power to launch a Mars mission."

"Excellent. That probably explains why I have nothing round here save for an iMac with a collection of music on it and a single iPad. No phones no anything really. I think I'll head over to you."

"No worries, see you soon."

Reynolds kept his phone out and called Moya in Wright and Tran's office.

"Hi Gov."

"Anything?"

"Nothing. I don't even have filing cabinets. Wherever they keep their records sure isn't here. There's not even a desktop PC although there is a docking station for a laptop and twin monitor screens. Just no laptop."

"Okay, leave John to look after the search team and head upstairs to Gary. I'll meet you there soon. Apparently he's found a stack of tech. If we're going to find anything to place her in Huntingdon it's likely to be there."

φ

Tien smiled to herself and killed the video and audio streams. The detective in Kara's apartment was obviously the senior officer. As soon as he met up with his team in Tien's apartment and they started dismantling all of her computers, then the camera feeds would end anyway. As it was she didn't

213

mind. She had already overheard enough to know they were looking for something to tie Kara to the Huntingdon killing. She had no idea how they had managed to put Kara in the frame but she was completely confident that not one scrap of electronic evidence could be recovered. She knew that Kara would have looked after any physical evidence that might have existed. All in all Tien was happy that the Police would find nothing to help them. Even better was that the office and her apartment would get a makeover to their front doors paid for by the taxpayer. She shut down the laptops and broke down all the rest of the IT equipment.

By 07:00 all their belongings had been packed into two of the six vehicles parked to the front of their rooms. They had a last run through of the plan and got ready to leave. Tien took Kara to one side.

"They're looking for something to tie you to the killing in Huntingdon. I already scrubbed all the electronic evidence that Saturday. They'll find nothing. Did you clear any physical evidence that you had?" Tien asked and knew that Kara wouldn't try to bullshit her. She had previously tapped out 'I know. It's ok.' in Morse on the back of Kara's hand and the time for being coy with one another was long gone.

"Yes. We're good."

"Good. Then as long as you don't break down in tears and start confessing we should be sweet."

Kara hugged her friend and whispered, "I might have known you'd have my back. And I think we can be safe in the knowledge that a confession isn't going to be wrung out of me. Thanks Tien."

They broke apart and went to the vehicles. Chaz and Sammi led them off, Tien followed on her own. Dan, Toby and Jacob left together, next Kara and lastly Eugene. Dinger's car stayed in the car park. It was 07:10.

30

Saturday Morning. Epping Forest

With five separate vehicles and Dinger being their eyes and ears the communications setup was difficult but manageable. Jacob listened to Dinger on his phone and Toby had all the others on a multi-way call on his, not that there would be much talking as soon as the word came that Nicolai, Carrie and Sunrise were on their way.

The call came at 07:55.

φ

Sunrise's real name was Uzy. He was unique within the men on Illy's security detail because he wasn't Russian. A veteran of the Israeli Defence Force's 202nd Viper Airborne Battalion, part of the elite 35th Paratrooper Brigade he was also an Expert Grade instructor in Krav Maga, the Israeli military's self-defence system. His many-times-broken nose testament to the violence of the realistic sparring that was a mainstay of the style.

Tired and just wanting to get home he pulled out of Illy's driveway, turned left and accelerated up the narrow Avey Lane.

Home was in the town of Woodford only five miles away and he had already covered one of those miles when he came round the long, shallow right hand bend and saw a car, half a mile ahead, indicating right at the crossroads. He didn't brake because the car would have turned long before he got to it. As he rapidly covered the distance to the crossroads he was a little surprised that the car hadn't moved. Avey Lane was still only a single car's width so there was no oncoming traffic to prevent the turn being made. Uzy's instincts kicked in and notched his attention levels up. He began to brake and began to focus, his tattooed hands flexed around the steering wheel.

The car ahead was a dark blue Vauxhall. Compact, two door. He thought it was called a Corsa or something similar. There were two people visible in it. A male behind the wheel, a female in the front passenger seat. Both their heads were turned to face each other. Uzy checked his left, right and rear. High hedgerows lined the sides of the lane and the road behind him was clear. The hedgerows dropped in height as he neared the crossroads revealing no other traffic approaching from left or right and no pedestrians. He switched his attention back to the little Vauxhall blocking his way. It remained stationary and he slowed down more. Reaching inside his jacket he drew his pistol out of its holster and set it between his legs.

As he slowed to a stop leaving a good ten yard gap between vehicles, he could see the couple were engaged in what appeared to be a full scale, highly animated argument. Another full check to his front, left, right and rear still revealed no other cars or people. He thought about pulling his mobile and ringing his day-shift colleagues back at the house but then he dismissed it. He'd look foolish if the car suddenly drove away. Apart from which it was just two people in a car. No other indications for him to be concerned about and he could look after two. Hell, he could look after six.

The argument was becoming increasingly volatile. The driver was gesticulating, displaying threatening and provocative behaviours. The woman's body language, or what Uzy could see of it, was looking cowed, intimidated, scared. His self-defence instructor's instincts were almost screaming inside his head for her to control the circumstances, take the initiative or at least put enough distance between her and the man so as to protect herself. His thoughts and musings were interrupted by a dark coloured BMW approaching him from behind. His senses sharpened even more. He dropped both hands from the steering wheel, took the pistol in his left and reached for the door handle with his right. He swore a little at himself for not calling in on his mobile. It was too late now if he was in the middle of something sinister. He paused.

Then he relaxed. The BMW was being driven by a young Asian woman who seemed to be barely able to see over the steering wheel. Uzy had the strange sensation that she was probably sitting on a booster cushion.

Moving his right hand to the electric window switch he cracked the seal a little and could now hear the shouting from the car ahead. He thought about sounding his horn but resisted. He'd give it another minute. As he watched the scene, framed in the small rear window of the Corsa he saw the driver shift position. He'd turned more towards the woman. Uzy knew what was coming and suddenly felt very powerless. The driver brought his right arm up and hit his passenger with a full force slap across her face. Her head smashed into the headrest. At the same time, in his wing mirror, Uzy saw the Asian woman getting out of the BMW, a confused look on her face. She was short, maybe five foot five, her long black hair fell straight to just below her shoulders. She wore a smart business suit, neat, well fitted, skirt, blouse, jacket, heels, but sensible height heels, not inappropriate. He switched his attention back to the front. The woman was scrabbling at the door. As she made to exit the car the driver reached over and tried to stop her. He grabbed her shirt. She pulled backwards, opened the door and fell backwards onto the road.

The Asian woman was now level with Uzy's car door but a few paces off it. She was gasping in shock with what she was seeing. Her hand had come to her mouth and she had turned to look at Uzy.

The Corsa passenger regained her feet. Uzy noted the broadness of the woman's shoulders and her height. It must have been a squeeze for her in the little car. She would have been five nine or ten. He saw she was wearing pumps, jeans and a white T-shirt that was now ripped from the left hand side of the crew neck down to almost the bottom seam. Mostly Uzy noticed that her left breast was fully exposed and she was caught between trying to stumble away from the car, cover her body and stifle the stream of blood that was coming from a smashed nose. Her right hand, against her nose, had blood pouring through it. Her short, mousey-blonde hair was matted with blood on the right side where it had sprayed back against the headrest. Her left hand was trying to use the torn fabric to cover her nakedness.

The Asian woman finally found her voice, "You. You Lady. You come here, come this way," she shouted, considerably louder than Uzy had imagined the diminutive woman could have yelled. Her Asian accent was thick and heavy.

The driver got out of the Vauxhall.

Uzy had a clear view. Probably mid-thirties, roughly the same age as the woman passenger but taller than her. Even more of a squeeze for him in the little Vauxhall. Maybe six foot. Lithe, long limbed. Short dark hair, jeans, shoes or boots, loose fitted English rugby top. Spots of blood splattered on the top consistent with more bounce back from the headrest. Gold ring on his right hand that would explain the damage done to the woman's nose. No watch. He seemed a little unsteady on his feet.

The passenger had run, almost fallen past Uzy's car. The Asian woman moved to shield her. The pair now stood just behind Uzy's door. The Vauxhall's driver had covered half the distance towards them.

"Do not come any closer. Do not dare," the now loud Asian shouted at him.

"Why don't you suck my fucking knob? Get the fuck away from her or I swear to fuck I'll go right through you," the driver yelled, seemingly slurring the last few words. He was level with the front of Uzy's car and seemed to have finally noticed Uzy sitting behind the wheel. He stopped and leant against the bonnet.

"And what the fuck are you looking at you fucking twat?" he yelled. Uzy was not only convinced he had heard the slurring that time but he was also convinced that he had seen enough.

He opened his door and stepped out. Leaving the pistol on the seat, he shut the door with his left hand. He moved in front of both women and as the Asian started to shout in a language he couldn't understand, he held his right hand out and shielded them backwards. He saw in the reflection of the windows to his left that they had gone back to the rear corner of his car.

The Vauxhall driver leant off the bonnet and took a single pace forward.

Uzy settled himself and focussed on the target approaching. Then he saw a brief flash of yellow in the reflections to his left. His mind processed the word Taser just as it discharged into his back. His world became a blur of noise and lights and then dark.

He was just regaining a semblance of consciousness when his mouth was taped with duct tape, as were his hands and feet. He was lifted into the boot of the BMW-3 Series and it all went dark.

φ

Carrie's real name was Emilia. She was a graduate of Russia's Ryazan Higher Airborne Command School and drove her 350Z like every road was a racetrack. As usual she was at the exit of the driveway before either of her two colleagues had even started their cars. She turned right and accelerated hard. As she rounded the second left-hander she came off the accelerator and onto the brakes.

Ahead, just in front of the left hand turning to the Avey Garden and Nursery Centre, was a silver Subaru Impreza saloon slewed completely across the road with its passenger side facing Emilia. The car's driver's side had been seemingly T-boned by a red car, the make and model of which she couldn't determine as it was mostly masked by the bigger Subaru. Thick black smoke was rising from the red car's engine. A woman was at the passenger door of the Subaru trying to wrench it open. Emilia checked her rear-view and side mirrors but the rest of Avey Lane was normal and empty.

As her Nissan decelerated rapidly she reached inside her jacket and undid the loop catch that held her pistol firmly in its holster. She stopped about twenty yards away from the destruction and scanned left to right.

The Impreza's passenger windows were gone and cubes of hardened glass littered the road where the woman, medium height, dark auburn hair, dressed in jeans and a jumper was still struggling with the door.

Emilia looked beyond her to what she could see of the red car. Its driver's door was wide open but the car seemed empty. She assessed the woman was the driver of the red car and had pulled out of the nursery turn without checking. Avey Lane was very quiet so it would probably have worked ninety-nine times out of a hundred but this morning her luck had given out. Emilia watched as the woman finally managed to wrench the passenger door of the Subaru open. The smoke was thickening and the driver of the Subaru, a large black man, wasn't moving to get away from the blaze about to engulf both cars. Emilia reached into her pocket for her mobile phone but as she moved she saw in her rear-view mirror a light blue Ford Mondeo approaching.

She pocketed her phone and got out. Her large colleague Anatoly had come to a stop behind her. He would have her back if this wasn't what it looked like. If it was a straightforward accident then they needed to get the driver out of the Subaru now. She could call the emergency services later. Either way she was comfortable with the situation. She waved for Anatoly to come and help, then she went to assist the auburn haired woman.

As Anatoly stepped out of his car and made to come to Emilia's assistance a white transit van came around the bend behind him.

Anatoly was big and sometimes slowed by his size but he carried no excess fat nor was he a slack operator. He had served in the 76th Guards Air Assault Division, was a three-tour veteran of the Chechen insurgency and had fought in Georgia in 2008 before leaving the Russian Army and joining Illy's security detail. He turned quickly at the sound of the van and appraised the likelihood he was being ambushed. His adrenaline spiked and he used the rush to focus on details. There were two men visible through the windscreen. He thought they looked similar enough to perhaps be brothers. Both were stocky, both wore high-visibility work shirts. The passenger had a cardboard coffee container still to his lips and both he and the driver looked shocked at the carnage in front of them. Anatoly dismissed them and turned back towards the Subaru.

Emilia and the other woman had the Impreza's driver by an arm each and were trying to twist and pull him out of his seat across to the passenger side with little success.

Anatoly came up behind her and spoke in Russian, telling her to step away. She did as requested and took the other woman with her.

"Come, leave it alone, my friend will do it," she said in her heavily accented English and put her arm around the woman's shoulders, guiding her back from the cars. The woman seemed incapable of saying anything other than, 'Oh my God! Oh I'm sorry! I didn't see him!' over and over. As Emilia forcibly turned her away from the thick smoke and moved out of Anatoly's way she got a strange sensation that something wasn't right.

Two men in high-visibility shirts, jeans and work boots ran past her. She looked up and saw their van parked behind Anatoly's car. When she was level with her own Nissan, Emilia turned back towards the crash and looked again at the scene. The auburn haired woman had walked a few feet further on. Emilia could hear her sobbing.

Anatoly and the two men who flanked him were struggling to get the driver out of the enclosed space. Emilia stared hard at the cars and suddenly realised what was wrong. The passenger windows in the Subaru had been smashed but the windscreens of both cars were intact and the airbag of the Impreza hadn't been deployed. Reaching inside her jacket for her pistol she yelled out, "Anatoly, it's an ambu-". She was cut off by the twin probes of the X2 Defender Taser discharging 50,000 volts into her back.

Anatoly straightened up at the shout of his name. As he began to turn, the men either side of him placed direct contact Tasers on his neck. The pain, bad from a single contact let alone a double hit, was debilitating even for a man of his size. He sank onto his knees next to the Impreza. The driver, who had been seemingly unconscious, suddenly sat upright, produced a Taser from the central console and discharged it into Anatoly's chest. The big man slumped sideways and swore in his native Russian as the darkness enveloped him.

Jacob Harrop walked round to the completely undamaged driver's side of the Impreza and got into the equally undamaged red Audi A4. As he reversed it back up the approach road to the garden nursery his brother extinguished the small can of burning oil that had been positioned under its engine compartment. The last wisp of trailing black smoke rose and was blown away in the morning breeze. Jacob took two brushes from the boot of the Audi and he and his brother swept the carpet of glass fragments into the verge. Once clear they gave the thumbs-up to Eugene who sat patiently behind the Impreza's wheel.

He reversed, straightened up and pulled forward alongside Kara. He pushed the boot release catch and stepped out to help his brother.

Dan, who had climbed out from the rear of the transit van, had helped Kara gag and bind the Russian woman with duct tape. Once they had retrieved the keyless remote for the woman's Nissan and taken the Glock-17 from her shoulder holster, the brothers lifted the still unconscious body into the boot. Eugene handed Kara the Subaru's keys.

"See you there," she said and executed a reverse turn in the nursery side road before accelerating away.

Eugene got into the Transit van and moved it as close to the unconscious body of the large Russian as he could. It took Toby, Jacob, Dan and him all their strength to gag, bind and manhandle the deadweight of the guard they now knew as Anatoly. With a struggle they finally got him into the rear of the transit and secured him with a set of cargo chains that had been bolted to the floor.

Eugene drove the van, Dan drove Anatoly's Mondeo, Toby slipped into the 350Z and Jacob followed in the Audi.

At the far end of Avey Lane, Sammi had thrown the fake blood capsules into the hedge, washed her face with bottled water and dried it using her torn T-shirt, pulled on a spare shirt and was now behind the wheel of Sunrise's VW Scirocco.

Chaz was back behind the wheel of the Corsa and Tien was following them in the BMW-3 with the seat raised back to its normal height. She called Kara first and then Dinger, "All done, no hassles, we're clear."

"See you tonight, clock's ticking," Dinger said and ended the call. It was 08:07.

31

Saturday Mid-Morning. Arlesey

A floodlight spot, normally used for under lighting of portrait subjects was turned on. The bright glare picked out the conscious figure of Emilia Shibkova. She was firmly bound to a wooden dining chair positioned just in front of a full width black backdrop. Behind this partition, in the rear third of Chris Sterling's workshop-cum-studio, were Emilia's two colleagues, Uzy Jabarin and Anatoly Maltsev, also conscious and also bound to chairs.

Kara stood at a side bench where the three security guards' personal belongings were laid out. She was flicking through the two men's wallets and Emilia's slimline card holder. The driving licences of all three lay on the bench.

Emilia's chair was central to the tableau Kara and her team had planned. To the Russian's front, on either side of the workshop, stood Dan and Eugene. Both wore white T-shirts that revealed their impressive physiques. Behind them, in partial shadow sat Sammi. Her face half turned away. Directly to Sammi's rear stood Chaz. He wore an open-necked shirt and his shoulder holster was prominent.

Kara walked across to the other side of the space that she

thought of like a stage. Set and lit for effect. She watched Emilia's head turn to follow her. The Russian woman's eyes gave no indication of fear. Her face was a little distorted by the heavy duct tape that still clamped her mouth shut but the overall impression was one of complete indifference.

Kara dragged a chair to almost directly in front of Emilia but offset enough so that the Russian would still have a sightline through to Sammi. Kara sat down and crossed her legs, left over right. Her left shoe pointing at the bound woman. Settling herself, she concentrated on making her voice conversational, yet cold.

"Emilia. Emilia Shibkova. Welcome back to this little abode." Kara cast her hand around the workshop. "I know you and your colleagues have been here before," Kara lied, knowing nothing of certainty and hoping their assumptions about who had taken the Sterlings would prove correct. But she kept any trace of doubt out of her voice.

"I know you came here and took Chris and Brenda Sterling. I know all of that. But..." she paused and was quite impressed that during her opening statement there had not been one flicker of emotion in the Russian's eyes. She let the pause draw out, "What I don't know is where you took them. That's all I want to know. Simple." She gestured with her hand and both Eugene and Dan stepped forward to be either side of Emilia's chair. Again Kara was impressed. Two big men like that walking forward, with all their latent aggressiveness on show and still the Russian never flinched.

"The thing is Emilia, you might be thinking that you will be the hero. Or heroine. That you will say nothing, tell me nothing and thereby prove to your male colleagues behind you that you are tough. Even tougher than they are. But..." again Kara paused for effect. Again she let the pause drag on, "You'd be foolish. For that's the point. I have two of your colleagues. If you don't tell me what I want," Kara reached down to her left ankle. In full view of Emilia's watchful eyes, she raised the leg of her jeans up and drew her pistol from the concealed-carry leg holster strapped to her shin, "I'll just shoot you."

Kara uncrossed her legs and leant back in her chair. She nestled the pistol on her lap. "And I don't mean shoot you in the arm or the leg or any of that nonsense." Kara shook her head to add emphasis.

"No, I mean shoot you through the head. Your life will end here. In this shed. You will die inside a little box in England and it will be for nothing. Truly a waste. For I will kick your body to one side and go get another of your colleagues and they *will* tell me." Kara rubbed the sole of her right shoe across the floor. "Your blood will seep through these floorboards and they will have told me what I want and you will have wasted the one life you have," she paused again and looked into Emilia's eyes. There was still nothing but a focused dismissiveness. "That's why I brought you all together. I have spares. I assure you, you will die for nothing, for if the second one I choose doesn't tell me, sure as hell is waiting for both you and me, the third one will."

Emilia blinked slowly and then breathed deeply through her nose and shut her eyes, as if she had decided to go to sleep. Kara wanted to applaud. Emilia was one resilient lady. Shame it would all be for nothing. She had been picked first for a reason. They expected her to be the least likely to give them anything. It was ever the way. Kara remembered reading about the advice of the German anti-terrorist teams in the 1970's; 'Kill the women fighters first, for they're the most vicious, the most hard-line, the least likely to surrender peacefully.'

Kara stood, "Now Emilia, I'm going to have my friends here take off your gag. You will answer my question. If you don't I shall kill you. If you do answer it then I shall simply hold you and your friends here for twelve hours and then I shall let you go. Disposal of bodies is such a pain. I would much prefer to let you walk away. Oh and a final word, as you know, this workshop is in a secluded garden of an isolated house. If you insist on screaming out then feel free. No one's coming to help."

She nodded at Dan and Eugene. Eugene held the woman's head and Dan ripped the tape off in one quick movement.

Emilia grunted with the pain, took a deep breath and began to shout, "You are all dead, fucking dead. You have no fucking clue who you are fucking with." Her pronunciation of the expletives was ferocious. She seemed to fill them with loathing, contempt and hatred. Kara had to suppress a smile. The woman was a mini-tornado.

"Fucking all of you fucking people are dead. I shall watch your bodies burn in piss. Vy chertovski shlyukha, ya budu rvat' vas na dva." Kara nodded at Dan and Eugene and they reapplied the duct tape.

"Now, now Emilia. What did I say? Before I give you a second, and last, chance I'd like to correct a few things. Firstly, I'm not sure you *can* burn people in piss but I'll let that slide. English isn't your first language. Secondly, on the contrary, I know exactly who you are. The problem is that you don't know who *you're* dealing with. And thirdly, I'm not a prostitute, never have been and believe me, even if I was, you wouldn't get close to ripping me in two before I razorval tvoyu golovu i kormila tvoyu mat'. Alright?"

Kara noticed the first real jolt to Emilia. She didn't think the threat to 'tear her head off and feed it to her mother' had shocked her. More it was the fact that her interrogator had the ability to understand and reply in Russian. It had thrown the woman. Her eyes had darted up to Kara's and there was the first hint of confusion.

"So, take two. Where did you take the Sterlings to?"

Kara walked quietly to just behind Eugene. She tapped him on the arm. He held Emilia's head, Dan ripped off the sticky gag.

Emilia was no quieter than before, "You are fucking dead. I will tell you fucking nothing I w-"

"SHUT THE FUCK UP!" Kara yelled at the top of her voice right next to Emilia's ear and by sheer volume overwhelmed the Russian's voice. Allowing a moment of quiet to spread across the workshop, Kara spoke slowly and deliberately, "Are.. you.. going to.. tell me.. where.. the Sterlings.. are?"

"Go fuck yourse- "

Kara fired once. The noise of the Sig Sauer P239 was deafening in the workshop but its report was lost in the wind before it reached any of the neighbouring properties.

φ

Tony Reynolds and his team had five cartons of potential interest lifted out of Tien Tran's apartment, including a drawer full of mobile phones. Out of Kara Wright's they had taken three box loads, including a pair of red high heels that were either the ones from the CCTV or a very close match. After almost three hours they had all they were going to get. It was a good effort but the one thing they were missing was Kara Wright.

He sent the rest of the team back to Huntingdon to start the review of the technical items and to fast-track the lab work on the red shoes whilst he and Moya headed to New Scotland Yard. It only took them half an hour in the light Saturday morning traffic.

Ringing ahead took a little of the processing time off their arrival but it was still a good five minutes to get through the reception area. Eventually they found themselves on the seventh floor and being ushered into an office that had the name of DCI Matthew Sexton stencilled on the glass.

A heavy set man rose and came around from behind his desk.

"How you doin'? I'm Matt," he said in a broad Northern Irish accent.

Tony shook the offered hand, "Tony Reynolds and this is Detective Sergeant Moya Little."

"Good to meet you, please sit," Sexton said returning to his seat behind the desk. "You have me at a bit of a disadvantage. I know we helped out on some raids this morning, our DCS requested it, but I'm not too sure what it's all about. The whole thing was handled on a real need to know basis. And I didn't, so I don't," he spoke in a friendly tone, not giving any indication that he was annoyed at the shut out from the operation.

Tony and he shared the same rank but having never met before, Reynolds had to hope the man was being genuine. He decided to play it as straight as he could, "Well, you're right in that it was delicate. Not for any other reason than the person of interest has a brother who's one of us. We needed to make sure there were no leaks, real or imagined."

Sexton sat a little straighter, "By one of us, you mean Police?"

"Yes, but even more so. He's a detective," Reynolds said.

"In here?" Sexton asked and looked through the glass walls of his office to the detective desks of the Met's Homicide and Serious Crime Command. "He's in SCD1?"

Reynolds nodded.

"Ah fuck," Sexton said under his breath. "Who is it?"

Tony brought Sexton up to speed on the case and ended with the fact that they could find no trace of Kara Wright at home or work.

"I can't see him tipping her off to run. He's not on the duty squad this weekend so he wouldn't even have known about this morning's raid," Sexton said a little defensively.

Reynolds couldn't blame him for his tone. If the tables were turned he'd be giving Gary Mason or Moya the benefit of the doubt. "No, I don't think he tipped her. I can't see how he would have known. So no. But I do need to talk to him because I have no idea where his sister is and he's my only real option."

"And that's why you're here, to lift him?" Sexton said with quite a sad look on his face.

"No. I'm here to ask you to help me. I don't want this to be formal. She's only a person of interest at the minute. We have no proof that she was involved and all I want to do is talk to her. To do that I'm going to need her brother's help to find her. To do that, I thought we could work together?"

Sexton seemed to brighten a little, "Oh right. I see. Well then yes, that's dead on so it is. I'd be happy to. Do you want to go to him or get him to come here?"

"Where's he live?"

"Out in Epsom, about an hour away."

"Family?" Reynolds asked trying to determine what would be easier and quicker for him and Moya.

"Wife, two little kids."

"Do you want to ring him and make sure he's home, then we'll go to him?" Reynolds asked.

"No problem," Sexton said and pulled his mobile phone.

"But no mention of why we want to talk. We can't risk him ringing his sister."

"Understood."

Ten minutes later Tony and Moya were following Sexton to David Wright's home.

φ

As the acoustic shock from Kara's pistol was still reverberating through the workshop and assaulting the ears of all those inside, Dan clamped the duct tape back over the open mouth of the shocked but otherwise unharmed Emilia before she could react. He put his hand completely over the woman's mouth and nose for added sound-proofing and Eugene lifted her and the chair together. They moved quickly yet quietly to the front of the workshop and out the door being held open by Tien. Crossing the garden to the main house they left the chair and a rapidly blinking Emilia propped against the rear wall. Then they sprinted back to the workshop.

Sammi and Chaz moved forward and standing where Kara had fired from, sprayed a bag of fake blood across the space. Then reaching into a small bag of shredded offal that the Harrop brothers had bought from the butchery-counter in the all-night Tesco's in nearby Baldock, Chaz added substance to the scene. The effect was gruesome and wholly believable.

As the ringing in her ears was diminishing Kara was joined by Tien, who was barefoot but dressed in an old grey overall.

"Get me some light. Cut her fucking loose and get that shit out of here," Kara yelled to no one. After a few seconds all the fluorescent lights in the workshop came on.

Chaz held out a section of duct tape and Tien ripped at it noisily with a knife. Then she slumped onto the ground in the midst of the blood and bits. The crump of the falling body was convincing. Chaz dragged her messily through the gore and up the length of the workshop.

Dan and Eugene returned with another dining room chair, dressed with shreds of duct tape hanging from it. They also brought Emilia's shoes. Leaving one halfway along the smeared trail of blood, they put the other at the foot of the chair that was set quietly back in the space where Emilia had been.

Sammi took her seat again, Chaz stood behind her. Dan and Eugene returned to outside the workshop and Tien gave a thumbs-up from the door before ducking back out of sight. Kara, with pistol in hand, pulled up the backdrop partition and opened the scene to Anatoly and Uzy, still strapped to their own chairs. Their already wide-eyed expressions widened more as they took in the details of the scene in front of them. The effect was heightened when Dan and Eugene came back in to the workshop and walked its length, wiping red hands on their T-shirts.

Kara looked at both of the bound men in turn, "Who's next?"

She gazed into their eyes, watched their pupils. The small beads of perspiration building on each of their brows. Small twitches in their cheek muscles, the veins popping on their necks, jaws trying to flex under the tension of the duct tape. She turned to Dan and Eugene, "Take the big fella."

Both Uzy and Anatoly moaned through their gags and became as animated as their predicament allowed. The big man started trying to bounce his chair backwards. His bulk and momentum tipped him over. Eugene and Dan dragged him by the legs of the chair and heaved him up into the sitting position. Anatoly's eyes darted sideways to the chair that sat beside him. The shreds of duct tape still attached to it and red pearls of blood dripping from the frame. Kara dropped the partition back in place, isolating Anatoly from Uzy. The fluorescent lights were switched off by Chaz. The floodlight spot was left as the only illumination.

"Hello Anatoly," Kara said.

The large man blinked in the glare of the lamp.

"Now you're probably thinking that if you tell me what you're female companion wasn't able to, then Illy, or shall we call him Chekov?" Kara noticed the flicker of surprise in Anatoly's eyes at the mention of Illy's name and alias. "Either or, doesn't matter. You probably think that he will have you killed," she paused and let the silence sink in.

"But here's the thing Anatoly. You and your friend behind there, what's his name?" She tapped the pistol's muzzle against her temple as if thinking, "Oh yeah, Uzy, like the gun but different. Well, you and Uzy can always say it was Miss Emilia that told me and you killed her as punishment. Or you can say no one talked and she was killed in crossfire as you tried to escape heroically. Or, you can say whatever the fuck you want to say really. Illy might kill you, he might not. To be honest, who knows? But that is all in the future. All of that is just maybes. None of it is certain. What I can tell you with absolute certainty is this."

Kara walked a complete circle around the man, carefully picking her feet up in an exaggerated manner so as not to step in the bloody debris. Anatoly tried to follow her movements as best he could, like a frightened mouse trying to watch the movements of a predatory cat.

Once back in front of him she continued in a deliberate, almost rhythmic manner, "When I tell my colleagues to remove that tape from your mouth; if the first words out of you; and I mean the very first words; if they are not where you took the Sterlings; then I will do to you; just what I did to Emilia."

She looked directly into his eyes, "Now you're a big fucking lad aren't you, so it might take two bullets to go through that fucking thick skull of yours, but the end result will be the same. I assure you. Then I shall get Uzy out here and he *will* tell me and both you and little Emilia will have died for nothing."

She waved Dan and Eugene into place, moved to the side and raised her pistol to Anatoly's head, "Now concentrate and think really hard about your next sentence." Kara indicated for Dan to remove the duct tape gag.

Anatoly Maltsev had seen death up close in two war zones and had lost five friends whilst on active service. Two in a gun battle near Gudermes in the Chechen Republic during the later years of the insurgency and another to a suicide bomber in that Republic's capital, Grozny. The last two comrades fell as a result of friendly fire outside Tskhinvali in Georgia. It was that incident that had taken his best friend since childhood. They had joined up together and Anatoly had cradled him as his life slipped away. The big man had discovered on that hot August day in a grimy field in South Ossetia how desperately he didn't want to die. He knew it, craved it. Tasted it. Sensed his own weakness and fear and knew that he would do anything to live.

He'd left the Army as soon as he could after that and it meant he'd avoided going to the Crimea and later the Ukraine, but more of his friends hadn't been so lucky. Nine of his former comrades were lost in a single engagement in Donbass in 2014. Anatoly was devastated. Big as he was, strong, quick and lethal if necessary, he was sick of the senselessness. His role as Illy's chief enforcer meant standing at the back, looking aggressive and in the years since he had come to Britain no one had ever challenged him. His ability to intimidate was paid for by sheer physical presence but, in truth, the fight had long gone from him. Uzy was more aggressive by far and even he paled in comparison to Emilia. She was the real terrifying force out of the three. Vicious and relentless when called on to administer violence. It had done her no good in the end, he thought as he looked at her blood, dripping from the chair alongside. Her fate was just one more horror and he wanted none of it. He hadn't survived this long to die protecting Illy and his sordid business dealings.

Bound, gagged and helpless for all his size, his only option was to cooperate and pray to whatever God would listen to him, that they let him go, or gave him an opportunity to save himself. His mind was made up even before the female interrogator had asked him her question.

He spoke as clearly as his fear and his heavy Russian accent would allow, "We took them to office. They are still there. I swear."

Kara managed not to smile in triumph as she lowered the pistol and sat down in her original chair, "What office?"

"In the Waltham Cross, small, near river. I show you."

"Well that would be nice, wouldn't it? A little daytrip out. Is that what you're thinking? Me and you on a jaunt into the countryside?

Anatoly looked confused. He repeated himself, "I show you where they are."

"You can show me on a map Anatoly, but we're not going to be going for a drive together."

As it happened, Kara was wrong.

φ

David Wright was showered and dressed. He had decided that if his boss was coming out to talk to him about some unspecified issue and bringing some visiting Cambridge police with him, it might be a good idea not to be lying on his sofa wearing just boxers and a dressing gown.

The Saturday mornings when he wasn't on weekend duty cover were alternately swapped with Alice in taking the kids to the local pool for their swimming lessons. It allowed her one or two Saturday mornings a month to do what she wanted and one or two for him to do the same. Albeit their ideas of a relaxing morning were somewhat different. On her free-Saturdays Alice would normally go food shopping, or spend the morning cleaning the house or very, very occasionally meet up with some of her girlfriends for coffee. David invariably slept late, got up, had a casual and relaxed breakfast, fed scraps of bacon to the family's pet Chihuahua, then settled down on the sofa with the little dog lying next to him, watched some recorded TV he hadn't seen during the week and generally lazed about until almost midday. Then he'd have a quick shower, tidy away the breakfast debris and be sitting back in front of the TV when Alice and the kids returned.

Now he was in the kitchen making coffee and trying not to be pissed off at the disturbance to his Saturday routine. He was also trying, and failing, not to worry about what the hell was going on. Sexton coming to see him was unusual enough. A unique occurrence in fact. Bringing extra police was simply adding to the dread. The only saving grace was that on a Saturday, heading out of London to Epsom, the journey wouldn't take that long and so he should be put out of his misery sooner rather than later.

It was approaching 11:30 when the doorbell rang and the furious, albeit ambitious, barking of the pint-sized Chihuahua greeted his guests. After the usual formalities and an offered and accepted round of coffees, they all sat at the dining room table.

It took Tony Reynolds less than ten minutes to outline the case and highlight Kara's potential as a witness. Reynolds didn't mention that they had raided Kara's home and office, nor did he mention she was actually a suspect. They needed David's help to find his sister, not give him reasons to be obstructive.

For his part David knew they were holding something back. Had it been as simple as he was being told they could have just asked him for Kara's number when they phoned him earlier. He surmised they hadn't told him until they got here so that he had no opportunity to warn her. That meant Kara was potentially in trouble. A lot of trouble. Reynolds and Sexton had played it well. He had no choice now but to give them her number. He made to hand his mobile over.

"No David, I'd prefer if you could ring her. Then you can let her know who I am and that I want a word. Is that okay?" Reynolds asked.

"Certainly," David said. He ignored the pounding he could feel in his chest. He tried to remember all those tricks Kara had struggled to teach him about staying calm, especially in the face of aggressive questioning but the hammering of his heart continued unabated. He called her number.

$$\phi$$

Tien had wiped her 'bloody' feet on the grass, stripped off the overalls and walked, dressed only in her underwear, past the bemused Emilia and in to the house. She used the Sterling's en-suite and when clean, dressed in jeans and T-shirt. By the time she was finished, Toby was guarding Emilia, who had been brought into the conservatory and Jacob was babysitting the still tethered Anatoly and Uzy who remained in the workshop. The rest of the team had also washed and changed before gathering in the Sterling's bright and spacious kitchen.

Various tablets and laptops were open on the bench and imagery of the office that Anatoly had described was up on each of the devices. Sammi was shaking her head, "There's no way we make that approach in daylight without being seen."

Eugene, Dan and Chaz were all nodding in agreement. Kara reckoned Toby and Jacob would have agreed too had they been there.

Tien leant over to look at the images. The office was a former administration building for a plumbing company. It was housed in a small brick-built unit located on the light industrial estate next to the Lea River in Waltham Cross. Only a mile from the office of the modelling agency and so in some ways its location made sense. The problem was it sat right on the edge of the estate. There was a small parking area to the front of the office but it was approached by a main road that ran for a straight one hundred yards to left and right. The rear of the building backed onto a towpath that ran alongside the river.

The office had a single door at the front and one large, half-height window next to it. The rear wall of the building wasn't visible on the imagery but according to the layout told to them by Anatoly it had a single rear door that led into a small yard, less than ten feet deep. That yard, perhaps the best option for a clandestine approach, was impossible to get into during the day as it was surrounded by a corrugated fence that looked to be at least ten feet in height and would only be scalable from the towpath. That towpath was also a footpath and a cycleway which on any day might be busy but on a sunny July Saturday such as they had, it would be packed.

"And we can't leave it until dark as Illy will miss his nightshift before then and the alarm bells will sound," Sammi continued.

Tien sat up on the kitchen stool and continued to gaze at the Google Earth image of the plumbing office building.

"Time to call in the cops?" asked Dan.

"I'd love to but we don't have any evidence other than the word of some folk we've," Kara paused trying to find a word.

"Slightly coerced with tenderness?" Eugene offered.

They laughed but soon fell quiet, looking at the images, trying to figure how they would get in to the office.

After a few minutes Tien broke the silence, "Sammi's right," she said. "We don't approach that without being seen. So we get seen. Anatoly said there's a main room to the front, a smaller office, kitchenette and bathroom to the rear. If we believe him that there's only one or two guards on site then the answer is to drive straight up. If we do it right then they'll see what they expect to see. Everybody does. So we give them something easy and they'll do our work for us."

Kara's phone began to ring. She indicated for them to continue planning as she walked outside to take the call.

"Hi Sis, how's you?"

"I'm good, but in the middle of something, 'sup?"

"Nothing, but I've got a detective from Cambridgeshire with me who wants to talk to you."

Kara guessed she was about to talk to the man she had watched authorise the use of door rams this morning. She checked her watch and reckoned he hadn't wasted much time in getting to David. Saying no to talking to him would send the wrong signal and she wanted to begin the process of dominating their interactions. Taking a breath she reminded herself that she knew nothing.

"Fine by me, want to put him on speaker?"

"Sure. There's a couple of others here too. My boss DCI Matt Sexton, and a Detective Sergeant Little from Cambridge-shire."

"The more the merrier David."

There was a small delay as David selected speaker and set the phone down.

"Hello Miss Wright."

"Hello Mr Wrong."

"Pardon?"

"Never mind. Who are you and what do you want?"

"I'm Detective Chief Inspector Tony Reynolds from the Tri-County Major Crimes Unit. Where are you Miss Wright?"

"Okay, enough with the Miss. Call me Kara. And I'm currently in the middle of a job. Why do you want to know?"

"I'd like to meet you so I can ask you some questions."

"Tony, you don't mind if I call you Tony?" She didn't pause for his answer, "Good, so Tony, what do you want to talk to me about?"

"I'd rather keep that until we meet Miss Wr-, I mean Kara."

"Nice. So you can surprise me? Is that it?" Again she didn't wait for his answer. "Listen, I'll come see you if you want, not a problem, even if you do want to possibly ambush me, but, for now I really am quite busy so you're going to have to wait."

"I'm afraid I'm going to have to insist."

"Really? Am I under arrest?"

"No."

"Then you can insist all you like Tony, but I'll come in and talk to you when I'm good and ready. Now, I'm sorry but I have a job to do, so you give your number to my brother and I'll ring you as soon as I can, I promise."

"That's not a smart move Kara," Reynolds said calmly.

Kara wasn't too sure why, perhaps it was tiredness, or that she still hadn't found, let alone secured, Chris or Brenda Sterling or that this Detective Reynolds had smashed in the doors to her apartment, Tien's apartment and their office all for some scum who would have assaulted, raped and maybe killed her. Whatever the reason her temper flared.

"Oi! Don't tell me what is and isn't smart. You don't even know where I am, you don't know what I'm in the middle of and if you had anything on me for whatever bullshit reason you're ringing me for you'd have nicked me already. So at the minute you're the last person to be telling me what's smart. I'll phone David when I'm good and fucking ready and he'll contact you. Until then, you have yourself a nice fucking day." She hung up the call and walked down through the garden to let her temper dissipate. Her phone rang again after a couple of minutes. David's number was displayed. She thought about declining it but decided to answer, she could always hang up if Reynolds annoyed her.

"Yes, what is it?" she asked abruptly.

"It's me Sis. Reynolds wanted to apologise but he didn't think you'd listen to him. He said it's fine, he trusts you to call when you're ready. Okay?"

She never could stay angry with her baby brother, especially when this wasn't even his fault. "Okay David. And I will, I promise, I just need to concentrate on what I'm doing."

"Do I want to know?"

"Probably not."

"Just be safe, hey Sis?"

"Always. You too. Love ya."

"Yeah, you too."

As she was about to hang up she suddenly realised what Tony Reynolds had said about his unit.

"David," she shouted, "David are you still there?"

"Yes Kara, what is it?"

"Listen, tell Reynolds not to leave London. In fact can you and your boss take him to your office? Keep him there. I promise I'll ring you this afternoon. Not sure when but certainly before seven-thirty."

"What's going on Kara?"

"I can't tell you yet, but the hairs on the back of my neck are up and I need your help."

There was a short pause, "Okay Sis."

A becalmed Kara ended the call and rejoined her team in the kitchen.

32

Saturday Midday. Arlesey

The planning took another half hour, the argument about which of Illy's three people to use added another fifteen minutes. Eventually Kara took charge and made the decision that was obvious but dangerous.

"Right, that's enough. We all know it has to be Anatoly. Sammi, you're taller than Emilia and broader in the shoulder and your hair isn't as long as hers, but you're a blonde and when it comes down to a quick glance through a car window you'll do. Chaz, you're taller than Uzy, slimmer and your nose is still in the middle of your face. I hate to say it, but compared to him you're actually quite handsome."

Chaz waggled his fingers in a V-sign at her by way of acknowledging the back-handed compliment.

"Your hair's the same colour and if you keep your head down then the same applies as Sammi, you're close enough. A quick glance through a window and you'll pass. But there's none of us look anywhere near the size of Anatoly. So we have to use the real thing. He seems compliant, but that might be a ruse, so Tien folds in to the backseat behind him and we keep a gun on him. Convince him we'll use it even if he's driving."

She held her hand up as if to ward off any continued protests but there were none.

"I know it's a risk and he might decide to try to punch his way out but it's really all we've got and the clock isn't stopping. We turn something up by the time Illy expects his three nightshift to be back on duty or we're all too late."

The team nodded their acceptance.

"Right, let's go and get our Russian giant."

ϕ

The drive took just over an hour. The convoy headed south along the A1, joined the A10 at Knebworth and entered Waltham Cross from the north. It slowly negotiated its way through the busy Saturday afternoon traffic to the industrial estate that lay to the south east.

"So far so good," Kara said to Tien as they pulled into a small circular spur road. It was home to a timber yard that according to the Internet was shut on a Saturday. The chained and padlocked yard doors and the prominent closed sign in the shop door confirmed it.

Tien pulled the BMW round so that it pointed back out towards the main estate road. Sammi arrived next in the Audi and did the same, ending up just behind Kara and Tien. The Transit, with Eugene and Dan up front pulled in and parked nose-on to the kerb, the rear pointing towards the light blue Mondeo that Chaz was just arriving in.

"Yeah," said Tien, "but now the fun starts. Do you think he'll try it?"

"Who knows, but it's a short drive and we're out of options," Kara said as she got out of the car.

Sammi got into the front passenger seat of the Mondeo, Chaz got into the back seat behind her. Tien, the smallest of them by a margin sat crouched behind the driver's seat. Invisible from view by anyone unless they were stood next to the car she had her Glock pistol out and pointing forward.

Eugene, by far the biggest of them, opened the rear door of

242

the Transit. Climbing in he released the shackles that had held Anatoly in place. The man's legs were now free but his hands remained taped together. Dan remained at the open door of the van, his sidearm drawn and held down by his side.

"Okay Anatoly, nice and easy, slide yourself to the door then feet on the ground and walk around to the driver seat of your car. Get in and relax. When we're ready we'll cut the tape and you do what we've talked about. You understand?" Eugene asked.

"Yes. Yes, I understand."

The Mondeo's suspension strained under the weight of the man. Anatoly looked at his passengers. Both Sammi and Chaz held Tasers in their hands. He twisted round and saw Tien pointing her pistol at the small of his back.

Dan locked up the van and waited next to the boot of the Mondeo. Eugene walked to the driver's door and stooped down to talk to Anatoly.

"You remember what you have to do and then we all walk away?" Eugene asked quietly.

"Yes. I know," the Russian answered.

Reaching in to slit the tape on Anatoly's wrists the sleeve of Eugene's T-shirt rode up. Anatoly saw the tattoo of the winged parachute on the black man's arm. "You are paratrooper?" he asked.

Eugene glanced down at the tattoo of the cap badge he had earned years ago, "Yeah. 3-Para, British Army. Why's that?"

The Russian tore the last shreds of tape off and rubbed his hands to get the circulation moving, then he rolled up his left sleeve and turned his arm so Eugene could see. The tattoo was of an Ilyushin-76 transport aircraft flying under a parachute. A scroll twisted around the aircraft with what looked like '76 rb BAB' etched into it. Sammi, sitting next to Anatoly, read the Cyrillic symbols.

"76th Guards Air Assault Division," she said to Eugene.

"Yes, this is right." Anatoly looked between Sammi and Eugene. "I am airborne guard. Paratrooper too," he said and gave a half smile.

Eugene looked at the Russian's tattoo again and gave a small nod of acknowledgment.

"You give word that I walk away?" Anatoly asked.

Eugene frowned, "What's that?"

"You give word. I trust paratrooper to keep word. We are honourable men," Anatoly said and held Eugene's gaze.

Without blinking Eugene said, "Yes Anatoly. You do exactly what we talked about and I give you my word, you will walk away."

Anatoly held his right hand out awkwardly in the cramped space behind the wheel.

Eugene put his knife away and tried to determine if the big Russian was being genuine. He held Anatoly's gaze then glanced across him to Sammi who gave him the slightest of nods and patted the top of the Taser to let him know she had him covered, just in case.

Eugene shook the Russian's hand.

"I could help," Anatoly said.

"Well you're going to help us anyway," Sammi said.

Anatoly turned a little in his seat. Sammi gripped the Taser a little tighter.

"No, I mean, I help. Properly. I could go to door. Get the man inside to come out. I can, um," Anatoly struggled for the word. He swapped to Russian, "Ya budu razoruzhit' yevo."

Sammi checked she had heard him right, "You mean disarm, you'll disarm him?"

"Da, yes, I will dis… arm him. No need to kill."

For no reason he could put his finger on Eugene reckoned the Russian was being truthful but allowing the big man to get back out of the car and have two or maybe three adversaries in the open wasn't a good idea. Even if he did believe him. It wasn't a choice he was going to make.

"Thanks, but all you need to do is drive us up there and angle the car the way we told you. If they look out through the curtains like you said they will, then you just wave and we'll take it from there."

Anatoly gave a resigned nod of his head.

"Okay, so pop the boot and when the BMW leaves, you follow. Good?" Eugene said, smiled and gave a 'thumbs-up'.

"Pop the boot?" Anatoly repeated slowly and frowned.

"Open the trunk," Sammi said. "American Eugene, they speak American. I blame the movies."

Anatoly reached for the release catch.

Eugene walked to the rear of the car and helped his older brother into the boot. He lowered the lid so Dan could hold the catch but not have it fully closed, then he climbed into the passenger seat of the BMW, next to Kara who had slipped in behind the wheel.

She led them out of the spur road and turned right onto the main estate thoroughfare. Two hundred yards later she pulled over just twenty yards short of the target. The Mondeo passed her and slewed into the small parking area to the front of the brick-built plumbing office. The curtains covering the barred window twitched and a head appeared like some bizarre prisoner in a glass cage. Anatoly waved nonchalantly as Sammi twisted towards the passenger door, balancing her need not to have her face seen with being able to watch both Anatoly and the office. Chaz was almost perfectly blocked by Anatoly's large frame but had his head bent anyway. Tien scrunched even further down into the foot well of the rear seat.

The curtains dropped back into place.

"Go, Go, Go," Sammi said quietly.

Looking from her vantage point back down the road, Kara felt a twinge of unease but pushed it to one side as she saw the boot of the Mondeo come up and Dan scramble out. His feet landed on the tarmac of the parking area at the same time as Sammi and Chaz both exited the car. Kara put the BMW into drive and pulled forward.

Sammi and Dan moved to either side of the door and went tight against the wall. Chaz stood a little to the side but in front of the door. He could hear a couple of bolt locks being drawn, top and bottom, then a chain and finally the main key lock being turned.

The door opened inward and the man opening it was instantly confused by what confronted him. He had seen Anatoly from his quick look out the window and thought Emilia and Uzy were in the car with the big man. He'd expected to see one of them at the door. Now there was somebody he didn't recognise standing between him and Anatoly's car and there was the loud blast of a horn. He looked past the stranger and over Anatoly's car to a BMW with a large black man leaning out the passenger side window giving him the finger. The car, driven by a woman, was moving slowly with horn blaring. Suitably distracted he didn't see Chaz move until he was being pulled out of the office by him.

Chaz had a good few inches of height advantage but was a good few pounds lighter. He spun the guard round and put him into a choke hold. Sammi and Dan, weapons drawn, moved into the office.

Chaz's opponent had obviously been trained reasonably well, for after the initial disorientation and surprise he began to react. Reaching up he tried to get his hands in between the crushing forearm and his throat, whilst trying to crunch down and sink his chin into the crook of the elbow at his windpipe. In turn, Chaz knew the next thing the guard would try was to step behind him, execute a simple circular half-step and the result would be Chaz on the deck and his opponent in control.

But Chaz was altogether faster in thought and movement. He spun the guard out of the choke hold and punched him full force in the solar plexus. The man promptly sank to his knees, badly winded.

Kara had swung the BMW around and pulled onto the parking apron. Eugene went to help Chaz whilst Kara moved quickly to the open office door and yelled out to Dan and Sammi that she was coming in.

"It's okay. It's all clear. Nobody else in here apart from the good guys," Dan yelled back from the rooms behind the main office.

Kara relaxed and holstered her pistol. "Where are you?" she called as she entered the curtained room. To her immediate front was a tired, worn and badly stained brown couch, next to it a long oval table was set against the back wall, a television, muted but showing a horse race, sat on it along with a random collection of newspapers and soft-porn magazines. In the corner to the far side of the long window a desk and two fixed-leg chairs seemed to huddle together like they were scared of encroaching into the main space. In the far corner between them and the television, diagonally opposite the door Kara had just come through was the door that Dan's voice had come from. Kara moved towards it but was met by Dan coming back in.

"Well?" she asked.

"We're halfway home Kara," he said as he stepped to one side. Sammi came through the door behind him leading a bruised and battered Chris Sterling.

33

Saturday Afternoon. Waltham Cross

Eugene had lifted Chaz's now taped-up opponent into the small back office that had been used to hold Chris Sterling. He'd then escorted Anatoly into the same space and explained that they would let him go as soon as they found Brenda Sterling, but for now he had to stay put. The big Russian accepted it with no outward show of emotion. He even held his hands out to be resecured.

Dan and Tien moved the Audi and BMW to less conspicuous parking spots and Chaz positioned the Transit so he could keep an overwatch on the office. They left Anatoly's Mondeo parked out front. Tien and Dan rejoined Kara inside the small kitchenette where she was making coffees whilst Sammi tended and dressed Chris Sterling's injuries. When all had been done to make him as comfortable as possible Sammi joined them.

"Couple of teeth knocked out, probably two or three ribs gone and a nose that'll need straightening at some point but it's functioning so I'll leave it. Extensive bruising all over. Apparently he was pissing blood a few days ago but it's stopped now. Says they started hitting him a week ago but I couldn't really gather why. They've been hitting and kicking him every day since but it's been slacking off lately. I assume the guards are under orders from Illy to do it but losing the will. Guess you can only batter someone so much. Anyways, he really needs to go to a hospital but not straight away. For now, he's all yours," Sammi said.

"What have you told him?"

"Not a lot. I just said we've come to get him out of here. Nothing else. To be honest, he just cried for most of the time I was with him."

Kara drained the last of her coffee and went out to the main room. She pulled one of the fixed-leg chairs over to the couch where Chris Sterling was awkwardly moving, trying to find a comfortable way for his punished body to sit. His head bent down, he looked submissive and scared. She could see the dried blood, that despite Sammi's best attempts to clean, was still crusted at his nose and, more worryingly, on his earlobes and inside the ear. His left eye was half closed under a purple and black eyelid that was grotesquely deformed and his bottom lip was swollen and sported a zig-zag split that would have benefited from proper stitches but which Sammi had closed with tiny Steristrip Butterfly versions.

"Hi Chris, I'm Kara. Zoe and Michael sent us." The man gave a strange wail and tears spilled down his cheeks.

Kara went to the small toilet out the back and retrieved a roll of paper. By the time she came back in Sterling's sobs had calmed a little. He very gently wiped his eyes and nose, gasping each time he touched his face.

"Ssshh now Chris, everything's going to be okay."

"Who are you? Are you the Police?" he asked in a strange, hoarse whisper, his eyes still staring at the ground.

"No, not police. Just people Zoe and Michael reached out to. Understand?"

"Yes," Sterling's voice sounded confused. "Have you found Brenda?"

"Not yet. That's why I'm talking to you. Where is she?"

"At the camp."

"What camp Chris? Where are you talking about?"

"The camp he keeps his girls at. You need to get her out of there. You have to go now. You need to leave. You have to go." His voice was still husky but he was getting louder, agitated.

"Take it easy Chris, calm yourself." Kara's voice had raised a little and she placed a hand on his knee.

He flinched, like a small puppy who was patted too aggressively. "Okay," he said much softer. "Sorry."

"First things first, tell me about your guard. When does his relief turn up?"

His voice was vague, disjointed, "They hand over at night. About seven or eight. EastEnders is on the TV. I can always hear the theme tune. They all seem to like it. Strange really. Then in the morning they all hand over again."

"What do you mean they all? Is it just a one for one handover?"

"The two of them change."

Kara suddenly realised what had caused her unease as she first approached the office. "Chris, listen to me. Concentrate," she reached out and took his chin in her hand, forcing his head up. "Do you normally have two guards?"

"Yes."

The open mic she was wearing was transmitting to the rest of her team in the rear kitchenette. "Head's up! Where the fuck's the other one? Tien, get Chaz on the phone and tell him to be on his toes. I knew there was something not right, there's no car out front." As she finished the sentence she heard a mobile ringing in the back room.

Then she heard Dan shouting, "It's Chaz, we have company turning up. Red Toyota slowing as it's approaching. Think it's going to swing in next to the Mondeo. Driver, white male, short hair, almost skinned. Mid to late twenties."

Several things happened at once. Eugene and Dan hustled into the front room and Sammi followed. She helped Chris Sterling up and moved him out to the kitchenette. Tien moved to the door of the small rear office and kept an eye on Anatoly and the other guard whilst Kara moved back to the door between the kitchenette and the main room to cover Dan and Eugene.

Dan threw the still live phone onto the long table, so that Chaz could provide a commentary to events outside. They heard the engine of the car as it pulled onto the parking area. Eugene twitched the curtains for effect but didn't look out. The engine turned off. After a short delay, the car door slammed shut.

"Just a single male, not looking like he's expecting anything other than his mate to open the door, you're good to go," Chaz's voice came from the phone speaker.

Dan withdrew the bolts top and bottom of the door. He made the sign for OK to his younger, but bigger, brother. When Eugene nodded his confirmation, Dan turned the main door lock and swung the door in.

All six foot three and sixteen and a half stone of Eugene erupted in fury through the opening. The newly arrived guard stood three feet away from the door's threshold. It was just enough distance for him to half raise both his hands before Eugene's right hook smashed into the side of his head. He was out before he hit the ground.

Dan helped his brother scoop up the new arrival. They were back inside with the door shut in a few seconds. After a few minutes the guard had started to come around but by then he'd been secured with duct tape and settled into the small room with Anatoly and his other colleague.

Kara swore softly under her breath. She knew they were tired but that was no excuse for missing the obvious.

"Right folks," she said into the radio-mic and the phone line still open to Chaz. "Lesson learnt. We nearly fucked that up. So let's switch on. I need you to think if we've missed anything else. Tien and Eugene, talk to Anatoly. I want to know what he knows about this camp Chris is talking about. Where is it? What is it? Sammi, bring Chris back in here."

When Sterling had settled back on the couch, his head bent down to the ground and his whole appearance once more one of defeat, she began again, "Chris, where's Brenda?"

"She's not here."

Kara waited for him to add something but he didn't. She stifled her frustration and kept her voice neutral, "Obviously Chris, I can see that. Where is she?"

"She's still at the other place. He's keeping her there," his voice was heavy with emotion.

Kara heard the tiredness, stress and desperation in his tone but she needed to get as much information from him as possible so she pressed on.

"What other place Chris?"

"The camp, I told you the ca-"

"Chris! You were in the Forces, yes?" Kara asked in a stern tone that cut off his whined response.

"What?"

"Royal Navy. You were in the Service?"

"Yes."

"For twenty plus years?"

"Yes."

"You ended up in intelligence work?"

"Yes." His answers, shocked by the change in direction of the questions, had become succinct.

"Okay. My friends and I were all in too. We've been sent by your kids because they were clever enough to recognise the message you left on your phone was bollocks. I know it was pure luck that the cover story chosen to hide your disappearance didn't factor in Brenda's fear of flying, but at least you had the presence of mind to stress the flying part. If we're going to sort this out I need you to remember that presence of mind. So harden the fuck up and stop being a fucking victim. Do I make myself clear?" Her voice carried a distinct edge, a firmness that was beyond anything a parent might use with a disappointing child.

He didn't answer.

"Or Chris, I can just go back out and wander away. Then you can stay here and probably get killed when whatever the fuck is going on has played itself out. Now do yourself a fucking favour and dig in. Clear?"

Another silence. Kara waited.

For the first time on his own volition Chris raised his head and met her eyes, his voice was steadier, calmer, stronger, "Clear."

"Good. Now what's going on? What do you do for Illy Sultanov?"

"I take photos."

"Why?"

"For passports," he said and coughed, wincing with the pain the simple action caused.

"Fake passports I presume?"

"Yes."

"For who?"

"His girls mostly." Sterling looked back down at the ground. His lips pursed together and he looked like he would cry again.

Kara felt a surge of anger. The intensity of it was like a migraine penetrating her temples. She concentrated on steering the conversation to the information she needed but her tone was brusque, "Chris, I don't give a flying fuck what remorse you feel or what guilt you're suffering. You stay strong and tell me what's going on or I swear to God I'm off out the door." His head came back up, he coughed again and once more the pain of it was etched into his face. "Good," Kara said. "Use that pain and concentrate. Tell me what I need to know and we'll repay the people that kicked the shit out of you."

Sterling breathed as deeply as his battered ribs would allow and then continued, "Illy has photos sent over via the modelling agency. They're large format, full-face shots. I re-photograph them, retouch them and turn them into passport standard."

"What else?"

"Nothing. That's all I do," he paused and Kara was about to press him but he added, "Brenda does the rest."

"What?" Kara's voice had raised a little. "What do you mean Brenda does the rest?"

"It was Brenda that got us involved. Years ago."

"Given our present circumstances Chris, I need the abridged version. Make it quick."

"I met Illy years ago. He would come to dinner and we were friends. His little daughter and our-"

Kara interrupted him, "I know all this Chris. Zoe told me. Skip to making false passports for a Russian gangster."

"We didn't know he was that," Sterling said defensively, almost pathetically. "He had a sister-in-law that he couldn't get into the country. He needed her to look after Nat but she didn't have the papers. He broke down in tears one night in our house, at dinner. Brenda worked for the passport office in Peterborough and said she could help. She stole a passport blank. I got Illy to get a picture of Yanina. I re-photographed it and we did the rest at home. It was easy."

"What's a passport blank?"

"It's a passport before it's had the personal details added. The purple book with all the pages save the last. It even has the holographic overlay that goes over the photo."

"And Brenda supplied it?"

"Yes. It was easy for her. That's what she worked with every day. She was even responsible for the inventory."

"But what about the electronic chips. I thought they made forgery impossible?"

"They do. But this is back before they came in. The passports we did only had a piece of machine-readable code and that was easy to forge if you knew the system and how it worked. Brenda knew it because that's what she did for a job. She typed in all the details in the right formats, forged the readable code, added the photo and finished it off." Sterling breathed deeply and winced again with the pain it caused.

Kara waited. Once he had settled from the waves of pain etched on his face, he continued, "It was perfect because it wasn't a forgery. It was, for all purposes, real. Illy posted it to Yanina and she used it to walk through the airport. There are no databases to check machine-readable passports against. When they're scanned they just display the data that's printed on the page. It matched, the photo was of her, so she was in."

Kara was slightly shocked at how seemingly unconcerned Sterling was in his recounting of the story. But she needed him to give up the rest. "Okay, so how do you go from getting Yanina in to the country to sitting in this place?"

"We did the one passport and Illy paid us a lot of money. A few months later he said he had young models wanting to come over but they couldn't get out of Russia. The country was falling apart under the Russian Mafia, there were no jobs and no hope for the youth. We thought we were doing a good thing, helping them escape poverty and a fracturing country. We started supplying him passports. Only a few at first. But then more. The money he paid was a lot. I mean thousands for each," he paused, his mouth downturned, his eyes sad.

"Yeah I know. We found it in your loft," Kara said, trying to suppress a mounting anger.

The man's one open eye focussed on her with a clarity of purpose that had been absent thus far. His victimhood instantly forgotten.

"You found it? How th-"

"Not really relevant at the minute Chris," Kara interrupted. Her anger surged with an almost instantaneous contempt. But she knew she had to rein in her emotions and keep him talking.

"But yes, I found your money and I thought it was why you were being held so I moved it. It's safe. We'll come to some arrangement after all of this is done and dusted. Let's get back to passports. When did you figure out what they were really for? Not models but human trafficking?" Kara asked with a harshness that she couldn't hide despite her best efforts.

All the time she'd been trying to find Chris and Brenda Sterling she knew they had to be doing something illegal, the money was proof of that, but she hadn't imagined they'd be implicitly involved in enabling Sultanov's activities. She was furious and struggled to concentrate as Sterling began to speak again.

"A couple of years into it. We'd been doing two or three passports a week. Then the photos stopped being just Russians and started to include Asian girls, Africans, all sorts."

"Yet you continued?"

"By then we had more money than we needed. We told him we wanted out. Illy took both Brenda and me out for a meal. Afterwards, instead of coming home, he took us to the camp. Made us watch what he did to one of his former associates who had disappointed him. He shot him in both knees. There was no way we were getting out," Chris said with a hint of the dread he still felt remembering the screams and the blood.

"He took you to other examples?" Kara asked recalling Ty's experience.

"Yes. But only me. In a way it was even worse on Brenda knowing that I had to go and see things she only imagined. He kept paying us the money but he said we needed the occasional reminder to keep us properly focussed."

Kara's anger was causing a physical pain in her chest. She spoke through gritted teeth, "And at no fucking time did you decide that just turning yourself in to the cops would be a way out?"

Sterling said nothing.

"No, obviously fucking not. You just kept taking the money and being persuaded?"

He looked up and spoke with a surly edge to his voice, "You think if we'd turned ourselves in and confessed that we would have made it to a courtroom to testify?"

She knew it was true but it didn't make her feel any more sympathy for him. Forcing herself to focus she replayed in her mind what he had told her. Something was out of place. She remembered back to her conversation with Wendy Mead, the simpering security consultant with the likely crush on her brother. Wendy had said that the old passports were being phased out. "How can you still be making forgeries if you're both retired and the new passports are being chipped?"

"Brenda knew that chip technology was going to be mandatory from March 2006. We told Illy there was no way we could forge them. They'd all be electronically recorded on verifiable databases. But he said that a passport issued before the chips became mandatory would still be valid for ten years. He ordered Brenda to steal as many blanks as she could. All she had to do was forge them as normal but date them before March 2006."

"How many did she get?"

"We had to wait until January 2006 so Brenda could match the correct machine-readable code formats. By then the stock of non-chipped blanks was being drawn down but she still managed to get a full box."

"How many?" Kara asked sternly, her frustration evident.

"Fifteen hundred."

"You're fucking kidding?" She stood up and moved to the other side of the room. She needed to put a little distance between herself and this man she desperately wanted to punch.

"No," Sterling said and looked forlorn again. "We've been supplying him since."

"Okay. So why are you here now?"

"We had a hundred and twenty blanks left and they're still good until March 2016. Brenda and I were making plans to get far away before either the blanks or the clock ran out. I guess Illy decided to act early. He wants us to make a last batch and then once we're finished…," he stopped.

Kara thought he was going to cry again and vowed that if he did she would slap him. But instead he just gave a little shrug and was racked by pain for the gesture. She came back and retook her seat, completing his sentence for him, "When you're finished making them you'd both be finished?"

"I guess so. I'm pretty sure he wouldn't want us hanging around. Not with what we know and being of no further use to him."

"So he came and took you?" Kara asked.

"Three of his people arrived in the middle of Monday night, Tuesday morning. It's been almost two weeks. They brought us here. Then Illy came and moved us up to the camp."

"What's this camp? Like an army camp?"

"No. It's the place he keeps his girls and what he uses for

his shows. That's what he calls it when he punishes someone and makes us watch. His shows of persuasion he calls them. They brought all my camera gear and the old printer Brenda uses for the passports. I had to make one hundred and seven photos and then he set Brenda to work and brought me back here. Told her not to screw it up or he'd hurt me. Last week she messed up one of the holder pages and they started hitting me. Showed pictures of me to Brenda, to make her concentrate more. Illy knows it's delicate work, careful work. Told her that she could talk to me on the phone everyday but if she fucked up again he'd fuck me up more. He also knows how many passports she can produce in a day so if she slacks off I get hurt again."

"But surely she knows what happens when she finishes?"

"Yes, but…," Chris muffled a sob.

"Chris?" Kara said through gritted teeth. She waited and heard him breathe deeply, battling against the pain of his ribs, recovering his voice.

"He said that if she worked properly I wouldn't get hurt anymore and if she finished them all then he'd only kill us, and quickly."

"As opposed to?" Kara asked half guessing the answer.

"As opposed to him torturing both of us. Killing us but not doing it until he makes us watch Zoe and Michael die in front of us," Chris' voice had become strangely devoid of emotion as he repeated the worst of Illy's threats. The flatness told Kara that for the days he had sat in this makeshift prison the prospect of watching his kids die had been consuming him.

Kara's temper subsided a little. She knew that regardless of what she thought about Chris or Brenda's actions, she wasn't going to expose Zoe or Michael to risk. "That's not going to happen Chris. I can absolutely assure you. But he's had you for nearly two weeks. How many passports can Brenda make in a day?"

"If you're asking how long we have left, not long. She can normally do about five a day. It's fiddly, not like the automatic printers at her work. They used to do one passport every couple of seconds, but she needs to set each one up manually and figure out the old machine codes. Thing is, Illy's had her working longer hours so she's done seven or eight in a day. He's kept his word and let us talk on the phone at night and Brenda tries to tell me how many if she can. When we spoke yesterday she had sixteen left. Maybe two days. At the most."

Kara nodded as she thought about the options open to her. She knew the rest of the team, listening in on the open radio net to the conversation, would be doing the same. She forced herself to speak encouragingly to him, "That's great Chris. It tells me we have time but I'm going to need some information on Illy's security. How many have you seen? Describe them."

"The three that took us originally. One woman, two men. One of them was that big bloke you brought in here. The woman was a blonde-"

"A blonde, medium height, athletic build, other guy was dark haired, face like a thug, broken nose?" Kara interrupted him with a succinct description of Emilia and Uzy.

"Uh, yeah, how di-"

"Never mind how, just tell me the rest."

"There's the two you have tied up out back and the other two on the night shift. They're all young guys, mid-twenties. Neck tattoos. Hard looking. They've guarded me since I got here. They sound Russian I think. I'm not too sure, but Russian would be my guess. That's it, that's all I've seen."

"What about before. How many security does Illy have in total?"

"He always has at least three with him on the show nights, but they're different ones. I've not seen any of them here."

"The big guy, did he ever show up at the camp?"

"I'd not seen him before he came to my house."

Tien's voice sounded in Kara's ear, "Sounds right. Anatoly insists he's never been near the place. Says Illy is tight on keeping his security to specific areas and operations." Kara didn't acknowledge the news.

"Chris, think. How many different faces have you seen?"

"I'm not sure but I've probably taken about twenty or

thirty passport photos of men over the years. Most of them looked like security."

"Looked like security?" she asked slightly confused.

"Some looked young, delicate, like rent boys. Some looked tough, mean, tattoos and broken noses is what I meant."

She nodded, "Okay Chris, so what's the camp like and where is it?"

"It's only a couple of miles from here but it might as well be on the dark side of the moon. Illy must pay off the local authorities for no one has ever come near it. It's a big warehouse shed that used to be a distribution hub for a supermarket. Sits in the middle of a small wood and has one road in. Has a smaller outbuilding that I think is used for the security people, but I've never been inside that. I've only been in the main warehouse. It's like a big open plan dormitory. Split into sections. There's about twenty or thirty small living spaces. The girls share them, two to a space."

"You mean they use them to turn tricks?" Kara asked, sickened anew at the prospect of the women being forced to use an open dormitory for prostitution.

"God no. These girls are kept expensive-looking. Good clothes, hair and make-up all top notch. Their clients expect top services in good quality surroundings. They do their tricks at hotels and private addresses. The camp is just where they live temporarily when they first arrive. Before they get moved on into apartments or other houses."

Kara's anger rose instantly again, "Brothels Chris. Fucking say it like it is. They get moved to brothels."

Sterling's head dropped again and he mumbled, "Yes, I suppose so."

Kara was aching to shout and yell but she heard Tien's voice in her ear, "Let it go Kara, concentrate on what we need."

Kara settled herself. "Okay, so what else is in this warehouse?" she asked.

"There's a partitioned off kitchen and a canteen, it'd

remind you of a transport café. A whole side of the place is bathrooms and showers and at the back there's a set of rooms used for video."

"What do you mean video?"

"Webcams. When the girls aren't working as escorts they're on camera doing private shows."

Kara paused. Something wasn't right and she didn't ignore the sensation this time. Instead she replayed in her head what Chris Sterling had been telling her. She felt her jaw clenching, the tightness in her neck muscles, the heat in her hands that were now involuntarily forming fists. She dreaded asking but knew she needed to, "How do you know this Chris?"

His hesitation told her more than anything he said. "I told you, Illy took us there when he was punishing others."

"Yeah, I get that but I wouldn't have imagined he gave you a guided tour."

"It's all open plan, mostly. A massive warehouse, you can see everything," he said, rather too hurriedly. His eyes were looking anywhere but at her. Discomfort, not caused by his injuries, was evident in his face.

"Yeah, I get the picture but the rooms at the back, how do you know what they're used for?" she asked, a lot calmer and colder than her insides felt.

"I ah, I just, the girls mu-"

"Did you take other photos for him Chris?" Kara watched as his head dropped lower and he stared at the floor.

The anger she had felt before was nothing compared to the emotion that swept through her now. She felt like punching and kicking Chris Sterling in all the places he was hurting. Instead, she just stood up.

"You're daughter hired me to find you and her mother. I'm going to fulfil my contract and then you can fuck off. These girls that you photograph, provide passports for, they come here probably thinking they're coming to a better life and they end up as whores. You can call them escorts and say they're doing webcasts but all they're doing is being held hostage until they're of no more use. Then what the fuck happens to them?"

She was raging inside but had managed to keep her voice relatively calm. But when Chris Sterling remained looking at the floor she suddenly shouted, "I'M FUCKING TALKING TO YOU."

He involuntarily jumped in his seat and the pain that shot through him caused him to cry out. Tien, listening from the kitchenette came in and turned Kara away, leading her out of the room.

"It's alright Kara. I'll get the rest."

Tien went back into the room with an iPad that had Google Earth open on it. It took her less than ten minutes. When she returned to the kitchen Kara was being handed another cup of coffee by Eugene.

"Do we know where this fucking camp is?" Kara asked, her voice still raw with anger.

"It's about a five mile drive from here, about two miles as the crow flies. Set in the middle of Shield Wood," Tien said turning the iPad for them to see. "That's it in the middle of the screen. Gets its name from being shaped like a medieval shield."

"That's a big warehouse," Sammi said leaning over to look.

"I pulled up the street view from that road leading up to it," Tien said and brought up a second browser window on the tablet.

"For fuck's sake, is he for real?" Eugene asked.

The image showed the entrance to the camp. There was a five-bar gate across the roadway, supported by two large, circular posts on either side. They provided the base of a wooden archway that was mounted over the road, reminiscent of a western ranch. Beneath the arch hung a large carved sign that read 'New Start Resort.'

"That's what he calls the place," Tien continued. "According to Sterling, Illy has contacts in various countries. He uses them to advertise for these girls to come over. Tells them there's a luxury resort they can stay in until they get established. Sells them the dream of freedom, a new start.

Shows them pictures of some top quality resort, certainly not this warehouse. Signs them up, gets the passports for them and arranges their transport. Says they can pay him back when they start modelling. But of course they don't get a contract because Yanina doesn't give them one. The promised dream life disappears into mist. He leans on them to pay back his investment and soon they're turning tricks. He takes what they earn so they never have enough to get away. The lower-level girls he supplies with drugs to keep them under control. The high-end he simply threatens to cut or maim."

"What decides if you are low or high?" Sammi asked.

"How pretty they are on arrival. Apparently Yanina puts a value on their looks," Tien answered flatly.

"For fuck's sake, it's the twenty-first century how can they not realise it's all a con? How can they sign up and get on a plane?" Kara said angrily but she was beginning to feel a weight in the pit of her stomach. Like a nausea brought on by sadness. "That bastard in there and his wife have supplied fifteen hundred passports. That's fifteen hundred lives fucking ruined over the last ten years. And what's happened to them? According to that fucker there's only forty or sixty at most in this shed. Fucking hundreds moved on, or more likely fucking sold on to other brothels and fuck knows what fate."

Eugene walked over to her and put a comforting hand on her shoulder, "We'll get Illy and Yanina and all the rest Kara. They'll not be able to do this anymore."

Kara swallowed hard, the lump in her throat physically hurt. She checked her watch. It was coming up to two-thirty.

"It ends today," Kara said and pulled out her mobile phone.

34

Waltham Cross

The call was answered on the second ring.

"You okay Sis?"

"Yeah, I'm good," she lied to her brother. "Are they with you?"

"Yep. Are you heading in here?"

"Not quite. Put me on speaker David." Kara waited until she heard the background hum of noise. "Good afternoon gents, I take it you can all hear me?"

They all confirmed they could.

"Excellent, I-"

"What's going on here Miss Wright? I told you I needed you to come in and see me," Tony Reynolds interrupted.

Kara swallowed her anger and sadness and succeeded in keeping the emotion out of her voice, "I did and I will Tony, but indulge me, you said you were Tri-County MCU?"

"Yes, why?"

"That covers Hertfordshire?"

"Yes, Bedfordshire, Cambridgeshire and Herts."

"Great. I think what's likely to happen is that you and your colleagues will probably come to me first," she paused and when no one said anything in response she pressed on. "Tell me Tony, have you ever heard of a thug called Chekov?"

"No. No I don- "

The soft Cambridge lilt of Reynolds was cut-off by a harsher Ulster accent, "Kara, I'm Matt Sexton, David's boss. I know who Chekov is. What do you know about him?"

"I know exactly who he really is and that he currently has one person held hostage. I know that the Police in Fulham refused to believe the report of a disappearance and said the people involved were just on holiday. I know that it's likely Chekov's going to kill his hostage and I know that I might just know where they are."

"Okay, give us the details."

"The place that he's holding the hostage is near Waltham Cross, just inside the Herts border. But I guess it being so close to London it might be quicker for Tony to request the Met send in SCO19," Kara referred to the Metropolitan Police's specialist firearms readiness group. "The place is big, might have some major security in and around it. If you can sort out the necessary force and meet me and my team, then we can guide you in. Do you think you and your colleagues from the sticks can sort that out?"

"Or you tell us exactly what you know now and we'll take it from there," Sexton said, a bit too forcibly for Kara's liking.

"Hey Matt, love your ideas but let's take a minute. You don't know where I am, you don't know where Chekov is and you don't even know who the hostage is let alone where she is. So, I'd suggest you help me to help you. Perhaps take a minute to ask my brother who I am and what me and my team specialise in. Then get back to me."

"Wait, wait," Sexton shouted down the phone. His accent made the words sound truncated and harsh. "Don't hang up Kara. You're right," he paused to check she hadn't ended the call. "What do you suggest?"

Kara thought that the speed of Sexton's capitulation underlined how big an arrest Chekov would be for a career detective.

"We have five hours to pull this off. After that Chekov will know he's compromised. So I suggest you both warn off your response teams and meet me where I am now. I'll text you the location and when you get here we can run through what needs to happen. Then it's all over to you."

Tony Reynolds could barely contain his temper and certainly couldn't hide it from his voice, "That all sounds very exciting, but you and I need to sit down and talk. Are you just wanting me to arrest you, Miss Wright?"

"No Tony I'm not. But I swear to fuck, you keep calling me Miss Wright and I might not say one more fucking word."

"Fine! Kara then. Do you want me to arrest you... *Kara*?"

She was actually quite impressed with how much disdain he had managed to get into her name given the shortness of the syllables. "No Tony, I don't and if you'll take your head out of your arse, it's simple. If you and Matt get me the help I need to take down this prick Chekov then I'll happily come talk to you afterwards. Guides honour."

The line went quiet for a good few seconds.

Finally Sexton said, "Hang on Kara." There was a faint click as the line was muted.

"Guess they're having a pissing contest," Sammi said.

"Guess so," Kara agreed.

After a few minutes the line came live again.

"Kara?" It was Matt Sexton.

"Yes."

"Okay, it's a deal."

"Excellent. One last thing. As well as where I am, I'll also text you another address. It's in Fulham. You'll need to go there and pick someone up. I'll have them warned and standing by. Lovely chatting but gotta rush." She hung up before anyone else could reply.

266

35

Waltham Cross

The red Toyota sat alone on the parking area in front of the plumbing office. Chris Sterling's two erstwhile guards sat in the holding cells of Waltham Cross Police Station. Uzy and Emilia sat in similar cells in Bedford. Anatoly wasn't with them. Kara hadn't been thrilled but Eugene insisted that he had given his word, so he'd made separate arrangements for the big Russian before the authorities turned up. And they had turned up. In numbers.

It had taken a few hours to sort things out and move the various players into place. One of the first to go was Chris Sterling. After Kara explained his role in things he was moved to the nearby St Margaret's Hospital for treatment. He was also put under Police guard and was soon to be under arrest. That had pleased Kara quite a lot.

As had the lack of argument or resistance to her and her team's involvement in what was coming. Interestingly it had been Tony Reynolds that had been the easiest to convince. That was significant as, by dint of being the senior ranking officer from the correct jurisdiction, he was in overall charge. Kara had first met him when she entered the Police Mobile

Command Centre, parked at the heart of the light industrial area, about a mile from the plumbing office. The vehicle was cramped and a lot less salubrious than she had expected but the multiple screens, phones and radios seemed to be enough to control a small army let alone the twenty or so SCO19 operators that were currently resting against, or sitting in, a variety of cars parked in the adjacent street. Dressed in blue overalls, boots and body armour, equipped with web-slung machine pistols, assault rifles and holstered sidearms, their blue combat helmets resting on their knees or on the bonnets of their cars, they looked more like a bizarre future-tech cartoon of paramilitary forces come to life than the tourist image of the good old British Bobby.

Inside the command centre Kara and Tien were greeted by Reynolds, Moya Little, Matt Sexton and Craig Harrison, the Inspector in command of the SCO19 detachments. The discussions that Kara had prepared for, a frustrating fight with civilian Police against her team's particular military skills, didn't materialise. Tony Reynolds had asked her to outline her thoughts. She had. There were a few clarifying questions.

The only real point of concern was if Illy didn't play by their hoped-for rules and simply used phone calls to get the job done. Harrison alleviated that by guaranteeing his teams could deploy mobile jammers around an isolated target like the camp. He had complete confidence that no cell-based phone call would get through. A follow-up check to ensure there were no landlines going into the place confirmed that they could isolate it. Once that had been dealt with, Reynolds looked at Sexton and Harrison, received nods of agreement from both and that was it. Kara's team were in.

Now, some two hours after that initial discussion, Kara, Tien, Reynolds, Little, Sexton and Harrison sat at the planning table in the middle of the command vehicle, but in addition all the desks and consoles along the sides were now occupied. There was a faint hum of anticipation and a charge of nervous tension in the space. Kara looked to her right, to the two most recent arrivals, her brother and the person he had been sent to collect.

"Ready?" Kara asked.

"Yes, more than." Zoe Sterling's voice was flat and hard. A firmness that, along with the expression on her face, betrayed a disgust and fury. These had replaced the shock and tears that had been her first reaction when David had explained the role 'Uncle Illy' had played in her family's problems.

Craig Harrison moved to behind one of the console operators. He tapped the man on the shoulder and said, "Now."

The operator spoke quietly into his head-mounted boom-mic and then waited for confirmation. After a few minutes, during which Kara sat with her hand overlaid on Zoe's, the operator swivelled in his chair and gave an "OK" to Harrison.

He in turn nodded to Zoe, "The camp's isolated, there's no calls can get through to it now. You're on."

"Remember, light and happy," Kara said.

"It's okay Kara. I might be a dancer but we're trained to act with our whole being." Zoe picked up her mobile carefully, making sure not to detach the trailing lead that ran to a digital recording device. Easing herself back into the chair she sat straighter and breathed deeply a couple of times. Then she raised her head, extending her neck muscles and smiled broadly. Kara thought of a line of ballerinas about to rise and take to the stage. Instead, Zoe punched Illy's number.

"Uncle Illy, it's me Zoe. I've got great news."

Kara and the rest had headphones held to their ears so they could hear Illy's responses. His accent, rounded by his many years in Britain, was nonetheless still heavy with Russian pronunciation.

"My dear, it is good to hear from you. What is this news?"

Zoe took a deep but unobtrusive breath and started speaking rapidly, in an overly excited, rushed manner, "The lady private investigator I hired, she says she's found Mum, she's at some resort, health camp sort of thing, oh I'm not too sure what's going on because she says she hasn't found Dad but she's found Mum but I just had to tell someone but Michael's playing rugby today somewhere in Hampshire and won't be home till late so I just had to phone you, oh I'm so excited." Eventually she paused and allowed Illy to get a word in.

"Zoe, Zoe, calm down, calm down child."

"Oh yes, I'm sorry but it's simply brilliant news isn't it?"

"Yes, yes it is. Now start again. You have seen your Mother?"

"No not yet."

"So this lady PI, she has seen her?"

"Well no, but she says her people are driving out there now. She rang me from her office in Camden. They're all just about to leave. She said that they have a lead on Mum being at some resort place just north of the M25. Isn't it fantastic? Anyway, they reckoned they would be able to get her within an hour or so. I just knew Mum hadn't gone on a plane."

Zoe sounded so happy and plausible that Kara had difficulty squaring the sound of her voice with the furious look in the woman's eyes. She listened intently to Illy Sultanov in the headphone to her ear and heard an increase in his respiratory rate. When he spoke again his accent had thickened, his voice sounded a little tighter, more forced. He wasn't a patch on faking it compared to his quasi-niece.

"Um, Zoe, listen this is great news. It really is. Terrific. I could not be more pleased. Thank you for phoning me, but I am sorry, I am just trying to finish a meeting with some clients. Let me get rid of them straightaway and then I will come see you. You are at home, yes?"

"Yes. At home and yes, that would be super. Michael's not due back for hours so it'll be great to have you and Aunt Yanina here. We can all be together when they find Mum and bring her here. Thank you Uncle Illy, that's so kind."

"Please, Zoe, it is nothing. You wait at home. I shall see you soon."

The line disconnected and Kara gave Zoe a broad smile, "Excellent, well done."

"And now we wait," Sexton said.

The background hum of the centre seemed to fade as Kara concentrated on the slow moving second hand of an analogue clock mounted on the wall. The longer the delay the more certain she was that Illy was trying to initiate everything by phone. She could almost feel the frustration he would be experiencing as each time he tried to call any of his people at the 'New Start Resort' he would have got a 'Network Unavailable' pre-recorded message. She watched and waited as the seconds dragged on.

After what had seemed like an hour but had only been four and a half minutes, Matt Sexton said, "He might just decide to cut his losses you know."

"You mean he knows something weird is going on with the phones and he's going to keep his distance?" asked David.

Sexton nodded. Kara knew the Ulsterman could be right. If Illy thought he was being lured into a trap then he might just stay away. If he didn't turn up at either location then the police wouldn't be able to pin much on him. They'd still rescue Brenda and maybe she and Chris would testify but given Illy's likely approach to dealing with witnesses, and their families, the case could fall apart before it began. Kara checked the clock on the wall. It showed 18:36.

At 18:40, Kara was realising that the one thing they hadn't decided on was how long they would wait before moving. She was about to ask the question when one of the mobiles that sat in the middle of the table began to ring.

"That belongs to the older of the two guards that was with Chris Sterling," Tien said. "I'd guess Illy's tried everyone at the camp and now he's going to try everyone else."

They all waited for the phone to stop vibrating against the laminate top of the briefing table. As soon as it ceased, the one next to it lit up and began to play an unidentifiable rock track.

"And that's the younger one's phone," Tien said. It vibrated so violently that Zoe reached out and steadied it from bouncing its way off the table.

"Shall we take bets?" asked David gazing at the other phones on the table.

But there was no next call to either of the last two mobiles. Kara knew there might be eventually but if Illy was ringing in an order then there would be a delay, for she'd had Eugene take Anatoly's phone to prevent awkward questions about five confiscated mobiles and only four security personnel.

As it was, Tien's mobile started ringing before anything else happened. She slid it over to Kara.

"Hi Dinger," Kara said and put him on speaker.

"I have all sorts of people hustling out the door. Reggie, Ronnie, Smirnoff and Penny now standing at the foot of the front door steps. Wait," Dinger reported from his secluded observation point in the grounds of Illy and Yanina's house. Cold, uncomfortable and hungry he'd had little else to do up to that point as neither Yanina nor Illy had left the house all day.

Tien pointed up to the series of A4 photos that she had downloaded and printed out. The names they had christened Illy's security personnel were written in black marker under them. All except Anatoly. He didn't appear on the wall. The set of photos in the command centre was one of eight Tien had produced. The rest were in the possession of the various SCO19 teams now waiting in four separate locations.

The atmosphere in the command vehicle was almost unbearable. Kara cast her eyes around and could see that even Tien, the calmest and most centred person she knew, or had ever known, was sitting forward in her seat. Her body leaning over the table, a small tremor of movement seemingly pulsing through her. The fingers of her right hand flexing in and out, forming a loose fist. David had risen and was actually pacing up and down, like some weird expectant father, Harrison remained standing behind his operator, but was rocking back and forward on the balls of his feet. Reynolds was still sitting down, but his brow was creased like a worried Shar Pei and he was twitching a pen through his fingers. Next to him Moya Little, who Kara had really only exchanged pleasantries with, had her head bowed, her hands interlaced and other than her thumbs tapping out a very fast rhythm could have been mistaken for praying. Sexton, his big frame sitting back in his chair, arms crossed over his barrel chest, his ruddy complexion showing traces of sweat on his top lip, had his eyes closed but the tension in his jaw was the giveaway that he was not asleep nor near it.

Kara wondered how she appeared to them. She knew her heart rate was up, her breathing rapid. She desperately wanted this prick of a thug to make a move but there was nothing more she could do to influence his actions. It was the lack of control that she knew was eating into her. She looked to her immediate right and realised that Zoe, out of all, sat the stillest, calmest, breathing deeply, face like a mask, poised like a porcelain statue of the finest cast and finish.

But even she jumped a little when the next of the mobiles on the table began to ring. It was Emilia's phone and Tien reached out quickly and silenced it.

Dinger's voice sounded calm and quiet in the midst of the jarring tension, "Thor's out with Illy. Illy has a mobile up to his ear. He's looking agitated, in fact he's looking very, very pissed off. Standby… Okay, so Illy's pocketed his phone but is doing a lot of shouting and arm waving. Not too sure what he's saying 'cos I'm no linguist but I'm guessing he's not happy. He's got into the back of the Merc. Thor's behind the wheel. I have Smirnoff driving the Range Rover, Penny in the passenger seat, the Twins are getting into the Red Golf GTI. That's Ronnie's personal car. Wait."

The seconds seemed to crawl again in the command centre.

"Okay, the Merc's gone right, right, right out of the gate. Seems Illy's on his way to the Cross," Dinger said but was cut off from saying anything else as a collective cry of "YES!!" sounded around the whole command vehicle.

Kara felt the tension drain from her, even though she knew there was still a way to go, "Sorry Dinger, but that's the news we wanted. What else have you got?"

"No worries, I'm sure my ear drum will recover," he said jokingly. "By the way that pony-tailed Viking might be freaky looking but he can drive, he's just pulled a sweet reverse handbrake in that Merc. The Range Rover's gone left, left, left and the Twins in the Golf have turned right, right, right, following Illy."

"Makes sense," said Kara to both Dinger and those assembled in the room with her. "Assume he's sent the two in the Range Rover off to Fulham to pick up Zoe. He thinks there's no Michael to deal with so two of them will be more than adequate. The bigger vehicle would allow them to hide her on the return journey."

Tien gave Kara the subtlest of signals, unobserved by anyone else. Kara understood her friend was telling her not to say anything more. She looked round and saw Zoe was already looking slightly shaken at the prospect that thugs had been sent after her. The fact that Michael was in New Scotland Yard, having been intercepted after his rugby match and furnished with a protective detail that took him to the central London location didn't seem to be much of a consolation.

Kara changed tack, "Okay Dinger. Who's left?"

"Well the front door is shut and the only occupants I can account for are Yanina, Cinders and Mrs Beeton. I've seen nobody else."

"Cheers, you stay in place until it's busted then come find us?"

"Roger that Kara. Be safe."

The phone line went dead and Kara watched as Tony Reynolds stood and crossed to one of the operator consoles. She appraised the man that she had taken such an instant dislike to on the phone and yet now found herself watching with a different appreciation. He wore no uniform, no visible rank, was of average height, quite trim for a man she guessed to be near fifty, but he possessed that rare quality; a command presence. Her initial dislike of him hadn't mollified, it would take much more than a few good decisions and an obvious ability to get things done quickly, but she was a little impressed.

Reynolds bent and keyed a desktop mic, "Trojan call signs, this is Papa Mike Two One One. Time is 18:44. Tactical authority is now passed to Trojan Control. Acknowledge."

The seven team leaders called in and confirmed the information that their boss, Craig Harrison, was now in charge.

The console operator in front of Reynolds pressed a button on the touch screen in front of her, "Delta Team from Trojan Control. Potential incursion your location. ETA fifteen to twenty minutes. Recce screens will advise." The woman, who Kara reckoned had a soft trace of Scottish in her accent, had just warned off the SCO19 squad assigned to the plumbing office location.

Harrison turned to look at Kara, "Get your teams moving."

She slid Tien's mobile back to her and waited a few seconds until Tien had initiated the multi-way call. Tien slid the phone back across, switched to speaker.

"Jacob, advise when you have him," Kara said.

"Roger."

Jacob Harrop had driven the Impreza with the smashed passenger side windows down to Waltham Cross as soon as the Bedfordshire Police had taken custody of Uzy and Emilia. Given the July evening and a weather forecast of light breezes, scudding clouds and no rain he felt confident that the vehicle wouldn't draw any undue attention. It just looked like he had the windows down to enjoy the evening. He'd made his way south of the town to a layby on the main A112 road that concealed him but gave a view of the junction with Avey Lane. After a few minutes he reported in.

"Jesus wept. That Merc's shifting. It's just hit the A112 heading north. There's no way I'm getting after it from here. It'll be at the roundabout before I get a hundred yards. Dan, you'll have to pick it up. But the Golf is appearing now. I'm in trail of it. Copy?"

"Copy," said Dan. He was in the red Audi A4 and currently positioned in the McDonald's car park that Dinger had been in back on Thursday when they had followed Yanina home. It was the obvious pick up for Illy if he decided to head north to Waltham Cross which was seemingly what he was doing. Dan would be able to drop in on his tail and see if he headed to the industrial estate or proceeded further west to the New Start Resort. Either one would be a result, but they all knew it would be easier and cleaner if he went to the industrial estate's office. They had to hope fate would be kind.

Kara felt that familiar operational thrill. She even felt like time, that had dragged and scraped past as she waited to see if Illy would bite, had sped up. All her senses were intensified and she could 'see' the map of vehicles and tail cars unfolding in her mind's eye. She realised she had a half-smile on her face and as she looked around the room she noticed that only two other people seemed to share her expression. One was Tien. The two friend's eyes met and they shared a broader smile. The other was Craig Harrison. Kara was surprised that the rest, including her brother, had faces that showed concentration, even concern for what was happening, but there was no hint of the joy or the thrill that she felt.

Kara allowed her mind to consider this slight revelation. It wasn't that she hadn't, long ago, realised how much she enjoyed the operational tension; it was more that she hadn't realised not everyone felt the same way. Tien, Sammi and her team, the O'Neill brothers, Jacob and Toby and all the other operators she had worked with knew the thrill, the buzz. They all loved it. All of them would be half-smiling. But for the first time she was working alongside people who weren't all ex-military. This room, this operation was made up of different types. She looked back at Harrison and thought, 'Mostly different types.'

Dan's voice refocussed her, "I'm in." As the Mercedes powered past the fast food outlet Dan shifted the Audi into its wake. Jacob followed the Golf until it turned left onto the main road into Waltham Cross.

"Toby, the Twins are all yours," he called to his brother, "I'm out of here."

"Roger, all mine," Toby answered from the Corsa he had driven back down from Arlesey and as the Red Golf GTI pulled past him he slotted in neatly behind it.

"All callsigns," Dan said reverting to standard radio procedure. Kara could hear the tension and concentration in his voice. "This Merc driver's a maniac, but I'm still in contact.

Just about. He's blown through the turn to the industrial estate. Repeat Illy is not going to the estate. He's heading north through the town."

The female operator with the Scottish accent keyed her mic, "Sierra One from Trojan Control. Be advised potential incursion your location. ETA twelve minutes. Recce screens will advise." Kara was impressed with the woman's understated yet engaging manner as she warned the SCO19 teams out at the warehouse location that they might be having company soon.

"Chaz?" Dan called.

"Go ahead," Chaz answered.

"Be aware this boy can drive. He's all yours in two. Copy?"

Chaz, pre-positioned in the BMW that Tien had driven that morning when they had mounted the ambush on Uzy, acknowledged, "Roger that Dan. Back off, I'll take him from here."

"Heads up all, the Golf is slowing to take the estate turn," called Toby from the little Corsa that was now three cars behind the red Golf that the Twins were driving. "Confirm the Golf is left, left, left into the estate. I'm out."

Kara, Tien and the rest of the command centre team had so far been following the communications via Tien's phone, set up for a multi-way call. But as Toby disengaged his tail on the Golf the speaker high up in the corner of the command centre, hooked up to the SCO19 net, clicked into operation.

"Trojan Control from Trojan One. I have eyes on red Golf, two males on board. Confirm targets identified as the Twins. South on main thoroughfare. ETA plumbing office location one minute."

The male SCO19 officer at the console next to where Craig Harrison was, keyed his mic, "Trojan One, roger. Delta Team Leader, from Trojan Control, be advised. Targets now one minute, repeat one minute, from your location."

"Trojan Control, Delta Team Leader. One minute. Roger."

The central screen in the command vehicle flicked across

to an external CCTV feed from a temporary camera that had been mounted with oversight of the office where Chris Sterling had been held hostage. From a vantage point on a roof opposite it showed the parking apron and the lone red Toyota parked on it. The curtains remained drawn over the main windows and it looked as normal as it had when Kara and her team had pulled up to it that afternoon.

The red Golf with the Twins in it pulled into the parking space next to the Toyota. The CCTV showed a faint flick of the curtains at the window.

Reggie and Ronnie stepped from their car cautiously and drew weapons from their shoulder holsters.

Craig Harrison leant across the console operator and keyed the console's desk mounted mic. His voice was clipped, but clear, "Delta call signs, targets have weapons drawn. I repeat, targets have weapons drawn. This is Trojan Control authorising Command Protocol Three. Go live. Go live."

"Roger, Trojan Control, this is Delta Team Leader, acknowledged, Protocol Three. We are weapons live."

Kara was intensely focussed on the screen to her front. Reggie and Ronnie were approaching the door with weapons up. She instantly recognised the reason the Twins worked as a team. Reggie was left handed, Ronnie right. Between them they had full situational awareness for a gunfight. Kara got up and moved over to be beside Harrison. Without waiting she reached forward and pressed the transmit button on the console mic.

"Delta Teams, be aware, both assailants using mirror weaver stance. Assess ex-military, high-end operators."

Kara had no idea who the Delta team leader was but from his answer of, "Roger that. All Delta call signs, warn once," she knew they had the message.

The speaker and CCTV feed gave a disjointed and rather out-of-sync picture and sound show to the command centre. But it was effective.

The distinctive wail of an old fashioned, handheld megaphone exploded through the speaker, "ARMED POLICE,

ARMED POLICE! YOU ARE SURROUNDED! PUT YOUR WEAPONS DOWN AND RAISE YOUR HANDS IMMEDI-ATELY."

The CCTV showed that the effect on the Twins was as instant as desired. They halted in their approach to the door. Reggie, his tattoo showing on his lead hand, looked across to his partner. Even on the CCTV's rather grainy image the red laser dots of Police snipers were evident on Ronnie's back and head. Reggie crouched and placed his weapon on the ground, then stood up again and raised his hands high. Although the sound wasn't audible they could see his mouth moving. After a momentary delay Ronnie followed suit.

One blue overall-clad SCO19 operator came from the left of the office building, another from the right and two out of the front door. They held machine pistols at the high ready and ordered the two targets onto the ground. The Twins were cuffed and taken into custody with no further trouble.

Just as Kara breathed a deep sigh, Chaz came through on the phone.

"The Merc's taking the approach road to the Resort. Activate your teams."

Harrison leant forward and once more keyed his mic, "Sierra One, this is Trojan Control. Standby, standby."

The commander of the three SCO19 teams out at the New Start Resort acknowledged him.

With Tien's phone having the maximum number of open lines in use, Kara pulled her mobile out and called Sammi and Eugene on a similar multi-way setup, "Heads up, they're on their way. Illy in the Merc, with Thor."

"You sure it's not Professor Plum in the Ballroom with the lead piping?" Sammi replied.

"Pretty sure," Kara said and gave a small laugh. "Guide them in."

"Roger that."

36

Tien had been correct in her description of Shield Wood. Two miles long by two miles wide at its extremities, it was shaped almost exactly like a mediaeval shield, even having a wishbone curve on its top, northern-most edge. That salient marked the entrance to the New Start Resort with its five-bar gate and western-ranch style arch.

The one road that led from the gate was about three hundred yards long and ended in an expansive concrete apron with an extended raised platform running three quarters of its length. It had once been used as the loading dock and turning area for supermarket distribution trucks. The space would have allowed an articulated lorry to swing round as easily as a London cab. Now it was a vastly oversized carpark that swallowed a fleet of more than a dozen cars, all high-end saloons, of various models but all dark blue or black. Butting up against the raised platform and running beyond it was the large warehouse whose structure, some one hundred yards wide on its northern wall by fifty yards deep, dominated the space. To the east, west and south sides the dense wood was separated from the large metal shed by cleared areas, also concreted, about ten yards in width.

Halfway between the gate and the apron on the eastern side of the road was what had been the administration block for the supermarket operation but was now, according to Chris Sterling, home to the on-site security staff. It was a long, brick-built rectangle, about forty by fifteen yards in size and depending on how the inside had been fitted, could have played host to a considerable number of personnel.

Although Illy used the camp as a practical but invisible prison and therefore the security personnel were employed inside the buildings and not along the perimeter, the fence erected when it had been a distribution hub was still present. Ten feet high and running through the woods about sixty yards back from the warehouse, it was in a relatively poor state of repair and boasted no sophistication or electronic alarm measures. It had taken Eugene and Sammi about two minutes to get through it and move to the woods on the eastern side of the warehouse, directly behind the security block.

In the first hour after arriving they'd established that the north wall of the warehouse, where it extended past the raised loading dock, had a small Judas gate that was the only entrance in use. The massive roller door that had been in operation during the distribution days didn't look as if it had been opened in years. There were no windows at all in any wall of the structure and the six emergency exit doors, spaced at regular intervals to meet Health and Safety regulations, were now all heavily barred on the outside.

The separate security block had no windows along its rear, eastern facing wall either, but did have a non-barred emergency exit door set into the narrow southern wall. Eugene made the long trek around to the western woods, and observed from across the wide concrete apron that the front of the security block had eight windows, four either side of a centrally placed double door that opened inwards. He'd assessed it as probably having eight rooms, likely once offices that were now possible sleeping quarters but there was no guarantee. He couldn't observe the narrow northern wall at all as the trees thinned considerably the closer they got to the front of the site and he didn't risk being exposed.

Once he had rejoined Sammi they had reported all they knew to Kara, including that they had seen no sign of Brenda Sterling. However, for each working girl that went out one of the guards would leave from the security block, walk up to the main building, enter through the Judas gate, then shortly after they'd leave together in one of the cars. Just before Zoe made her call to Uncle Illy there had been twelve cars left in the large carpark.

Now, following Kara's orders, Sammi and Eugene moved swiftly. Sammi went back through the hole in the fence she and Eugene had made earlier. She turned on the small GPS beacon that Tien had given to her. Less than a minute later the SCO19 detachment leader, who held the other half of Tien's small locator system, emerged from the depths of the wood. He was followed by three squads, a total of twenty-four officers, all wearing full assault kit, including helmets and with their goggles pulled down into place. Sammi turned and led them back through the fence to where Eugene was waiting.

A squad member handed both Sammi and Eugene a tactical radio set of the type all the SCO19 operators had. Then Eugene led two squads off whilst Sammi took the commander and the remaining squad down to the trees that faced the rear of the security block. She knelt on the ground and the commander came next to her.

"I'm Mark Stroller."

Sammi liked him already as he hadn't bothered with rank.

"I'm Sammi. This is as far as we go until you're ready to move. The trees get steadily thinner, so you'll be spotted any further forward. You good to go?"

"Yep, all we've been doing is playing in the sand."

Sammi gave a small laugh, understanding that the commander and his assault teams had been practising their drills over and over since the likely tasking had come through. Back in the day she had actually used sand tables to draw out operational scenarios and practise them. Now she knew they'd more likely used electronic tablets and screens but it was nice to know the phrasing hadn't changed. She definitely knew that they'd studied the images that were available and with the information she and Eugene had passed back via Kara they would have been resolving their action-on plans until they'd been relatively happy with them. There was never a time they'd be completely happy, but the time available for planning always had to be balanced by the time for actually doing.

"What's our call signs Mark Stroller?"

"I'm Sierra One, you're two and your oppo is three," he whispered.

Sammi's trailing mic and earphone connected to the phone in her pocket. She keyed the mic-button, "Kara, I'm in place, designate me Sierra Two. Eugene is Sierra Three. I'm now handing control to Sierra One." Then she disconnected her phone line and switched the tactical radio on.

Eugene, slightly out of breath by his swift transit in escorting the other two SCO19 squads to the area of the woods directly behind the rear, south-facing wall of the warehouse called in, "Roger. Likewise. Confirm I'm Sierra Three and I'm going to site the recce position."

He then took a deep breath and set off on his own to get to the western side of the woods. He'd be the only one with eyes on the front of the security block.

"Sierra One this is Trojan Control. Confirm status," said the female operator with the trace of a Scottish accent.

"Alpha, Bravo, Charlie, this is Sierra One, check in, over," Stroller whispered into his throat mic.

The man just five yards behind where Sammi knelt, said, "Alpha One roger."

The two team leaders kneeling in the southern wood also keyed their mics, "Bravo One roger."

"Charlie One roger."

"Trojan Control from Sierra One. Status Green," Stroller said.

"Roger Sierra One. You have TacCon. Acknowledge."

"Roger Trojan Control, Sierra One has TacCon," Mark Stroller said and with that took full command authority to launch any action within the Resort area.

Sammi focussed on quieting her breathing and concentrating on her surroundings.

The woods were never completely silent. The faintest of breezes disturbed the summer fullness of the leaves and set up mutual and continued rustling. Sammi gazed upwards through the briefest of gaps in the foliage above. She glimpsed chunky clouds bumbling their way across a deepening blue backdrop as the sky began to acknowledge the sun's passage to the horizon. But it wasn't the sight or sounds of nature that drew her attention. She was struck by the amount of fidgeting she could hear from the squad behind her. Used to a much more rigorous noise discipline, she glanced sideways at Stroller, but he seemed oblivious. She understood why the assault teams had arrived into the last staging point as late as possible. Had they come in earlier she was certain someone would have heard them. But now it wouldn't matter, for she reckoned it was about to get quite noisy before much longer.

"Sierra One, from Trojan Two. One Mercedes, confirmed driver is Thor, no identification on passenger. Now west on small approach turning to Camp location. ETA Camp one minute."

"Trojan Two, Sierra One. One minute. Roger."

Sammi had a limited line of sight to the arched gateway at the entrance but she could see the Mercedes travelling at speed along the small lane that ran past the camp. As it approached the entrance point it slewed to a violent, skewed halt on the far side of the five-bar gate. Thor got out.

"All teams, this is Sierra One. Targets are on site. Standby. Standby."

Sammi watched as Thor went out of view, masked from her sightline by the security block. She guessed he was opening the gate, for he was quickly back in the car and it was powering up the single road towards the security block and the warehouse. Almost immediately the Mercedes started blaring its horn.

"Sierra One, this is Sierra Three," Eugene's deep voice sounded mellow, almost relaxed despite his efforts to make his position in time. "Central doors on security block are open. I have four, check that, six personnel, all trying to hurriedly put jackets on and straighten ties. Be aware at least three of those are confirmed armed, pistols in shoulder holsters. Mercedes is braking hard… Thor is out of the vehicle… As is Illy. We have target confirmation. Copy?"

"Roger Sierra Three, we have target confirmation," Stroller said.

Sammi reached out and put her hand on Stroller's arm. They were shielded by the security block but in direct line they were only about fifteen yards from where the Mercedes sat on the other side of the building. It wasn't far enough to attenuate Illy's raised voice and his near-hysterical raving in Russian. Sammi leant in to Stroller so she could whisper, "He's yelling about none of them answering their phones. He's telling all of them that he will," she paused, "Nice, he's going to cut their cocks off and feed them to their wives or sisters or mothers if they do that to him again. Charming. More importantly, he wants two of them to come with him, the rest are to get," she paused again, "Nope, didn't get that bit, but whatever he wants them, oh he wants four of them to go down to the gate and wait there for, ha," Sammi laughed quietly. "He wants them to wait for some PI bitch and her friends who think they're going to walk in here and take what's his."

"Sierra One, this is Sierra Three. You have a total of ten security now in front of the building. I guess some of them were asleep. The last four look somewhat dishevelled. Illy, Thor and two of them are heading up to the warehouse. The other eight are hustling back into the security block."

"Sierra Three, are weapons drawn by target and his escorts?" Stroller asked.

"Negative Sierra One. No weapons visible at this time," Eugene answered.

Stroller knew the walk from the security block to the

warehouse was about one hundred and fifty yards. He had a clear line of sight on most of it. All he needed to do was wait a few seconds for Illy to come into full view.

"Bravo and Charlie teams, from Sierra One, move to jump off. Advise when in position."

Unsighted by the bulk of the warehouse, Illy had no idea that as he was walking towards the building, sixteen heavily armed personnel were moving across the ten yards of open ground from the woods behind it over to the rear wall. Once there, Bravo team moved to the eastern corner and Charlie to the west.

"Sierra One, Bravo in position."

"Sierra One, Charlie in position."

"Sierra One this is Sierra Three. The four guys Illy is sending down to the gate have reappeared at the door to the block. They're armed with assault rifles. Look like AK's. They're heading down the road on foot. Nil sighting of the other four. Assess they're still in the block building."

"Roger, Sierra Three."

Stroller was watching Illy carefully through a set of small field glasses. He was about fifty yards from the Judas gate.

"Alpha Team, move to jump off."

"Roger."

The confirmation was hardly needed as eight people moved past Stroller and Sammi and made their way across the clearing to nestle up against the rear wall of the security block. Half went left and half went right. The leader of the squad looked back at Stroller and gave him a thumbs up.

Illy was almost at the small Judas gate.

"Bravo, Charlie, position two."

From where Sammi was she could see the eight-strong Bravo Squad moving along the eastern wall of the warehouse to the northern most corner. She knew that Charlie Squad was doing the same on the opposite side.

Even from over a hundred yards away they could hear the massive thumping Illy had started on the metal frame of the warehouse wall.

"All call signs, standby, standby," Stroller said. Sammi noticed the hand he was holding the small field glasses in was shaking slightly.

'Good,' she thought. 'You're about to send people into harm's way, you should be nervous.'

Libby Cooper was designated as Bravo Two and as such she stood directly behind her squad leader with her left hand up on his shoulder and her right controlling the weapon she wore across her chest. The twenty-six year old Police Constable had been a member of the Met for eight years. Having grown up in rural Suffolk she had wanted to join the Force since visiting London with her parents during the Queen's Golden Jubilee celebrations in June 2002. The then thirteen year old had been awestruck by the Police horses. She had fallen in love with the image of the beautiful female constable atop the jet black Irish Warmblood. The horse, standing almost seventeen hands high, had serenely guided the swarming crowd with the occasional nudge of its long head. It seemed so strong, yet glamorous and combined perfectly the young Libby's love of horses with her sense of adventure.

She had joined the Met one month past her eighteenth birthday. After a two year probation she had spent a year and a half in the crime squad, planning how best to work her way into the Mounted Branch. Then, because a colleague was nervous going on her own, she tagged along to a familiarisation day with SCO19. Having never fired a gun in her life it came as a revelation to her and a surprise to the Sergeant controlling the range that PC Libby Cooper was a natural. The lure of the Mounted Branch was replaced by the pull of SCO19. Now a three-year veteran of the unit, she had been deployed on more than two hundred operations but not once had fired either her Glock17 pistol or the Heckler & Koch MP5 sub-machine gun in anger.

She felt the tremor of anticipation flowing from her squad leader, through her and onto Bravo Three who held his hand on her shoulder. She focused on the actions she would carry out and the drills that she had practised time and time and time again. The soft hum in her ears from the small integrated headset in her helmet provided a static accompaniment to the rising tension and the flow of adrenaline that her training tried to control. She heard the banging of a fist on the aluminium of the warehouse and heard a raised voice shouting in a foreign language that she guessed was Russian. The tension notched up further, she could feel her heart beat increase and the hum in her ears seemed to buzz.

"Go. Go. Go."

Her squad leader was moving by the end of the first word. He broke from her hand and she moved immediately after him. They came round the front corner of the building and raised their weapons into their shoulders. Libby moved slightly to the right to get clear lines of sight. Immediately to her front she could see two men. Both wore dark suits and both stood outside the small open door that had swung inward to the warehouse.

Beyond them she could see the lead elements of Charlie Squad rounding the far corner of the building. Both Bravo and Charlie closed the gap on the door rapidly.

The two men, in the process of going through the open door, hadn't noticed what was closing in on them. That lasted for another second. The one furthest forward was just about to step over the threshold when he turned his head to the left and seemed to look straight at Libby. She heard her squad leader yell, "ARMED POLICE. ARMED POLICE. STAND STILL." The call was also taken up by Charlie Squad's leader.

The two men at the door seemed to be caught in a comedic double take, looking from one side to the other. The one furthest back from the opening immediately raised his hands and stood very still indeed. The man to his front, stocky and wearing a pinstripe suit that Libby thought looked more appropriate for a banker in the city, finally decided that ducking in to the shed was a better option. But he'd left it a fraction too long.

Alerted by the calls of 'Armed Police' someone inside the

warehouse decided to slam the door shut and did it with force. They would have succeeded had it not been for Pinstripe's hand that was gripping the doorframe. He yelled out as three of his four fingers were fractured, let go of the frame and stepped backward. Libby's squad leader caught the left hand flap of the immaculately tailored suit and unceremoniously flung him backward. The adrenaline-filled power of the action caused the stocky man to crash into his partner and sent both of them spiralling backwards. Libby saw them fall but ignored them. Securing the men was someone else's job.

Her squad leader pushed the swinging door back on its hinges and entered the bright, halogen-lit interior of the large warehouse. He immediately stepped to his right and swung back around a full 180 degrees, thereby ensuring he wasn't silhouetted in the doorway and checking that no one was nestled behind it about to take a shot at him or his squad. "Clear."

Libby hadn't even broken stride as the call came to her. She went through the door and moved to her left, knowing without looking that the remainder of Bravo and Charlie Squads were following close behind her.

Her eyes swept over an interior that could have comfortably accommodated a football pitch and her mind processed the scene, looking for targets and threats. Since her very first live operation she'd never ceased to be amazed at the phenomenon that occurred when she stepped into a threat environment. It was true for her that time dragged into slow motion. She found the rapid assimilation of scenes and movement was achieved almost effortlessly.

To her far left, along the long wall, were a series of openings that separated into four distinct blocks. At the opening nearest to her was a young girl, Libby assessed her as probably no older than twenty, just stepping out into the main space. She was wrapped in a towel with another wrapped around her head. The vents that ran along the length of a false ceiling had steam rising from them. Libby's mind registered it as a shower block. Nil threat.

To her rear right quarter she heard shouts of 'Armed Police. Stand Still.' But they were of no concern to her, she had her own area of responsibility. Her eyes, moving left to right from the shower block, took in a broad sweep of half-height cubicles that filled the main expanse of floor. Young women, in various states of dress, were standing at random points throughout the space. Each block of cubicles had clear laneways running in a grid pattern throughout them, giving free access to the whole. She could hear some screams, high-pitched, terrified. A few of the women that had been visible were beginning to drop out of sight. Libby thought it looked a little like one of those fairground games where the gophers ducked before you could hit them with a mallet.

As her eyes swept past the cubicles she saw, in the third laneway, a man with a blond ponytail standing still, his hands raised. A shoulder holster visible under his open jacket.

She began to move directly for him, "ARMED POLICE. PUT YOUR HANDS ON YOUR HEAD. GET DOWN ON YOUR KNEES. DO IT NOW." Her sights were on the central mass of the target she knew had been designated Thor but her peripheral vision was still searching left and right.

Thor complied with her shouted instruction almost in time with her words.

"Charlie, from Bravo Two, confirm you have Thor," she called, knowing that the large number two painted in Day-Glo yellow on the rear of her helmet and back of her flak jacket would identify her whereabouts to the members of Charlie Squad coming behind her. They had been tasked with the securing of any prisoners.

"Bravo Two, Charlie Five. I have him, you're clear."

Libby moved past Thor, leaving him kneeling in the laneway as she moved deeper into the space. She didn't look behind, knowing that her back was covered. To her left she saw Bravo Three moving forward in line with her and beyond him, Bravo Four. To her right was a large gap that should have been filled with Bravo Five and Six but further over was Bravo Seven and Eight.

As she passed each cubicle she could see two single beds, topped and tailed into the space. A couple of cheap drawer units doubled as bedside cabinets to separate the sleeping spaces. In most cubicles the young women were crouching down beside, or hiding under, the beds. As she passed one space two boys, maybe in their late teens and dressed in sweat pants and singlets, were huddled together on the floor.

Moving quickly she was now almost halfway to the rear wall. It was host to about fifteen doors and presumably was the area that housed the video rooms they had been briefed about.

A sound of a shot, rapidly followed by two more came from way behind her to the right and the high-pitched screams of the women, which had been lessening, increased in their intensity again. Libby's heart rate spiked. Almost simultaneously she had movement to her immediate front left and right.

With all her training Libby knew that rapid movement meant one of two things, both of which were initiated by an evolutionary desire to survive.

The first type of movement was to flee, but it took speed of thought and an ability to process events quickly. That meant it was much less common than she had first thought when starting out with SCO19.

Hence, out of all the women visible when she had entered the building, very, very few had dropped down inside the first three seconds. Most took much longer to react and some, by virtue of them still standing and screaming even now, almost half a minute later, would have, in by-gone days, been trampled by a mammoth.

The second type of rapid movement in an emergency situation was much more of a concern for Libby. It showed a speed of thought and reaction that was honed by either training or a naturally gifted predatory instinct. At worst, both things combined. In by-gone days these were the people who had brought down the mammoths.

Libby saw two men rise up in front of her, almost exactly positioned at her eleven and one o'clock positions. The one on her left was Illy Sultanov. Seemingly spurred on by the gunfire that had just sounded he was turning away and making to run. To her front right was a tall, well-built man probably about the same age as she was. Dressed in jeans and a black T-shirt his physique was impressive. He wore a shoulder holster but it was hanging empty and the pistol it had been home to was in his hands. The muzzle was rapidly coming round to Libby.

Pavel Ivanovich Leshev was a gifted soldier who had physically survived the Crimea and Ukrainian campaigns as a member of the elite GRU 45th Spetsnaz Regiment. A born fighter with natural aggression he was very proud of his marksmanship. Clever and quick he had survived many an engagement by being aggressive and accurate. He had joined Illy's security on the recommendation of his cousin who had worked for the gangster, as Pavel thought of Illy, for about five years. Enjoying some post-operational leave from his latest trip into the Ukrainian border region, Pavel had come to visit his cousin in London the previous year. Impressed with his cousin's fancy car and fancier apartment he decided that money, cars and girls seemed like a better reward for work than being shot at by Ukrainians. It took him a while to resign and another couple of months to get a fake passport sorted. He'd joined Illy's team just six weeks ago. His body had left the Spetsnaz but his mind was still firmly in the combat zones that surrounded the Sea of Azov.

As the first shouts had reached his non-English under-standing ears he had done what any good operator would do; taken cover and observed.

He'd seen his employer running and sliding into the space just across the open laneway from him. Pavel had signalled for him to be quiet.

Through the gaps in the cubicle walls he had seen blue-clad combat soldiers moving into the warehouse. He'd watched as they had quickly overpowered one of his comrades who, with him, had guarded the whores in the warehouse. Then he'd watched them take the surrender of the little prick with the ponytail who was Illy's personal bodyguard. Pavel thought that was disgraceful. He had given up without even a slight effort. Pavel hadn't worked for the gangster for long but his military mind said the gangster was in charge. That meant he was the Officer running the show. He would be loyal to Pavel. Every Spetsnaz Officer had sworn his life to die for his troops. Pavel was sure Illy would do the same. Of that Pavel had no doubt and so Pavel would be loyal to him. Regardless of how short a time he had been here.

As the seconds ticked by Pavel assessed his options. He could see only two. One was not acceptable to him. The Ukrainians were rumoured to torture and execute any Russian Special Forces prisoners. He peered out through the gaps and watched the line of blue soldiers moving forward. He saw, far in the bottom corner of the warehouse, his cousin rise up. He heard shouts and saw his cousin fire a shot at one of the enemy soldiers. Then two more shots sounded and he saw his cousin's head spray a crimson cloud into the air.

Pavel signalled to the gangster to get ready to run. He raised three fingers up, then two then one, then signalled for Illy to go. At the same time he stood up and prepared to buy his commanding officer time in the face of an enemy attack.

Libby's eyes were sighted along the barrel of her MP5, yet she could see above, below and to the sides of it as her field of vision seemed to expand in the threat environment. She saw the dense, black metal of a pistol muzzle come through the last degrees of travel toward her. She saw in high definition the fractional movement of the physically impressive man's hands as he began to squeeze the trigger.

At a distance of fifteen feet she fired once and observed a hole, neat and precise form instantly in the middle of the man's forehead. A puff of red bloomed behind him. Life left his eyes like a switch had been flicked.

She registered another four rounds hitting the man's wide torso as her colleagues to right and left engaged a fraction of a second later. With still no break in stride Libby continued moving through the space.

"ILLY SULTANOV, ILLY SULTANOV. STAND STILL. ARMED POLICE. STAND STILL OR I FIRE," she yelled at the slightly overweight man who was running for the rooms at the rear. He didn't slow but angled towards the door to the far left. Libby broke into a sprint. She thought about firing but he had presented no threat, she had seen no weapon and her rules of engagement didn't allow her to just shoot a fleeing subject in the back of the head. Not unless she thought he was a suicide bomber and the rational part of her brain dismissed that as an option.

She was younger and much, much fitter so closed the gap to the man very quickly. He had opened the door, stepped inside and was trying to ram it shut when Libby hit it with her left shoulder. The wood flew open and the leading edge caught the Russian high on his brow sending him splaying backwards. Libby stepped in to the room in time to see Illy skidding back across the cheap linoleum floor. His already bleeding head cannoned into a video camera tripod positioned at the foot of a sagging double bed that was covered in a gaudy and cheap looking bedspread.

Keeping her weapon trained on the seemingly unconscious body she scanned the room. Cowering in the corner, between the bed and a long wall-mounted bench that held a printer, various small knives, scissors, cut-outs of photos and what looked like a stack of passports, was a middle-aged woman. Her eyes were heavy with dark bags and her mouth was drawn back in a silent study of terror. Yet Libby was mostly struck by how so out-of-place she looked in this room. From her hair and clothes she would have been more suited to a Woman's Institute meeting rather than a video sex suite.

"PUT YOUR HANDS ON YOUR HEAD. HANDS ON YOUR HEAD NOW. DO IT NOW."

The woman did as she was ordered.

Libby dropped the volume of her voice and asked the question she already knew the answer to, "What's your name?"

"Brenda. Brenda Sterling."

After a further ten minutes Libby walked out of the Judas gate back into the late evening sun. Her goggles down around her neck and her helmet in her left hand. The scene to her front showed Alpha Squad arrayed in front of a row of eight men lying outside the security block, their hands cuffed with plastic ties and a collection of assault rifles piled behind them.

In front of the loading dock, half of Charlie Squad were standing in front of a similar scene but with only six prisoners laid out on the ground. Illy was sat separately from them whilst a medic patched up the deep gash on his brow.

In the middle of the concrete apron five police vans were disgorging what looked to be about fifty uniformed officers. Their Sergeants calling them into groups to brief them on what they would be doing up at the warehouse. Libby squinted and wiped the sweat from her eyes with the back of her leather glove. Mark Stroller was coming up to her accompanied by the man and woman who had met the assault squads in the woods.

"You okay Libby?" Stroller asked.

"Yes Gov," she paused and considered what she had said. She knew there and then that she was completely okay. The killing of the man in the black T-shirt was justified. She had no doubt that he was going to kill her, so she had killed him. She looked between Stroller and the two civilians. The man, a large black guy with a gentle smile and soft eyes, held her gaze.

"Yes Gov. I'm fine," she repeated more for herself than her boss.

"Good, Libby. Good," Stroller said.

The black man nodded at her and the blonde woman patted her on the shoulder as she walked past.

Libby walked the short distance to the duty forensics supervisor and handed her firearm over, along with the other six members of SCO19 Bravo Squad who had fired during the raid. As she waited for the paperwork to begin she turned and looked back at Stroller and the two civilians. They had stopped just short of the Judas gate. As a member of Charlie Squad escorted Brenda Sterling out of the warehouse, Stroller stepped forward and introduced himself and his two companions.

Kara was hugging her brother and feeling truly thrilled at the outcome. She raised her head from his shoulder and looked around the command vehicle. Tony Reynolds was shaking hands with Moya Little, Matt Sexton was shaking hands with Tien, Craig Harrison was making his way down the line of console operators, congratulating each in turn. The atmosphere was relaxed and exuberant. But as Kara turned her gaze she suddenly felt flat. She stepped back from her brother and gave him a kiss on the cheek, "Thanks Bro. It was great working with you."

"You too. Hey where ar-" but he stopped from asking her the question as he followed her movement and saw Zoe sitting at the table. The dancer's poise was unbowed but tears were running freely down her face. David moved over to where Tien and Matt were.

Kara sat, reached her hand onto Zoe's arm and received a sad, forced smile in reply.

"Is there anything I can do for you?" Kara asked quietly.

Zoe shook her head.

"I'm truly sorry Zoe."

A small sniff and a smaller nod were all Zoe could manage.

"Would you like to go to Michael?"

Zoe shut her eyes, "Oh God Kara. What am I going to tell him?"

"Tell him your parents are alive and well," Kara said trying to make her voice sound lighter than she felt.

"And then tell him they're cheats and forgers? Tell him that they've been responsible for making the lives of hundreds of girls a tortured misery? That they've been lying to both of us since we were little kids?" Her voice was brittle, but in it was the beginning of the edge that Kara had noticed when she first met her. A strength, that once the tears stopped, would reassert itself, take control. Zoe brushed the tears away with her fingers. "How long do you think they'll get?"

"I'm not sure. DCI Reynolds is probably the best person to

ask but they'll want your parents to testify, so there's likely a deal to cut. I'm sure it's your Uncle Illy they'd rather get."

"I think we'll drop the Uncle. We may just call him Illy the Bastard from now on," Zoe said it quite politely and gave a little half-smile.

Kara reciprocated.

"To be honest, I don't think my parents deserve a deal," Zoe said.

Kara looked at her and had an intuition that it was unlikely Zoe's attitude would mellow over time.

"When shall Michael and I come round to settle your fee?"

"Take your time, there's no rush," Kara said and thought that the whole topic of money would make an interesting conversation when the time came. She became aware that the background celebratory noises in the vehicle had quietened.

She turned to see Craig Harrison bending over the console mic, "Foxtrot One, say again."

"Trojan Control from Foxtrot One, we have eyes on targets. Confirm Smirnoff and Penny are at the Fulham residence. Permission to intercept?"

"Roger that Foxtrot One. Proceed when ready."

The tension returned to the command vehicle but it was relatively short lived. A full squad of heavily armed SCO19 operators was an overwhelming force for the two unprepared occupants of the Range Rover. Less than a minute had passed before the call came in.

"Trojan Control, this is Foxtrot. Targets secured. Nil force."

Harrison, understanding the latest arrest had proceeded with no resort to firearms, authorised the last Police action of the operation.

"Echo Team Lead, from Trojan Control. Proceed when ready."

Two and a half miles directly south east of the command vehicle the final squad of SCO19 operators accelerated their cars down Avey Lane and swung hard into Illy's driveway. Dinger had a ringside seat for an almost textbook house assault. As Yanina, Mrs Beeton and Cinders were being led away, a Police Sergeant called him by name and Dinger stood up and stretched for the first time in days.

Kara texted Eugene that all was complete and he could keep his word.

It took Eugene another fifteen minutes to get back to his car and drive into Waltham Cross. He parked between the transit van and the light blue Mondeo. Swinging the rear doors of the van open he stood back while Anatoly stepped down.

"Thank you," the Russian said as he took the offered car key.

"One other thing," Eugene said. "We're the good guys. Emilia's not dead. She's not even harmed but she and all the rest of Illy's team are under arrest."

Anatoly stared at him and Eugene wondered if the big man was contemplating hitting out in payment for the cruel subterfuge, but instead the Russian merely laughed.

"Ha, that is good. You did it well. Is Illy under arrest too?"

"Yes."

"Shame you didn't kill him for real. He is a bad man."

Eugene considered that as he watched Anatoly drive away.

As Kara checked the text from Eugene confirming all was complete, Tony Reynolds came over to her.

"I need you to come up to Huntingdon with me now."

"Now? Will tomorrow morning not do?"

"Not really. We can do this politely or I can have my DS there," he indicated Moya Little who was currently talking to David, "place you under arrest. Which do you prefer?"

"I think polite always wins. I'll come with you and have Tien follow me up. She can drive me home when we're finished." She saw the slight doubt pass through his eyes and thought, 'Advantage me.'

37

Saturday Night. Huntingdon

Kara sat comfortably in the chair on one side of the table. Her hands were in her lap. The tips of her fingers and thumbs pressing together with the lightest of pressures. She was concentrating completely on that pressure. Focusing her mind on it, listening to the rhythm of her heart in her ears and matching it to the rhythm of the pulse she could feel in her thumbs. She slowed her breathing, but not so any external observer could see. Just slowed it and then held it for four seconds, then breathed out. Again she controlled it so it wouldn't be noticed. Again to a count of four, then once her lungs were empty she held for another four. Then in again. All the time focussing on the tips of her fingers, listening, feeling, focussing. She gazed across the table.

Moya Little and Tony Reynolds sat opposite. The tape recorder was on and above it a little green light glowed softly. Kara gave them her best smile.

"Kara, have you ever been in Huntingdon before?" Moya asked.

"Yes, a few times I'm sure."

"What about last week?"

"Yes. Definitely. I was here carrying out a surveillance operation for a client. Her name was Boon and I was asked to follow her girlfriend. To find out if she was cheating."

"What time did you finish?"

"About two or three in the morning."

"Did you- "

Kara raised her hand up and stopped Moya in mid-sentence. "Listen folks, I'm not silly. You have a dead body on the ground near to where I parked my car. I do read the news. I would have come forward and volunteered any information had I had it. But I didn't. And I still haven't. So let's cut to the chase. I will volunteer a complete file detailing all my movements. I'll tell you or even take you to the site where I parked my car. I'll reconstruct every aspect of my Friday night, Saturday morning. But I have to tell you, it won't put me anywhere close to a dead body, wherever it was, because I can tell you one thing with certainty. I'm observant. I'm pretty sure I'd have seen a body on the ground. So all my help won't actually help."

Moya looked sideways to Reynolds. It was a subtle glance but Kara was quite happy she had rattled the Sergeant. Kara continued, "Unless of course, you have some evidence on me. I know you raided my office, my home and Tien's home this morning. Seems so much longer ago doesn't it?"

This time Kara saw Reynolds react. She watched him racking his brain trying to figure out if he had let that nugget slip out during their long day. She thought about letting him hang but decided to just move things along.

"I know about the raid because Tien and I have surveil-lance measures that alert us to break-ins. Oh and you'll have to pay for nice new doors, you know that Tony, don't you?" She had to stop a smile crossing her face as she watched Tony almost involuntarily nod in response to her question.

"So, do you have any evidence? We know you took lots of things away. PCs and mobiles and a pair of my shoes. Nice new ones that I specifically bought for the Huntingdon job. You'll see there's very little wear on them. About one night's worth of walking around this town." 'Or a couple of hours of walking around my little courtyard at home since buying them at Camden Markets last Saturday,' she thought but decided not to add.

"Do you have any evidence? Because Tien wondered about the PCs and mobiles you took. She told me they were all blank. All of them set up by her to be able to clone to mine when we need to do a new job."

She watched both Reynolds and Little struggling to process where the interview was going.

"That's not illegal by the way. We do it for client confidentiality. Now, you took my mobile off me when I arrived here. That's," she checked her watch, "an hour and a half ago. I'd have thought that was enough time for your tech-heads to figure out if there's anything of worth on it. Wouldn't you?" She didn't give either a chance to respond, "So, either front up some evidence or let me go. What do you say?"

Reynolds seemed to finally have recovered his composure. "Kara, that's all very good but I have questions for you."

Again she raised her hand, "No actually you don't. Am I under arrest?"

"No," he answered through gritted teeth.

"Am I free to go?"

"Yes," he said in the same tight manner.

"Well then, I'll be off. I've cooperated fully and offered you a complete portfolio of my whereabouts and movements. I have no information of use to you and I need to go to bed. I'm tired as I'm sure you both are too. Good job today by the way. Awesome result. And when it comes to locking all of Illy's crew up I'll be glad to be a star witness. Likewise when you lock the Sterlings up. You will be doing that won't you?"

Reynolds nodded.

"Excellent. Because I have to say I think they're almost more to blame than that sad bastard of a Russian. Anyway, have a nice night." Kara stood and waited for Reynolds to terminate the interview and escort her out of the station.

Reynolds took his time shutting down the formalities. Kara

imagined he was trying desperately to come up with a reason to keep her. Once he concluded he didn't have anything, he stood and opened the door. As he led her up the corridor, DCS Laura Mitchell came out from the video monitoring suite. She stepped in front of Reynolds.

"It's okay Tony. I'll take Miss Wright from here." Kara saw the confusion on Reynolds face as he stepped aside.

"Hello. My name's Laura Mitchell. I'm the Detective Chief Superintendent here. Can I show you out Kara?"

Kara was intently aware that Reynolds had not been expecting this. She looked at the woman in front of her. The DCS was in uniform, her shoes, skirt, white shirt and black tie all pristine even given the lateness of the hour. Her rank slides with the pip and crown above were the same as a Lieutenant Colonel's rank from the military and familiar to Kara. Both women were a similar height but the DCS had lighter hair, a few flecks of grey visible at the roots and Kara estimated she was probably in her mid-forties. She still had a young complexion and a pleasant smile. There was an intelligence in her eyes and Kara sensed a firmness of purpose.

"It's fine by me Laura. Thank you."

Mitchell led and Kara followed. But as Kara half expected they didn't head to the station's entrance. Instead she found herself following Laura into an office on the second floor. The nameplate on the door showed it was Mitchell's own. An older man, thin, with a receding hairline, long features, a straight nose and a faded scar on his chin was standing to the side of the desk. He was dressed in a dark three-piece suit, white shirt and banded red and blue tie. His open jacket revealed he had a fob watch in his waistcoat pocket, the gold chain of which looped across his middle. He extended a long hand, the liver spots showing on his leathery skin. Kara reached out and accepted his greeting.

"Good evening Kara. My name's Franklyn. I have a proposition for you, if you would be so kind as to hear me out?" He spoke with no accent. Such a rare occurrence that on the occasions Kara encountered it her interest was immediately piqued. She prided herself on logical analysis, in-depth preparation and always, always taking the extra precautions to be safe. But she was also a sucker for an enigma and sometimes she just went with her gut. Her gut was telling her that Franklyn was a man she wanted to get to know.

"Go on," she said.

"Please sit." He extended his hand to one of the visitor chairs in front of the desk. Kara sat. Mitchell didn't. Instead she patted Kara gently on the shoulder and left the office, shutting the door with a gentle click. Kara glanced round and then returned her focus to Franklyn. He settled into the adjacent visitor's chair and turned to face her.

"There are no tape devices in here. There are no tricks, this is not entrapment. I do not expect you to believe me so I will not expect you to acknowledge anything one way or the other. However," Kara watched as he placed his long, slim fingers into the exact position she had put her own into at the beginning of her interview with Reynolds. The tips just pressing together. "I am thoroughly impressed. Whoever killed a drug dealer in Huntingdon a week ago was an expert in certain skills and more importantly," Franklyn paused and gave her the most endearing smile, "much more importantly, Kara, they knew how to clean up so that there was nothing," he separated his fingers one by one and placed his now cupped hands in his lap, "absolutely nothing left for anyone to find."

Kara waited.

"That's a rare skillset," he continued. "An even rarer one if it turns out that an individual like that also has a knack for investigating incidents. Perhaps using different methods to the norm. Gaining information, tracking people, observing them, making arrests possible on occasions that otherwise would never have materialised. Almost exactly what happened today with our old friend Chekov."

Franklyn leant back a little in his chair but didn't add anything more. Kara knew the tactic. Say nothing, see if she would fill in the space, see if she would engage further. Her training told her to say nothing, do nothing, give nothing. But as she sat in the office and looked around, looked at the photos and certificates on Mitchell's walls and much more so, looked at Franklyn, she knew that her training was dependant on circumstance. It was designed to not engage, not give anything away, not open up, not betray her comrades when in the face of an enemy. This was different. This was intriguing. She actually wanted to know more, especially about the man to her left.

"Go on," she said again.

Franklyn allowed himself another smile. A warm expression that Kara found herself reciprocating. "I am long retired," he said. "But Laura and I represent some people who would find a combination of skillsets such as I have described, very attractive. Very useable. Very worthwhile."

"Yet I notice Laura isn't here," Kara said.

"Yes. That is a little tenet of ours, self-imposed. We see it as a matter of honourable necessity. Call it a separation of powers. A protection of the rightful forces of law and order from," he paused and smirked. "Well, shall we just say from those forces that would be able to take a fresh approach, and leave it at that?"

Kara thought about the implications of what he had said. She finally spoke, "So Franklyn, what would these people you represent need these skills for? What might this fresh approach be used for?"

"The skills could be convenient on those occasions when the normal system has difficulty investigating. Difficulty apprehending. Difficulty achieving a just outcome. The freshness of the approach could be all the difference."

"And would these people protect their fresh and skilful asset?" Kara asked and held the gaze of the old, yet vibrant, blue eyes that stared back at her.

Franklyn said it almost imperceptibly, "No, not at all. But the rewards would be handsome."

"I don't think I need money, for once in my life," Kara said with a self-deprecating sarcasm.

"That's good to know Kara. Well done if it's true. But money and materialism is always more fun when underpinned by even more money. However, I wasn't only referring to financial rewards. There would be opportunities to exercise skills that might otherwise become rusty. Perhaps the chance to do something that matters. And I suppose, not to be over-looked, the altruistic reward of making the world a better place. Even in a small way."

Kara gave no outward indication but she reflected that whoever had briefed Franklyn had done it well. She had been read, profiled. He was hitting all those pressure points that she would respond to. She was being recruited. She should have felt manipulated, potentially used. But she didn't.

He continued, "And I realise it is of no interest to you, but I'm told the death of a Huntingdon drug dealer would be classified as unsolved and closed forever. There would be no follow-up. Ever."

Kara sat very still and thought through the proposition. Despite her best efforts she felt the thrill of operations, the rush of going into harm's way, the excitement of danger building in her.

She knew she had a half-smile on her face as she turned to look at the old man. "And how Franklyn, would you know when you've found the person to take on these tasks?"

"Oh, I think I'd know when I'd met the right person," he stood and extended his hand again, "Miss Wright."

Acknowledgements

Quite simply this book couldn't have been written without the generous time, enduring patience and good humoured tolerance afforded to me by the following people:

To Sara for all the advice, in-depth information and not least, the patient proof-reading. The thin blue line is being ably supported by safe hands.

To Kirrilee for taking the time to write gory emails about an enthralling subject. I am glad you enjoyed it as much as I was intrigued by it.

To my happy-go-lucky, ex-colleague Sam for the reminders of how it was in her early days and for the Russian insults, 'spasibo'.

To Mark and Guy for the latest information in an ever-changing arena and for the never-ending banter on Facebook. I only mention you two in this acknowledgment to see if you actually notice. This not being a pop-up book, it is doubtful.

To Giles for the help with the inner workings of little books and to Rhiannon for the inside track of what happens behind reception desks. Thank you both for taking the time to answer my bizarre queries.

To Anne and her 200 students who have dissected Chapter One for their coursework. I can only hope you enjoyed it as much as I was terrified by the prospect of it.

I also want to belatedly thank Elaine Fry, Will Yeoman, Xan Ashbury, John Wyatt, Stephen Gamble, Roy Forbes and the staff at my local Libraries. Thanks for taking the time to review, interview me about, and support my former offering.

Finally, to Jacki. Your support, encouragement, patience and sense of humour keeps me sane. Not only when I'm writing but in all of my life. Thanks honey, I love you very much.

About the Author

Ian was born in Northern Ireland in 1966. At eighteen he joined the Royal Air Force; originally training as an aircraft technician he was later commissioned as an Intelligence Officer. Throughout his Service he had the pleasure of working alongside some "right eejits" whom he still feels lucky to call friends. On leaving the Service he relocated to Western Australia and is now surrounded by a resident mob of Kangaroos who bounce past his house each day. They remind him of his previous colleagues.

His first novel **A Time To Every Purpose**, an alternative history with a religious twist, was published independently in 2014 and gained positive critical acclaim.

He is currently working on the next in the Wright & Tran Series of detective novels.

Enjoyed the Book?
Leave a review

Follow Ian at:

Web: www.ianandrewauthor.com

Blog: www.viewsfromtheridge.com

Twitter: @ianandrewauthor

Facebook: facebook.com/viewsfromtheridge

Email: ian@viewsfromtheridge.com

Flight Path
The Second Wright & Tran Novel

Kara Wright and Tien Tran, combat veterans of an elite intelligence unit, now make their living as Private Investigators. Often working the mundane, just occasionally they get to use all their former training.

*"I'd like you to make sure
the dead are really dead."*

So it is that the enigmatic Franklyn tasks Kara and Tien to investigate the apparent suicide of a local celebrity. Within days the women are embarked on a pursuit that leads halfway around the globe and into the darkest recesses of the human condition. Kara, Tien and their team will endure mental stress worse than anything they experienced from combat and, like combat, not everyone makes it home.

...Wright and Tran are the best in the business. Andrew's own experience working with Military Intelligence provides his work with authenticity and heart... He is an author who can be relied upon to deliver a good – no, much more than that – a great read.
The West Australian

Fall Guys
The Third Wright & Tran Novel

Kara Wright and Tien Tran, combat veterans of an elite
intelligence unit, now make their living as Private Investigators. Often working the mundane, just occasionally they get to
use all their former training.

*"We want to know why the Brits
are selling weapons to ISIS"*

When a break-in threatens Britain's National Security,
Franklyn calls on Wright & Tran but Kara will have to take
this case on her own. Tien wants nothing to do with the world
of Private Investigations and less to do with the world of
Franklyn. Kara goes solo, but finding who is responsible for
the break-in is the easy part. Finding who the real criminals are
is much, much harder.

Isolated in a world of half-truths and lies, international arms
deals and power politics, she is quick to discover that she's
been working for the wrong side. What she didn't figure on
was that making amends will place her, and those she loves, in
the sights of those who have everything to lose.

A Time To Every Purpose

What if Jesus hadn't been crucified?

For two thousand years humanity has been enveloped in Nirvana. But in the early decades of the twentieth century, natural disasters, famine, disease and economic collapse bring catastrophe and a fledgling Nazi Party sweeps to power. Now, almost a century later, their brutal persecution of millions is a never-ending holocaust.

Yet a few heroes remain.

Leigh Wilson, the preeminent scientist of her generation, has kept a secret all her life. But plunged into the aftermath of the cold-blooded murder of a Nazi official, she is forced to make a choice. Will she destroy what she loves to save what she can only imagine?

A Time to Every Purpose is a thrilling mix of science and action, good versus evil, and the eternal question all humans face: Is this my time to act?

"A thriller with heart... Gifted storytelling combines with meticulous scientific and historical research to produce a memorable and profoundly moving story."
(Elaine Fry, The West Australian)

"A Time To Every Purpose by Ian Andrew deals with huge concepts, looking at the broad sweep of history... a well-executed alternate history novel with some great action scenes."
(John Wyatt, News UK)

The Little Book
of
Silly Rhymes
&
Odd Verses

An illustrated collection of humorous, daft, sometimes sad and occasionally thought provoking verses from the pen of Ian Andrew. Illustrations by Alison Mutton.

CPSIA information can be obtained
at www.ICGtesting.com
Printed in the USA
LVOW11s1112120317
526914LV00003B/522/P